THE APOCALYPSE GENE

THE APOCALYPSE GENE

BY

WILLIAM V. CROCKETT

This is a work of historical fiction. All the characters and events portrayed in this book are fictitious, and any resemblance to real people or events is purely coincidental.

THE APOCALYPSE GENE

Hudson Publishing

ApocalypseGene.com
wvcnovel@gmail.com

ISBN: 0692784497
ISBN-13:   978-0692784495

To my son, Richard, whose creative mind, knowledge of science, and familiarity with Yale made this writing possible.

I thank him for what we humorously call his thankless labor.

Acknowledgments

I would like to thank the many people who took the time to read through my manuscript. Your proofreading and comments, I am sure, saved me some embarrassment. Diane Mariash and Sueihn Lee were exceedingly helpful in the beginning stages, and most importantly, I say "thank you" to my incomparable research assistant, Julie Hodsdon. I'm sure if I had taken *all* her advice, this novel would have been better. Lastly, I thank my wife, Karen, who has always been my support.

"Then the kings of the earth,
and the moguls,
and the generals,
and the rich and the powerful,
and everyone, great and small,
hid in the caves and the mountains
... for the great day of wrath had come."

Apocalypse of John 6

1

Early one morning while still dark, Professor Robert Westover arrived at his office, excited to examine his new creation. He called it, *Alpha*, because in his mind, it was the beginning of everything, the dawn of a new age. Westover opened his office door eagerly, his entire body trembling as he felt for the switch. But almost immediately, he withdrew his hand. Something was wrong. Several of the lab doors had been opened, and in the central lab where he stored *Alpha*, a faint glow lit the edges.

Professor Westover shuffled a few feet into the threatening dark, his brow furrowing. "Hello?" he called, striving for a confident tone, but the silence that followed unnerved him. He wished he had said nothing. He took a calming breath, and moved into the main complex. A shadow slid eerily across the room, and Westover jerked his head around, swallowing hard. His eyes darted to the stainless steel chamber where he stored his new creation, and immediately he began fumbling for the lights to the rear labs, flipping them on one by one.

A man stepped out of the chamber.

Westover's shoulders slumped in relief. "Oh, it's you," he said. "You gave me a fright."

"I am sorry I startled you."

"Yes, well, I thought you were in Detroit, at the conference."

"Change of the plans." His accent seemed thicker than usual.

The old professor stared, confused. "But we agreed you wouldn't get involved at this stage. If something goes wrong—"

"Nothing will go wrong. Besides, I want to see our project completed. I have worked on it since I was a graduate student."

Westover mumbled his thanks but felt uneasy with Dr. Jozef Krakauer involved, especially on this of all mornings. Krakauer had been a physician in the Czech Republic before relocating to the United States, and was doubtless the brightest Ph.D. student to have come through Yale in Westover's fifty years of teaching. But his odd mannerisms made for an uneasy relationship, and the professor wished his assistant had gone to the conference as planned.

"I have prepared everything," Krakauer said with an awkward sweep of his hand.

"You need not have done that," Westover said as the other disappeared into the polished cavern. Alone, he glanced around the familiar room with its racks of test tubes and glass beakers, its ebony tables and brown wooden stools. He exhaled slowly and smiled. It was as if he were surrounded by a comfortable coat. Yes, he was old now, and many would say his time had passed. But they were all so wrong. In days—no, minutes— he would shake the foundations of science. He had discovered the Holy Grail: a flawless delivery system for genetic engineering. In his lab he had created what others had thought impossible—a synthetic vehicle that would evade the body's immune system.

Robert Westover plopped down on a stool and extracted a rubber tourniquet from his jacket pocket, twisting it one way, then the other. The possibilities of his discovery were staggering. It would be the end of genetic diseases like cystic fibrosis, muscular dystrophy, and Down syndrome. Inherited scourges like Alzheimer's and many cancers would become a footnote in humanity's gruesome past. Even obesity and baldness would become curious testimonies to the pre-genetic era, and he would be the catalyst for that wonderful revolution in science.

There were dangers, of course, the chance happenings that often surfaced when mortals skirmished with Nature, and Nature refused to bare her secrets. But *Alpha* was harmless, nothing more than a proof of concept. It carried a simple inert gene, a kind of cell marker that served no function except to show that the gene had indeed been incorporated into the body. *Alpha* would jeopardize no one.

But the scientific establishment would not allow him to move forward. If he followed the rules, *Alpha* would enter its next phase of trials, where it would languish for decades. Robert Westover knew he would never live to see his creation help anyone. And millions would die waiting while the politicians bickered. An unbearable thought. Enough to push him to the edge. He bit his lip, knowing what he had to do.

He would become the proof they needed. Once in his bloodstream, *Alpha* would evade the immune system and replicate in the trillions, until like a silent roaring inferno, it would edit the DNA of every cell in his body. That event—that proof—would be enough to overcome any opposition.

He slipped off his tweed coat, rolled up a wrinkled white sleeve, and bound the tourniquet tightly around his upper arm. The sudden pressure hit him, an angry throb from his elbow to his fingers, and he rubbed his arm vigorously, trying to relieve the bulging blue lines that looked like a subway map. "Krakauer?" he called.

"Coming." The voice sounded terse.

"Is something wrong?"

No reply.

Westover looked around uncertainly. "I appreciate your help," he said, stretching his arm, "but I don't understand why a simple injection is taking so long."

Silence.

Westover sighed, unhappy with his peevish tone. As he'd grown older he had noticed an increasing lack of patience. He remembered his crotchety grandfather and the endless complaints that tumbled from his purple lips as he stuffed tobacco in his pipe. Is that who he had become, his grandfather?

The door opened and a silhouette appeared, uniformly black against the well-lit inner room. "I am ready now," Krakauer said, syringe in hand. "Careful preparation takes time, yes?"

Westover dropped his eyes, embarrassed. "It does," he said in muted voice.

Krakauer stepped out of the alcove as the professor began swabbing his arm with alcohol. "Should be a beautiful day."

Westover raised an eyebrow, knowing that this man's whole life lay within the walls of the science building. He nodded, and Krakauer's hawk-like eyes held him fast. His peculiar habit of staring had always bothered the professor. The younger man often conducted an entire conversation without shifting his eyes, like a bird of prey engaging a quarry. Westover dropped the cotton swab into a sink stained green from nitric acid and said, "I'm eager to conclude this part of the morning."

"Of course."

"I've never been overly fond of injections," Westover said gamely, searching for a kindlier tone. "I think it harkens back to Woodridge Elementary and Nurse Clemens, who delighted in poking us with needles." He managed a weak laugh and said, "That was in the day of reusable needles, big square ones with burrs on them."

Krakauer smiled thinly as he slipped on a second pair of sterile gloves. "The world will never be the same," he said, examining the veins in the professor's arm. "It is unfortunate that you must experiment on yourself. But self-experimentation has an honorable history; people forget that."

"Honorable or not, if something happens to me, I charge you with finding my little Synapse a good home. I don't think she could run the streets again."

"Your cat has nothing to worry about," Krakauer said, then added in a soothing voice, "and neither do you. *Alpha* is flawless. Our masterpiece. You will be fine."

Westover grunted. That was the second time Krakauer had used the word *our*, and he didn't like it. He had worked himself to the bone developing the delivery system, yet it seemed as if his assistant jumped at any chance to claim ownership, despite contributing only minor elements to the enterprise.

"You are certain, then," Krakauer whispered, his eyes seeming to glow as he slipped off the plastic syringe cover and leaned forward.

Westover looked away and sighed, "Proskin will pull the grant money if I don't come up with something concrete. I don't like it, but this is my last opportunity. I'm out of time." He plucked his glasses from his shirt pocket and held them above his nose to study the amber liquid shining like honey in the syringe. "It seems a darker color than in the flask."

"Syringe glass is thinner," Krakauer said calmly.

Westover thrust an arm of his glasses into his mouth, chewing the curved end, a habit he had been trying to break since he started teaching. "I don't see how glass thickness would make a difference."

"I can draw your blood tomorrow morning," Krakauer said, changing subjects, "but we should do it sooner if there is some immune response, like your temperature elevating ...."

"Tomorrow will be fine."

"Of course. Meantime, I suggest you cancel classes for the week." His mouth smiled. "You need a quiet place to rest." Getting no reply, he continued, "Even though we expect no reaction, one can never predict the body's response, especially in older people. Rest is always a wise safeguard."

Westover moved his arm to accommodate the needle, but he didn't appreciate Krakauer playing physician to him, and even less the comment about his age. It was true, of course. He was old, and he did have a less robust constitution. But the reminder still miffed him. And Krakauer's inflated concern for his health seemed nothing if not hypocritical. Three times in the past five years his assistant had gone over his head to the administration, to discuss procedures for assuming Westover's professorship in the event of his retirement. The old professor had no doubt that were he to expire on the laboratory floor, Krakauer would leap-frog over his body in a wild rush to the Chairman's office.

The needle broke through his skin, flooding his bloodstream with microscopic life eager inside its new host, and in that moment, as Westover glanced up, he noticed that Krakauer's face was glistening with perspiration.

* * *

Four days later, Professor Westover felt normal. Other than a mild headache and a touch of diarrhea on the second day, he might have been given a placebo. His assistant took blood every twelve hours, and from his results, it looked as if their experiment had succeeded in altering Westover's DNA sequence perfectly. Oddly, Jozef Krakauer grew more anxious each day. When taking a skin biopsy, the man's fingers trembled, and then like a startled fox he would scurry off to the lab.

Professor Westover knew he had to address the situation, but for the moment, as he walked down Science Hill, he was enjoying the sound of leaves crunching under his feet. He had done it. After so many years of trying, it was hard to take in. He paused at the corner, watching a group of students crossing the street. They were so full of life and promise.

Westover nodded to himself. Everything he had done, all the effort, the risks, the sacrifices, all of it was worth it. He had given the world a better future. He smiled, feeling truly content for the first time in years.

"Professor," a voice called, breathless, interrupting his thoughts.

Westover turned to see Krakauer chasing after him.

"I looked for you in your office," his assistant said. "Why are you out here?"

"I have a class," Westover replied with a quizzical frown.

"A class!" Krakauer blanched. "You can't … you said you had cancelled your classes until Monday—"

"And then I changed my mind."

"You cannot teach your class today—you should be resting."

"I feel fine."

"Your face is flushed."

"It is not. I feel perfectly fine." He turned to continue walking.

"I … most strongly recommend—" Krakauer croaked, reaching for him.

Professor Westover withdrew his arm. "Dr. Krakauer," he said formally, the heat rising in his face, "you might have been a practicing physician at one time, but need I remind you that I am the principal investigator here. I've seen the same data you have. *Alpha* is in essentially every cell of my body. And there have been no sequelae for days. I feel perfectly fine. So while I appreciate your concern, be assured, I intend to teach my class. I'll be back in the lab this evening and we will talk about this obsessive behavior of yours."

Westover turned abruptly and continued down the hill.

* * *

The theater-style room was packed, one hundred sixty eager-faced students waiting as their professor stepped to the podium. Robert Westover ran his tired eyes over them wistfully, remembering how he had once been one of them: youthful, enthusiastic, impatient to learn everything he could about molecular biology and the structure of genes and chromosomes. He loved teaching intro classes. A tiny smile crinkled the corners of his mouth as he recalled the uproar his own professor had caused by telling a risqué joke about how to observe a female chromosome. "You pull down her genes," he had said. His smile broadened. Yes, much had changed since then. That was a long time ago.

Westover flipped open his briefcase and retrieved his glasses. Reflexively, he stuck the well-chewed arm into his mouth to ponder the situation. The plastic had a metallic taste and he quickly pulled it out to look at it, wondering if someone might be playing a joke on him. He glanced around the hall but everything seemed normal.

Opening his folder, he began his lecture on epigenetics. The students tapped furiously on their laptops and tablets. He passed over the first of his witty remarks, fearing it wasn't as entertaining as he had supposed. Then, ten minutes into his lecture, his mouth felt unusually dry.

He licked his lips, his tongue scraping like sandpaper.

A headache suddenly throbbed at the base of his skull and he was having trouble focusing on his notes. He resumed speaking in a strangled voice, then trailed off. What point was he making? He couldn't remember. That brought a flash of panic, immediately suppressed.

Then his nose began to drip. He stared at a bright red starburst on the notepad before him.

Blood.

Blood was dripping from his nose.

Westover hadn't had a nosebleed since he was a child. He clutched his handkerchief to his nose, swaying against the podium. Students were now rising from their seats; something was desperately wrong. He reached for the glass of water beside the podium but lost his balance, tipping it over and staggering as it smashed on the wood floor. He grasped the edge of the table and stood there rigidly, dizzy and confused. His limbs had now puffed up like the bloated flesh of the dead, and a wrenching pain chopped through his entire body. His inner organs seemed to burn with intense heat and his eyeballs bulged until he thought they would burst.

The injection!

Something had gone wrong.

He could see the students crowding forward.

"Stay back!" he coughed, crumpling to the floor, shirt and tie stained with blood. "Don't touch me."

His eyes stared without seeing, while his racing mind began inexorably to slow. He had been so careful ... *Alpha* was harmless. This couldn't be an immune reaction. Nothing was making sense.

He seemed to hear Krakauer's voice directing students out of the lecture hall. *Krakauer!* The name flared like a dying light bulb. What was he doing here? Had he been watching, waiting? His strange behavior since the injection .... Could he have altered the gene, created something deadly, something designed to destroy?

The elderly professor was now curled into a tight ball, eyes half shut, his world spinning wildly around him. His stomach tightened and, with a violent convulsion, huge quantities of black liquid spewed from his mouth, while a warm, wet sensation flowed from his ears and bowels. In the gathering darkness, Robert Westover thought about his lifelong quest to change the world ... and he wondered who would care for his ragged old cat, Synapse.

Then he sank into the numbing void.

Two Years Later

2

The taxi splashed to a halt.

Heavy rain pummeled the streets, beating on the cab's metal roof, making Nicole Van Buren feel as if she were inside a kettledrum. She scrubbed the fog off the window and squinted at the entrance to her college. Deserted. Students usually roamed the streets until well past midnight, but on a night like this, they were all indoors. And who could blame them? Even with an oversized umbrella, Nicole couldn't bring herself to leave the cab.

"Want me to walk you to the gate, lady?" the cab driver asked sarcastically.

"Gee, thanks for your patience," Nicole replied. Good thing she hadn't tipped the guy. She grabbed her bags, cracked the door, and popped her umbrella. "Don't bother helping," she said. "I can manage." She stepped out of the cab and into a puddle three inches deep. Icy water flooded her shoe. "What is your problem?" she shrieked, her foot recoiling. "We're sitting in the middle of Lake Michigan! Move up!"

"Yeah, yeah," he said as he pulled forward.

Nicole climbed out into the rain and slammed the door, hoping she had made her point. As the taxi started away she remembered her plant in the back seat, and thumped the trunk with her fist. He stopped. She sighed as she opened the back door and hoisted out her Pepper Elder.

"You should have checked the seat before you left," the driver said.

"Oh, that is truly helpful. Thank you."

"Next time I won't stop."

"Next time I won't pay!" she said, and left him to close his own door.

She struggled toward the iron gate, clutching her bags with one arm, the Pepper Elder with the other, and all the while trying to hold the umbrella erect with her chin. It didn't work. When she reached for her key card, a torrent of water cascaded off the umbrella, and down her neck.

"This is ridiculous," Nicole mumbled as she hobbled toward the gate, rain slashing her face.

She passed the card across the electronic key box and bumped the gate with her shoulder. It didn't open. She shook the rain off her proxy card and tried again. The tiny lights blinked red and green. "No, no," Nicole moaned. Red and green meant out of order. She thrust her face between the metal bars of the locked gate. "Anyone in there?" she called to the archway beyond, but the wind and rain swallowed her voice.

She shivered, feeling a slight bit sorry for herself as she swept her eyes across the empty roadway, the rain bouncing like ball bearings off the pavement. The only signs of life were a few cars plowing through the puddles at the far end of the street. She thought about the phone in her purse, dialing 911, but decided that the Yale emergency system might be the better choice.

Suddenly, a sharp gust of wind ripped the umbrella from her hand, flipping it end over end down the street. "I can't believe this," she muttered as she chased after her umbrella, the Pepper Elder flailing madly in her arm. By the time she got her hands on the umbrella, she was completely soaked, and felt like smashing the Pepper Elder on the pavement. Her better judgment prevailed. Truth be told, the Pepper Elder was more important to her than most people. She took a breath and tried to calm herself.

Sloshing over to the panic button, as Yale students called it, she butted the red knob on the emergency box with her elbow. A brilliant blue light flashed silently above on the stone wall, like the beacon of a deserted lighthouse.

Seconds later a police cruiser cut across the intersection and pulled up on the sidewalk across the street. The driver's side door flew open and an officer came thundering across the pavement. He was a heavyset black man who moved quickly for his size. "What's wrong?" he demanded, rapidly scanning the area.

"The electronic key isn't working," Nicole said.

"You called in an emergency because your card didn't work?"

"No," Nicole said in an overly patient tone, "my card works fine. This wonderful system of yours is crap—it doesn't work in the rain. You might want to report it."

"You can be sure of that," he said, turning his back and speaking into his radio: "Station eleven, all clear. Le Beau, out." Then he punched some buttons on the emergency box and the blue light stopped flashing. He unlocked the college gate with a bronze key and motioned for her to step into the lighted archway out of the rain. "I'll need your name and student ID number," he said, wiping water off his face.

She whirled. "What?"

"Misuse of the Emergency System is a ticketable offense."

"How else was I supposed to get inside?"

"Patrols come by here regularly. Students are expected to wait a few minutes—"

"At night? This is absurd."

"ID card, please."

She put her bags and Pepper Elder against the wall. "What is your name?"

"My name is Officer Le Beau, as you can see on my lapel." He tapped the embroidered patch on his chest, his other hand fishing inside his jacket for a pen.

She put her hands on her hips. "Well, Officer Le Beau, I would not want to be you when certain people hear about this harassment."

He paused, notepad halfway out of his jacket, and looked at her. "I am asking for your ID card, Miss, that's all."

She thrust her chin toward him. "Outright harassment if you ask me."

"Harassment, is it?" He acknowledged the threat with a patronizing smile that irritated her.

She stepped forward and returned his smile. "You won't think this is so funny tomorrow when you find out who my father is."

"I know who your father is," he said calmly.

Nicole tried but failed to conceal her shock. After a moment she snapped her mouth shut.

"Yes, I know exactly who he is—he's somebody important. Yale is filled with the kids of important fathers." He paused. "Do you know what this is?" He plucked at a lapel mic. "Everything is being recorded in that police car over there. So let's stop the nonsense and you give me your ID card."

Nicole glanced toward the car, then at the officer and back at the car again. "This is clearly a form of intimidation, which I don't appreciate," she sputtered, trying to reestablish her authority.

"Well, the Masters of each college handle violations involving the Emergency System. You will have ample opportunity to explain your situation. ID card, please." He held his hand toward her and waggled his fingers.

Nicole bit her lip, angry at being so easily trapped. "Look," she said softly, "I don't think you understand ... I was worried." She located her card and handed it to him.

He wrote down her name and ID number without responding, then returned the card.

"I was worried," she repeated. "I thought I saw someone—a grubby looking guy—hiding in that stairwell over there."

He turned his head. "Someone in the stairwell? You said you used the Emergency System because the electronic key malfunctioned."

"That's right," Nicole said indignantly. "I walked up to the gate, tried my key, it didn't work, and then I saw a man watching me."

He gazed at her, face blank, his eyes filled with disbelief.

She crossed her arms, thrust one foot forward. "Well, aren't you going to check it out? See if someone's hiding in the stairwell?" She shot a glance toward the place of the danger.

A pained expression crossed his face. "Wait here," he said and exited the gate. Minutes later he returned. "There's no one there. You playing games?"

"I am shocked and offended that you would say something like that."

"There's no one there," he repeated.

"Yeah? Well, you tell me what a woman is supposed to do when it's late at night and the gate's not working, and she sees someone stalking her. He might have had a butcher knife or a gun. How could a slender thing like me fight him off? I could have been robbed here tonight, or maybe even ..." she dropped her voice for effect and said quietly into his lapel mic, "murdered!"

He rolled his eyes.

"Oh, you don't think so, officer? This is New Haven—it happens every day!"

He didn't say a word, just looked at her.

She stared him down.

"Well, Ms. Van Buren," he said at last, "I don't see anyone out there. But I will report this as a security mistake. See that it doesn't happen again, because I have a good memory."

"I really don't understand your attitude. Are you saying that if I'm about to be murdered—"

"If you are about to be murdered," he said with a scowl, "by all means, press every button you see."

Nicole's smile of satisfaction lingered the whole length of the vaulted walkway. Policemen like that need straightening out, she thought. He probably bullies students all day long. Well, he picked the wrong girl this time. The fact that she had lied about a man being in the stairwell had nothing to do with the issue. There *might* have been a real man waiting to murder her, and that policeman still would have acted the same, and that infuriated her most of all.

But she had work to do. It was the first day of the semester and she had yet to unpack a ton of boxes delivered during the day. She was determined to have everything in order, even if it took all night. Turning into the quadrangle she stopped abruptly. Heaped under the towering elm tree were scores of boxes that looked very much like the ones she had watched being packed two days earlier in Greenwich, Connecticut.

"What. Is. Going. On?" she spat through clenched teeth. "These were supposed to be delivered to my room!"

She blew out in frustration, and lugged her bags and plant back to the arch where they would be protected from the rain. That done, she splashed across the grass and ripped the tag off one of the boxes—not hard to do, since the cardboard sagged forlornly in its sodden condition. "Van Buren," she read by the weak light of one of the quad lamps, "Calhoun College, Room 496, Yale University." She mopped the rain off her face, flung a soaked rope of hair over her shoulder, and looked for help. Of course, the quad was as deserted as a cemetery at sundown. "Unbelievable!" she muttered as she hefted the closest box to the slate walkway. She rescued two more boxes from the edge of a rapidly forming pond, then a garment bag that had once contained expensive, but now, she had little doubt, ruined shirts and coats.

Her microscope! Where was her microscope? As equipment went, it was useless, almost a toy, but it had been a gift from her brother who had died several years earlier. She scrambled through the boxes until she found the plastic carton lying flat in the water. "Oh no," she wailed, yanking open the top, and instantly slicing her thumb on the jagged edge. She stared at the blood trickling down her wrist, now mingled with the rain, and then, blinking back tears, she inspected the microscope, and carefully placed it on the walkway.

"Are these your boxes?"

Nicole turned to see a tall, well-muscled student holding open the oak door leading to her dorm. He had an unassuming air about him that suggested hard-working middle-class values. Just what she needed. "Yes, unfortunately, these are my boxes," she said, squeezing her thumb into her palm, not wanting dripping blood to scare away a potential helper. Everything was supposed to be delivered to my room and I'm not sure what to do." She smiled sweetly, hoping he would volunteer.

"I charge two dollars a box."

She laughed. *I'm soaked, and he jokes.* But still, if he helped .... She maintained the smile.

He smiled back.

She made to give her hair a playful flip, realized the matted mess would be anything but sexy, and instead said flirtatiously, "Well, there is no doubt the damsel's in distress. I suppose you could demand almost anything."

He stepped out into the rain. "Do you know your hand is bleeding?"

Nicole glanced down. Blood now stained the cuff of her jacket and one of the boxes in front of her. She shrugged, and dismissed his observation with, "Oh, this is nothing. I was about to get a bandage." She met his eyes and said as warmly as she could, "Thank you for your help. If you hadn't happened along—"

"Who left your boxes in the rain?" he asked as he ambled forward.

"Delivery guys got mixed up, I guess. But what's done is done. I don't like to complain." She turned toward the door. "My room number is 496."

"Oh, fourth floor," he said, processing the information. "That's an extra dollar per box."

She stopped, turned back, mouth open and eyes wide. "Are you serious? You want money to help me?" He looked embarrassed, she was happy to see.

"I told you I charged."

"I thought you were joking."

"Well, I'm not."

"You should be." She could feel heat rising from her neck. Actual heat rising. "I have never heard of a fellow student wanting money to help with a few boxes." She glanced around the quad at the warm squares of lighted windows surrounding them, then turned back and said, "What are you doing here, anyway? Lurking behind the door like some miscreant, spying in windows? Or do you just wander the campus trying to make money off the misfortunes of others? Does the Master of the College know about this?" She snorted and added, "Are you even a student here?"

He held up his hands in surrender. "I'm not trying to—"

"Y'know," she said, swiping at the rain on her face with one hand, eyes never leaving his, "this has not been a pleasant day for me. I'm wet. I'm tired. And I'm not in an especially jolly mood. I sliced my hand on a shard of metal—no doubt tetanus bacilli are already racing through my veins. I've been hounded by police and abused by a taxi driver. Somebody dumped my books in the mud. And you ... you want money." She was standing inches from his face by the time she finished. "So how much do you want?" she snapped.

He waved a hand and started to turn away. "Forget it. I don't need—"

"No, no, I am happy to pay."

He stopped, shifted awkwardly. "Look, I'm sorry for—"

"Yes, yes, apology accepted," she said in a tone that indicated otherwise. "Now, let's do business. I have about sixty boxes, and that, if I am not mistaken, comes to one hundred eighty dollars in highwayman economy. I'll round that up to an even two hundred if you hustle your butt and get my belongings upstairs quickly. I'll even throw in an extra twenty if you haul the cardboard away. No doubt an enterprising fellow like yourself can scurry for a couple Ben Franklins when necessary."

He stood quietly, unmoving. Nicole detected anger in his eyes and she wondered whether she had gone too far. Then, without a word, he walked away.

"Wait!"

He kept walking.

"So, what am I supposed to do? I've injured my hand. Please, I can't carry ...." Her voice died as he reached for the door. "Okay, I shouldn't have said what I did. I ... I'm sorry. Did you hear me? I said I was sorry."

He propped open the thick door and said, "I don't know what your problem is. All day I've charged three dollars a box for the fourth floor. It's a fair price. Now it's pouring. Your boxes are soaked, and you act like I'm the bad guy. You can do it yourself. I really don't care."

"I can't do it myself," Nicole said, gesturing feebly toward the confusion of boxes, hoping to invoke pity. "I'll pay you five dollars a box if you want, but I—"

"Three dollars is what I charge. I don't want a dime more."

"Whatever you say," she said meekly. "I just want you to be happy."

"And I wasn't lurking behind the door. I was setting up someone's bookshelves on the first level."

"Fine by me," she said crisply, opening her wallet and extracting two bills. She walked slowly toward him and smiled as she slipped the bills into his shirt pocket. "Room 496. I'll make sure it's open." She collected her bags, tucked the Pepper Elder under her arm, and blew out in relief as she left the courtyard.

3 ᐁᐁᐁᐁᐁᐁᐁᐁᐁᐁᐁᐁᐁᐁᐁᐁᐁᐁᐁᐁᐁᐁᐁᐁᐁᐁ

Ryan Taylor smashed his hand down on the alarm clock. He had chosen the clock for its particularly irritating buzzing sound, and at five in the morning, it was superbly irritating. He lay on his back, eyes still closed, listening to the wind whining in the cracks around the window, then slid open the slider. A blast of rain spattered his face. He slammed the slider shut. How many hours had he slept? Two? Three? And now he had to leave his warm bed to do a five mile run through the streets of New Haven. He groaned, and flopped back into the enfolding warmth of his down blanket, his eyes heavy with sleep. A couple more minutes, that's all he needed.

Thud! Thud! Thud!

The pounding on his door rattled the light fixture overhead, discharging a puff of dust that dispersed slowly in the grizzled morning light. "Taylor! You still in there? Better get moving. Coach is running with us this morning."

Ryan bounded out of bed. "I'm ready," he called as alertly as his croaking voice would allow, then cleared his throat before adding, "Just need my shoes." He took two quick steps toward the closet where his sweats hung, and plowed his toe into the metal bedpost.

"Shit!" he growled through a clenched jaw. He reached down and massaged his foot. How could one toe hurt so much? A sudden burst of rain pummeled the window, sounding hollow, like mocking laughter. Man, he hated morning workouts, especially when middle-aged coaches ran with the team. They piled up the miles to show that their incredible abilities hadn't changed since their storied youths. Of course, they avoided the weightlifting and killer sprints afterwards.

The rain reminded him of Nicole Van Buren and her boxes. What an insufferable bitch. Rich and pretty—a noxious combination. Yale always had a large share of her type. Well, rich and bitchy, anyway. He was glad she was a biology major and not in computer science, with him. If he were forced to deal with her every day, he might end up with his fingers around her throat—a satisfying fantasy.

Hours later, after a predictably miserable run, followed by his breakfast duties in the dining hall, Ryan called his mother. The last time they talked, a week ago, he had lost his temper and said things he shouldn't have, and he wanted to apologize. The money from Yale, the twenty-thousand-dollars Yale had given him for school was gone. Somehow his mom had talked the local bank manager into giving her the money, and "loaned" it to Ryan's father, who promptly gambled away every last cent and then some. What a fucking shocker.

Now Ryan was in trouble. He had bills but no money.

"I tried to phone you," his mother said.

"I know, I got the messages," he said, dropping his eyes to study a short length of thread that had strayed from a button. "I should have called back. I'm sorry."

"Oh Ryan, it's my fault," she moaned. "I don't know what to say. I thought this time he would try to ...." She sighed. "I'm sorry. I wish I could get some money out of the house, but there's nothing there."

"That's fine, Mom," he said, giving the thread an experimental tug. It wasn't her fault, not really; his father was the one who had blown the money.

"Maybe you can talk to the school?"

Ryan abandoned the button to run a hand through his hair. Not likely, he thought. If he told anyone, they'd probably arrest her for fraud. He stifled a sigh. "Don't worry about it," he said in a confident voice. "I've already worked everything out. Yale's got tons of money. Anyway, I shouldn't have said what I did. I know you were just trying to help Dad."

Ryan talked several minutes longer, assuring her everything was fine. But it was not fine. He was in trouble and had no idea how he would handle the school year. He faked a cheerful good-bye to his mother, and headed for the Student Employment Office. He had been there several times before, but never carrying a notice that described irregularities in his work forms. This day just kept getting better.

He pulled open the door and passed a long line of students getting ID photos. Others sat in cubicles, discussing employment opportunities. Ryan's heart sank; he'd be here for hours.

A pleasant looking girl with auburn hair wended her way through the cluttered desks, her arms stacked with folders. He glanced at her nametag and leaned over the counter, saying with a polite smile, "Amy? My name's Ryan Taylor, and I have an appointment—"

"I'm sorry," Amy interrupted, "you'll have to wait."

"I understand, but I have a notice—"

"You-will-have-to-wait," she repeated in a staccato voice, eyes blazing. "Take a number like everyone else!"

Ryan flushed at the sudden outburst. "Okay," he said, smiling weakly. "I'll ... ah ... just take one of these numbers." He peeled the number fifty-two off a large paper block resting on the counter. "I'll be sitting over there," he said, motioning to a row of chairs against the wall, "in case there's a cancellation or something ...." His voice trailed off. She had already turned away.

For the next hour he watched students come and leave and still he sat. He'd opened his backpack and taken out a book on compilers, trying to make up for the class he was missing, but he couldn't concentrate. The big clock on the back wall was nearing eleven. He would be late for lunch duties.

Stuffing the book back into his bag, he elbowed between two students waiting at the counter, who moved aside with annoyed glares. "Amy," he called, using the student worker's name purposely to irritate her, "thanks for your help, but I can't wait any longer. Tell Ms. Edwards I'll phone her tomorrow."

Amy stopped and focused all her attention on him. "Dr. Edwards? Your appointment is with *Dr. Edwards?*" She snatched the notice from his hand and stared at the words IMMEDIATE ATTENTION. "Why didn't you say that in the first place!" she sputtered, and hurried off toward the back rooms. She returned as speedily as she had left, and seconds later Ryan found himself in a tiny room, three feet distant from a thin, severe-faced woman sitting behind a gray metal desk. She had the best posture he had ever seen.

"Ah, yes, Mr. Taylor," she said, enunciating the words precisely, as if each syllable carried momentous meaning, "please seat yourself." Her long, bony fingers were interlaced and resting on a manila folder. "Now, why do you suppose I've called you here?" Piercing black eyes moved slowly from the folder until they locked onto his.

"I'm not sure," Ryan said.

"You're not sure."

Ryan waited.

"How many hours are you working each week?"

"About nineteen."

"Thirty-eight."

Ryan's brows rose. "I don't think so."

"Thirty-eight hours, Mr. Taylor. You are working two shifts at the Calhoun dining hall. It's all here in your file." One finger tapped the document in front of her.

Ryan pulled his eyes from hers and glanced around the somber little room. "Thirty-eight hours," he said. "I had no idea."

She folded her arms and inspected him as one would a cockroach caught in a pair of tweezers. "Mr. Taylor," she said at length, "you are treading in hazardous waters."

Ryan stared at her, motionless, thinking it better to stay silent.

"Someone altered the names and ID numbers in our system—I am not quite sure how—but now the computer thinks there are two Ryan Taylors registered at Yale University. Same W2, same address. Our system is supposed to catch that, but for some reason it didn't." She straightened her back so that she was sitting even more erect than before. "Every few years we get someone like you, Mr. Taylor; someone who imagines he is above the system. Don't be so naïve to think you're the first one to try it."

"If you think I had anything to do with—"

"Please," she held up her hand, "do not insult me with your denials. I know you altered the database—how, I don't know, and I have no desire to waste my time finding out. But be assured that your adolescent shenanigans fool no one. I have never trusted computers and in this office we check everything by hand."

Ryan swallowed. "May I continue working the extra shift--"

"No, you may not."

"I desperately need the money."

"Nineteen hours, Mr. Taylor, is the maximum this university allows." She made a note in his file. "You will discharge your obligations in the lunch room today, but beginning tomorrow, breakfast duties only. Is that clear?"

Ryan stared at her.

"Ten hours a week," she said, "that is what I will allow."

"You said the maximum was nineteen!"

"Yes, but you are a member of the lacrosse team, are you not? And that takes up a significant block of your time."

"Ten hours! What good will that do?"

"The rules are for your benefit. You cannot maintain the high caliber of study this university requires if—"

"I do well in my studies," Ryan blurted.

"You cannot," she repeated, entirely unruffled, "maintain the high caliber of study this university requires if you are involved in multitudinous distractions. Perhaps you might consider discontinuing lacrosse."

"Coach Waldhart got me into Yale," Ryan said. "I can't just walk out on him. Besides, I need the financial aid."

"Your financial aid isn't tied to playing lacrosse, Mr. Taylor."

Ryan snorted but said nothing. Without lacrosse he knew his scholarship would last about two minutes.

"Well, there you have it," she said, rising. She smiled and gestured towards the door.

* * *

"Veal or chicken?" Ryan asked for the hundredth time. He had been serving lunch for over an hour and faces had begun to blur.

"I'll take *ossobuco* with *risotto*, light on the sauce."

Ryan looked up to see Nicole Van Buren in the line of students. "This is a cafeteria," he said, "not a French restaurant."

"*Ossobuco* is Milanese," Nicole said.

"Milanese? Really?" Ryan yawned, trying to show that he didn't care his smart remark had backfired.

"It wasn't on the menu the last time I dined at Per Se," the fellow beside her said. He walked over to the sandwich line, chortling and repeating the name Per Se as if it were a hilarious joke. Ryan didn't get it.

"Per Se is a French restaurant in Manhattan," Nicole said by way of explanation.

"Clever," Ryan said, squinting through a cloud of steam as he pushed aside the lid on the chicken. "A friend of yours?"

"Yes, as a matter of fact. Basil Meryash." She pronounced *Basil* the English way, *Baah-zul*. "Actually, it's Basil Meryash the Fourth. He's junior year and," dropping her voice to a whisper, "he's all but a member of Skull and Bones." She paused, stepped back and waved a trio of students with trays past her. "Can you imagine?" she added, raising her eyebrows to make the point.

"Impressive," Ryan said, slapping chicken onto three more plates and burying them with rice.

She stared at him, incredulous. "You've never have heard of Skull and Bones, have you?"

"I've seen them on some of the ingredients we put in the chicken. Think that's important?" He slid the plates across the counter to students as they moved past Nicole.

"Very funny," Nicole said, tipping her head and looking down her nose at him. "It's only Yale's most secret society."

"I guess that's why I haven't heard about it," Ryan replied with a lopsided grin.

Basil made a big show of taking his tray to the outer room.

"We're not supposed to talk about Skull and Bones," she said, explaining why Basil had left. She kept her voice low. "Those on the inside call it, *The Order*. Not many know that. Some still call it, *The Brotherhood of Death*, although that's a misnomer because they've been tapping women since 1991. I'm hoping to be tapped myself next year." She paused. "Haven't you noticed that mysterious-looking building on High Street with no identification marks?"

"Is that the secret clubhouse?"

"*Tomb!* They call it, *The Tomb.* You must have seen it."

"Nope."

"No? It's right in the middle of campus, a nearly windowless Greco-Egyptian mausoleum with padlocked iron doors."

Ryan held up his hand and looked over his shoulder at the steamer table, making it clear that the level of the mushroom soup was more important than her pretentious chatter. "So who's in this club that makes it so important?"

"It's a *Society*," she said. "It's not a club."

"Yeah, I got it. So who's in the club?"

She paused to register her displeasure, then said, "Most of them would probably be unfamiliar—"

"I knew it," Ryan crowed. "You can't even name one person—"

"I could, but—"

"A name. Give me a name."

She crossed her arms and leaned forward. "How about Former Presidents George Sr. and George W. Bush? Both were tapped to become members when they were here. As was President Taft, John Kerry, and half of the President's advisors."

"Really?" He shrugged. "Then I suppose I should be impressed that ol' Baah-zul is a member of the same club."

"The same society," she corrected. "And you should be impressed."

He surveyed Basil Meryash the Fourth, who had returned and was now picking through the salad bar. A vegetarian, no doubt; Ryan would have bet his last dime on it. The guy wore boat shoes with no socks, a monogrammed brown leather jacket that probably cost a zillion dollars, and over his left shoulder, he carried a long-strapped purse. Just like a vegetarian, he thought, decked out in the most expensive leather. He noted the prissy-looking face, the kind one always associated with the privileged. Ryan definitely wanted to hurt him.

"Basil also rows crew," Nicole informed him.

"Why am I not surprised?" Ryan mumbled. It figured that someone named Basil Meryash would be on the rowing team. Of course, they would never allow themselves to be called the rowing team. No, they were members of the crew, an exclusive club devoted to the ancient traditions of Yale. He took another gander at Basil and said, "Most rowers at least have some muscle. Basil's neck looks like a starved chicken's."

Her eyes narrowed. "Basil doesn't do the actual rowing. He's the coxswain."

Ryan pushed past her and replaced a tray of steamed beans. "I don't want to be harsh," he said, clearly wanting to be, "but isn't the coxswain the midget that sits in the back of the boat talking a lot and doing nothing?"

"He steers the racing shell," Nicole said, indignantly. "What do you do besides serving lunch?"

Ryan overlooked the dig. "I play lacrosse," he said.

Her eyes slid down, then back up to his face. "I thought people of your sort played football."

Your sort. So typical. "You don't like football?"

"Actually, I do like football, certainly more than lacrosse, a sport no one has ever heard of," she said, screwing up her nose.

"Ever heard of Jim Brown?"

She looked blank. "No."

He raised his brows in mock incredulity. "You like football and you have never heard of Jim Brown? He was the greatest running back ever."

She lifted her chin. "So?"

Ryan grinned. "Guess what sport he liked best?"

"Lacrosse?" she asked in mock surprise.

"An All-American lacrosse player at Syracuse, but he played football because he couldn't make a living at lacrosse."

"Wow," she said in a bored voice, then held up a twenty. "I have something for you," she sang with an impish smile.

Students in the line stared at Nicole and the twenty she was waving around, then shifted their attention to Ryan.

He groaned, his eyes darting across the faces now looking at him. "You don't owe me anything," Ryan said flatly.

Nicole's emerald eyes danced in delight. "Oh, yes, I do." She was back in charge and enjoying it. "You hauled away every bit of those old boxes—and so here is the extra twenty I promised."

She dangled the bill in front of him. "Of course, I shouldn't hand over money to a total stranger," she said, drawing her hand back and clearly relishing the spectacle she was making. "I don't even know your name—Mr. Boxman, I suppose."

"Ryan Taylor," he said evenly.

"Well, Ryan Taylor, here's your money." She placed the bill neatly on the counter, her eyes sparkling.

He eyed the twenty, and then had an overwhelming urge to fling a spoonful of green beans at her. Of course, in the cold light of day, someone might call him an opportunist for demanding money to help a desperate woman in a rainstorm. But it wasn't a fair assessment. He had been working all day, as had a dozen others like him. Students were happy to pay someone to lug their boxes up three or four flights of stairs. It was hard work and he deserved every dollar he made. A wave of righteous indignation swept over him as he pulled the plastic glove off his hand and reached for the twenty.

Nicole tossed her brown hair and said to a female student beside her, "You would think I'd be the one getting paid for my services, but last night this young lad worked so hard to please me that I thought he deserved the money."

Ryan avoided the other woman's glance, tucked the twenty in his pocket, and grimly busied himself with the chicken.

4 ᖯᖯᖯᖯᖯᖯᖯᖯᖯᖯᖯᖯᖯᖯᖯᖯᖯᖯ

Officer Le Beau parked his police car in a strip mall on the outskirts of New Haven, his eyes sliding up to the Citibank clock. Fifteen minutes late. Perfect. He strolled across the parking lot toward a collection of vehicles parked illegally along the fence. He didn't care—this wasn't his jurisdiction, and even if it were, he would soon be in the same meeting with these people. He patted his ample middle, knowing he couldn't wedge a dime between his shirt and belt, so tightly stretched was the polyester. But he kept a positive attitude as he sucked in his stomach and entered the door emblazoned with huge red letters: Weight Watchers.

Inside, he headed for the table against the wall and fingered through Wednesday's cards until he found his own. Then, turning, he scanned the room. The meeting was already in progress; thirty, maybe thirty-five women in folding chairs, heads inclined toward the speaker, listening. Again, not a man in the hall. He didn't count the skinny guy with the nervous eyes sitting in the shadow of his enormous mean-eyed wife. Put a German uniform on her and she'd fit right in at Treblinka.

"Good morning," the woman behind the counter said, drawing his attention. She had a smile that would cheer even the most defeated fatty. "A little late, but don't worry, the meeting just started," she said, her voice encouraging.

Le Beau nodded. "I don't like standing in line with all the women." He glanced around. "Why aren't there ever any men here?"

"We do have one over there," she said, pointing to the skinny guy.

"I said, *men.*"

She dropped her voice to a conspiratorial level. "We *are* working on that very thing," she said. "You might see an improvement in the coming months."

Le Beau grunted, handed over his card, and paid his weekly fee.

"Well, Elijah," she said, glancing at his name, "let's see how we did this week." She motioned to the scale beside the counter and waited, smiling.

Le Beau removed his police belt with its gun and cuffs, emptied his pockets, shed his watch, and kicked off his shoes. He'd have turned his lungs inside out if he'd thought it would help.

The scale—one of those reliable, electronic kinds—shook as he stepped up and awaited the verdict.

She recorded his weight and stamped the card.

"Well?" he prompted, stepping off.

"Up a tad," she said.

Le Beau looked at the card. "Two and a half pounds!" He rubbed his face, hardly believing it. He had tried so hard this week, even went to bed hungry a few times. He shrugged. "I, uh, well ... you know, couldn't avoid some food events. I'll do better next Wednesday ... stick to my points."

"I'm sure you will," the cheery woman said. "A few pounds is nothing for a strong man like you."

Le Beau managed a smile, gathered his things and took a chair at the back. Someone was showing a chart on meal portions, but all he could think about was his two and a half pound gain. He had done so well the first couple of weeks, lost nearly eight pounds. But now ... well, it wasn't his fault! How could he lose weight when he spent so much time sitting in cars, taking care of spoiled rich kids like that little Ms. Van Buren. And she was rich, no doubt about that. He'd run a check on Yale's major donor list, and her father had contributed millions to the university over the years. Le Beau couldn't afford to lose his job over some misunderstanding, especially now that his wife, Helena, had been diagnosed with multiple sclerosis. He just wanted to make retirement, leave behind New Haven's miserable weather, and head for Arizona where he and Helena could settle into their desert dream house.

Le Beau left the meeting determined to keep his points low during the coming week. He stopped at a Popeye's Chicken for a salad, but ended up getting the eight-piece combo with buttermilk biscuits, Cajun gravy, and coleslaw. The points were a little high, but he wouldn't eat the rest of the day.

* * *

Nearly a month passed before Ryan saw Nicole Van Buren again, and that suited him fine. Not that she was boring or unattractive—far from either. But her type had a way of making him feel impoverished, as if he were Jean Valjean gazing into a bakery window. And he felt poor enough already. In truth, a financial gloom had settled over him like a choking fog: he was desperate for money. The university couldn't provide him with any more grants or loans, so he needed work. In spite of the Student Employment Office he had managed to find odd jobs elsewhere, but at this rate he would soon need a bread line of his own.

He decided to market himself as the campus computer expert, and printed up a small stack of notices:

Computer problem? ITS not helping you?
You need The Amazing Ryan. I can fix anything!
PCs, Macs, Linux.
Speedy service. Reasonable rates.

He had just begun tacking up his notices when he heard a familiar voice behind him.

"My, my, a computer genius! I had no idea you were so talented."

Ryan sighed and turned to face Nicole. She was reading one of his notices, and beside her stood Basil Meryash. "You get a discount," Ryan said, "because you're a repeat customer."

Basil looked at Nicole and said, "Just what your family needs, a discount. Maybe we should all consider joining Costco."

Ryan said nothing, but he imagined his fist flattening Basil's prissy face.

"I wouldn't mind a discount myself," Basil said, chuckling, "but— bad luck—I'm not a repeat customer."

"Basil," Nicole interjected, "why don't we meet at my room around seven?"

"Ooh, that sounds delicious," Basil said with a lecherous grin, kissing her on the lips and then growling like a lion. He glanced at Ryan. "Well, Amazing Ryan, keep up the good work." He left laughing.

"He's got a lively sense of humor," Ryan said, as he watched Meryash swagger away.

"A little tactless at times," Nicole conceded, turning to follow his gaze, "but he has his good points."

Ryan looked back at her. "Really? What are they?"

"They are too numerous to mention." Her mouth creased into a fake smile.

"So you can't even think of one good point."

She bristled. "He comes from an upscale family—"

"That means he's rich."

"And ..." she drew out the word, making it clear she didn't like being interrupted, "he is brilliant."

"Wow," Ryan said.

Her arms crossed. "He has a beautiful singing voice, so good in fact that he's a member of the Whiffenpoofs."

Ryan stifled a smile.

Her face changed, anger hardening her green eyes. "Okay," she snapped, "why the big smirk?"

He held out his hands in mock surrender. "I didn't smirk."

"Yes, you did! What's so funny?"

"About the *Whiffenpoofs?*" He burst out laughing, no longer trying to contain himself. "*Whiffenpoofs?* Are you kidding me?"

"You really don't know anything, do you?" she said, her hands dropping to her hips. "The Whiffenpoofs are the oldest collegiate *a cappella* singing group in the nation. Only fourteen are chosen, usually seniors—I remind you Basel is still a junior—and believe me, people would kill their grandmothers to secure a spot on the Whiffenpoofs."

"My grandmother would kill me if I joined a group called the Whiffenpoofs."

"No offense to your family heritage, but that doesn't surprise me."

Ryan laughed, this time not holding back at all.

She gave him another insincere smile and said, "Even you, I am sure, can see that Basil is associated with the two groups that are *de facto* Yale University: Skull and Bones and the Whiffenpoofs. He's also captain of the Yale Trap and Skeet team, which means he's a superior marksman and, as you know, he's a member of the crew team. Furthermore, if I'm allowed to add a personal note, he is incredibly handsome, extremely interesting, has fascinating insights—"

"He's a toad."

"He's not a toad! And none of this is your business anyway."

Ryan didn't reply and the silence hung awkwardly between them. He bent over to retrieve his notices.

"I looked for you in the cafeteria," she said.

"I work mornings now." He stuffed the notices under his arm.

"That explains it. I never eat breakfast. Makes me hungry all day. I work-out mornings."

"Me too. I've never seen you at the gym. We start at 5:30."

Nicole glanced up at Ryan. "Well, I dance. At a studio." She paused, tipping her head, so that her hair cascaded over one shoulder. "I saw you mopping stairs in Woolsey Hall. How many jobs do you have?"

"Only the cafeteria. But I fill in for friends." This conversation had gone on a lot longer than he expected. *Where was she going with this?* he wondered.

Nicole idly twisted a lock of her hair around one finger. "When do you get time to study?"

He sighed. "It's been a challenge. The load at Yale is definitely not like Yorktown."

"Your high school?"

"Best lacrosse school in the nation," he said with a grin, dropping his guard.

"I went to Choate Rosemary Hall." She paused for a reaction; when Ryan offered none she added, "Where John F. Kennedy attended."

"Oh, that Choate," he said, wanting her to think he'd never heard of it.

She shook her head.

Tired of her nonsense, he motioned toward the sheaf of notices under his arm. "I'd better put these up."

"You expect to do a dozen jobs and still pass your courses?" she asked as he turned away.

He stopped and looked at her, feeling as he had in the face of Dr. Edwards' implacable doubt. "My grades are excellent," he replied, trying not to sound defensive. "I have a knack for computers."

"I can see that," she said, not entirely unkindly, eyeing the bold printed slogan on his notices. "You just have no idea how to make money."

"What's that supposed to mean?"

Her eyes returned to his. "It means you should find a job that pays more for fewer hours."

"Oh, that's brilliant, Ms. My-Daddy-Pays-Everything. What do you know about finding jobs?" He clapped his elbow against his side as the pile of notices started slipping out from under his arm.

"More than you," she countered, leaning forward.

"Really," Ryan said, desperately wanting to say something clever, but making do with sarcasm.

"I don't want to hurt your feelings," she said, "but anyone with modest brain cell activity could see the problem. You dash around campus raking leaves, washing stairs, collecting garbage, and now you're putting up computer notices—you probably spend more time looking for jobs than actually doing them. You work hard, but not smart." She laughed, her face rising in disdain. "Has it ever occurred to you that maybe, just maybe, one job at ten times the pay would solve the problem?"

"Has it ever occurred to you," he said caustically, "that there are no student jobs like that, not even off campus?"

"Well, I know—"

"What do you know?" Ryan snarled. "You know nothing!" His hand came up to stab a finger at her, and half the notices slipped from his grasp. He bent over to pick them up, dropped a few more, then abruptly pitched the rest onto the ground. His hands curled; he very much wanted to smash something, but managed to say in a controlled voice, "There are no jobs like that. None. And even if there were, the Student Employment Office would probably have them on their restricted list. Maybe your *fascinating* Whiffenpoof boyfriend could explain this to you." He didn't bother telling her he had recently been hauled into the Employment Office—again—and given a lecture by Dr. Edwards' assistant, Amy something or other, on how they would be "watching him closely in the future."

Nicole drew a long breath and expelled it slowly. "What I was trying to say is, I know of a position that has no restrictions."

Ryan stared at her.

Her brow lifted. "Have I got your attention now?"

He felt his face flush.

"Good," she said. "If you listen, I might be able to help you."

The phrase, *I might be able to help you*, really got under his skin, but he managed to hold his tongue. "What kind of pay?" he asked.

"High pay," she said. "For you, very high pay. Up front." She opened her eyes wide, as if amazed by her own comment.

He was still skeptical. "What's the job?" he asked, his tone neutral.

"Maybe I won't tell you," she said coyly. "You seem very ungrateful."

Ryan sighed. "Okay, what is this wonderful job?"

"No, no," she said, wagging a finger at him. "Not without an apology. And it better be sincere."

Ryan ignored her teasing. "Do you really know of a job like that, that has no restrictions?"

"I'm wai-ting," she said in a sing-song voice.

"Oh for ..." and Ryan turned away, lifting his eyes skyward.

"Well?"

He turned back. "'Well' what?"

"You know what. An apology, or I'll tell you nothing."

"Okay, I'm sorry."

"Not sincere enough," and Nicole's mouth had a hint of a smile.

Ryan grimaced. "Ms. Van Buren," he began, "I am deeply sorry for my appallingly ungrateful attitude. Please, if you can find it in your heart, forgive me."

"That's better. You should practice that demeanor. It's more attractive."

He sighed. "So tell me about the job."

"It's a biology position—"

"Oh, great!" Ryan said, frowning. "What do I know about biology?"

"Nothing, probably. But you don't need to know anything. Just run a few tests, clean up after the professor, and fill in charts." She paused. "I knew the student who used to assist in the lab, Fraser Samuels. He worked far less than the nineteen hours, and he paid his tuition." Her eyebrows rose for emphasis. "Interested now?"

"How is that even ... I mean ... the university pays a standard amount—"

"All I know is that Fraser received a wage outside Student Employment restrictions. He said the work was uncomplicated—mostly cleanup—but that the professor was a little odd."

Ryan made a face. "Nothing new around here. Who's the professor?"

"Dr. Jozef Krakauer."

"Never heard of him, but he must be a fine human being." He grinned, daring to believe he might actually get the job. He only hoped his high school biology would carry him through.

"Apparently, Krakauer tends to hire undocumented workers rather than Yale students."

"Really? Why?"

She shrugged. "Like I said, he is a bit weird. But, no matter, the university pressures professors to use at least one student worker."

"Which is me," he said with a wry smile.

"Exactly."

"Are you sure the position is still open?"

"That's the best part," she said, her lips widening into a mischievous smile. "Krakauer posted only one note at Kline Biology." She pulled a crumpled paper out of her jeans pocket.

"Aha!" Ryan said, snatching the job advertisement from her hand.

"Just tell his secretary you saw the note at Kline and they'll probably take you. But whatever you do, don't mention my name. My father is a benefactor of sorts to the science program and—well—just don't mention me. Krakauer is very particular about his privacy."

Ryan hesitated, his mood suddenly darkening. Nicole was helping him. She probably expected him to bubble out his thanks, but he couldn't bring himself to say the words. This is what rich kids did. They rallied round the less fortunate and then crowed about it later. Well, he hadn't asked for any help, and he didn't need it. He didn't need anybody, especially Nicole Van Buren.

"Is something wrong?" she asked.

Ryan stared at the ground, angry at himself, at Nicole, at the whole situation. He knew a job of this sort could change everything, but he couldn't say thank you. He swallowed hard. "No, nothing's wrong," he murmured.

She shrugged off his discomfort and continued speaking, "It also might be wise not to mention anything about Fraser. Apparently, Krakauer kicked him out of the lab at some point. Fraser said that Krakauer's a bit paranoid about people meddling in his business."

"Sounds mysterious."

Nicole laughed. "Yes, everything about Professor Krakauer is mysterious, either that or just plain strange. You'll find out. He's from Eastern Europe, suspicious of everybody, and has a habit of staring. The biology students call him Dr. Crackpot."

"But he pays well."

"Yes, he pays well." Her smile was warm now, not at all condescending.

"I should phone this Fraser to find out—"

Nicole put a hand on his arm and inclined her head slightly. "That's why the position is open," she said. "Fraser was in a car accident two weeks ago. He's dead."

5

The chateau had stood imperiously for a hundred and fifty years, a stone fortress overlooking the choppy waters of Chesapeake Bay, the only structure along Maryland's eastern coast that had withstood the constant pounding storms. At the front of the house, the well-tended lawn seemed out of character with the surrounding acres of forbidding marshlands and waterways.

Four mammoth gates controlled access, and everywhere dotting its two-mile approach, cameras and sensors observed the slightest movement.

The general had often wondered about the previous owners and their penchant for security. They obviously lacked military training, because anyone seriously wanting to attack the chateau could have mounted a rear offensive from the bay, quickly neutralizing the few sensors and cameras pointed toward the water. Civilians for you, he thought, as he punched the security buttons to open the final set of gates.

The general waited patiently as the black Lincoln rolled silently through the arched entryway. The man who stepped from the car didn't offer his hand but saluted crisply and barked, "With my shield or on it!"

The general saluted back, his eyes fixed on the man. "With my shield or on it," he replied quietly.

The man smiled. "Good to see you, sir."

"You as well, Mr. Secretary," the general said, inviting his guest into the study for brandy.

The general chose a hard chair, shunning the softer stuffed ones into which visitors usually settled. His guest understood this loathing of soft chairs and the people who slumped into them, choosing for himself a heavy bench in the center of the room and placing his brandy glass soundlessly upon its smooth varnished surface.

"How's Washington these days?" the general asked, dispensing with the obligatory questions about family.

"I want out."

"So you said on the phone."

The man's eyes moved restlessly around the room, as if he were searching for something. "I have two years left in my term as Secretary of Agriculture," he said, "but I'm considering leaving earlier to pursue other interests."

"Go on."

He hesitated. "General, we've known each other for a long time. During my years as your adjutant I worked hard and served you well. We retired from the army the same month fourteen years ago and have remained, I think, good friends. I know you appreciate straight talk and that's why I asked for this meeting." He took a swallow of brandy, his hands now fidgeting with the glass.

The general sipped some brandy himself, eyes expressionless. The Secretary's speech sounded rehearsed, but he gestured for the other man to proceed.

After a deep breath, the Secretary continued, "I have no illusions about myself. Without you and your influence I would never have become Secretary of Agriculture. I know that." He shifted uncomfortably on the bench. "Overall, I think I have done a credible job at Agriculture—people say I've accomplished more than my predecessors, if that's any endorsement."

The general waited, knowing the power of silence.

"It's this genetic engineering business," the man said, his face scrunching in embarrassment. "You know how these bleeding hearts are, always looking for someone to blame. This woman who died from eating pizza in Philadelphia? The investigation is going to show that, yes, the proteins used to engineer the plump red tomatoes were peanut-derived. It won't matter whether it contributed or not at that point. It's been leaked and the anti-GMO groups are having a field day; there's real money behind them now. I'm getting calls from the Hill all the time. Another lawsuit was filed in California on Monday, and the media can't get enough. My department screens over a thousand calls a week and I was the one who sanctioned the framework for the new Transgenic Crops Initiative in the first place. Now it's all unraveling."

"A tough spot."

"Very tough," said the Secretary, swallowing more brandy and then reflexively topping up his glass.

"But that wasn't Proskin Pharmaceutical."

"That's true, your company had no ties to this tomato fiasco or TCI, but ...." He laughed awkwardly. "Agriculture is getting hammered. These watchdog groups are all over us. The administration is calling for heads." He reached into his pocket for a pack of cigarettes, found nothing, and then mumbled something about having quit. "I'm worried, you see?"

"Of course," the general said.

The man wiped beads of sweat from his upper lip. "You know I have always responded favorably to your requests, but right now, well, I'm under the gun. This recent application by Proskin for field-testing of your new biosynthetic lines—I just can't do it, General. Not now." He wagged his head anxiously. "You have to understand, the political winds are changing. The damn eco-nuts and religious groups—they're actually together on this! Sue-for-hire firms are in full throttle, and they're carrying a big stick. Hell, General, they've got a howitzer! They're on the news every night claiming that genetic material—from humans—has already been introduced into the US food supply chain."

"Not from Proskin."

He paused, then asked nervously. "So you don't have anything like that in development?"

"I believe we do, in our synthetic dermis project."

"Human skin!" The Secretary looked sick.

"Bits of DNA, Bruce. A few proteins." The general waved his hand. "Everyone's got a dermis project going these days. Half of them are in food crops."

"But that's what I'm saying. These people are frightened to death about eating animal flesh, and now," he rubbed both hands across his face, "now I've got to tell them they're cannibals?"

The general took a long look at his guest whose sunken eyes avoided his. "Nothing has left the lab," he said, "and you have no obligation to provide them with any information. Let them file FOIA requests—none of this is in the official pipeline yet."

The other man gulped down a large amount of brandy and again refilled his glass. "Well, they seem to know something about what's going on at Proskin—they're calling your recent application for genetically altered animals a freak show—a Frankenfarm."

"Frankenfarm?" The general laughed. "Can't they come up with anything new?"

"This is no laughing matter," the Secretary said. "Not in Washington. There's no political cover on this."

The general bolted from his chair. "You think I find this funny?" he roared, irked that his former adjutant would presume to reprimand him. "What I do at Proskin has nothing to do with a freak show! We are creating a better world! Do I make myself clear?"

"Please," the Secretary said deferentially, holding up a hand and bowing his head slightly. "These are not my words, General. You know how these alarmist groups work, they beat their propaganda drums day and night. The average citizen hasn't a clue what any of this science means, and that's what keeps these groups in business, that and the money they raise from their scare tactics." He shook his head. "Everyone else in Washington gets by because they play ball, but I can tell you this, I am fast becoming the scapegoat."

The general slowly returned to his seat. "Anything else? he asked.

"Well," the Secretary said, gathering himself, "Proskin has created animal models that—to be blunt, they suffer their whole life through. There's been nothing submitted to Ag, but the word is that you're maintaining huge populations of blind and crippled animals that are reproducing with the same defective genes."

"Not *defective* genes. The genes have simply been altered."

"Altered! General, the animals are blind and crippled!"

"And what is the problem with that? We eat animals, make belts and shoes out of them."

The Secretary slumped back on his bench. "It's the suffering aspect. Creating a blind animal whose offspring will always be blind sounds cruel to the public."

"What the hell do they know? It's not like we let the blind stocks wander the nation's highways. The populations you reference aren't even in U.S. jurisdiction. We're following the letter of the law, Bruce.

The Secretary shrugged weakly. "What I'm saying is that Proskin's current application could be more than just a straw to break the camel's back—it could be a time bomb. You have to understand that these animal rights activists don't care about the research benefit; they see geneticists as the anti-Christ. Nobody in the administration wants to hear about it. Frankly, I don't know what to tell them."

"You tell them to drop by any institution for the sightless and ask those poor wretches if they mind the Proskin Pharmaceutical Company altering the genetic codes of animals to help blind people see. I will trade a pig's rights for a human's any day. Humans look at Monet, pigs look at shit."

The Secretary nodded vigorously and said, "General, believe me, I agree with you a thousand percent. I'm just worried about a domino effect." He licked his lips.

"These aren't new concerns, Bruce. This is old news. What's on your mind?"

"Well, to be frank, General, there's the other problem, you know … with all the scrutiny, someone's bound to discover that I fast-tracked Proskin's early requests. We could both be in trouble." He leaned forward. "That's why I was thinking, maybe if I step down—"

"Don't be absurd," snapped the general. "How long do you think it'll be before the new Secretary of Agriculture discovers the fast-tracking arrangement?"

The Secretary looked surprised, as if he hadn't thought about the new Secretary. He drained the bottom half of his drink, his eyes on the black walnut flooring. "The Green political agenda is out of control," he said. "There's always some reporter or headline-seeking judge out to nail your hide to the Washington Monument. All of a sudden, no one cares about immigration, or health care, or entitlements. Everything is about the Greens. You know how Washington works better than I do, General. How long do you think I can keep this up?"

The general rose and walked over to the window, his eyes drawn to the sun hanging low over the marshlands and the distant cattails that appeared to be on fire. His former adjutant had trusted him to make sound decisions, and now those decisions had come back to bite them both. He ran his fingers through his graying hair, thinking. One thing was certain: he was not about to stand by idly while a fellow officer twisted in the wind.

The general had created the problem and he would solve it. Besides, the last thing he wanted was for some special interest group to focus a light on Proskin, looking for blemishes; too much was at stake. "Let me make a suggestion," he said, turning to face the Secretary. "I want you to deny Proskin's request for field-testing these ..." he gestured with his hand, "freak-show animals. That should take the heat off you."

The Secretary's head lifted. "Are you sure? That's a major item for you."

"We'll submit it—you reject it. Who can accuse you of favoring Proskin when you have denied such an important application?"

"I don't know what to say." The Secretary looked stunned.

"Naturally, I expect to hear no more about you stepping down from your post. I still like having old friends in high places." The Secretary opened his mouth to speak but the general waved him quiet. "I value your friendship, Bruce," he said trying to be personal. Opening the drawer of a small table, he removed an item wrapped in a scarlet cloth and handed it to the other man. "A watch," the general said.

The Secretary stood to receive the gift, opened the cloth, and smiled. "Like the old days," he said. "An MTM Special Forces watch." He squinted. "But I don't think I've seen this kind." He took out his glasses to examine the watch more closely, then read the single word printed on the faceplate: "Thermopylae." He looked up.

"Made especially for us. Slightly better craftsmanship. Read the inscription."

The Secretary turned the watch over and nodded as he murmured, "With my shield or on it."

"I'm giving them to people I value."

"A good reminder," the Secretary said. "Thank you."

The general clasped his hands behind his back and squared his shoulders. "One last thing. These final two years at Agriculture could be tough—we can't predict the future—but if it'll help you sleep at night, know that when you leave, you'll be stepping into a senior vice-president's job at Proskin." He allowed a smile to flicker across his face. "That's seven million take-home, Bruce, with stock options. On a good year, with bonuses, you could be making upwards of fifteen."

Bruce stared at the general.

"Old soldiers should stick together, don't you agree?"

"Yes, most definitely," the Secretary whispered, smiling for the first time since he arrived. "I suspect I can survive the rigors of Washington two more years."

"Good," the general said, offering his friend more brandy. "I have a feeling the future will be very bright indeed."

"With you," said Bruce, "how could it be otherwise?"

6

The chimps scampered around their sealed containers, each with a separate air supply to prevent cross-contamination. Through the thick window, Dr. Jozef Krakauer studied the female in the corner compartment who was cautiously approaching a glass vial attached to the wall. Chimps were always curious.

Krakauer poured himself a cup of tea, one hand holding the steaming pot, the other hand directing the computer controls that moved the mechanical arms in the corner compartment. He swallowed some tea, and then manipulated the arms to open the vial of colorless liquid. Fishing out his stopwatch, he clicked start, and recorded the time in his notes. Eight minutes should do it. No different from his tests on smaller primates like marmosets and lemurs; they had metabolized the trigger chemicals in seven to eight minutes. Larger primates should perform about the same.

The professor tipped back his chair, sipped some more tea, and listened to the sweeping strains of Mozart's *Nachtmusik*. He massaged his neck, tiny circular movements that relaxed his shoulders and filled his mind with thoughts of sleep. He wished he had the stamina of the energetic chimp, now screeching and swinging on the mechanical arms.

Yes, it had been a long process, but he was pleased with the airborne trials. At the beginning, when he hijacked Westover's delivery system, Krakauer had made certain the newly introduced deadly gene needed physical contact to trigger it—safer that way. A small amount of trigger on the arm of the old fool's glasses had worked well and presented little danger to anyone else. But that time had passed. Now he had perfected an airborne trigger.

As the chimp bounced playfully around the cage, Krakauer's mind drifted back to Westover and his nasty old cat. What satisfaction he had felt when collecting that fleabag to use in his experiments, and not because he'd had some perverse desire to see Westover's cat die. Krakauer had fully expected the animal to survive the trials and live out the remainder of her days on the streets. The satisfaction came in knowing that Westover, his cat, and everything about the man would finally be gone, and a new era would begin.

But Krakauer's satisfaction turned to horror when Westover's cat collapsed like baked cheese. Krakauer had engineered *Alpha* (*Omega*, as Krakauer now called it, because the gene was the end of life, the destroyer), he had engineered the gene to infect only human and animal primates. So how could a feline be affected? The whole thing puzzled him, and for many months he reworked his experiments, making certain it never ranged beyond primates, which would have been the ultimate disaster. Once triggered, it could have spread rapidly through the animal and bird population, destroying most life forms on the planet. Such was the power of genetic engineering, and why Krakauer was determined to stop it.

He felt no remorse for Westover's grisly death. Scientists like Westover, who scrambled the genetic codes of species, deserved the grave.

Let them rot!

Every one of them!

Rot in the bowels of the earth!

The world was better off without the Westovers of this age. They were not true scientists but destroyers of creation. They reduced life to bits of information, scrabble chits to arrange at whim. They thought nothing of introducing human genes into animals and animal genes into vegetables, all the while trumpeting the magnificent benefits that would come from the process. Yet they had no idea what their genetic pollution would produce, and scoffed at those who warned of the hideous surprises stalking the human race.

Worst of all they took no responsibility for the new life forms they created, and acted as if their abominations could be recalled like defective car parts. But you cannot recall new life forms; once out there genes replicate indefinitely. Over the years, Krakauer had come to realize that biotechnology would be the final step in humanity's collapse.

The public didn't understand, but like blind people strolling toward a cliff, they continued merrily onward. They anguished over fruit flies and African "killer" bees in the ecological mix, when hidden away in labs from New York to New Delhi, a thousand swarming life forms were being prepared to gobble up their precious world. They had no idea what was being done in the name of science, no idea of the coming apocalypse. Their ignorance of genetics was staggering.

How he wished he had chosen to study something other than genetics, something like mathematics or music perhaps, anything but genetics. Then he would be like everyone else—ignorant of the destruction that lay ahead. He would be like the poor souls that awful morning in the Trade Towers, oblivious of the conflagration about to engulf them.

But Krakauer was not oblivious. He knew! Yes, Jozef Krakauer knew the dark possibilities very well, and he was determined to stop the insanity.

But at what cost?

What cost indeed!

His thin lips tightened across his teeth. Sentimentality was not an option; he could serve humanity only if he steeled his mind and applied a sharp mercy, a mercy that would require some to die so the majority might live. He sighed. Einstein had been right when he had said the world was a dangerous place—not because of evil people, but because of good people who did nothing to stop evil. Krakauer remembered the numbered tattoo on his grandmother's arm. She had seen an entire nation do nothing when her people were herded into cattle cars destined for Hitler's ovens. "Stand and be counted!" his grandmother used to say. "What more can God expect of us, than to stand and be counted?"

Krakauer's eyes stared at the chimp without seeing, and he wondered what his grandmother would say now. Would she put her arms around her grandson and tell him he was doing the right thing? Krakauer didn't know. He folded his hands. He was not without feelings, and well knew what his actions would produce. But what choice did he have? A line from an ancient Hebrew poem nibbled at the edges of his mind:

> Who has beheld the gates of deep darkness?
> Has anyone seen the gates of death?

Now he could answer those questions. *He had*—Dr. Jozef Krakauer had seen the gates of deep darkness looming at the end of a twisting roadway, on which genetic scientists walked. No one else seemed able, or willing, to peer into that future land where the souls of innocent people cried out for release. He knew the earth would become a distortion of itself if genetic engineering were allowed to continue to its inevitable conclusion, and so with trembling fingers and a steely resolve, he cracked those gates—slightly—to test the earth for a season.

Krakauer paused. The chimp had begun to screech inside the glass enclosure, its body suddenly trembling. He studied her briefly, recording in his notes: *four minutes.* She was starting to feel the effects of the open vial after four minutes. Restlessness was always a precursor. Krakauer shifted his eyes to the other animals, but they were calm. He leaned back in his chair and thought about the strange road he had been traveling, a lonely road, but a road that led directly to the Eternal One.

The professor knew he might sound like a religious screwball, but in truth, he was not a religious man. He never attended synagogue, and rarely, if ever, prayed, though he sometimes did read the Hebrew Scriptures at night to pass the time. Still, he had no doubts that the Ancient of Days had chosen him. He remembered sitting rigidly on the commuter train from New Haven to Grand Central Station, clutching his carrying case to his chest, and wondering whether he should proceed. That's when he'd first heard the voice, a gravelly resonance calling out to him.

He remembered whipping his head around and looking intently at the man sitting next to him. "Did God send you?" he had asked.

"What?" The man appeared shaken by the question.

"God," Krakauer repeated. "Did God send you?"

The man stared at him but said nothing. At that moment, Krakauer felt a flame searing his body, as if it were sanctifying him, consecrating him for his mission, and he welcomed the pain. It was a cleansing flame, he knew, preparing him for the trying days ahead. Yes, the Eternal One was about to weigh his soul in the balance and he was determined not to be found wanting. Closing his eyes, he answered the voice, saying out loud: "I am the apostle of the Almighty."

The voice replied, "I have roamed the earth sifting the hearts of men. You will alert the people."

"Yes," Krakauer said eagerly. "I will alert the people." The man next to him gathered his things and left, but Jozef paid him no mind, squeezing his eyes shut and reserving his full attention for the voice.

"Do you believe I am calling you?" the voice asked.

"Yes, I believe."

"And your resolve will not waver when I am silent?"

"I will never waver."

"My people are in danger."

Krakauer wiped the sweat streaking his face.

"My people are in danger!" The voice sounded upset.

"They ... they will not listen," Krakauer stammered.

"Make them listen."

"But how?"

The voice did not reply.

Krakauer sat in awkward silence, eyes still closed, waiting.

"I have chosen you from many."

Krakauer swallowed. "Can I make the blind see and the deaf hear?"

"You can."

"But how—"

"You know how," the voice whispered.

Krakauer slumped in his seat. "Many will die ...."

"All flesh is grass," the voice crooned.

Krakauer opened his eyes and stared at the ribbed ceiling of the train. "I understand," he said in full voice. "The grass withers, the flower fades."

People all over the train were turning their heads.

"Yes! Yes!" the voice prodded. "Speak it out!"

"The grass withers, the flower fades," Krakauer repeated, locking his eyes onto the few people who dared look in his direction. "They shrivel because the breath of the Lord blows upon them." He raised his voice on the last phrase and smiled as the train faces stared at the floor. "Yes," he laughed, understanding, "I am the breath of Yahweh!"

For the rest of his trip to New York, Krakauer slouched in silence, hugging his case. No one so much as glanced at him, and his fear had vanished. At Grand Central he left the train quickly to lose himself in the crowds, but his caution was unnecessary; no one had alerted the police.

The hand of the Almighty was upon him.

Krakauer opened his case and extracted a stack of one dollar bills he had previously sprayed. He purchased several cakes, a dozen coffees and a straw doll, all of which he promptly dumped into a refuse bin. He saw a janitor mopping floors in the cavernous train station, and scores of people crisscrossing from every direction, ignoring the yellow caution signs and caring little whether the janitor had to redo his floors, and again he opened his case, this time to retrieve a small flask of amber liquid. He covered it with his hand, an unnecessary caution, as it turned out. Not one person looked his way. People were too preoccupied with their own lives to worry about 9/11 events. That was the job of government.

Krakauer waited for the janitor to turn his back before emptying the flask into the bucket. He then splashed two more flasks, one on the ramps leading to the trains and the other at the station exits.

He took a hack cab to Kennedy Airport, and purchased more items with another batch of singles. Then he emptied his remaining flasks at the ports of international destinations. He sprinkled *Omega* at all entrances and exits, and used a sponge to coat door handles and the black rubber handrails of the escalators. Some might have thought it strange to see a man holding a sponge against the moving handrail, but no one said a word. In New York people still kept to themselves.

* * *

His eyes focused on the chimp again, and the events unfolding inside the glass enclosure. She had begun her death dance, as Krakauer thought of it. He glanced at his watch—seven minutes. Marmosets, chimps—it made no difference. The trigger amplified in about the same time. Krakauer sipped his tea as the animal threw herself against the glass walls and sprinted mindlessly around the cage. Seconds later she lost her motor capability and began to spin sideways until, eyes bulging, she dropped in a heap on the floor. Krakauer pushed his face toward the glass. The chimp was now clearly dead but its body continued to move inside the fur. Cells were exploding everywhere as the deadly trigger spread, and within seconds the animal melted into an unrecognizable puddle of fur and dark liquid.

Krakauer checked his watch again and took another sip of tea, then grunted in satisfaction. Everything was proceeding nicely. He opened the airshafts to three other chimps in the corner compartments. Minutes later the three began to experience symptoms, and soon they too lay in formless lumps on the glass floor. Krakauer smiled. The chemical agent had triggered the deadly gene efficiently and quickly, and as an airborne droplet, it migrated extraordinarily well in spite of a seeming lack of air movement. He rechecked his watch, waited twenty minutes, and then opened all the airshafts inside the chamber.

The remaining two chimps in the center compartments scampered about unaware that contaminated air from the other cages was entering their compartments. As the minutes ticked by the chimps continued their playful movements, but were not visibly affected by the incoming air. Eight minutes grew to fifteen and still the chimps appeared robust and healthy. Krakauer waited until the half-hour mark before directing the computer to raise the glass walls, leaving two bewildered chimps surrounded by four lumps of muck-encased fur.

One of the more curious chimps poked at the carcasses as if his efforts would somehow produce a reaction. Krakauer noticed that its feet were tracking bloodied tissue everywhere, but neither remaining animal suffered ill effects.

"Excellent," he murmured.

He leaned forward and let his forehead rest against the cool glass. With the perfection of the airborne trigger, *Omega*, his masterpiece, was now complete.

The trigger had broken down in less than an hour, probably in fifteen to twenty minutes. It could no longer harm anyone, and more importantly, no one could detect it. Any researcher examining the liquefied remains would find only harmless proteins present everywhere in nature. In two short years he had performed a miracle, taking Westover's crude efforts and transforming them into something that would make the world tremble. Westover might have been ignorant about the devastating possibilities of his research, but Krakauer was not. And he was determined to put an end to it.

The alternative was unthinkable.

Left to themselves, geneticists would destroy the world. The unsuspecting public could be roused to action only if they understood the shocking potential of genetic research. After a season of instruction, Krakauer felt certain that the whole world would force scientists to abandon genetic research forever.

At the New York airports Krakauer had unleashed a life-form so infectious and so proficient at avoiding the immune system that one year later he had not found a single New Haven blood donor whose cells had not been altered. Even the hundreds of samples sent to him by the Red Cross under the guise of other research projects—from every corner of the world—were more than ninety-nine percent positive. Everybody, including himself, now carried the potentially destructive gene. All Krakauer needed to do was provide the chemical trigger, and the people of the earth would melt like wax, liquefy like the monkeys in the cage.

Judgment was at hand.

7

Three days after talking with Nicole Van Buren, Ryan had secured an interview with Dr. Jozef Krakauer. He had been studying biology around the clock, even bought *Cliffs Quick Review for Biology*, but it was not quick enough. He rubbed his red-rimmed eyes in despair, and left his dorm for the interview.

After some searching, Ryan found the basement entrance to Sterling Library and pressed the combination of numbers given him by Professor Krakauer's secretary. The mag lock released and he made his way down the empty passageway, eventually coming to a hulking brute of a door that looked like the entrance to a vault. Above the doorbell in tiny letters he read *Krakauer, Principal Investigator*. What was a science lab doing in the basement of the library? he wondered. But here it was.

Peering along the dimly lit hall, Ryan spotted a wooden crate in an alcove, and sat down to rehearse his newly acquired biology knowledge. At exactly 2:00 p.m. he rang the bell. Punctuality would impress a scientist, he reasoned.

Nobody answered.

Ryan instinctively looked at his watch. Two o'clock. Tapping the bell again, he leaned close to hear if it rang on the inside, thought he heard something, but couldn't be certain. He glanced the length of the hall, then waited a few minutes before ringing the bell again. Appearing impatient wouldn't be helpful. What if Dr. Krakauer were in the middle of an important experiment and heard him assaulting the bell like a New York trucker? How infuriating would that be? On the other hand, he didn't want to seem unsure of himself, so he pushed the button again.

Nothing.

Ryan was now pacing up and down the hall, wondering what to do. Yale professors were notorious for neglecting their appointments. The thought annoyed him. He popped the button a few more times. Still no answer. He walked over to the wooden crate and sat down. He needed this job, and wasn't about to give up. Thirty minutes passed. More bell ringing and more silence, and the deserted corridor was beginning to look spooky. At forty-five minutes Ryan began ringing the bell in angry clusters, and then as he held the button down one last, long, irritating time, the door opened.

"Oh!" Ryan stammered. "I ... I thought—"

A hawked-faced man with pronounced acne scarring stood in the doorway.

"Are you Dr. Krakauer?" Ryan asked haltingly. "I have an

appointment with Dr. Krakauer ... for two o'clock." His words emerged as a weak dribble.

"Come in." The two briskly spoken words were tinged with an accent Ryan couldn't quite identify.

He followed the professor through a coatroom and into a large lab cluttered with empty crates and packing materials. On the opposite side of the lab were double doors with slit windows, and from what Ryan could see, a central hallway that led away to other labs. The professor mumbled something, gesturing loosely with his hand, then disappeared through the doors. Ryan waited, unsure whether he was supposed to follow, decided he was, and pushed through the doors. The hallway had five or six smaller rooms on one side, an oversized lab on the other, door partly open, and what seemed to be a huge room at the end. From the smell of disinfectant and the sound of feet scampering in cages, Ryan guessed the end room housed the animals.

Ryan poked his head inside the oversized room, a brightly lit area that housed two stainless steel chambers with thick glass windows and rubber-sealed doors. He spotted the bent form of the professor leaning over a computer, and immediately stepped back. Too late. The professor jerked his head around, and took several steps toward Ryan, his eyes flashing. "I told you to wait in the main lab," he snarled.

"Sorry," Ryan said to the rapidly closing door, "I didn't hear you." He headed back to the main lab, concerned about how his interview was progressing. When the professor returned, Ryan smiled, trying to give the impression he thought everything was moving along smoothly. He cast his eyes around the room, as if he had suddenly noticed the chaos of empty boxes, bubble wrap, twisted tape, and Styrofoam littering the tables and floors. If nothing else, thought Ryan, the professor needed a good assistant to clean up after him.

"You have an appointment with me, yes?" the professor asked.

"I made it with your secretary at Kline," Ryan said. He was trying to sound casual, but he knew the professor had heard the angry bell ringing.

Krakauer took a seat at the only clean table in the room. "We can talk here," he said.

Ryan swung his leg over a tall stool and found himself staring at a balding man with a closely trimmed beard, and brilliant blue eyes.

"Your name is Taylor?"

"Yes, Ryan Taylor."

"And you have interest in the student research position?"

"Yes."

"My secretary was uncertain about your status. You are a third-year biology student?"

"Not exactly," Ryan said, clearing his throat and remembering how he had danced around the secretary's questions. "I'm actually in my second year and ... well, I'm in my second year."

"I see. Second-year biology." His words sounded like a statement so Ryan remained silent. "The position is not dedicated research," he continued, "mostly basic duties, and since you would be my only lab assistant, a significant amount of cleanup would be required."

"I don't mind cleanup," Ryan said, smiling again and looking toward the muddle of boxes in the corner. "Looks like you could use a good cleanup person."

Ryan's smile met with silence. He wished he hadn't tried to be personable. "I understand you've been several weeks without an assistant," he said, trying to recover.

"How would you know that?" Krakauer asked sharply, the blue eyes fixing on him.

Ryan stared blankly, stunned into silence by the question.

"How did you know about my assistant?" The professor's body was now completely rigid.

"I don't remember," Ryan said, avoiding any reference to Nicole Van Buren. "Somebody at Kline must have mentioned it."

Krakauer's face twisted. "You've been asking about me and my lab, haven't you?"

"With respect, sir," Ryan said, anger seeping into his voice, "I've been trying to find a job, checking bulletin boards all over campus. Before I saw your note, I had never heard of you or your lab." He realized he had better curb his pride or he'd be back to slinging beans.

The professor seemed satisfied and Ryan wondered whether his anger had somehow made his story more believable. "I hire specific cleaners when I need them," Krakauer said in a measured tone, "and if I do select you, you will allow no one to enter this lab without my authorization. Is that clear?"

"Of course," Ryan said.

"No one," he repeated.

An awkward silence followed, so Ryan said as neutrally as he could, "You just tell me what needs doing and I'll get it done."

"Have you assisted other professors in their labs?"

"No, not really." He wanted to sound like he had at least some lab experience.

"Have you or not?" Krakauer's voice was cold and flat.

Ryan shifted awkwardly on his stool, uncertain how to answer, then opted for the truth. "I did some lab work in high school," he said.

"And here at Yale?" The professor leaned forward, eyes boring into him.

Ryan shook his head.

"Because I will soon discover if you have assisted for anyone else."

"No, no I have never—"

"Good." His mouth smiled, although his eyes remained, not cold, but distant, as if focused inward. "No harm done, yes? I have little tolerance for other professors sending their research assistants to meddle in my work."

"I just have high school lab experience," Ryan repeated, thankful he'd opted to be truthful.

The professor's gleaming eyes now held him fast, as if probing for hidden information. Ryan pulled his own gaze away and glanced around the lab, trying to approximate a relaxed manner. "So," he said, "what kind of research do you do?"

The professor made no response.

"Doesn't matter of course," Ryan said, shrugging, "Just wondering."

"Immunomics," he said at length, "and immunomodulation."

Ryan nodded, as if he understood. "That's very interesting."

"Yes. I have hope my research might be useful for developing gene therapy approaches."

"Gene therapy," Ryan repeated, nodding. Then, thoughtfully, he said "So you want to fix genetic disorders."

The professor studied him a moment and then said, "Yes, exactly, I want to fix genetic disorders."

Ryan let out a snort, obviously pleased with himself, and then to cover up he said, "Well, of course, you did say, ah … immuno … work."

"I did."

Ryan couldn't control the grin that spread across his face.

Professor Krakauer smiled and said, "You are acceptable to me. Very acceptable."

* * *

Elijah Le Beau thumped out of another Weight Watcher's meeting, patting his middle. Down four-tenths of a pound. Not bad, considering what he had eaten that week, but not what he'd hoped. He thought about his football days at Florida State, how lean and strong he'd been. Never could he have imagined himself growing old and fat. But that's what he was. Old and fat. There was no other way to put it. Too many burgers and fries, topped off with cheesecake at Claire's. He slammed the car door and sped off, determined to change his ways. Why shouldn't he be thin? All he had to do was stop stuffing Popeye's biscuits into his mouth every time he drove down Whalley Avenue. "You didn't get here in a day," the woman leading the meeting had said, "and it won't come off in a day. Just gotta keep at it."

Le Beau cut across town and soon found himself driving through the heart of New Haven's Little Italy. He hadn't eaten all day because of the weigh-in so he still had all his points to use, and if he was going to eat something, it might as well be good. Pepe's Pizza had the best white clam pizza in the world, tender clams with soft-cooked bits of garlic sprinkled on a chewy crust. Basically, fish with a dash of cheese, he reasoned, and everyone knew garlic was incredibly healthy for you. Maybe he would add a salad to make it a balanced meal, and if the points were a little high, he wouldn't eat the rest of the day.

Later that afternoon, the skies darkened, threatening rain. Le Beau made his rounds, writing a few tickets for double-parking, and blaring his horn at a townie sawing a lock off some student's bike. When the rain finally came, it splashed street grime onto his glossy cruiser, depressing his mood, which made him think yet again about his weight. He remembered ruefully the pizza and fried crostoli pastry he had eaten earlier. His lack of discipline was sickening; he was the biggest rationalizer on the planet! Here he'd had a good day going and what did he do? Congratulate himself for losing weight by filling his face with pizza and crostoli. He looked gloomily past the rhythmic swaying of his windshield wipers.

The storm passed quickly but not before downing some trees, which in turn knocked out power to a dozen blocks in central New Haven. Dispatch said the situation would be remedied in two hours but all police officers were to continue rounds until seven that evening. Le Beau wanted to check on his wife, but with dozens of calls coming in, he had little time.

An hour later his cell phone buzzed. He looked at it and saw it was Helena. "Hi, honey!" he said. "Are you calling to check on my weight?"

"Of course," she said, but her voice sounded subdued.

"Down half a pound," he said without mentioning his stop in Little Italy.

"Wonderful," she said, but this time he could hardly hear her.

"Is everything okay? You sound—"

"I think you should come home."

His heart jumped. "What's happened?" he asked. Helena was not the kind of person to complain about trivialities.

No reply.

"Helena?" He swung the car around and flicked on his overheads. He suspected her call had something to do with the multiple sclerosis, which had clearly worsened over the past few months. "Helena? Listen to me, honey, I'm on my way." He glanced at the phone, waiting for a response. Getting none, he said, "Talk to me, now. Tell me what happened. Are you hurt? Should I call an ambulance?" He spoke in his police voice, hoping to snap her out of her silence.

It did.

"I had a fall," she said.

"A fall," he repeated. In the last year she'd been having trouble walking. "What kind of fall?"

"Down the basement stairs," she said.

Le Beau's fingers tightened on the wheel.

"I was ... and ... stairs ...."

"Honey, I'm sorry, I can't hear you. You have to speak up."

"The wash," she said, "I was doing the wash."

Le Beau swept his eyes across an intersection and sped through. "Are you all right?"

"A little dizzy."

"Where are you? In the basement?"

"Bottom of the stairs," she said.

"Okay. Are you sitting down?"

"I feel dizzy," she said.

"Are you bleeding?"

"I don't know," she said. "Please hurry."

"Hang on," he said. "I'm on Maple now. Be there in a minute." He gunned it around a Ford being driven by an old man whose head barely cleared the steering wheel. Where did these people get their licenses? Minutes later he was on Ellsworth and heading toward his house at the end of the block. He slowed. It was already dark and the street deserted, trees still dripping with rain, but with a neighborhood knee-deep in kids, he worried about someone darting in front of his cruiser. Parents were funny—some let their kids run the streets at all hours.

When Le Beau arrived at his house, the red oak in his front yard had snapped in two, pulling down the electrical wires leading to the house. He radioed for a work crew to clean up the problem, though he knew it would be hours before anyone came. All he could do was tape off the area.

But first, he had to check on Helena. A wave of unease swept through him as he eyed their two-story frame house, now looking starkly unfamiliar in its blackness. Pushing his bulk out of the car, he elbowed the door closed, and charged up the porch steps like a linebacker. Helena hated "big scenes" and would be manifestly unhappy that he had left the overheads flashing on the police car, alerting all the neighbors that Helena Le Beau's MS was acting up. He'd deal with that later. Right now, he needed to make sure she wasn't lying in a pool of blood, or worse.

Inside, he swept his flashlight across the living room, slowly, carefully, the beam eerily illuminating one item after another, then returning it to darkness. One of the lamps had been knocked onto the floor. He moved into the room, clicking several light switches up and down, but none worked, though most had been switched on. Lately, Helena had been leaving the lights on everywhere, as if she were having trouble seeing. Le Beau had wondered if it had something to do with the MS, but he never voiced his concerns. He followed his beam of light through the kitchen and started down the basement stairs.

"Helena!" he called.

"Elijah?" Her voice sounded very small.

He huffed down the stairs and caught his foot on a knit sweater draped across one of the steps. Scooping it up without pausing, he suddenly realized that Helena must have tripped on that same sweater earlier. He arced his light across the floor but saw nothing.

"Honey, where are?" Then he saw her, sitting on a chair against the wall. "Are you okay?" he asked, dropping on one knee in front of her. He cupped his hand over the light to keep the glare out of her eyes, but angled it so he could see part of her face. She had a broad scrape running from her cheekbone to her chin, and her lips were swollen, but neither injury looked serious. "Are you okay?" he repeated softly.

"I think so," she said.

"Your back and neck?"

She nodded slightly to say they were fine.

"Close your eyes," he said. "I need to examine your face." He removed his hand from shielding the light and turned it a little.

Her eyes remained wide open.

Something bothered him about her fixed gaze. He allowed more light onto her face, and then more until the full beam shone directly into her eyes.

He waved the light back and forth.

She didn't blink.

She didn't move.

His wife was blind.

8

At Payne Whitney Gym, Ryan paused before knocking on Coach Waldhart's office door. He breathed out, trying to calm his nerves. The coach had asked him to stop by, and when Coach asked someone to "stop by," it was never good. Waldhart's big thing was priorities. "You've got lacrosse, your studies, and your mother," he often said, "and you might want to put your mother before studies." Last year a new player had made the mistake of laughing, only to choke under the steely gaze that bored into him. Waldhart was serious.

Ryan took a shallow breath as he knocked on the door.

During the past few weeks, his erratic work schedule had caused him to miss several practices, and now his new lab job would probably cost him more. Lacrosse was a spring sport but players were expected to participate in "voluntary" captains' practices and scrimmages during the fall, and to work out regularly with weights. Thus far Ryan had managed to attend most of the practices, but missing even a few caused Waldhart's ears to turn red. And one thing Ryan had learned during his first year of Yale lacrosse: you *really* did not want to be anywhere near Waldhart when his ears turned red.

"Take a seat," Waldhart said coolly as Ryan entered his office.

Ryan slipped into a club chair that had seen better days, his eyes darting nervously over the older man's face.

"Captains tell me you're having some problems."

"I've been meaning to talk to you—"

"You're here now, so talk."

"Okay," Ryan said, swallowing. "My work schedule is petty demanding and ah ... it's caused me to miss a few practices which ... well, what I mean is that I don't expect the problem to continue in the future." Ryan had no idea how he was going to achieve this expectation.

Waldhart's alert eyes explored Ryan's face, but he said nothing.

Ryan glanced around the tiny office uncomfortably and added, "I wanted to say I was sorry and ah ..." he shrugged, "well, just that I'm sorry if I let you down."

Waldhart expelled a long breath before speaking. "Y'know, Ryan, I attended a little school in upstate New York. Made lifelong friends. But I always dreamed of places like Yale and Harvard." He pressed his lips together. "You've made it, Son. A Yale education! Do you know that Yale rejects seventy percent of valedictorians? Seventy percent! And yet you're here, because of lacrosse."

Ryan didn't know what to say so he just nodded.

"Any problems with your grant money?" Waldhart asked.

The question hit Ryan like a truck. "What do you mean?"

"Your twenty thousand dollar grant. Any problems with it?"

"No, everything's fine," he managed to say, but he wondered if Waldhart knew he no longer had the twenty thousand. His face felt hot.

"It's good to remember the money is a grant, not an entitlement," Waldhart said. "Ultimately, it comes from big donors and sometimes these people become interested in certain recipients. Know what I'm saying? You don't want these people making calls because you never know where it's going to end. It's just better to keep under the radar, not ruffle anyone's feathers, and so on."

"I'll do my best."

"I'm sure you will," Waldhart said. "Keep my conversation in mind as you plan your day."

Ryan nodded, but wasn't at all certain what the coach meant.

"You're a superb lacrosse player," Waldhart said, rising. "Not some prep school sissy. Don't piss it away."

Ryan tried to smile, but his lips stuck to his teeth.

* * *

"Elijah! Are you there?"

Le Beau jerked forward in his seat and rubbed his eyes. For a moment, he wasn't sure where he was, then realized he had fallen asleep in the hospital room. "I'm here, Helena," he said brightly as he stumbled toward her bedside. "I was just waiting for you to wake up."

"How long have you ... oh, Elijah, you've been here all night, haven't you?" Her voice was tender and sad.

"Never mind me," he said, brushing a few loose strands off her face, "how are you feeling?"

"Okay, I think."

"What happened yesterday, hon?"

She blinked several times, her eyes looking like glass orbs, entirely unfocused. "I've been losing sight for a while now," she said. "I kept turning on more lights, but it didn't help."

"You should have told me."

"I thought it would come back," she said softly. "Then yesterday," she took a breath, "I was doing laundry when everything around me suddenly faded into grays and browns—like shadows—and then the shadows seemed to blend into the darkness and disappear." Tears filled her eyes. "I never realized how awful it is to be blind!"

Le Beau didn't know what to do so he kissed her hand then held it firmly in both of his, hoping the gesture would bring her some comfort.

"I thought I was calm, but apparently not. I blundered right into that heavy lamp in the living room." She touched her swollen lips. "And then I tripped going down the stairs."

"You'll be all right, honey," he said, as he lugged a chair toward the bed. "We'll get through this together. Okay?"

"Okay," she whispered.

Her hand searched for his, and tightened on his fingers when she said, "I can't help it, Elijah. I'm scared."

"I'm scared too, baby," was all he could say.

For a long time Le Beau sat quietly, holding his wife. He talked about Arizona, where they had gone for their honeymoon, where the night skies glittered with stars, about the house they would build, and the fish he would catch. But mostly he just held her and prayed she would get better.

He had been inside Yale-New Haven Hospital a thousand times, had stood guard over violent felons with blood bubbling out of their chests, had rushed pregnant women and vomiting children through the emergency room doors, and had watched men die, but never had he felt like this. Utterly powerless. He stared down at his wife and wondered if she would ever see again.

A voice came from the doorway, "Elijah!"

"Dr. Mokosh," Le Beau said, rising.

"What's this 'Dr. Mokosh' stuff?" she said, greeting him with a kiss on each cheek. "You used to call me 'Katarina.' Haven't we spent enough time together in the ER to be on a first-name basis? And why didn't you page me last night?" She then turned and introduced herself to Le Beau's wife. "Katarina Mokosh," she said, gently laying her hand on Helena's arm, "neurologist, and veteran, with Elijah here, of some long nights in the emergency room." She gave Le Beau an encouraging smile and said, "Now you relax, Elijah, and if you don't mind, Mrs. Le Beau, I'll examine your eyes."

Twenty minutes later Dr. Mokosh explained that Helena had inflammation of the optic nerve. Light was having difficulty moving from the retina to the brain, but in time the condition would improve, and Helena would regain her sight. The news was as good as Le Beau could expect, but he knew the real problem was the underlying MS. The disease could manifest itself in a hundred different symptoms, and if they didn't get it under control, Helena would dwindle away into a very unpleasant death.

Le Beau left the hospital that morning determined to find some kind of treatment for his precious Helena. He would beat on every doctor's door in New Haven, if he had to, scour every lab, but he would make her better.

9

After his conversation with Coach Waldhart, Ryan headed for the lab. He continued to mull over the coach's remarks about his tuition grant, knowing that if they found out what had happened, he'd be finished at Yale. He wondered if this was Waldhart's way of telling him he had better not skip practices. Or was there something deeper? Somehow, he would have to attend lacrosse practices and still make a good impression on Krakauer. He couldn't afford any mistake.

This time at the lab, Krakauer opened the door immediately, and Ryan followed him into the main lab with its jumble of old packaging. "You will clean this room," Professor Krakauer said, skipping any greetings or pleasantries. "Plastic bags and biohazard stickers are over there." He pointed toward a wooden cabinet. "Brooms, mops, cleaning fluids are in the hall closet. Fill the bags with trash and display the biohazard stickers prominently on the sides. Then use a cart to transport them to the Central Power Plant at the end of the block. The employees there will tell you the normal procedure for scientific refuse is autoclave, that the autoclave will sterilize everything. But inform them that your materials are from Dr. Krakauer's lab and everything must be incinerated." His eyes gleamed. "I want *nothing* left. Do you understand?"

"I understand," Ryan said, feeling slightly uneasy that Krakauer hadn't blinked during the entire conversation.

"Good," Krakauer said, eyes still staring with reptilian fixity. "You are to number the pieces of refuse you take to the Power Plant and make certain every one of those pieces goes into the incinerator."

"I'll take care of it," Ryan said.

Krakauer lifted his finger. "Every single piece goes in, yes? And you count them, every last piece. Understood?"

"Yes, sir."

"Also, before you leave, clean the cages in the housing room. Instructions are on the wall for feeding and watering."

Ryan nodded.

Just then, the outside laboratory door buzzed. The professor glanced at his watch, rose, and yanked open the door. He scowled at two heavily tattooed workers whose eyes were on their boots. "*Apúrate!*" he shouted as they scurried down the corridor.

Krakauer's eyes followed them.

"Day laborers," he said, "very unreliable. Understand that they come only when I call them for cleanup duties. No other times. None. They come, they bag animal refuse, then they go. They don't take anything to the Power Plant. You do that. If you see them do something unusual, or if they try to enter the lab complex when I am not present, you report it to me. They have no key cards," Krakauer said, glancing around, "and no way to enter the complex."

The nickname "Dr. Crackpot" crossed Ryan's mind. He wondered whether the professor might actually be clinically paranoid.

Krakauer seemed to sense Ryan's unease. His face softened. "You will make a high-quality assistant," he said. "But remember, you must destroy every last bag from the lab. The Animal Care and Use Committee insists on it, you understand."

"I understand," Ryan said solemnly, not sure what else to say.

"There is something else. Due to new regulations, it is important that you wear a full face mask while in the core labs." Krakauer lifted a mask gingerly from the lab bench behind him, like a magician revealing his prize. "Here, try it on."

"It's wet," Ryan said, frowning.

"I apply a small amount of disinfectant to the filters every morning. Keep you safe, yes? It also helps to cover the odor of deceased animals. You will get used to it."

Ryan pulled the mask on while Krakauer watched him intently. After a few seconds he offered, "It seems to fit, yes?"

Ryan grunted.

Jozef Krakauer's eyes sparkled. "Excellent. You feel fine wearing the mask? No breathing problems ... headaches, nausea?"

"No. It's fine. Can I take it off?"

Krakauer nodded. "Wonderful."

Ryan felt foolish being praised for just standing there with a mask on like some circus clown, but he was relieved all the same.

"You will need access to the outside laboratory door and the rooms within this complex. I have directed the ID Center to add appropriate codes to your key card, so you can tend to the animals." His cobalt eyes surveyed the room. "But concentrate on this lab. There is ample work here."

Ryan asked, "So my key card will work at the Power Plant?"

"Yes, of course," the professor said impatiently. "I just now indicated your card has appropriate codes to conduct your work. Everything is operable today."

Ryan kept silent. He thought he had asked a reasonable question, and was not about to compound his mistake by asking another—namely, whether the university had approved him to handle contaminated materials. It turned out to be a good decision.

"One other item," the professor continued, narrowing his eyes. "The university requires a safety course on handling animal waste, but the substance is basic so I submitted paperwork stating that you have taken it. Saves you time, yes?"

Ryan nodded.

Krakauer turned abruptly, saying over his shoulder, "I will be in my lab and I do not like being disturbed when working."

"Certainly," Ryan said as the professor disappeared down the corridor, door closing behind him. Alone, Ryan swept his eyes around the room and blew out silently. He knew that first impressions were critical so he tore into his cleanup duties as if goblins were chasing him. He slashed every box and piece of Styrofoam he could find, cutting them into squares and dumping them together with the rest of the trash into the orange plastic bags. By the end of the day, the men at the Central Power Plant jokingly told Ryan that they'd have to work overtime just to get their regular work done. But Ryan had managed to rid the room of every vestige of trash, and had scrubbed the tables and floors until they glistened. Even the sink fixtures sparkled beneath the deadening gleam of the fluorescent lighting.

Before he left for the night, Ryan wandered down the central hall, checking out the smaller labs, and unlocking and propping open doors. Most of the rooms were empty and unused, and surprisingly free of the sort of mess Ryan had found in the main lab, probably because that area doubled as a delivery room. In one lab near the back, he noticed a steel door with a faded sign overhead, indicating that it led to the steam tunnels under Yale's campus.

As a first-year student, he and a friend had explored the warren of tunnels, emerging two hours later at the other end of the campus. The doors were vital links to life. Fire marshals had designed them as emergency exits from the tunnels in case a heating pipe ruptured. Four-hundred-degree steam flowed through the pipes, burning vapor, that could engulf a tunnel in seconds, cooking workers like Thanksgiving turkeys.

Ryan stared at the emergency exit, frowning. Normally, the steel doors were dead-bolted on one side only, the steam tunnel side, to prevent students from entering the tunnels. This door, however, was bolted from inside the lab, in which case anyone looking to escape from the steam tunnels would be in for an unhappy surprise.

Ryan concluded his inspection by checking out Dr. Krakauer's personal lab. The heavy windows of the chambers had been blocked out, but slivers of light around the edges told him the professor was still inside the main one. The two workers who had scuttled away earlier were cleaning the smaller chamber, filling medium-sized plastic bags with something, and depositing them on the animal cart. When they headed back into the chamber, Ryan bent over the bags to get a better view. What he saw turned his stomach. The bags were filled with mashed animal parts—or mucky fur—it was hard to tell which, so thick was the plastic.

Ryan took a deep breath and shifted his eyes away to a narrow desk crowded with computers and stacks of old CDs. Classical music was playing softly, and the pleasant sounds helped soothe his upset stomach.

He glanced around. On the far side of the lab a door hung open, like a gaping tomb, although on closer inspection the tomb proved less sinister, nothing more than a back exit propped open with a baseball bat. It led to the main hall.

Then Ryan noticed two closed storage rooms. He turned the handle on the larger door. Locked. He slid his key card through the slot and the red light blinked several times. No access. Curious, he peered through the tiny window but in the gray light he could see nothing. He tried his card on the smaller door, but it too blinked silently and remained locked.

The workers had now finished in the chamber and were placing the plastic bags into larger orange biohazard coverings. Ryan headed off for the cages in the back to make certain he had watered and fed every animal. When he returned fifteen minutes later, the men had gone and the cart was pushed up against one of the walls. He tried both locked doors again, wondering why they wouldn't open.

A bolt clunked and Ryan whipped his head around. The heavy door behind him cracked open, and Professor Krakauer stepped out of the chamber and into the lab.

"What are you doing?" he asked.

Ryan swallowed.

"What are you doing at that door?" Krakauer was leaning forward and, despite his height, resembled a crouching animal.

"Nothing," Ryan said, anxiously furrowing his brow. "I finished my work and—"

"You cleaned the entire room?" Krakauer's face showed his skepticism. He had straightened perceptibly, although his demeanor remained aggressive.

"Yes, everything's done and I thought—"

Krakauer turned on his heel. "Wait here," he said and disappeared up the hall. Moments later, he was back. "A reasonable job," he said grudgingly. "You work quickly. But I still want to know what you were doing at that door." His lips twisted in suspicion.

Ryan shrugged nervously. "I was just looking around to see if there was anything else to clean up," he said, motioning over his shoulder, "and my card worked everywhere, except on these doors. I was checking again to see if the card wasn't reading or something."

Krakauer studied him for a long awkward moment, then visibly relaxed. "I store refuse in these rooms," he said calmly, swiping his card. "You will soon receive the codes for these rooms." With that, he pulled open the walk-in freezer, flipped on the lights, and entered.

A cold blast of air chilled Ryan as he followed Krakauer into the freezer. They were standing at one end of a twelve-foot rectangular room choked with orange plastic body bags. "The workers store refuse here," he said. "My research can be inventory depleting, but I expect I will need fewer subjects in the future." He glanced around the room. "On another day you will incinerate these bags at the Power Plant."

When they exited the freezer, the professor mumbled something about the smaller room being of no great concern.

* * *

As the days passed, Ryan worked hard to impress Dr. Krakauer with his industry. He received two checks, one from the university and another—immensely larger—from the Proskin Pharmaceutical Company. Now he understood how Krakauer's first lab assistant, Fraser Samuels, had avoided the university's work restrictions. The Proskin Company paid their money directly; it was like an outside job. In the following weeks, Ryan cleaned up the lab, sterilized equipment and gathered materials for the professor. He never found out what was in the smaller room beside the large freezer, and soon forgot about it.

10

By the time Nicole Van Buren arrived at Coxe Cage field house, the afternoon skies had turned a deep purple. The wind swirled, coming in gusts, and shook the barren lilac bushes along the roadway. She pulled open the side door, threw back her hood, and entered the cavernous building.

Nicole had heard about Coxe Cage but this was her first time inside the athletic complex, a gigantic building with lofty glass walls encircling a two-hundred-meter rubber track that wrapped around a central practice field. She moved closer to the practice area. Twenty lacrosse players wearing helmets and gloves raced up and down the field, cutting and turning, whipping a lacrosse ball through the air at tremendous speeds.

She eyed the players. Ryan was definitely here somewhere, but with everyone wearing helmets, she had no idea which player he might be. Then she spotted him, sweeping around the goal, stick tucked under his shoulder, trying to protect the ball from a huge defenseman who was chopping at him with a long stick.

"Ryan!" she hollered and waved her hand.

He glanced in her direction and was hit almost instantly by another defenseman, who slid across the crease. Ryan flopped to the ground like a broken doll.

"Oh!" Nicole's hand flew to her mouth.

"Hey!" a man yelled from across the field. "This is a closed practice." His hat and whistle told her he was a coach.

Nicole's eyes shifted to Ryan, who was getting to his feet shakily. He seemed all right but remained bent over, hands on knees, for a few moments.

"Did you hear me?" the coach called as he started across the field in her direction. "You have to leave."

Nicole ignored him. "Ryan, are you okay?" she called.

The man stopped in front of her and snapped his fingers a couple of times to get her attention. "Hello," he said testily. "Ya gotta go." His aggressive attitude and Long Island accent irritated her.

When he snapped his fingers again, this time in front of her face, she leveled her eyes at him. "I don't have to go anywhere," she said. "This is a university building, open to all Yale students."

"I don't know about that," he said. "But you can't stay here."

She frowned. "This is Coxe Cage, right? Newly renovated? Well, my father paid for most of the renovation." Her mouth smiled while her eyes said, "Up yours! I don't have to go anywhere."

The coach glanced around indecisively, then drifted away with a shrug when a thin man in his forties approached. "Can I help you?" the man asked.

"Yes," Nicole said, "I'm looking for Ryan Taylor."

"He's practicing now. You can talk to him in about an hour."

He spoke with a quiet authority, the kind of man no one questioned. Must be the head coach, she thought. "I need to speak to Ryan," she said, furrowing her brow earnestly, "Just for a few minutes." Her intuition said that "serious" might be more effective than "seductive" with this guy.

He exhaled slowly and then turned toward the players. "Taylor!" he shouted, jerking his thumb in her direction. "Get over here."

"Thank you," Nicole intoned sweetly.

His gray eyes saw through her but he said nothing as he returned to the practice field.

"What are you doing here?"

Nicole could see the anger in Ryan's eyes, and of course, a healthy dose of anxiety. He was obviously afraid of the head coach with the quiet but piercing demeanor. She pointed to the reddening bruise on his neck and asked, "Did I cause that?"

He scrunched his face up impatiently. "What do you want? I need to get back to practice."

"That's a nasty bruise."

"Nicole..." he scowled.

"I want to talk to you," she said calmly.

"Are you kidding?" He glanced over his shoulder. "Waldhart is not someone to fool with. I'll call you later," and he turned to go.

"Not good enough," Nicole said, stepping in his path.

He glanced again toward Waldhart, who had resumed the scrimmage. "This is ridiculous! We can talk after practice."

"Where?"

He hesitated.

"How about Ras Dashen," she said, "eight o'clock after your lab work."

"Ah, yeah, okay," he said, trying to leave.

"Do you know where it is?" she asked, pressing forward.

"Yes, I know where it is," he said defensively. "You're not the only person who eats at restaurants."

She tapped him on the chest. "You better be there, box-boy, or I'll bring a lawn chair to your next practice."

* * *

Le Beau glanced up from his desk and groaned. Captain Barton was threading his way through the desks, glad-handing everyone along the way as he headed for Le Beau's office. An outside appointee, Barton had his nose in everything and acted more like an advocate for the university administration than for his own officers. No one liked or trusted him.

"Elijah!" Barton said, cheerfully.

Le Beau rose and greeted the captain with his best smile.

"So nice to see you," Barton said. "Sit down, sit down."

Le Beau took his seat uneasily. Barton always sounded more like a politician than a cop.

The captain pulled out a chair for himself and said, "It's rare in my position to be the bearer of good news. But today is a happy occasion for me."

"Am I getting a raise?" Le Beau asked, trying to match the captain's light-hearted banter, and hating every second of it.

"Of course not," the other man said, his teeth gleaming. "But I did receive a call from a Dr. Mokosh at Yale-New Haven Hospital. Apparently, she keeps missing you, left messages, etc."

"Dr. Mokosh?" Le Beau was surprised. "I've been having trouble with my phone-message system."

"I see. So I gather this doctor has been treating Helena."

"Yes, Dr. Mokosh is one of the best neurologists in the country," Le Beau said, nauseated by Captain Barton's use of Helena's name, as if they were old friends.

"And how are Helena's eyes doing?" the captain asked.

"A lot better these last weeks."

"Starting to see, eh? That's what I've heard."

"From Dr. Mokosh?"

"No, no, you know how doctors are—all tied up with ethics. Other sources. I keep my ear to the ground." He crossed his legs and leaned back in his chair, his face creased with concern, "You've been through some tough days, Elijah. I'm so happy things are turning around."

"Thank you," Le Beau said cautiously.

"Back to the good doctor," the captain said, simulating a chuckle. "She wants you to call her. Apparently, some company has been conducting trials on multiple sclerosis, and she thinks their work could be helpful."

Le Beau sat up and gave Captain Barton a genuine smile. Finally, his letters and phone calls had paid off. "What company?" he asked.

"A drug company," the captain said. "Proskin Pharmaceutical."

11

Ryan arrived at Ras Dashen thirty minutes late. It turned out that he was pronouncing it wrong and nobody knew where it was. Not that he cared about being late for Nicole. In fact, he had toyed with blowing her off and heading back to his room, but decided against it. Nicole was a pain—no doubt about that—but she had found him the lab job and he felt as if he owed her. Besides, she was incredibly good looking, and he had to admit that counted for something.

He pushed through the crowds of suits and black dresses, fresh from the Schubert Theater around the corner, and vaguely wondered if he should have worn a sweater rather than his lacrosse jacket and black tee. He scanned the room for Nicole and found her on the upper level, dressed in an expensive navy suit, hair pulled back with a wide mother-of-pearl hair clip, and sipping a glass of red wine. She looked good. Too bad he had to set her straight.

A waiter who had eaten too many dinners pulled out a dark wooden chair and ushered Ryan into his seat, then whisked off to another patron who was calling him.

"Nice of you to come," Nicole said, arching an eyebrow.

"Krakauer kept me late," Ryan lied. "Nothing I could do." He glanced around at the lighted candles on each table. "Eritrean food, eh? Nice place."

"Ten more minutes and you were dead."

"I said I was sorry."

"No, you didn't."

"Well, I thought it." He said the words flatly, with no hint of an apology.

"Do you know what I was thinking about during the last half-hour?" Her eyes locked on him.

"No idea."

"I was thinking up ways to punish you."

"Oh, yeah? Like hanging out at my practices?"

"Maybe. Or maybe I'll phone Waldhart and tell him my boyfriend Ryan is finding practices too strenuous. Way too much running, I'll say."

Ryan said nothing, but knew he had to nip this in the bud before she got completely out of control. No way could he have her stirring the pot with his coaches, especially Waldhart; his whole existence at Yale depended on lacrosse money.

Nicole was slowly swirling her wine, head tilted downward but eyes fixed on his face. "Maybe I'll tell your coach you need to cut a few practices because we have this beach thing going on in Tobago."

Ryan wondered whether she might be serious. She seemed capable of anything, the narcissistic bitch. He leaned forward and said evenly, "You've never worked a day in your life, have you?"

She took a sip of wine. "Aw, Ryan's trying to hurt me, and after all I've done for him." Her lips pouted. It flashed through Ryan's mind that her lipstick made a perfect line around the contour of her lips.

Taking a deep breath, he tried to focus on his objective. "Look," he said, "I appreciate your help in getting me the lab job. I really do. But I don't want you at my practices. Okay?"

Her eyes widened.

"I'm serious," he said. "No more."

"Of course, if that's what you want. How was I to know you would be so sensitive about it?"

"Well, now you know."

"Any other complaints?"

"No—well, actually, yes—stay away from my coaches. One of the assistants thought you were trying to intimidate him when you said your father funded the renovation of Coxe Cage."

"Just stating a fact."

"That kind of fact gets me into trouble."

"Is it possible you're being a tad melodramatic?"

"Maybe, but when my financial aid for next year is on the line, this is how I react. You might find it difficult to understand, but without that money, Yale gets a little pricey. I need to keep my coaches happy."

"You worry too much about the wrong people," she said.

"What is that supposed to mean?"

She stared at him, as if she were gauging her response.

He gestured for her to speak.

"Think about it," she said. "You worry about your coaches, when what you really should worry about are the people behind the scenes, people with money and power. They make one call and everything changes. One call—that's all it takes, and you either get your grant or you don't, depending on that call."

He frowned.

"Your lacrosse money," she said, "even the grants that pay for your lab job, come from donors, from people like my father. Piss them off, and you do have trouble."

"Yeah, but in reality, it's Coach Waldhart I have to deal with. The money and power people, as you call them, haven't a clue who I am."

"You never know," she said, pausing to sip. "You'd think a coach would caution his players to keep a low profile."

He stiffened, looking at her intently.

Nicole's eyes met his but betrayed nothing.

"What are you saying?" he asked.

"Nothing. Just that when you receive money from these sources, it's just common sense to avoid conflict with similarly positioned people."

He snorted. "So I'd better not piss you off. Is that your message?"

She smiled. "No, but maybe you should be nicer to people like me. As I said, you never know."

"Wine list sir?" The portly waiter was back.

"I'll ... ah ... drink this," Ryan said, motioning to the open bottle on the table. His mind was still on Nicole's comments. He couldn't tell if she was serious or joking, and he worried that someone might have called his coach about the twenty-thousand-dollar grant. He swallowed the finger of wine the waiter had poured for him. "Fine," he said as he motioned for the waiter to fill his goblet to a proper height. The waiter did so and watched silently as Ryan drained the glass. After this weird conversation, he needed a drink.

"More sir?" the waiter asked with what Ryan perceived to be an air of condescension.

"Another would be good," Ryan said, looking directly at him. He wasn't going to take crap from this pudgy peddler of exotic foods. The waiter met his gaze then looked away, refilled his glass, topped up Nicole's, and finally left. Ryan gulped down more wine, smacked his lips, and said, "Yes siree, real fine."

"Glad you approve." She fluttered her fingers in the direction of his neck. "That bruise looks gruesome. You should talk to the player who hit you."

He laughed. "You mean, ask him to be gentle?"

"No, but he should recognize that you're both teammates. Someone his size could easily hurt you."

Ryan lifted his eyes, unsure whether he was being mocked for getting knocked on his butt, decided he wasn't, and glanced at the menu of odd-sounding meals. They both ordered Tsebhi, the Eritrean version of curried chicken. As they waited for it to arrive, Ryan listened without interest to her thoughts about dancing at Green Hall. Apparently, she liked jumping around. Halfway through the meal, which turned out to be surprisingly good, he began to wonder what she really wanted to talk about. Then, abruptly, she set her silverware down, placed both hands on the table, and said, "So tell me, Ryan, how's it going at the lab?"

"Good," he said, between bites. "I'm making money at least."

"And how's Dr. Crackpot?"

"Strange as ever, makes me wear this mask that smells like rotten oysters; I swear the thing gave me pneumonia the second week, and I've had a cough ever since. On the plus side, he must submit scores of extra hours to Proskin for me—more than I worked—because they overpay, a lot. So I guess that means we're pals."

"I wanted to ask a small favor," she said, appearing to switch mental gears as her tone became warmer. "Third-year biology majors are required to observe a lab and write a report on how it functions. It's really just a make-work assignment—not very important, but it has to be done." She waved her hand dismissively. "It's such a waste of time that most biology students just fudge it." Her eyes drifted across the restaurant before returning to his. "Fraser was supplying me with details about Krakauer's lab, but now, obviously, he's gone. I've already submitted Krakauer's lab as the one I'm observing, filed initial reports, etc., so it would be awkward to switch labs. You understand." She stated the last as a foregone fact, and one that would naturally determine his actions. "I thought you might help me fill in the gaps."

He hesitated.

"It won't take long," she said, tilting her head coquettishly, "just a few questions." Ryan wondered at her ability to change so quickly from one demeanor to another.

"Well, I certainly don't want to piss you off," Ryan said with a snort, "but the truth is I'm a little concerned about Krakauer, you know, that he might get wind of a false report coming from his lab. He's so paranoid about—"

"He'll never know. Graduate assistants check off these reports and nobody cares." Amazingly, she actually looked vulnerable as she added, "I can't believe I've gotten myself into this mess, but I have no one else to turn to. I know we don't get along, Ryan, but you'll help me out here, won't you?"

"Nicole ...."

"It would mean a lot to me."

Ryan exhaled heavily. "Isn't there some other way you can finish this project?"

Nicole's fingers ran over her now-empty wine glass, slowly. "Of course there is." She looked at him across the table. "But that would mean finding someone else for the job at Krakauer's lab—and I really don't want to do that to you, Ryan. I want to help you. Just like I know you want to help me."

Ryan leaned back in his chair and emptied the rest of his glass in one swallow. This wasn't dinner, it was a chess match, and Ryan did not like the look of the board. He thought about his lacrosse aid, and met her glance, swearing silently. It wasn't a bluff; he could tell by her eyes.

"Sure, I'll help you," he said, choking down the anger. "What do you want to know?"

"Thank you, Ryan," she said warmly, as if he had reached his decision without coercion. "I appreciate your help so much. You know I would never do anything to jeopardize your financial aid, I really wouldn't."

He nodded, but knew no such thing. He'd be a fool to trust her.

"Okay," she said, "Krakauer does immune research, and you clean up after him, right?"

"Yeah."

"Any other cleaners?"

"Day laborers—Mexican guys, I think—for the serious stuff."

"The undocumented—"

"That's it."

"What exactly do they do?"

"Clean up the mess after his experiments. He goes through a lot of animals—"

"These animals are dying?"

He nodded.

"How many?"

"All of them."

"Really." She gazed into the flickering flame of the candle and asked slowly, "None of the animals ever survive? Inside his lab, I mean."

Ryan shook his head. "Dead as dirt."

"None?"

"Well," Ryan said, thinking, "he mostly uses primates now. The rats and birds might have survived in earlier trials, but I don't know."

"Interesting," she said, still staring at the candle.

"Yes, but don't put that in your report," he said. "If some graduate assistant sees—"

"Don't worry," she said. "Only vague, boring material will appear in my report. Anyone reading it will fall asleep. I promise. Now, about the undocumented: what do they wear during cleanup?"

"Their regular blue cleaning uniforms, I guess."

"Not masks or positive pressure suits?"

"Nope. Just Krakauer and me."

"And you take the bags ...?" She trailed off, waiting.

"Every few days—after the monkeys are bagged and frozen—I take them to the incinerator." He stirred his chicken with his fork. The image of dead monkeys was dampening his appetite.

"More wine?" she said, smiling.

He grunted.

"I'm curious about Krakauer's notes," she said. "Where does he put them?"

"The notes," he said, trying to provide a thoughtful expression. "I think he writes stuff on index cards."

"What does he do with the cards?"

"Don't know. Maybe takes them home. He doesn't leave them in the lab. Not that I've seen."

Nicole sipped her wine and licked her lips approvingly. "Tell me about his experiments," she said. "Does he inject the animals with something? Or take slices of the brain?"

"I have no idea. Krakauer does everything inside the lab core. I've never been there—never even seen inside. All the windows are blacked out."

She leaned forward. "Ok, but I know he has an electron microscope—it's a computer that has a big vacuum pump."

"Yeah, I've seen it—heard it. He uses it a lot. A couple of times a day."

"Have you ever heard him call something a neutralization assay?"

"A what?"

"Does he run a lot of gels?"

"You've lost me. All he does is kill monkeys in the lab core. And he never lets anyone in there when he's working. Just for cleanup."

She patted his hand and said, "You've been patient. Thanks."

It felt odd having her fingers touch his. They were smooth and warm.

She was looking at him now. "One last thing. Maybe you could do something for me, to satisfy my curiosity."

"Okay," although he felt a twinge of unease. "What?"

"Are you ready for this?"

"Let's hear it."

"Well, you know how you don't like doing things out of your comfort zone—"

"What are you talking about?"

"I'm just saying you prefer to play it safe rather than do something risky."

Ryan screwed up his face.

"You disagree?"

"I never disagree with bullshit because the people shoveling it are having so much fun."

"Really. Then what have you ever done that's wild, or risky?" she said with skeptical amusement.

"I need to answer this?"

"Tell me the last time you did something outrageous. I'll bet you never have."

"Outrageous ... let me see ... well, I decided to show up for this dinner."

"Skirt the issue if you want but you know I'm right. You don't like taking risks."

"Maybe it's because I don't have a daddy to bail me out if I make a mistake." The full truth of this sent a pang through Ryan as he spoke, but his face remained sardonic.

"That's a fair point," she said. "All I'm saying is that you like to feel safe, which means you'll probably get enormously defensive about my request."

He sighed. "What is this – your attempt at Psych 101? Guess what, you fail. What's your request?"

"Peek into Krakauer's lab core. See what he's doing."

Ryan gaped at her. "I don't mean to be enormously defensive," he said, "but the answer is: No. No fucking way."

"Just to see what he's doing in there."

"First, I'm not a big fan of dead monkeys. Second, I am not losing this job because Nicole Van Buren is curious."

She lifted her hand in derision. "Don't be ridiculous. You said he's papered over the windows, so how difficult would it be to lift a corner and look?"

"Forget it."

"Why are you so afraid?"

"I'm not *afraid.*"

"Sure sounds like it."

"It's not just me in the lab," Ryan said. "The cleaners can show up at any time."

"They don't even have key cards. Not much of a surprise when they have to ring the bell."

Ryan placed his fork neatly on the edge of his plate. "How did you know that?"

She shrugged. "Just a guess."

"Well, whatever—it's not smart spying on Krakauer. He's constantly on guard. The guy's totally paranoid. What is your interest in all this?"

Nicole gave him a bored look.

"Listen, I'd like to help, but I can't start tearing off pieces of the contact paper—even if I could get in there."

She crossed her arms.

"Okay, fine," he said. "You want to hear something?"

Her eyes said she did.

Ryan moved the candle to one side and leaned closer as if his words might be overheard. "The first day when I was checking out the lab, I found two locked doors. Krakauer caught me trying to open them with my card and he freaked."

"Where were the locked doors?"

"Across from the lab core."

"And what did he say?"

"A lot of things, but the next day when I was about to leave, he called me back and said I ought to be careful, because science labs were dangerous places."

"So what did he mean by—"

Ryan held up his hand to silence her. "Then he told me that *Fraser Samuels never understood that.*"

Nicole laughed in ridicule. "And, what, you thought that was a threat?"

Ryan arched his eyebrows.

"That's absurd! Fraser died in a car accident."

"Krakauer is a weird guy, but I got his meaning—be careful around his lab because bad things can happen."

"In other words, don't poke around."

"Right."

"And you took it as a threat."

"Yeah, I did."

"And that's why you're afraid."

Ryan flopped back in his chair, and half smiled. He knew she was button-pushing so he kept his mouth shut. He had said enough already. No point in bringing up the other strange shit he had seen in the lab. Through slivers of frost in one of the biohazard bags, he'd spotted what looked like tattoo markings on some of the chimps. It was hard to see and could have been blood dried in a strange pattern, but Ryan remembered the chill that went through him when he saw it. It looked like the same tattoo he had seen on one of the cleaners. A crazy thought, maybe, but Krakauer had recently brought in new cleaners, and Ryan hadn't seen the old ones since.

"So, Ryan." Nicole asked, interrupting his thoughts. "Will you take a little peek in the window for me?"

"Nope."

"C'mon," Nicole said with amusement in her eyes. "What's the worst that could happen?"

"He'd fire me," Ryan said flatly.

"Look," she said, "if you're nervous about sneaking a peek, I understand. Who'd blame you? Krakauer spooks a lot of people."

"That's not it," Ryan said, knowing he sounded like a coward. "I'm not kidding that Krakauer's paranoid. Who knows if he has cameras mounted somewhere? I cannot lose this job, I just can't."

"Sure." She finished the last of her wine.

One word, but Ryan felt the threat in her voice. He hated that she had leverage on him. Mounting a hidden camera in a lab of concrete and polished steel probably would have been impossible—even cell phones didn't work—but it was still a risk. Then again, he realized, so was saying no to Nicole Van Buren. He closed his eyes in defeat.

"Okay," he heard himself saying, "I'll check it out. Maybe ... maybe I'll take a look, we'll see." His words dribbled off. Opening his eyes, he glanced at his watch, feeling uncomfortable with her again.

She noticed and called for the check.

Their waiter brought the check on a pewter plate and placed it in front of Nicole, utterly ignoring Ryan, who flushed at the snub. "I got it," he said, reaching for the plate.

Nicole placed her American Express Centurion on the check and said, "I don't think so, Ryan. It's over seven hundred, you know, with the wine and all."

"Seven hundred!" He stared at her in disbelief.

She shrugged. "They opened an 89 Montrose for me, my father's favorite. They keep a small stock in their wine cellar for when he visits."

Ryan said nothing, but he felt the waiter's eyes on him and hoped the candlelight would conceal his burning face.

12

"This is the manager of the Northlight Motel," Krakauer said into the phone. "I have been trying—without success—to deliver a simple message. What is the matter with you people? If you don't want my help, that's fine with me."

Talking like a desk clerk didn't come easily to the professor. He had written out several phrases he hoped would strike the right mixture of impatience and indifference. "What? I already explained everything to the other fellow on the line ... that's right, one of your employees stayed here last night ... he left his watch in the motel room. What? Speak up! See here, all I know is Carefree Dream Liner ... he works as an air conditioning technician, and he departs on a cruise next Thursday morning. No, I can't read his name on the ledger, but I would know it if I heard it ... sure, I'll wait."

Minutes later Jozef Krakauer placed the phone back on its rest. The Purser's office at Carefree Dream Liner was more than happy to supply him with the names of a dozen air conditioning technicians, and now Krakauer could deliver his package with ease. More importantly, the package would be opened only after the ship was at sea.

Krakauer glanced down at the three plastic bags tucked innocently in their cotton packing, then placed them carefully into cigar boxes. He examined the twenty-dollar bills in each pouch. Perfect. He had no doubt someone would open the plastic bags, and eagerly at that. And then, finally, people would understand the terrifying power of genetic research. Three little plastic pouches would change everything. Once opened, the chemical mixture on the money would trigger *Omega* in the people nearby, and their genetically altered cells would reproduce more chemical trigger until each cell in its turn exploded, leaving the hosts indecipherable masses of sludge.

The professor sighed, feeling for the first time, real hope for the human race.

He quickly sealed the boxes, addressed them, and placed them in a shopping bag. That done, he peeled off his surgical gloves and plastic gown, tossing them in the wastebasket. No one would likely trace the boxes to him, but vigilance was the god of secrets.

Early the next morning Krakauer took the train to Philadelphia for a conference on, "The Future of Eukaryotic Genetics." He changed coaches several times, watching carefully to see if someone might be following. In recent months he had noticed Proskin Pharmaceutical agents nosing around campus. They presumed he was oblivious to their spying, as if he didn't know they were observing his research. No matter, they could not know his intentions to protect earth's children. By his extreme actions, he would rescue faceless billions from the hands of arrogant fools intoxicated with their power to manipulate the basic components of life.

Krakauer surfaced from these thoughts and listened to the clacking of the train while he studied the few passengers in the car. Satisfied he was not being observed, he settled on the perfect person to mail his boxes: a man in his twenties with a beard and guitar, and hands swollen like leather mitts. Obviously a heroin addict. Krakauer took the seat across from him and struck up a conversation.

"You ever been to the Philadelphia train station?" he asked.

"Huh?"

"The train station, yes, ever been there?"

"Piss off!"

"Tell me if you've been to this train station!" Krakauer demanded in a loud voice.

The man spit on the floor and curled his lip. "Practically live there," he mumbled without glancing up.

"Then you know where the post office is located near the station. Right?" Getting no reply, Krakauer continued, tapping the parcels in his shopping bag. "I would like you to mail these for me. They already have postage. I'm in a bit of a hurry."

The other man looked through strings of dirty hair, his pupils tiny dots from the heroin. "And why would I do that, asshole?"

Krakauer extracted a twenty from his pocket and said, "Because I would be grateful."

The man's eyes stared greedily at the twenty.

"I will be across the street on a phone call, but I'll be watching to make certain the packages are mailed, yes? And if they are, I have three more twenties for you." He showed him the bills. "Come to the station coffee shop and I will leave your money on the table. Agreed?"

"No problem, man," he said, reaching for the twenty.

Krakauer gave him the money and the shopping bag and said, "Remember, if you fail to mail the packages, you get no more money."

"I'll mail them," he said.

Krakauer rose and stood by the door in the next car, where both he and the man could see each other. When the train arrived at the Thirtieth Street Station, he followed the man through the building toward the Market Street quadrant, making him acutely aware that he was being watched. After the packages had been posted, Krakauer returned to wait at the coffee shop. A minute or so later the man entered; they made eye contact and the scientist slipped sixty dollars under a newspaper, then left.

By ten o'clock that night, after attending the lectures at the University of Pennsylvania, Krakauer was back in New Haven, and by midnight, he slept soundly, confident his actions had begun to make the world a safer place.

* * *

Earlier that morning Le Beau noticed a car parking illegally on College Street a block from Sterling Library. Visitors often tried to park in this area and he spent a good deal of his time shooing them away.

"Can't park here," Le Beau said to the two men emerging from a plain brown Chevrolet.

"Thank you officer," the shorter one said. He turned his back and motioned the other to proceed across campus. As the taller man scurried away, his windbreaker pulled across his waist, outlining what seemed to be a firearm.

"Sir!" Le Beau called to the man already fifteen paces away. "Remain where you are please."

The man glanced over his shoulder but kept moving.

"Sir! I am ordering you to stop." Le Beau dropped his hand to his nine-millimeter automatic, a gesture more for show than anything else. In his sixteen years as a Yale police officer, he had never once unholstered his gun in the line of duty.

"Gonzales!" the shorter man barked.

The man stopped and turned back to face the officer.

Le Beau shifted his eyes between the men, trying to keep them both in view. He reached for his radio.

"No cause for alarm," the closer man said smoothly, opening his hands in a relaxed gesture. "We're on official business. My identification." He moved his hand slowly to his hip pocket, turning his body so Le Beau could see. Removing his wallet with two fingers and flipping it open, he said, "Military police, Civil Liaison Office. I'm Colonel Donovan, he's Sergeant Gonzales."

Le Beau beckoned the sergeant to come closer. He ran his eyes over their identifications, then glanced up. "Why are you here?"

"AWOL apprehension."

"Some nutjob?"

"No, it's just a routine pickup."

"But you think you've got someone hiding on campus?"

"My thoughts are unimportant. Civil Liaison has its reasons and we do what we're told."

"What's the name?" Le Beau asked.

"Not at liberty to say. Civil Liaison cleared our investigation with Captain Barton of Yale Police. I assume you know him." Face blank, words laden with inference.

"Yeah."

"Check with him. He'll fill you in."

Le Beau pursed his lips. "Okay," he said, "go ahead. But move your car by noon. We have a fleet of buses coming in here."

"Plenty of time," Donovan responded with a slight nod.

As Le Beau watched the two men move rapidly across the campus, he felt mildly uncomfortable. The colonel had a cold bearing, something beyond routine military demeanor. Taking out his notebook, Le Beau recorded their Maryland license plate for good measure. It seemed odd for the US Army to be hunting a deserter at Yale, but in his years as a police officer, Le Beau had come across many odd situations. He returned to his car and continued patrol.

* * *

That same morning at around eight, Ryan submitted his computer cryptography assignment and made his way to class. Some TA was jabbering about linear and differential cryptanalysis—their exciting differences—but his accent was so bad that Ryan couldn't understand a word. He tried to concentrate, but his mind kept wandering back to his dinner with Nicole, her veiled threats about not upsetting people like her father, people with money and power. Ryan disliked—no, loathed—being pushed around. But he knew that if he didn't bridle his anger he'd ruin everything. Better to do a little spying for Nicole than lose his job.

What really pissed him off was being labeled a coward, even if it was purely a ploy for Nicole to get her way. She had no idea what it was like to scrounge for money, taking odd jobs where you could. And now that he had a good job—sure, thanks to her—he wanted to keep it. None of this fazed her. She obviously enjoyed saying he was afraid of Krakauer, that he played everything safe. Nothing sinister in her comments, of course, just a rich girl's idea of fun. Still, he wished he could put her in the same position, see how she liked it.

Ryan glanced at his watch and smiled, thinking. Eight-thirty. Time enough if he hurried. More than once Nicole had talked about her dancing class at Green Hall, how important it was to her. Now might be a good time for a visit. He slipped out of class, and five minutes later was climbing the dozen or so steps of Green Hall. Almost immediately, he could hear music, someone playing a piano. He crept past an open door with about twenty women stretching and working on routines. At the end of the corridor a custodian directed him to the lost and found where he rummaged through a cardboard box until he found a pair of pink dancer tights, a checkered elastic leotard, and a tutu.

Ryan could feel the janitor's eyes on him as he stripped down to his boxers, and pulled on the outfit. "Do I look fetching?" he asked as he tied a scarf under his chin. The janitor turned back to his cleaning. No doubt his years in Yale's Fine Arts buildings had taught him to keep his thoughts to himself.

"Nicole!" Ryan shrieked, as he burst onto the dance floor. "Nicole Van Buren! You corrupt thing! How do you manage such a scandalous body? I hate you!" Although unpracticed, he did his best to sound utterly camp.

Nicole's mouth was hanging open as she unhooked her heel from the waist-high wooden barre. The whole room had stopped and everyone stared at Ryan, then Nicole.

"Oh, please," he said, waving his right hand dramatically. "Don't let me interrupt."

Nicole turned to face Ryan, her eyes squinting, her lips tightening at the corners. Just the reaction he was looking for. Let her be embarrassed for once.

His hand flew to his mouth. "Oh, crumples," he said. "What a disturbance my intrusion has caused! I shall never forgive myself." He whirled around with arms outstretched, trying to give his limp tutu some visibility. "Nicole, my sweet," he said, feeling good about his performance, "I simply must meet your instructor."

Nicole continued to stare at him, stunned, then burst out laughing. "This is pay-back, right?" She glanced around the room. "My friend, Ryan," she announced. "He has needs I never knew about."

Then everything went wrong. Nicole's dancemates surrounded him and began cooing about how beautiful and sensitive he was. One of them, a girl named Emily, cupped his butt. Nicole laughed pertly and said, "Are you enjoying yourself, Ryan?"

He pushed his face close to her ear and whispered, "This isn't working, is it?"

"No," she murmured, "but you certainly are a hit."

13 ∾∾∾∾∾∾∾∾∾∾∾∾∾∾∾∾∾∾∾∾∾∾∾∾∾∾

Ryan dressed and left the fine arts building with amazing speed. Instead of minor smiles from the dancers, maybe a rebuke from the instructor, Nicole's dancemates laughed and hooted as they snapped his leotard-top and tugged on his tutu. He might have proved he was a risk-taker, but he hadn't embarrassed Nicole in the least. A recreational dance class was far more laid back than a Division I lacrosse practice.

Now—he couldn't believe it—he found himself heading for the lab to see how he could spy on Krakauer. A colossal risk! Stupid beyond the outermost reaches of stupidity, actually. But he desperately needed the job. What would happen if he didn't check out the lab for Nicole? Would all the joking end? Would she ask her father to make that one phone call? Ryan grimaced. Probably not, but he couldn't be sure. It was a risk either way.

He opened the basement door to Sterling Library and hiked through the passageways until reaching the fortress entrance of Krakauer's lab. More than once, Ryan had smiled when he approached the forbidding door—a perfect image of Krakauer's paranoid mind. Too focused to care right now, Ryan entered and moved with purpose through the central lab, down the main hall, and into Krakauer's private area, flipping on lights as he went.

The professor was attending a conference in Philadelphia, which lent Ryan a calm he ordinarily wouldn't have had, but he still moved quickly, wanting to finish this unnerving task. He stopped at the thick windows of the main airlock chamber and examined the blue contact paper stuck to the glass. *How had he gotten himself into this?* He peeled back the lower corner and pushed his eye close to test the view. *One quick look, that's all he'd do.* Face pressed against the glass, he had a perfect angle to see the entire lab. *He should have said no.* Ryan folded back the corner and pressed on it to make sure it didn't pop loose.

Done.

He sighed in relief. Then paused. Something wasn't right.

He glanced over his shoulder and across the empty lab, unsure if he had heard something. A voice? A door opening? He listened, head inclined. *Nothing.* Ryan snorted at his imaginings, and turned back to the contact paper, a wasted effort because it was holding nicely.

A refrigeration unit suddenly kicked on and Ryan's heart jumped. He rubbed his face in embarrassment; he was clearly losing it. Stepping into the corridor, he peered both ways, first down the hall toward the animal room, sinister in its blackness, and then toward the entrance where he thought he had heard something. He steadied his breathing, his posture rigid as he strained to hear any aberrant sounds, and while he tried not to think about it, he remembered that Fraser Samuels, the last research assistant, had worked in this very lab—before he died.

The sudden clatter of rats' feet clawing over each other in the cages jerked his head back to the rear labs, the sounds unnerving him. He swallowed, wondering what had spooked them. Then, just as suddenly, they settled down.

Wiping his sweaty palms on his jeans, Ryan sucked in some air then exhaled slowly. *Might as well feed and clean the animals now,* he thought, and the normalcy of the idea calmed him. He punched the light switch and started down the hall toward the rear labs.

Then froze.

Whispers! A bolt of fear passed through his body as his eyes slid slowly back to the entrance area. Who could be there? Not Krakauer, he was in Philadelphia, and the cleaners didn't have a key card. Unease fluttered in the corners of his mind. The whispers were growing louder and more urgent, and Ryan had an overwhelming sense of vulnerability.

Hide!

He reached for the hall lights to switch them off, then changed his mind—he needed to see where he was going. A door opened, then closed softly. Ryan's breath caught in his throat. He darted down the corridor and ducked into one of the smaller labs. Light spilled in from the hall, glinting off the steel escape hatch that led to the steam tunnels. Ryan pounced on the dead bolt, and ripped it back, but the door wouldn't move. It was fastened on both sides.

"Think!" he kept saying to himself.

He swung his eyes around the tiny lab. *Nothing.* A few sinks with attached cupboards, a steel table in the center, and blank walls.

The cupboards! He pulled open the largest one, flinching when it squeaked, and looked inside. Fixed shelves. His heart sank. Desperate, he tore open the other cupboards, oblivious to their creaks and scrapes. No space anywhere! They were jammed with boxes of chemicals, beakers, and other junk.

Somebody coughed, and Ryan stiffened.

The man coughed again, the wheezing catarrh of a smoker. Then two voices began to speak in low tones and Ryan knew they had entered Krakauer's private lab. He had to hide! Quickly! But where? He stepped behind the open door and pressed his eye up toward the crack, looking intently down the hall. Two men emerged from Krakauer's lab. It was a sharp angle but he could see them moving carefully, eyes searching everywhere. One was tall and sinewy, with large pockmarks covering his face and nicotine-stained lips. The other was a solid, athletic-looking man with a broken nose and clipped blond hair. He carried a large gun under his coat—Ryan could see the butt end.

"Clean to this point," the thin man said in a hoarse whisper.

The shorter one turned slowly, surveying the hall and labs leading from it. His lifeless eyes seemed to pause on Ryan, who was still peering through the crack behind the door. Then he shifted his eyes to the other man. "Sweep the rear," he said, as if they were on a military mission. "I'll sift the computer."

The taller man flipped back his windbreaker, revealing what looked like an Uzi strapped to his side.

The other blocked his way and hissed, "I said, no blood."

Ryan recoiled. *No blood?* What did that mean? He whipped his head around, desperately scanning the blank walls and silver edges of the sinks. He really had nowhere to go. They were certain to find him. And what would they think? That he was spying on them, no doubt about it. He licked his lips and realized he was fighting for each breath. Maybe he should step out, pretend he had been innocently working in the back labs, certainly a better thing to do than getting caught behind a door.

The thin man started down the hall, checking each lab. Ryan bit his lip. Now was the time to step out. Maybe they were plain-clothed policemen? He frowned, knowing he was grasping at straws. What did the broken-nosed man say ... "no blood"?

Ryan's mind raced in a hundred directions, none of them good. He thought about Fraser Samuels, about whether he might have been murdered. *Stop it!* he told himself. *Just stop it right now!* Fraser died in a car accident, his body found at the scene. The whole thing was crazy. Ryan was just a Yale research assistant, and here he was hiding behind a door. How absurd! But absurd or not, he felt a cold shiver run up his back. He knew he had to make his presence known, now. What was the alternative? They would find him anyway. He swallowed and stepped away from the door.

The thin man shoved his face close to the doorpost, squinting into the crack where Ryan had been standing.

"What's left?" It was the aggressive man with the lifeless eyes.

The thin man turned and as he did, Ryan stepped back behind the door. "Just the animal room," he said, moving into the tiny lab and yanking open every cupboard. In that instant the man's right hand swung past, and in it was the baseball bat from the private lab.

Ryan's heart pounded. *No blood.* What was going on here? The footfalls of the shorter man were audible as he strode down the hall toward the animals.

The thin man now stood inches from the door, so close Ryan could smell the stink of cigarettes. His high cheekbones had a weathered look and a smattering of whiskers that darkened his gaunt face, a futile attempt to hide blotchy skin. Ryan wondered whether the man would hear him breathing behind the door.

Suddenly the man coughed. And again, this time a rolling cough that lasted three or four seconds. He disgorged a heavy piece of phlegm into one of the sinks, ran the water, and left.

"I don't like it," the shorter man said, his voice receding as they moved up the hall toward Krakauer's lab. "We've got to move fast. Five minutes, tops."

"I tell you, Colonel, I followed him to class. We've got at least thirty minutes."

"Negative. These lights should not be on. The plan's been breached."

The thin man mumbled something, then the colonel barked, "Move it!"

A flurry of activity followed. The men were concentrating on Krakauer's private lab, especially the airlock chambers. Then Ryan heard the colonel say, "Check these freezers first."

Ryan strained to hear what they were doing. The thin man said something that Ryan couldn't make out, and then he realized they had unlocked the freezer that Ryan's key card refused to open. Their key cards opened everything! Who were these guys?

"Well, well, well," the colonel said slowly.

"What are we going to do?" the thin man asked, clearly dismayed.

"Leave," the colonel said. "Close the fridge."

"Colonel, respectfully ...." The man paused as if asking permission to speak, and Ryan detected apprehension in his voice.

"Go ahead," the colonel said.

"Sir, I believe we have time to examine the contents thoroughly. The kid's been here, sure, but he's in class now. Maybe we can figure out—"

"The general wants a clean operation—"

"I understand, sir, but—"

"That means no complications, Gonzales. And no more foul-ups with lab assistants. Close it, *now*."

* * *

Ryan waited a full twenty minutes before emerging from behind the door. He had been motionless for so long his legs felt like hundred-pound logs, and he couldn't shake the feeling that the man with the dead eyes might suddenly step from the shadows and say, "I came back for you!"

For the next hour Ryan wandered the campus, oblivious to the students milling around him. When he had awakened that morning, he had been one of them, thinking only about sports and girls and how he would get through school. Eventually, his wanderings took him to the Central Power Plant, a Gothic brick facility dominated by two enormous smoke stacks, chimneys that had a menacing, crematorium appearance. He had been in the Power Plant many times, mostly to incinerate Krakauer's refuse animals, but now he was thinking about the men in the lab. Would they have killed him, maybe used the incinerator to get rid of his body? Could they be that dangerous? Or was he being ridiculous? He glanced around, telling himself that Yale probably had security agencies that no one knew anything about, but all he could see was the black outline of the Power Plant against the sky. It reminded him of death.

He knew his imagination was running wild, but he also knew that he had to do something to protect himself, and he had to do it now. He thought about the maze of tunnels that spidered out from the Power Plant to every part of the campus, and immediately started toward the side door.

A workman at the far end of the Plant craned his neck to see who had entered the building.

Ryan waved in his direction and shouted, "What's happening, Bill?"

Bill nodded and went back to work.

Ryan breathed easier, and strolled toward the gates that led to the steam tunnels. Open, just as he had hoped! The warning sign he ignored— *Enter With Hardhat and Two-Way Radio Only*—and slipped through the open gates, moving quickly into the tunnel system. The ninety-degree heat hit him like a wall. In the summer, the temperature often soared well above a hundred and thirty, and workmen told Ryan they kept their tools in water buckets to prevent burns.

The tunnel was long and narrow, two heavily wrapped steam pipes running along both sides, with pressure gauges jutting every so often into the walkway. Overhead, lights dotted the gloomy tunnel, and thick electrical cables hung loosely from the ceiling. The cables looked well insulated, but Ryan avoided touching them just the same. He also took particular care when passing the gauges, not only to avoid burning himself, but because he knew they broke easily. He wasn't interested in finding out what four-hundred-degree steam felt like.

He came to a bend in the tunnel, then a fork where it branched in three directions. He paused, mentally noting his progress. Every fifty feet or so he could see the rust-brown escape doors, looking much like cemetery gates on a crypt. He tried to concentrate, knowing how easy it would be to lose his way. At each junction he rehearsed where he had been, all the while keeping a sharp eye out for workers.

Fortunately, the Power Plant was near the library so that within minutes Ryan had found the door leading to the lab. He approached the metal barrier carefully, his fingers dusting lightly around the deadbolt, his eyes inspecting the encrusted moldings. He was searching for silent magnetic alarms that alerted the police.

For a hundred years, Yale students had considered it a rite of passage to sneak through the tunnels, if for no other reason than to say they had done it. Not infrequently, they lost their bearings, panicked, and tried the first door they found. A few decades ago, in their zeal to catch students on a Saturday night lark, Yale administrators had installed alarms and begun expelling students for the dangerous pursuit. You don't fool around with four-hundred-degree steam, officials said, echoing their lawyers. Unfortunately for the administration, students knew that most of the alarms didn't work. But no one was sure exactly how to tell a live one from a dud. From Ryan's point of view, he just had to move quickly. It took ten minutes, he had heard, ten minutes from the moment an alarmed door opened until the police arrived. Time enough to get back to the Power Plant gate.

He inspected the deadbolt again, then wrapped his hands around the rusty handle, and gave it a hard yank. It didn't budge, not even a bit.

"Wonderful escape door," Ryan muttered.

He glanced around for something he could use to loosen the deadbolt but found nothing except a heavy metal hook caked in dirt and partly hidden in the cobwebs. He picked it up, tapped off the dirt, and bashed the hook against the end of the bolt. A loud *crack* rang through the tunnels. Ryan checked over his shoulder, worried that some worker would hear him. He looked back at the bolt, which had moved only about a quarter of an inch, but it had moved. Another few blows and the bolt jumped all the way across.

"Okay," he said with enthusiasm. He pushed the door inward, opening it, then pulled it closed again. He checked his watch. Got to move! If the alarm had tripped, he had less than ten minutes. He started into the tunnel, and stopped, furrowing his brow. What if he had the wrong door? He hadn't actually looked into the lab. Suppose he was mistaken! One escape door looked like another in the tunnels. He hurried back to the unlatched door, shoved it open and took a good look inside. He breathed deeply in relief. It was Krakauer's lab, all right. Satisfied, he closed the door and returned to the tunnel.

Ryan felt better than he had all day— not good, but better. At least now he had a way to escape from the lab, not like earlier when he had been trembling behind the door like a hunted animal.

Movement!

Ryan dropped to the cement floor. Two workmen were coming around a corner, carrying rolls of wiring. He snapped his head around, searching for cover, then ducked under the steam pipes, pushing himself back as far as possible. It was the worst place. The heat from the insulated pipes burned into his back, while his cheek was jammed against something freezing cold. He dragged his face away to relieve the numbness, and realized he was squashed against the water piping system used for air conditioning. Bitter cold on one side, blistering hot on the other. But Ryan gritted his teeth and refused to move from his protective lair. The workmen sauntered by, oblivious, and soon disappeared down one of the many side tunnels.

Frozen and burnt, Ryan clambered out from under the pipes and back onto the walkway. He rubbed his face as he checked both ways, then set off at a gallop through the tunnel, hardly slowing at the intersections. He was nearly out of time. Two minutes later he rounded the final bend in the tunnel, the point from which he could see the gate to the Power Plant.

His face dropped. Locked—the gate was locked!

Ryan trotted in a daze toward the gate, staring at the chain and padlock. The thought of being booted from Yale twisted like a knife in his stomach.

The escape door! He started back to the lab.

"Hey! What are you doing in there?"

Ryan froze. His mind raced and he wondered if he should break for it.

"I'm warning you," the man shouted. "If you run I'll call the cops."

The voice sounded like Bill's. He turned back and forced a smile. "It's me," he said, "Ryan."

"Ryan?" Bill gaped at him. "What the hell you doing in there?"

Ryan laughed. "Never been in the tunnels," he said. "I saw the gate open so I thought I'd take a peek."

Bill opened the padlock. "You can get in trouble ... I'm supposed to report everything." He took a quick look around and said, "Come out of there before one of the supervisors sees you."

Ryan mumbled his thanks and headed toward the exit, his muscles as tense as violin strings, half expecting the police to burst in the doors. Outside, he checked the street for police, but saw none. After fifteen minutes of watching the street leading up to the lab, he finally relaxed. They weren't coming. More importantly, he now knew that the alarm on the lab door didn't work.

The rest of the day passed without incident, but Ryan found it difficult to focus on anything. At lacrosse practice, he felt as if he were encased in a bubble of fog, constantly missing the ball and cutting at the wrong time. He could see Waldhart's ears reddening and hear his strident voice, but the sound barely penetrated the mist. All he could think about was the men in the lab who had opened the freezers. One of them had followed him to class. They knew how Fraser Samuels had died. And they were prepared to kill to keep their secrets.

14

Loose ends bothered the general.

As a soldier, he knew the difference between honest ambition and fanatical obsession. Dr. Jozef Krakauer, he believed, was a fanatic, a loose end that needed pruning. Proskin scientists in the special projects division had dubbed Krakauer a loose nuke capable of destroying human civilization, and this wasn't an exaggeration—he had the machinery to do it. The general remembered sitting in stunned silence as his scientists explained the significance of Krakauer's genetic research, then asking, "Why not go in and grab him?" But it was too late. Krakauer had spread the vector everywhere and no one could be certain what he intended to do with it, or what might trigger the devastating hidden gene.

The general had to be careful. If Krakauer felt threatened, he might easily kill himself and take everyone with him. It would not be difficult to plant the trigger in simple but effective suicide modes. Better to let him continue his search for an antidote than to confront him and risk everything.

The general picked up the phone and buzzed his chief of operations. Within seconds, Colonel Michael Donovan appeared in his office, a powerfully built, stern-faced man in his forties who looked as if he could still compete on the UFC circuit. The general liked former military people. Most of Proskin's seventeen thousand employees had military connections, and not a few of them came by way of the Special Forces community. Donovan was a former Delta Force colonel who had been wounded during covert actions on five separate occasions, and had twice been awarded the Silver Star. There was a rumor about Donovan—that no single bullet could kill him—and the general half believed it. Anyone who looked into the dead-cold eyes of the man knew he would not die easily. In the six years since he had come on staff, Donovan had never been known to smile or participate in light conversation. He was the perfect chief of operations—goal-oriented and hell-bent on achieving his objectives. With the exception of the general, everyone feared him.

Pushing back the papers on his desk, the general grimaced. "Okay," he said, "let's hear it."

"Gonzales and I came up empty," Donovan said, taking a seat across from his boss.

"You got into the lab?"

Donovan nodded. "Into his freezer."

"And?"

"Krakauer had it packed with vials, hundreds of them."

The general leaned back. "Well, we guessed he would do something. Nothing labeled, I suppose?"

"Letters, numbers, nothing that helped. I took pictures and passed them on to intel. Their first impression is that it's not breakable without more data."

"Maybe something will turn up."

"I had a time situation ... less than a minute to examine the freezer."

"Oh?" The general raised an eyebrow.

"The new research kid must have done some early cleaning," Donovan said. "We found the lights on. I set a five-minute parameter because I figured he might return."

The general nodded. He remembered the night Samuels died. The general had used surrogates to pay the kid for copying Krakauer's notes, but Samuels had been caught with an armful. He managed to make a call, but it was too late. Krakauer apparently assured the boy that his breach of trust was unimportant, then exposed him to a rare conotoxin. Samuels didn't know what hit him—barely got out of the parking lot before he went into spasm. Krakauer had expected him to lose consciousness on the Interstate and crash the car, but he miscalculated. It was a disaster. Fortunately, Donovan found the car, strapped on a seatbelt, and piled Samuels's Volvo into a cement underpass. When the police arrived, Donovan was gone and they classified Samuels's death as a highway fatality.

The colonel had made the right decision with Samuels, and he made the right decision today. To eliminate a second Krakauer assistant would strain credulity and put the whole mission at risk.

"Notes?" the general asked, talking about Krakauer's research.

"No notes in the lab, his apartment, or at his other office in Kline Tower."

"You checked his car and the places he frequents?"

"Sir, the man is a recluse. He has no car and no life; when he leaves the lab, he goes straight to his apartment."

"What about his computer?"

Donovan shook his head, face remaining impassive. "Nothing."

"Nothing," the general repeated. He felt sick. "Are you certain?"

"I imaged the hard drive and had SIGINT look at it. It's clean."

"Flash drives or CDs?"

"Nothing of import anywhere."

The general ruminated on the information, searching for possible avenues he might have overlooked. "Recommendations?" he said at length.

"Send in a team to wire the lab. With video we can tell which vials he's been using."

"We've discussed this before. The inside of that room is too difficult to wire. If he even suspected an intrusion, he could become erratic."

Donovan stared at the floor, obviously troubled.

"Spit it out," the general said.

"Sir, if we have no eyes in the lab and no intel on his preparations, we could get blindsided. No one knows what this guy is capable of doing. I say we jock up, go into the lab and take him out."

"And if he releases the trigger?"

"Won't matter. We wear positive pressure suits. Our best intel says the trigger will decay in less than an hour—and we get control of the vials. Then we go through them one by one."

"Can't take the chance," the general said. "Not yet, anyway. The risk of collateral damage is too high. We have no reliable model of how this thing spreads. Even if we clear the building, a rat or something might carry it outside the perimeter. We could put a whole campus of students in harm's way, maybe worse."

"How about nabbing him outside, or using a sniper so he has no time to set off anything?"

"And if the trigger has a dispersion device that requires deactivation every day? He's smart enough *and* unstable enough to do that. And I suspect he knows we're observing him." The general shook his head. "No, for now we wait. We cannot afford a mistake. You know the potential."

"I do, sir."

"Intel still thinks he's working on an antidote?"

"They do—the number of animal corpses has remained fairly constant, which means the trigger is still collapsing their systems."

"So whatever antidotes he's testing, they're not working."

"Apparently not."

"Doesn't mean he hasn't found a partial solution."

"That is correct, sir. Dr. Wu in the lab thinks a partial antidote is quite likely, that he might take a dose in his coffee every day, or in his food."

"Colonel, if Krakauer has developed even a partial, or temporary, antidote—getting control of it is priority one."

"Yes, sir." Donovan's voice betrayed the slightest hesitation.

"Do you understand?"

"Yes, sir, but we would be better-positioned if we had the trigger."

"We would," the general agreed. "But securing the right vials is not the whole bag of apples."

Donovan frowned. "I don't understand, sir."

The general exhaled wearily. "Some of our research boys are saying that the vials might not contain the complete trigger, that it might be a combination of more stable precursors."

"Not sure I follow, sir."

"We know the trigger is unstable in the air. Krakauer might have to perform other steps to ready the precursors," the general said, rubbing the back of his neck.

"Like what?"

"It could be anything—some last step in the synthesis—like heating the reagents to a specific temperature for a certain length of time, and then combining them in a particular order. A physical or chemical cipher."

"If it takes all that to activate the trigger, he won't be booby-trapping anything soon."

"Unless we're wrong and he also has ready-made trigger that he somehow keeps stable. We just don't know." The general sighed. "For now, obtaining the antidote is our primary objective."

"So we can't neutralize Krakauer."

"Not yet," the general said. "And I bet he knows it. Still, my gut tells me he doesn't have a series of steps. I think some of those vials contain intact trigger right now. For the time being we're just going to have to take it slow, and err on the side of caution."

Donovan grunted his understanding.

The general reached into his desk and pulled out a cigar, Fuente Fuente OpusX, his favorite. The silken rosado tobacco leaves were the finest in the world, and the smooth draw never failed to calm him. He passed the OpusX under his nose to enjoy the aroma and then struck a match. "What we need right now," he said, exhaling a cloud of dense smoke, "is patience."

Donovan nodded.

"The trigger is important," the general said, "but ultimately it all comes down to the antidote. With that in our hands, I can tell you, we'll be singing in the sunshine. Without it ...." He shook his head. "Tough decisions, and a dark road. A grisly, dark road."

Donovan waited as the general puffed silently on his cigar, then asked, "And Krakauer?"

"We let him continue his research," the general said, "and pray he finds an antidote."

Donovan rose to leave. "What's our time frame, sir?"

"We'll give it three or four months to see what he comes up with."

"And if he doesn't find an antidote?" Donovan asked.

The general stared at his OpusX and took a long, slow puff before speaking. "Then we proceed with Thermopylae," he said. "Our duty to this country is supreme. With no antidote and no understanding of the situation, the White House is defenseless. That's the brutal truth. This thing acts too fast." He shifted his eyes to Donovan and said, "At the end of the day, I suspect our boys will have to step in."

Nicole ignored her ringing cell phone for the fourth time that evening. She knew it was Basil Meryash, wanting to talk "about us," as he had said in class that morning. No way was Nicole in the mood to have a big talk about their relationship. She took a steaming hot shower to get her mind off Basil, but it didn't work, and she was still thinking about him as she put on a flannel nightgown and brushed her teeth. He was pressing too hard and she didn't like it. The persistent calls—it was getting out of hand. Banking her bed with pillows, she pulled the covers up to her waist and began reviewing her Biology class notes.

The phone rang again.

Utterly exasperated, she snatched it off her night table. "What?" she said, spitting out the final "t" through her teeth.

Laughter spilled out of her phone. It was Emily, one of her dancemates. "That sounded positively inviting," she said, still laughing. "What's with you?"

Nicole took a deep breath. Should have checked the caller ID. She ran her fingers through her hair and briefly told Emily about her troubles with Basil. Far from being sympathetic, Emily dismissed her concerns out of hand. "You have the richest guy on campus after you, and now the cutest thing I've ever seen shows up at your dance class. I have no idea what you're whining about."

Their conversation lasted all of ten minutes, but Nicole felt better. Maybe she needed to "lighten up," as Emily said, have more fun, be more in the moment, get laid.

When the phone rang again and Nicole saw it was Basil, she picked it up and tried to sound upbeat. "Hi, Basil!" she said.

"I know it's late," he said, "but maybe I could drop over and we could talk a bit, you know, finish our conversation from this morning."

"Oh, Basil, I don't think so," she said, glancing at her clock. "It's almost midnight and I've got a test tomorrow."

"I could be there in a few minutes."

She started to object but he continued.

"C'mon, Nicole," he said, "I really would like to talk."

"I know," she said, "but not tonight." And then she added, lying, "I've been in bed asleep for an hour."

"You're in bed? That's the best place to talk, Nicole."

"No," she said more forcefully. "This is not a good time."

He made a sound of frustration.

"I'm sorry, Basil," she said. "I've just been so busy with studies and other things—"

"I never see you anymore."

"You see me every day in class."

"You know what I mean. We never seem to have time together."

"I know," she said quietly.

"Are you trying to tell me something?"

"You know me," Nicole said. "If I didn't want you around, I'd say so. I'm just really pressed right now. I feel like I'm being dragged in a hundred different directions and I can't satisfy anybody."

"Well, you satisfy me."

"Basil, that's sweet."

"Yeah, thanks." He sounded defeated.

"Listen," she said, "you know the Master at Calhoun is holding a Tea on Friday night, right?"

"Yes," he said with renewed hope.

"Maybe we can spend some time together afterwards. How does that sound?"

"First rate!" he said, "simply first rate!"

"Then let me get back to sleep and we'll call it a date."

"Yes," he said in an authoritative voice. "You get to sleep!" He hung up and Nicole turned off her phone, then gazed sightlessly at the wall for a long time before returning to her notes.

15

Ryan stared at the heavy fan above his bed, its blades moving slowly round and round. Sleep was impossible. He was still thinking about the two men with guns in the lab, searching for reasons why they had been there. He took a large breath, trying to think rationally. Dr. Krakauer was a bit odd, no doubt about it, but not much different from scores of other professors that populated the classrooms across the country. Universities seemed to collect his sort. He was just a scholar pursuing research on gene therapy. Nothing overly exciting.

But why the men with guns? Did pharmaceutical companies spy on competitors, maybe send out armed thugs to steal secrets? Ryan continued ruminating on possibilities, finally drifting into an uneasy sleep.

The next morning he rose early and headed to the lab, looking for answers. He had no idea what he expected to find, but since Krakauer's research seemed of such consuming interest, the lab might be a good place to begin. He couldn't face a morning of lectures when scant hours before, someone had been hunting him with a baseball bat.

Ryan slipped into the lab the way he supposed the two men had the day before, in total silence. The image of violent men creeping through the passageways spooked him, and more than once, he found himself looking over his shoulder. Strange, the sounds that emanated from a lab, as if each room were alive and listening. How could surroundings, once so familiar, now seem so alien?

As Ryan entered the hall that led to Krakauer's lab, he almost bumped into him. A small *yip* escaped his lips, despite himself.

"Did I frighten you?" Krakauer asked. He was standing beside the transport cart.

"No, of course not," Ryan said. "Well, maybe just a little." He smiled weakly. "I was thinking about something. Sorry."

"Why are you here so early?"

"I ... I didn't get time to clean all the cages last night."

The professor stared at him, his eyes narrowing in suspicion, the way he often looked when the unexpected occurred. "I need a chimp and four squirrel monkeys for this morning's tests," he said tersely, then turned away.

After Ryan transferred the animals, he spent the next hour cleaning and watering. But the picture of Krakauer conducting experiments persisted, and his curiosity grew. Nicole had asked him to sneak a look in the window, and now he was ready to do it.

He entered the private lab area quietly, as if Krakauer could somehow hear from inside the sealed airlock chamber. Immediately, his eyes darted to the contact paper. Still pasted down. He mopped his forehead, second thoughts creeping in. Just get it done, he told himself, and he dropped to his knees, peeled back the paper, and gazed into the lab.

The professor was sitting at the mechanical arms, working with four cute little squirrel monkeys and a chimpanzee. A standard experiment, Ryan supposed, and the thought made him feel queasy. He had seen too many bags of dead animals not to know what was coming. The subjects in the cages had probably been dosed with whatever Krakauer was using, and they would soon die. At least that's what Ryan imagined occurred inside Krakauer's lab. Chimps come in; biohazard bags go out.

He frowned. Something was happening. The tiny monkeys and chimp had begun to scuttle around the cage, as if the floor had turned scalding hot. The monkeys flung themselves against the glass barriers and flipped like fish on a dock until, exhausted, they lay twitching on the floor. Ryan grimaced and shifted his eyes to the chimp. His hand had caught in the food dispenser on the wall and he was jerking up and down like a clown on a rubber band.

Ryan drew his eye back from the peephole and wiped sweat from his forehead. He felt a pang of guilt for all the animals he had transferred from the back room. When he looked again, the chimp was dead, hanging limply from the dispenser on the wall. But strangely, his body still moved, as if infested with living things struggling under the skin. The body sagged increasingly until it bulged at the bottom, like a bag filled with voracious worms gobbling up the animal's innards.

"Eugh!" Ryan curled his lip. He tried to swallow, but his mouth was sticky, his tongue thick. Sweat poured off him as if he were in a steam room. He stared in disbelief as the animal's fur darkened and stretched, until finally, when it could no longer hold the watery muck, it burst like an overfilled leather balloon. The sight of black slime sliding down the glass wall, bones and skin dropping into the melted goo, made Ryan sick. He drew his face back from the peephole and pressed his palms into his eyes. If the professor was looking for a way to do gene therapy, what he had was an abysmal failure. The "therapy" had chopped through the animals' internal organs like a high-powered blender. It was now clear why Krakauer needed cleaners for his lab, and why there were so many frozen bags of mashed flesh.

Ryan thought about the Mexican workers that had stopped showing up all of a sudden. He told himself that they were just fine, that they hadn't ended up like those monkeys. But down deep, somehow, he knew the truth. They had died in the same sickening way, probably wondering what was happening to them ... maybe running and screaming, beating on the glass windows as Krakauer watched them dissolve from the inside out. And Krakauer had covered it up. Or worse.

Ryan managed one last look through the opening and saw Krakauer tipped back on his chair, a cup of tea in his hands. He had a pleasant look on his face as he sipped the tea and scribbled out his notes on a stack of index cards.

Patting the contact paper gently until it stuck closed, Ryan left the lab.

* * *

"What the hell is with you, Taylor?" Waldhart hollered, his ears scarlet. "You keep screwing up the ride. You've got to pressure the ball all the time, not just when you feel like it. Let's do it again." He flipped the ball to the goalie and blew his whistle. Ryan hesitated. Waldhart opened his hand in disgust. "Again," he said, blowing his whistle. Ryan took off after the goalie, trying to force him to make a mistake as he cleared the ball out of his defensive zone.

"No! No!" Waldhart screamed. "I just told you, Taylor, only go halfway toward the goalie and then back to the D-man. You are killing me, you know that? You'd better get your head out of your ass or you'll be riding the pine."

"Okay, Coach."

"Okay, Coach. Okay, Coach," Waldhart mimicked. "That doesn't cut it. Syracuse will be here in a few days, on this very field. You think they're going to lie down and die?"

Ryan looked at the ground.

"I asked you a question." Waldhart's face was stone. "Do you think Syracuse will be ready for us?"

"They'll be ready," Ryan said.

"Damn right, they'll be ready! You play like this and they'll rip your lips off. You understand me?"

"Yes, sir."

"Quit thinking about your little girlfriend and get down to business."

Ryan nodded.

Waldhart paused, his eyes fixed on Ryan. He moved closer and said quietly. "I don't know what's bothering you but you better get it straightened out." He took a breath. "Something I should know?"

Ryan shook his head. "I'm fine, Coach."

Waldhart stared at him, giving him an opportunity to speak.

"Really," Ryan said. "I'm okay."

Waldhart chewed at his lip. "Then let's get it together. Life is filled with problems. It's a matter of centering your mind. Concentrate on what you're doing and the other problems take care of themselves."

Ryan nodded. He wondered what Coach would say if he told him what was really bothering him.

Waldhart turned to the players strung out across the field and smacked his fist into the palm of his hand. "Priorities, gentlemen," he said, launching into his stock speech. "Priorities! That is what life is all about. You've got lacrosse, your studies, and your mother, and we all know what got you into Yale."

"Lacrosse," the players murmured in unison.

"That's right. And where's your girlfriend?"

"In the stands," the players said, but Ryan heard somebody say, "In bed where she belongs."

"What did you say, Conor?" Waldhart's eyes flashed as he fixed them on the guilty player.

"I said, 'In the stands where she belongs,' Coach."

Waldhart said nothing for several, long intimidating seconds, letting the silence do the chastening. "Y'see, this is what I'm talking about," he said finally. "Conor and Taylor are supposed to be our best players, and they're letting us down. They don't care that Syracuse is coming to town. They think the 'Cuse want to be our pals. Well, let me tell you, they don't like us, and I don't like them. I've never liked them. In fact, I hate every last one of those bastards. And do you know why? Because they want to humiliate us. Am I right?" he asked, glancing at his assistant coach.

"*Damn straight!*" the assistant growled.

"They want to make fools of us! Oh, make no mistake about it, people, they are laughing at you up there. They trot around in their big fancy Carrier Dome and are not impressed that you got into Yale. They see you guys as lacrosse rejects."

The assistant snorted.

Waldhart's face hardened. "This is the first time they've come to a fall tournament at Yale, and they think it'll be a cake walk. You're nothing but a bunch of losers to these guys. That's what they think you are. Couldn't play big-time lacrosse so your daddy sent you to Yale! That doesn't bother you? Well, it bothers me! And let me tell you what's going to happen. They're in for a wake-up call. We are going to run them like dogs, until they step on their tongues. We are going to get every ground ball, every face-off, and we are going to kick their orange butts back up north where they belong."

The players shouted their approval.

"All right, give me ten around the field—fast—and when your little hammy hams or some other injury starts acting up, you think about the 'Cuse."

* * *

Ryan sat alone in the back of Rudy's bar. Lacrosse practice had made him thirsty, and the memory of Krakauer's experiments made him want a stiff drink. He was beginning to understand why those guys had come snooping around the professor's lab. Krakauer had made something that melted people!

Ryan reached for another Jim Beam. He was feeling more relaxed and secure, the effects of dim lighting and several whiskies. At first he was thankful to be alone, but as the hours wore on, he couldn't help thinking about Nicole Van Buren. He knew where she was—at the Master's Tea. Every few months the Masters of Yale's residential colleges held teas, a place where distinguished speakers came to chat with selected students. There was supposed to be a lottery, but some people, like Nicole of course, were always invited, and right now she was sitting by a warm fire sipping tea and nibbling biscuits. Ryan downed his last Jim Beam.

"Yo! Over here!"

The bartender came to the table and cleared off the empties. "Another pair?" he asked.

"Yeah, and this time put some whiskey in it. Can't even taste it." Ryan had begun to slur.

"It's a standard ounce and a half with coke," the bartender said.

"Is that right? Well, put in a standard two-and-a-half ounces. And forget the coke. Can't even taste the whiskey."

"I'll have to charge more."

"So, charge more. I've got a great job." He laughed, enjoying his own joke. "Yes, sir," he said, laying a twenty on the tray, "can't beat my job!"

Minutes later Ryan threw back the first of his newly arrived drinks. "The Master's Tea," he mumbled. Nobody invited ol' Ryan Taylor. He drained the second glass. No, they wouldn't do that. He wasn't one of the elite. Not that he couldn't get himself invited if he really tried. But why bother? Where would he get the time? Every spare minute was consumed by work, or lacrosse, or studies. Masters' Teas were for the few with nothing else to do but soak in the Yale experience.

What bullshit!

Pretentious intellectuals—that's who went to Teas.

Rich pretentious name-droppers.

It was all bullshit.

He glanced around the empty bar and at his empty glasses. When did he drink that second double? He signaled for two more. It occurred to him that he might be feeling sorry for himself, but the thought passed quickly. He worked hard, damn hard for what he had. What had Nicole ever done to deserve her wealth? Or that prissy-faced Basil Meryash, for that matter? They belonged together, a pair of arrogant swine wallowing in money, chatting at the Master's Tea. But Ryan Taylor was alone in a bar, wondering whether someone was hiding in the bushes, waiting to kill him. They had killed Fraser Samuels and now they would kill him. By week's end his body would be lying cold in a grave. And who would care? Not Krakauer, that's for sure. Not Waldhart, who currently hated him. Maybe his mother. Yeah, his mother would care.

He gulped down another drink. It was all Nicole's fault. No doubt about that. She had gotten him this job with a mad scientist who melted monkeys and murdered Mexicans.

He paused, frowning into his glass.

"Murdered monkeys and melted Mexicans," he said aloud. He glanced around, laughing to himself. "Did you hear me?" he shouted to the bartender. "Melted Mexicans are murdering monkeys!" The bartender didn't seem to get the joke.

He wiped the wetness off his mouth, trying to focus his thoughts. How'd he get into this mess? The whole thing was insane. He eyed the door. It was time to squeeze some answers out of people, and the best place to start was with Princess Van Buren herself. He rose shakily, finished the better part of his last drink, and headed off to the Master's Tea.

16 ∾∾∾∾∾∾∾∾∾∾∾∾∾∾∾∾∾∾∾∾∾∾∾∾∾∾∾∾∾∾∾∾∾

The Master's house in Calhoun College was sparsely but richly decorated, a reception room with old leather chairs, brass lamps, and a baby grand piano that glistened as if it had been rubbed daily with mink oil. The room could hold about twenty students comfortably in the large wingbacks, but on this day many more were sprawled on the padded arms, or sat on folding chairs brought in for the occasion.

The television journalist, Chris Cuomo, had just finished his comments on America in the 21st Century, noting that everyone, whether in college or the workplace had a responsibility to enrich the world around them, to change situations for the better. He flipped his notes closed and swept his eyes around the room. "Questions?"

Nobody said a word.

"C'mon," he said with a smile, "You're not going to humiliate me by not asking questions. When I was a student here at Yale—"

"Excuse me," Nicole asked, rising, "I was wondering why you never mentioned that you saved a man's life from drowning? That's a good example, I would think, of helping others around you."

"A little self-serving, I would think, but thank you."

"I have a more serious question," she said. "How do you know what to do when, at times, your only options might be evil?"

He paused and looked at her. "Evil," he said, lifting his eyebrows. "Well, that definitely is a serious question." He took a breath. "Let me answer this way. Situations like this—'Sophie's Choice' dilemmas—are quite rare. But when they come, I think that in almost every situation, you will know what's right," and then he added, "at least you will know what is better."

Minutes later as he was expanding on his thoughts, the side door banged open and a late student staggered in. "Ah, yes," the newcomer said, swaying in the entryway, "the Master's Tea!"

Nicole froze.

She knew that voice.

She turned, and along with the whole room, watched Ryan stumble his way through the chairs, tripping on feet and apologizing as he came. "Sorry, sorry," he slurred as he bumped and elbowed toward her. Suddenly, he lost his balance and toppled over the arm of a heavily padded chair, knocking the girl sitting there onto the floor. He pushed off the chair and stood shakily. "My fault entirely," he announced with a lop-sided grin. "Please, forgive me."

Nicole dropped into her chair and closed her eyes. He was filthy drunk.

As the Master moved toward Ryan, Chris Cuomo quipped, "Reminds me of myself in my younger days."

Ryan staggered to a halt at Nicole's chair, the Master at his shoulder. "Ms. Van Buren!" Ryan said, pronouncing her name ostentatiously, as if he were in a Victorian ballroom. "I want to thank you publicly. Yes, I do. You are a wonderful person who got me a wonderful job!" He laughed insanely, gesturing toward her and clapping. "Isn't she wonderful?" Give her a hand folks."

"Ryan, will you please—"

"Time to go, son," the Master said gently but firmly.

"One minute," Ryan said, holding up his hand in a grand sweep. He craned his neck around the armchair next to her. "And of course, her shadow, Basil Happyass!" He clapped his hands enthusiastically and encouraged others to do the same. No one did, but several students had smirked at Ryan's remark.

The Master edged closer to Ryan and said, "This is not the time—"

"Happyass!" Ryan repeated with a hoot. "That's his name! I shit you not!" His face lit with pleasure.

The Master placed a hand briefly on Ryan's shoulder. "Remember where you are," he said, "and have some decorum." He crooked his fingers. "Follow me out."

"Certainly, sir," Ryan said with exaggerated sincerity. "But first I need to talk to Ms. Nicole here."

"You can talk to her later," the Master said.

"Now would be a good time, sir," Ryan said, grasping the chair for balance.

Nicole turned to the Master. "It's fine," she said, rising. "I'll walk him out. Sorry for the disturbance."

"Yes," Ryan agreed in nearly indecipherable slurs. "Sorry for the disturbance."

* * *

Nicole made her way out of the Master's house with as much dignity as she could manage. It wasn't easy with Ryan wobbling behind her, a stupid grin splashed across his face. Once in the courtyard, she turned on him.

"Well?" she said angrily.

"Well, what?"

She clenched her teeth and for a moment was seriously tempted to push him over. "I don't believe this," she said.

"I had a few, so what?"

"A few!"

"Yeah, a few."

"More like a few cases," a voice boomed behind them.

Nicole turned to see Basil striding across the grass.

"Uh-oh," Ryan said. "Here comes Dad."

"Ryan, be quiet," Nicole hissed.

"You are a drunken lout," Basil said in raised voice.

"A lout!" Ryan said, enunciating the word. "I am so offended."

"You're going to be more than offended."

Ryan laughed. "Really?"

"Yes, really."

"Okay," Nicole said, "enough of this—"

Basil stepped toward Ryan. "I ought to thrash you right here."

"Thrash away, you little gush-ball—"

Basil slammed his hands against Ryan's chest, knocking him easily to the ground. "I wouldn't lower myself. But I'm warning you," he said, pointing his finger, "stay away from my girl."

The words "my girl" irked Nicole. She whirled around to Basil and said, "Your girl! Like you own me?"

His face dropped. "I didn't mean it in the possessive sense," he said.

Nicole could hear Ryan giggling stupidly on the ground, and it grated on her. Then, of course, he started spouting in slurred speech: "Ol' Basil made a big mistake. This is an outrage! He acts like you're his pet frog."

"Ryan, shut up," she snapped.

"Okay, but it sure sounded like that to me."

She turned to Basil. "You had better go. I'll see you tomorrow."

"What? We were supposed to get together tonight."

"I know, but we'll have to do it another time."

"I don't understand," he said with a whining look on his face.

"I don't want any trouble between you two," she said. "Do me a favor and just go."

"Why should I be the one to go?"

"Because I need to talk to Ryan."

"You're kidding me, right? This drunken fool can't even pronounce his name, he's so blasted."

"Ryan! That's my name," the drunken fool said. "Amazing Ryan." He erupted into laughter.

Basil glared at Ryan, who was by now stretched out on the grass, trying to push himself up on one elbow. Basil turned toward Nicole, his face trembling with rage. "We were supposed to go out tonight! This assclown shows up, and all of a sudden you have to talk to him. Now you tell me why."

"I don't have to tell you anything," Nicole said, annoyed.

"Not acceptable," he shouted. "You tell me why!"

"Don't speak to me like that, Basil. If I want to talk to Ryan or anybody else, I'll talk to them. I don't need your permission."

"This is ridiculous," he said, scowling.

"Ridiculous or not, that's the way it's going to be. I'll see you tomorrow."

"I can't believe this."

"Basil! Please!" She gave him a look that said the discussion was over.

His lips curled in frustration, but he began shuffling toward the gate.

"Don't worry," Ryan said with an evil grin, "I'll take good care of your ... *girl*."

Basil swung around, eyes blazing. "I have had about enough—"

"*Real* good care," Ryan slurred.

"Ryan, keep your mouth shut! Basil, I asked you to leave!" Nicole had had enough too. She grabbed Basil by the arm and walked him briskly to the archway that led out of Calhoun College. "Goodbye," she said curtly. He now looked more chastened than angry, but she ignored this and turned abruptly back into the college without a backward glance.

When she returned, she found Ryan sprawled on the ground, asleep. Feeling in no way charitable, she booted him in the ribs. "Wake up!"

"*Stop!*" he said, his eyes still closed, his hands erratically pawing the air to fend off another attack.

Nicole wasn't in the mood for slobbering protests. She dropped to her knees and shook him violently until his head snapped back and forth.

He sat up, this time pushing her away forcefully. "Okay, okay," he mumbled. "What do you want?"

"I want to talk to you," she said, pulling him to his feet. "At the Tea you said something about your job. What happened?"

He stood swaying, looking around the empty quad as if uncertain where he was.

"Hello?" she said into his face. "Are you in there?"

He grinned, his eyes glistening with alcohol. "Hey, Nicole! You look very serious." He steadied himself on her shoulder.

She pushed his hand away. "You made a fool of yourself in there, you know ... and of me as well, I might add."

"Where?"

"At the Tea! At the Tea!" she shouted in his face.

"Oh, the Tea."

"Yes, the Master's Tea, in case you've forgotten."

"I just ... I have rights too, okay?" He gestured toward the Master's house. "What are you saying, I can't come to the Master's Tea?"

"You came drunk."

"Yeah, well ...."

"Well, what?" she asked.

"Hey, let's not make this my fault," he said. "You're ... you're the one who got me the job."

"What are you babbling about?"

"What am I ...?" He laughed crazily, the way he had at the Tea, as if he were privy to an inside joke. Then he abruptly lowered his voice and said, "I'm *babbling* about murder!"

Nicole looked into his barely focusing eyes. *How bizarre can this get?* she wondered. "Okay," she said in resignation. "Follow me. We'll go to my room."

His face twisted into a smile. "Got something exciting planned for ol' Ryan, have you?"

"Yeah, that's my big plan," she said. "I hope you can make it up the stairs."

"Don't worry about me," he said. "I'm fine."

"You look it."

"I am."

She grabbed him by the jacket and pulled him across the quad, maneuvering him through the oak door that led to the stairs. When they reached the fourth floor, Ryan wrapped his hands around the banister.

"What's the matter?" she asked.

"I feel sick."

"You're not sick," Nicole said evenly. "Just breathe."

His face turned ashen and his lower jaw began to quiver.

She grabbed his face. "Ryan," she said forcefully, "do not throw up."

"I'm okay," he said, and promptly vomited on the hardwood floor.

Nicole moaned. "Ten feet from my door."

"My bad."

"Don't even talk."

He wiped his mouth on the sleeve of his jacket.

"Oh, gross," Nicole said, curling her lip. She moved around to his other arm and steered him to her door.

"Room 496," he said, reading the brass number on the door. "I remember this room."

"Hooray for you."

"Lots of boxes."

As she helped him through the door, she turned her head aside to avoid his vomit breath. Three feet from the couch, she unhooked his arm from her neck, pushed him forward, and took a particular delight in watching him crash onto the couch. His head struck the wooden arm and bounced twice before coming to rest in an awkward position.

"That must hurt," she said without a shred of compassion, then whisked away her Pepper Elder from its perch at the end of the couch.

"This is your fault," he mumbled, his eyes half closed.

She shook her head in disgust. "I'll make some coffee."

When she returned with the coffee Ryan's head was propped back, mouth open and now emitting snores as well as noxious breath.

"Attractive," she muttered through pursed lips, and then returned the coffee to the sidebar. She called cleaning services and left a message that someone had vomited outside her door and she wanted the whole place steam-cleaned immediately. Not tomorrow. Immediately. Then, while Ryan slept, she studied till midnight. The only concession she made was to throw a blanket over him before she turned in for the night.

Shortly after six the next morning, Nicole awoke to the sounds of Ryan thumping around the living room, probably looking for the bathroom. She hollered through the bedroom door, "It's near the entrance."

As the bathroom door clunked closed, she pulled on a large T-shirt and headed for the fridge to see what she could fix for breakfast. She heard the shower turn on—at least he washed—and spent the next ten minutes fixing some eggs and bagels, then straightening up the apartment. When the bathroom door opened, she strolled over to see how he was doing. Ryan was standing in front of the sink with a towel wrapped around his waist, brushing his teeth. A good body, she couldn't help noticing.

"You found the toothbrushes," she said.

"No," he said, "I just used this one here."

"What? You used—I can't believe this—you used *my* toothbrush?"

"I'm gonna wash it off when I finish," he said, his lips dribbling toothpaste foam.

Nicole closed her mouth, which she realized had been hanging open. What an animal!

He stopped brushing, seeing her shocked look. "Relax," he said. "I told you I'd clean it."

"I don't want it now," she said, screwing up her face in revulsion. "I have a package of new ones in the cabinet."

"Oh, you have extras."

"Yeah, I have extras," she said, mimicking his dumb sounding voice.

"Anyway, thanks for letting me crash here last night."

"I didn't have much choice, did I? What did you think you were doing, stumbling into the Master's Tea like that?"

Ryan shrugged.

"Really. What was all that talk about murder?" She stretched out the last word and made a scary face to highlight her point.

"I can't remember much," he said, massaging the back of his head.

"Well, I remember it vividly."

"You can tell me about it sometime."

"I won't need to," she said. "The Master will give you a detailed account. Of that I am certain."

He flinched.

Nicole liked the nervous look in his eyes. She had finally gotten through to him. "Yes, the Master at Calhoun will be eager to have a nice sit-down chat with you," she said, enjoying the effect.

He collected his clothes. "Mind if I put my pants on?" he asked, trying to change the subject.

"Be my guest." She turned on her heel and walked away, saying, "If you're hungry, there's breakfast in the kitchen."

A few minutes later, Nicole watched him gobble down four eggs, two bagels smeared with grape jam, and a quart of orange juice. She sipped black coffee and remained silent.

"Didn't know these rooms had kitchens," he said at last, wiping the corners of his mouth with his fingers.

"They don't," she said. "I have a hotplate and a refrigerator."

"Clever."

"Yes," she said, studying him. He was essentially a nice guy, rather transparent, which could be refreshing. With Ryan, there wasn't much subtlety. But something had been bothering him the night before, something he now didn't want to talk about. "What was with you at the Tea?" she asked. "I mean ... why did you come looking for me?"

"Well, Nicole," he said, running his eyes over her body, "the truth is I was drunk and thought you'd be a good lay."

She didn't respond.

Embarrassed by his own boorishness, he took a slow breath and rubbed his face. "I don't know," he said finally, "maybe I just ...." He paused uncertainly. Then, spying the wine racks against the wall, he quipped, "That's a lot of wine. Maybe you're the one with the problem."

She smiled, a touch sadly. "My father doesn't visit me often," she said, "but when he does, he comes bearing wine."

"I'll bet some of them are worth a bundle."

"Nope. Just tasty, medium priced wines."

He studied the bottles as if interested, and then, avoiding her eyes, said, "Look, it doesn't matter why I came to see you. It really doesn't."

"It does," she said, moving closer and trying to appear sympathetic. "Tell me, Ryan."

"I haven't decided what to do."

Her instinct told her to stay silent.

After a few breaths, he rocked back on his chair and his eyes roamed the apartment as if searching for something. "I was thinking about going to the New Haven police," he said at length.

"The police."

"Yeah."

"Something in the lab? You said it was my fault, that I got you the job."

"The alcohol talking."

"Please, Ryan, don't shut me out. I want to help."

He pushed off his chair and paced the room.

"Please."

"It's insane," he said, "but there are these people ... with guns. Maybe government agents, or something, I don't know." He laughed tautly. "Sounds crazy—but they were there. And they weren't cops, I can tell you that."

"Who? What happened?"

"And if you stumble on them, I think they'd kill you." He looked at her, his voice going flat. "Can you believe that?"

Nicole could see he was agitated but she had no idea what to say—a novel experience.

"I know what happened to that Samuels friend of yours." Ryan was now standing in the center of the room and nodding to himself, as though he needed to affirm his own thoughts. "I heard them talking about it."

"Okay," she said quietly, encouraging him. "Fraser Samuels, what happened to him?"

Ryan remained standing, head tilted oddly, posture rigid.

Nicole tried to make eye contact. "You were saying?"

He looked like a statue, unblinking.

"Please tell me," she said in a gentle voice.

His face darkened.

"Ryan?" She moved toward him, hoping the gesture would break through whatever barriers his mind had erected. "I asked if you could tell me—"

"No!" he shouted angrily. "*You* tell *me* what's going on!"

Nicole felt her face flush at his outburst.

"You know something, don't you?"

She could see he was flipping out.

"Well?" he demanded. "All this interest—all these questions. What do you know about Krakauer's lab?" His eyes now glowed with anger and suspicion.

"I don't know anything," she said, frowning in confusion.

"Bullshit! You know more than you're saying."

"I don't, Ryan. Please believe me. I told you Krakauer was creepy, a bit odd, you know, but he's not dangerous."

"*Dangerous?*" Ryan spat, staring at her. "Why would you say that?"

"You just said there were men who would *kill* you."

"Yeah, but I didn't say it about Krakauer."

Nicole opened her hands. "Ryan, I don't know what you're driving at. I'm just trying to help."

His eyes searched her face, then glanced back towards the door. "Yeah."

"Do *you* think he's dangerous?"

"Krakauer? Damn right, I do."

"He's a Yale professor, for heaven's sake. What do you think ...." She stopped. "Oh, no, is that what you're saying? That Krakauer killed Fraser Samuels?"

"He might be involved, I don't know ... I think so."

Nicole forgot her attitude of sensitivity and rolled her eyes. "Sure, this is a sane conversation," she said with a laugh. "Professors often kill their students."

"You didn't see what I saw!" he blurted, anger flaring again. "And I'm really getting tired of your patronizing crap, Nicole. I might not understand what's going on, but I'll tell you this, you don't know either. So just drop the attitude."

Nicole closed her eyes and paused before speaking. She spoke softly, and tried to sound contrite when she said, "Fraser died in a car accident, pure and simple." She shrugged. "I know Krakauer made some comment about it, but he was just warning you to keep out of his business." She looked up. "Right?"

"This involves more than Krakauer," Ryan said with an edge to his voice.

"What do you mean?"

He stared at her but said nothing.

"Not secret agents from the government? Seriously?" She knew her words would very likely annoy him but she didn't care. At this point she needed him to talk, and Nicole gambled that an angry Ryan would tell her everything.

He grabbed a chair, twisted it backwards and banged it to the floor. He then sat down and said through tight lips, "Well, they weren't cops, and they weren't—you know—townies stealing lab equipment, okay? Military, homeland security, I have no idea. But two men with guns, one totting a baseball bat, were prowling the lab—and if they'd found me they would have killed me!"

Nicole took a seat as well. She hoped it would help him relax. "Those men," she said quietly, "don't you think they could have been Yale police checking out something?"

Ryan shook his head vigorously. "With a fucking baseball bat?"

"Well ...."

"One of them had an Uzi!"

"Oh, Ryan," she said, stifling a laugh.

"I'm serious. An Uzi! Except it had a round bottom."

"I don't even know what that means," she said.

"Yeah? Well I know what I saw. It wasn't a normal gun that a cop would carry."

Nicole saw no point in arguing. He was clearly upset, and possibly hung over. "Yale police have all kinds of weapons," she said, "especially now with terrorism. Can't you see you're overreacting?"

"No, I can't see it at all. One of the men was a colonel—that's what the other guy called him. And before you say it, yes, I know there are police colonels, but believe me, this was no cop. He moved and talked like a soldier, and he had the coldest eyes you ever saw. I have no doubts he would have killed me with about as much emotion as someone flattening an ant."

"Okay, I've heard enough," she said, inclining her head in a thoughtful manner. She feared that if she looked unsympathetic, he would become irrational. "You might be right about something strange happening. But I don't think it has anything to do with Fraser Samuels's car accident. The most important thing now is not to act rashly. There has to be a reasonable explanation." She smiled. "Can you imagine how foolish we'll look if we find out it was just the police investigating some break-in?"

He didn't respond.

She leaned forward on her chair. "I remember hearing about a man who entered a women's bathroom and was caught trying to open one of the stalls. A big woman clobbered him from behind with her briefcase and he was taken to the hospital with a concussion. Turned out he was blind." She looked at him. "See what I'm saying? There is usually a simple explanation for even the oddest behavior."

"There might be, but I'm going to the New Haven cops, and I'm doing it now."

"Maybe you should hold off, you know, for a week or so until we get more information on what happened?"

"No," he said, rising, "I'm finding out now."

"Ryan—"

"I'm gone," he said, heading for the door.

"Wait." Nicole heard herself say as though someone else was speaking. "I'm coming with you."

17

The general prided himself in living an austere life. Rarely did he indulge in the pleasures his enormous inherited wealth could buy. He liked a good cigar, a plain whiskey, and an interesting woman now and then, but mostly he liked the power to chart his own destiny. Unfortunately, events often ranged beyond his control. He could no more determine them, or predict their outcomes than he could the flow of the wind. They arose from nowhere—like this Professor Krakauer business—and threatened to overwhelm all his careful planning.

Still, even the most treacherous storms carried the seeds of opportunity, for those with eyes to see.

The orange light flashed twice on the general's phone.

"Secretary Thomkins on the line," came his adjutant's voice.

"I'll take it in my private office." He walked over to the bar in the corner of the room and reached for a crystal decanter shaped like an army canteen. A semblance of a smile crossed his face. His men had given him the canteen at retirement, that and a lone golf club. He'd never had occasion to use the golf club but he did justice to the canteen. He missed the army—none of what his wealth could buy compared to army life, with its code of behavior and system of accountability. As a member of 1st SFOD-D (Delta Force, to civilians), he had led countless missions in Iraq and Iran, and in later years had trained Special Forces units from a dozen allied countries. Those days were gone now, but at least at Proskin he had surrounded himself with the best the army had to offer.

The general poured himself an Old Crow and headed for the inner office, where he removed his coat, loosened his tie, and took a satisfying swig of his drink. Then, seating himself in a Shaker rocking chair from the 1800s, he picked up the phone.

"Bruce," he said after a slight pause, "good to hear from you."

The Agricultural Secretary's voice sounded strained on the other end. "I hope you feel that way by the end of our conversation."

"This a secure line?"

"Yes, of course, General."

"I presume you have denied Proskin Pharmaceutical's request for field-testing genetically altered animals."

"Finalized this morning, and already posted on the Department of Agriculture website," the Secretary said. "But that's not the worst of it, I'm afraid."

"Go on."

"Quite an explosive meeting."

The general swallowed some more whiskey.

"We've lost most of our support on the committee," continued the Secretary. His voice dropped. "They think I betrayed them. I know how they feel. They stood up to the animal rights devotees, took the heat, and then I stabbed them in the back. That's what they're saying."

The general grunted. "Even so, it's a better position than where you were, wouldn't you say?"

"No question," he said. "Denying your field-testing request gets me out of a legal mess. No one can say I've been sympathetic to Proskin."

"Exactly."

"So the major concern is finished with, as you predicted it would be. But, you should know, General, there are some who wonder, well, whether you—"

"Whether I had the stomach for the fight."

"Some are wondering that, yes. They think you're behind the scenes, pulling the strings, and if this string wasn't pulled then it might be because you've lost your nerve."

"Let them think what they want. It poses no problem."

"Not today, but I'm worried about future decisions, especially here at Agriculture. It'll be difficult to push proposals through if they think you—"

"Rest your mind, Bruce. Everything is moving along smoothly. You are doing a great job, and I am entirely satisfied with today's decision."

The general could hear the sigh of relief even through the phone.

"You realize," the Secretary said, "as a result of my actions today, we'll encounter problems—"

"Not worried, Bruce. Not worried at all." He swished some whiskey around in his mouth.

"That's good enough for me, General," he said, trying to sound optimistic. "Once again, I am in your debt. I wish I could repay you."

"You will, Bruce. I'm certain of it."

* * *

"Ryan," Nicole said, trying to slow his progress out the door, "I don't care whether you go to the police or not. I just have a question."

Ryan stopped, but refused to turn fully toward her, making it clear he was still on his way out. "What's your question?"

She grimaced. "First, I need to go to the bathroom. Okay? It'll just take a sec."

He breathed heavily.

"I know," she said, "but I won't be long."

He gestured for her to proceed.

In the bathroom Nicole closed her eyes, trying to think. She pushed back her hair and stared at herself in the mirror, as if the action would stimulate her mind. She needed to slow Ryan down. True, something had happened in the lab; that was evident. But Ryan was wound up like a clock and jumping to all the wrong conclusions. If he ran off half-cocked to the city police, spouting that tenured professors were murdering research assistants, and men with Uzis were roaming the campus, the whole ridiculous story would be splashed across the national media, and that would be bad for everyone, especially Ryan. She patted water on her face, fixed her mascara, applied some lipstick, and left the bathroom.

"Finally," Ryan said, starting toward the door.

"Wait, I wanted to ask if you really think it's a good idea to get the police involved—"

"I knew it! I knew you would start again."

"Okay, fine, we'll talk to the police, but it makes more sense to go to the Yale cops than a city precinct. If anything is going on, the Yale police will know."

His face tightened.

"What's the matter?"

"I don't trust the Yale police," he said.

"Ryan, really," Nicole said, trying not to sound patronizing. "How do you know who to trust or not? In the end, Yale officers will conduct the investigation anyway because they have jurisdiction over everything that occurs on university grounds. If you're not sure who to trust, best to keep it to the fewest possible, no?"

"Well ..." Ryan shrugged, acknowledging her point, "then we'll go to the Yale police," and with that he walked out the door, moving so quickly down the four flights of Calhoun and through the gates that Nicole was certain he was trying to leave her behind.

She hurried after him, determined to match him step for step. After a few minutes he slowed, and she tried to inject humor into the situation. "You think some broken-down lacrosse player can get away from a dancer?" she asked, doing a quick shuffle step.

He barely looked at her, and Nicole realized how deeply disturbing the whole situation had become for him. Walking alongside him in silence, she wondered what he would say to the police.

The wind picked up and there was a chill in the air as they passed the Grove Street Cemetery—Nicole tried to refocus his mind, chatting about petty thieves and how they often broke into university buildings. Most of the time they were harmless, she said, just looking for something not bolted down. She tried to talk reasonably, but if Ryan got the connection between thieves, break-ins, and police investigating labs, he didn't say so.

Directly ahead, she saw the red-brick police building, bordered by a few under-watered shrubs. Ryan cleared his throat nervously and entered the building.

A police officer with an unusually long head for his body sat behind a glass window. He looked tired, and the skin sagged around his eyes as if he were part bloodhound. Just finishing the night shift, Nicole figured.

"What can I do for you?" the officer asked.

Ryan shrugged and said, "I would like to—"

The hound's finger pointed toward a circular hole in the glass.

Ryan bent down to the hole and said, "I would like to talk to someone."

The police officer reached for a printed form and said in a bored voice, "State the nature of the problem."

"Do you have any plainclothes police officers?" Ryan asked, bending again.

The hound kneaded the loose skin on his face and blinked his eyes. "What is the problem, sir?"

"I'm asking if you have any plainclothes police officers."

"You mean on the street?"

"Anywhere."

"Can't hear you."

Ryan bent again. "Anywhere," he repeated. "Plainclothes officers, do you have any working at the university?"

"Why do you want to know that, sir?"

"Cause I want to chop them up for dinner," Ryan muttered to Nicole. "What's wrong with this guy?" She elbowed him aside, worried that Ryan's anger would bring trouble. Leaning over to the hole in the glass, she said, "It pertains to the nature of his report."

"I see." The hound's eyes drifted back and forth between them. "All our officers are uniformed," he said.

"I knew it!" Ryan flashed Nicole an I-told-you-so look. He bent over to the glass again. "I want to report that armed men entered the lab where I work." His voice sounded triumphant.

The officer jotted something on the form and asked, "Are they there now?"

"No."

"Name and address of your work?"

Ryan pressed his mouth so far into the hole his lips stuck out the other side. "Can I come in?" he calmly intoned. He was so obviously trying to make a point that the weary officer relented and let them both in.

The gate buzzed and Ryan and Nicole trundled down a hallway that led to a drab room full of cubicles. "Over here," a man's voice called from one of the side rooms.

They wove their way through a half-dozen metal desks covered with papers and dirty coffee cups. Nicole glanced over at three teens handcuffed to the metal struts of a bench. One of them was mumbling a rap song and gesturing with his free arm as if he were on stage. The others had their heads tipped back asleep. At the end of the bench, an old woman in a tattered dress sat staring at the floor, clutching a shopping bag.

"Come in," a deep voice directed.

Nicole followed Ryan into the tiny office and immediately blanched. *Oh great. Just great.* Coming around the desk was a heavy-set black officer, and his nametag read Officer Le Beau. He shook Ryan's hand, then turned to her with amused eyes and said, "And you must be Ms. Van Buren."

"You have a talent for names."

"Some," Le Beau replied smoothly.

Ryan looked quizzically at her.

"Officer Le Beau," she explained, "once helped me when I was in a desperate situation. He said he would never forget me and, true to his word, he has even remembered my name." She reached out her hand to Le Beau and tried to smile pleasantly as they shook.

Le Beau half-smiled, seeming to enjoy the awkward look on her face as he waited politely for the two of them to be seated. Nicole opened her mouth to say something but stopped when the officer moved back to his chair and pulled his laptop in front of him. He looked at Ryan. "Name?"

"Roger, ah, Roger Rumson," Ryan said.

Nicole sighed.

Le Beau typed something into his computer. "As I understand it, Mr. Rumson, you are reporting a break-in at a lab? Is that correct?"

"No," Ryan replied, "not a break-in. They had cards."

"Key cards?"

Ryan nodded.

"Men?"

"Two of them, white. One tall and skinny, the other medium height, face like a boxer, and in good shape. Both in their forties, I think. The tall one might have been Hispanic."

Le Beau paused. "Two men, you say?"

Ryan nodded.

Le Beau chewed on his lip, as if thinking, typed some more, then looked up. "If they had key cards, how do you know they weren't there for legitimate reasons?"

"Believe me they weren't."

"How do you know?"

Nicole answered. "They had weapons."

"Lots of official people carry weapons," Le Beau retorted with a frown.

"Yes," Nicole said, "that's what I told—"

"Uzis? Do they carry Uzis?" Ryan gripped his chair so tightly that his knuckles turned white.

The officer lifted up a book off the back table, flipping it open and handing it to Ryan. "An Uzi?" he asked, "like this?"

Ryan looked at it. "It wasn't exactly like that, no. It was more rounded."

"Uh huh."

Nicole felt vindicated and turned impulsively to Ryan. "See, maybe it was—"

Ryan gestured her away, clearly annoyed, and flipped through the book, stopping near the end. "*This.* This is what they had."

"P90?"

"Yeah, but with a longer tube on the front."

"A suppressed FN P90."

Le Beau shifted his eyes from Nicole to Ryan, then cupped his chin and leaned forward.

"Actually," Nicole interjected, "we really aren't certain about that."

"I am!" The veins popped out on his forehead. "You weren't even there."

"Ryan, this is ridiculous—"

"Hold on," and Le Beau lifted his hand. "Were you in the lab, Ms. Van Buren, when these men showed up?"

"No, but—"

"Then please be quiet."

"Dangerous looking men," she snorted, "probably part-time security guys that—"

"If you keep it up, I'll have to ask you to leave."

Nicole glared at Le Beau but held her tongue.

"You'd better start at the beginning," Le Beau said, focusing on Ryan. "This is a Yale lab, right?"

"It's a Yale lab, but I would prefer not to say where it is."

Le Beau frowned. "Why not?"

"It's complicated—the professor's a bit touchy." Ryan squirmed on his chair. "Look," he said, "all I really want to know is whether some police or government agency—I don't know, maybe the military or the CIA—might have reason to check on a professor's research."

Nicole mumbled, "I vote for the CIA."

"Please," Le Beau said, giving her a jaded look. He took a sip of nasty-looking coffee and said, "I think it's time one of you told me what is going on. We'll start with you," he said, jamming a thick finger at Ryan. "You're not Roger Rumson, are you?"

Nicole nearly laughed at the look of feigned indignation on Ryan's face.

"I don't understand," Ryan said. "Of course I'm Roger Rumson."

He was the worst liar Nicole had ever seen.

Le Beau pushed his computer around to show a florid-faced boy with a shock of red hair. "Meet Roger," he said in a deadpan voice.

Ryan coughed, stalling for time.

"It won't take long to ID you in Yale's photo database," Le Beau said. "Ms. Van Buren here called you Ryan, and believe me in short order I will know your full name and which lab you work in as well."

"He's Ryan Taylor," Nicole said. "He doesn't want to lose his lab job."

Le Beau nodded. "Be straight with me and I'll see what I can do to keep you out of this."

Ryan shot a glance at Nicole.

She ignored him. If Ryan thought he could keep his identity private at a police station when they already knew he was a registered student, he deserved a snoot full of reality. "Ryan," she said quietly, trying to assuage his anger, "tell the officer about the men in the lab." At this point, the best thing was to give Le Beau the bare facts and get out of there.

Ryan seemed to understand because he told Le Beau in some detail about the two men and their conversation. When he mentioned the name, Krakauer, Le Beau's demeanor abruptly changed. He leaned forward on his chair, his eyes narrowed to a slit. "Which Professor Krakauer is this?" he asked.

"Jozef Krakauer," Ryan replied.

Le Beau was silent, thinking.

"Does that name mean something to you?" Ryan asked at last.

"No, no," Le Beau said. "Yale has several Krakauers, one in the Philosophy department, one in European Studies, if I'm not mistaken. It's just hard to keep them straight."

But Nicole couldn't help noticing how the officer's face had tightened when Ryan mentioned Krakauer. He continued with his questions, speaking in lowered tones and cryptic phrases. Twice he rose and checked the area outside of his office doorway.

Near the end of their interview, Le Beau leaned closer to Ryan and said, "So what's being done there?"

"You mean in the research lab?"

Le Beau grunted.

"Krakauer's studying gene therapy—"

"Anything out of the ordinary?"

Nicole felt a growing unease. This man was fishing for something and she didn't like it. "Standard research," she chipped in.

He ignored Nicole's contribution. "Anything out of the ordinary?" he asked Ryan again.

Ryan avoided Nicole's eyes. "They melt," he said. "The animals melt like butter."

Le Beau bolted forward as if jabbed by a pin. After a moment's pause, he went to the door and closed it. "What do you mean, melt?" he asked, his eyes riveted on Ryan.

This was going too far, Nicole thought. "They don't melt," she said. "That's not possible."

"Bull!" Ryan said. "I saw a chimpanzee melt. Some black goo was eating it from the inside. In fifteen minutes there was nothing but bones, pieces of rotted fur, and black muck."

"That's not possible," Nicole repeated. She expelled a breath wearily. "The truth is that Ryan doesn't know the first thing about biology."

A quiet tap at the door hit Le Beau like a second pinprick. He spun around, facing the door.

What is with this guy? Nicole wondered.

Le Beau cleared his throat and visibly relaxed his body, then stepped forward and opened the door. "Captain," he said calmly.

"Have you stumbled on some robbers, Elijah?" a white-haired man asked.

Le Beau laughed, somewhat artificially, Nicole thought. "Yes, sir," Le Beau said with a broad smile. "We've got us a robbery, but these are not our thieves."

The man nodded and said, "A lab break-in, I hear."

"Robbery outside the lab, sir."

"Outside the lab?" the man repeated.

"Yes, sir. Mr. Taylor was robbed outside his lab by a townie, we think." He shifted on his feet, glancing around awkwardly. "A black male in his twenties accosted Mr. Taylor with a weapon and demanded his wallet."

"I see. What kind of weapon?"

"A knife."

The captain nodded. He shifted his eyes between Ryan and Nicole, and then he scratched his head. "A robbery, you say. Stole his wallet. Hmm." He moved closer to the chair in which Ryan was sitting and motioned toward his back pocket. "Looks like you've already managed to purchase a new one."

Nicole saw Ryan lick his lips tensely. She cleared her throat and said, "Same wallet, luckily. All the man wanted was money. He threw it down some basement stairs. Ryan didn't even need new ID."

"That is fortunate," the man said.

"Yes," Nicole replied, "and fortunate that Ryan wasn't killed! Makes you wonder how safe Yale students are when thieves run wild on campus, and there's no police anywhere."

The captain glanced around the room slowly and apologized for their trouble.

Le Beau turned to Ryan and Nicole, then said in an overly loud voice, "As I was saying, we have some ideas but we can't promise anything. I have your phone numbers so we'll be in touch."

Nicole thanked him, and she and Ryan left the station.

18

The building under construction looked very much like the West Wing of the White House, only it was sitting in the middle of a huge forced-air dome. The General couldn't help admiring the speed with which his engineers had accomplished their work, constructing three complete floors, and a series of tunnels to represent the basement levels. He signaled Colonel Donovan who was transferring biohazard suits to holding areas along the wall.

"Projections?" the general asked.

Donovan shifted his eyes to the workers moving briskly across the docks. "Assuming we're in here tomorrow—"

"You'll be in."

"Okay ... the troops have been over this thing a hundred times," he said. "So figure ten days of full scale maneuvers—that's a minimum, a month is better—but after that we can ratchet up in six hours."

The general nodded. "A first-rate job, Colonel."

"I have first-rate commanders," Donovan said. Then he added, "They appreciated the watches, sir, especially the inscription on the back."

"The Battle of Thermopylae, 480 B.C.," the general intoned, as if he were quoting from a history book. "King Leonidas and his tiny band of Spartan soldiers, surrounded by a quarter million Persians, refused to surrender. They vowed to go home carrying their shields, or on them. They fought to the last man."

The two soldiers stood silently on the catwalk, their eyes on the activity below, but their minds lost in the bravery of another age.

"CDC Atlanta will take care of outbreaks around the country," the general said at last. "We focus on the White House and the Secret Service. They'll need us because they aren't equipped to handle crises of this magnitude." He turned to face his chief of operations. "We cannot afford mistakes. Everything must be planned to the second."

"Understood."

"Closer to home, we might have a few loose ends."

"Oh?"

"Krakauer's new research assistant. You know the situation there."

"Yes, sir."

"The additional care we have to take, we've discussed this."

"Yes, sir."

"Problem is, I've received troubling information."

Donovan's eyes narrowed.

"The kid reported a break-in at the lab."

"Gonzales and me?"

"Possibly. It's a bit muddy right now. The official report has a robbery outside the lab."

"You want me to clean the situation?"

"If he proves difficult." The general looked away. "I would prefer to pass over him, but the larger picture takes priority. Use your judgment."

"Yes, sir."

"He's been talking to an officer named Le Beau. Yale PD."

"I'll take care of it."

"We don't want bodies at this stage, understood? Especially a police officer. We can do without investigations. Find an angle to keep him quiet. I'm told his wife has MS, that he's been to every doctor in New Haven about her condition, looking for cures. Interestingly, she's involved in one of our drug studies. See the lab boys downstairs. They might have some carrot you can use to bring him into line. But if you have to go the other route, set it up properly. The mission is everything."

Donovan nodded.

"On another front, Lieutenant Prator is definitely a go."

"Understood," Donovan said, his face expressionless.

The general frowned. "You have something to say, Colonel?"

"No, sir."

"I felt your hesitation before when we talked about Prator. Let's hear it."

"Sir, I don't work well with the lieutenant," Donovan said.

"Prator's a damn fine intelligence officer," the general said. "And loyal to the core."

"I know you raised her, sir, but—"

"I didn't raise her. I provided for her. There's a difference. I can count the times on one hand she was in my home."

Donovan's eyelids dropped, but he said nothing.

The general took a breath. "My objectivity's intact," he said. "From the first day I scooped her up in Iraq with a bullet in her gut, I saw something special in her. I brought her here, gave her my mother's name, provided for her education and other needs, but I let her choose her own path." He paused. "The point is, she can help us now."

"Yes, sir, but with respect, the lieutenant is primarily an interpreter, an over-trained babysitter at best. I don't see why—"

"She's Secret Service."

"I understand, sir, but—"

"What you don't know is that she's coming off a two year relationship with the Special Agent in Charge of White House Operations."

"Iverson?"

"Precisely, Darryl Iverson. That makes Prator the perfect liaison officer. With her talking to Iverson—when the crunch comes—she could tip the balance."

"I stand corrected. A good choice, sir."

"You'll still partner with Gonzales, but Prator's a godsend." He shifted his eyes to the construction below and said curtly, "If you have problems, work it out."

"Yes, sir."

"Also, I talked to Bruce at Agriculture this morning. His Department has formally denied Proskin's request for field-testing our new genetically altered animals, a major loss for us, but now, at least the Secretary isn't under the gun from these watchdog groups. The last thing we need is to hurt our friends."

"Is the Secretary on board?"

"He's on board, but he doesn't know the full story."

The colonel paused. "Will this be a problem?"

"When the time comes the Secretary will do his duty. We all will."

* * *

"Hello," Nicole said into her cell phone. The sun was too bright to see who was calling.

"How'd your talk go?"

She squinted at the phone. "Basil?"

"Yeah, it's just Basil."

"Sorry, I can't hear you. Everyone's leaving the lecture hall, and it's loud out here. Where are you? You've missed a lot of classes."

"I didn't think anyone would notice."

Nicole took a breath. "About Friday night—"

"How long did you and what's-his-name talk?"

"For a while," she said.

"A while. What's that mean? Five minutes? All night?"

"It means—"

"So where'd you go to have your *talk?* His room or yours?"

"Basil, you're misunderstanding the situation. Let's have lunch—"

"Sorry, gotta go. Another call coming in."

* * *

After teaching his biology class at Kline, Professor Krakauer stopped by Taft Cosmetics to buy Excedrin. The endless lab experiments and mounting apprehension over his packages had given him a headache. He swallowed three tablets dry and surveyed the newspapers beside the cash register. Nothing yet, but when it happened, he would have no need to check newspapers. In one devastating day, the words *genetic engineering* would burn themselves into the collective consciousness of billions of people.

He remembered how 9/11 had shaken America—planes crashing, buildings exploding—and suddenly the word "terrorist" became real. No longer were fanatics threatening some indefinable US interest abroad, they were threatening husbands and wives and children—ordinary people—and they were killing them here in America. Yes, 9/11 opened America's eyes to terrorism, and soon, very soon, his packages would alert everyone to the awesome power of genetic engineering.

The professor picked up *The New York Times* and turned to the financial section. He ran his eye down the ticker symbols, pausing at the countless biotech firms that specialized in genomics. The greedy of this age were pouring billions of dollars into genetic research, and no one thought about controls, no one asked whether a genetic project was advisable, only whether it might be profitable. And warnings had no effect, not with the bonanza that eugenics promised the person on the street. Newscasters continually ran stories about genetic engineering "getting close" to curing diseases like cystic fibrosis, muscular dystrophy, and sickle cell anemia. In this brave new world eugenics would give sight to the blind, make the crippled walk, and regrow body parts with the prick of a syringe, all using the DNA of salamanders, spiders and creatures from under the sea.

But Krakauer wasn't fooled. He knew these geneticists—saw them at conferences. They held nothing sacred, certainly not the human body. Left unchecked, he shuddered to think what the human race would be in a hundred years. For eons nature had vigilantly selected all the genes in the human genome, and in an afternoon science would sweep away that balanced order.

What could a lone professor do to halt the tide? He was like one crying in the wilderness. Who would listen? Would people heed the solo voice of Dr. Jozef Krakauer if he warned of impending disaster? He knew the answer: No. A thousand times no. When the Pope railed against genetic manipulation, calling it insane, risky and dangerous, and labeling it anti-Genesis, his words were met with yawns. If they didn't listen to the Pope, why would they listen to a simple professor? Like beasts of the field, people would do what they've always done, stumble along blindly and hope for the best. They foolishly believed science could be trusted to draw the line.

But "science" was about egos; large egos that knew nothing about drawing lines. These people would cure baldness under the guise of helping cancer patients recover their hair, and then they would sell the gene therapy to the pharma behemoths.

And they wouldn't stop there. Oh, no, science never stops. Next they would engineer hair to be a particular color, blond perhaps, and then compliment it with blue eyes, if the person wished. And what else? Skin color? Intelligence? Height? Muscle mass? Who could resist endowing one's child with firm muscles, uncommon beauty or an Aristotle-like mind? Certainly, people would select out unhappy features such as large noses and stooped postures. Why not create a race of drones that had enough intelligence to do manual labor, but not enough to notice their inferiority?

Fantasy? The professor knew better. The history of the human race proved they would do anything for money, fame, or power. After this, there would be no stopping human ingenuity. Maybe a simple-minded race of beautiful men and women, trained to fulfill the whims of their masters, or a warrior class that had no fear of death, or even a combination of human and animal life forms targeted for specific tasks.

And what happens when millions possess the capability of manipulating genes? Surely, hundreds—if not thousands—of future geneticists would surface with the sick mindset of hackers who now design computer viruses.

What then? Catastrophic biological disaster?

Yes, Krakauer had genuine fears for the human species. Few understood the breathtaking potential of genetic engineering, and those that did were standing in silence, watching the train to Auschwitz roll by.

Jozef Krakauer remembered the words of his grandmother, that every generation must stand and be counted. The test changed with each generation, turning up in oblique ways so that only the clear-eyed could see it. In the 1930s, an individual who perceived the evil of Adolf Hitler, and planted a bomb—say in a market place—that killed scores of innocent mothers and children along with the future leader, he would have been considered a murderous villain. A butcher. Not fit to live. Without Hitler, world events would have taken a drastically different course and no one would have ever heard of the Nazi party, death camps, or the swastika. Well-meaning people would have condemned this farsighted individual, and vilified his name forever, never realizing the nightmare that had almost engulfed their world.

Such was the fate of Jozef Krakauer, Yale professor. His part in the things to come would forever blacken his name—Jozef Krakauer, killer of women and sweet children. His crime? With the soul's eye, he perceived the currents of history, and not being able to abandon the human race as it slid into oblivion, he stepped forward and pruned its branches so the tree would live. He had heeded Einstein's warning from a malignant age, and he determined not to sit and let chaos happen.

And now his name would burn in infamy.

Jozef Krakauer, fanatic.

Murderer.

Slayer of children.

But in his heart, he knew the truth.

Yes, he had prayed, something new for him. Long hours into the night. "Do not be far from me," he had pleaded, "for my time of testing is near, and there is no one to help. I cry out by day, but you do not answer, and by night. Why do you not hear the words of my groaning?"

And then, as the cracks of dawn banished the night's darkness, he received his answer. "Dogs will surround you," the voice had said. "A band of evil men will encircle you. All who see you will mock you; they will hurl insults at you. Yes, they will count your bones."

The time of testing had fallen upon him, and he knew he must grasp the horns of the altar and never let go. He must face this generation's test, and not wither in the wind.

"Do you wish to buy the paper, sir?" the balding man at the counter asked.

Krakauer stared at him blankly, dropped the paper, still open to the financial section, and left the store. He stood on the sidewalk for a long time, watching the souls trudge by, oblivious to the gene that inhabited every cell of their bodies. Innocent fools. With a dusting of a few simple chemicals— his trigger—anyone could extinguish the entire population of the city. And it could happen within hours. Everyone gone. Such was the power of genetic research. Would they see? Would they awaken in time? He watched the crowds move. They would not.

Not without fire and pestilence.

Like a slumbering giant they would ignore the signs of approaching disaster until it was too late.

Krakauer closed his eyes and waited for the voices to come. Voices? Even now it sounded insane. How could he tell anyone he heard voices? Obviously, he could not. But at this very moment he could hear the collective cries of numberless people yet to be born—genetically clean people—pleading for him to act. "Help us," they murmured. "Who else but you?"

Krakauer glanced up and down the street, and straightened his back. He would not fail them. Somewhere out there his packages were moving to their destinations, and he rejoiced at his strength of character. He had become the giver of life.

19

Ryan stared at the email from Officer Le Beau. It was an evite for a fundraiser four months from now. The image contained the text: "Fourth floor of Payne-Whitney Gym, seven-thirty. Below it, "tonight" was underlined in bold. The message sounded odd, spooky even, but he grabbed his jacket and started for the door. It was already seven forty-five.

As he hurried past the rare book library, late afternoon shadows spilled across Beinecke Plaza, slanting along the pavement, and blending into the pulsing darkness on the far side. Ryan looked around, wondering suddenly if he was being followed, concluded he wasn't, and turned onto Grove, his head jerking with every gust of wind. The street was vacant except for a rapidly approaching man in a dark coat, a stooped, skeletal-looking creature in his fifties. Ryan squinted, thinking he had a menacing look, but the man passed by without even a sideways glance. Seconds later, Ryan was across from the Grove Street Cemetery. The image of thousands of eyes watching him from behind somber gravestones made him uneasy, though he knew he was being ridiculous.

Still, why would Le Beau want a secret meeting? And why would he lie to another cop? The questions were increasing, and Ryan didn't like the answers his mind was creating.

At Payne-Whitney the elevator creaked and popped on its way up, as if the cables would suddenly snap. Funny how everything seemed alien now. When he reached the fourth floor the door opened slowly to a dimly lit hall, and Ryan glanced both ways before stepping out. The painted walls glistened in circular patterns under the night lights, like lanterns on a deserted path. He sensed the heavy presence of stairwells and stone lintels, and along the corridor every door was shut except for a murky bathroom propped open with a waste barrel. He could hear his sneakers squeaking on the polished floors as he walked toward the open door, a light breeze from the bathroom window curling around his legs.

He paused.

Footsteps, he was sure of it. He leaned into the sound, head cocked, straining to pinpoint its direction. Definitely on this floor. Must be that way, he thought, his steps quickening toward an intersection in the corridor. Then, sensing something wasn't quite right, he stopped abruptly.

"Easy," Le Beau said, stepping out from the shadows. "Just making sure it was you." He gestured with his hand for Ryan to follow. Seconds later they arrived at a storage room near the end of the hall, Ryan blinking heavily under the fluorescents. Tables, desks, and chairs were piled everywhere, and in the center of the room, sitting on top of a desk, her feet resting on a chair, was Nicole. She looked troubled.

"Let me start again," Le Beau said, pulling out an oversized office chair for himself. "Two years ago we had an officer on the Yale police force named Fred Romano. He was doing routine patrols in Kline Biology Tower when he saw students running from a classroom. He tried to enter, but Professor Jozef Krakauer stopped him, insisting he wait until certain specialists arrived."

"What kind of specialists?" Ryan asked.

"Germ guys, with air suits," Le Beau said. "Anyway, if you ever met Romano, you'd know some scarecrow scientist wasn't about to tell him how to do his job. He pushed his way in and found something unbelievable." Le Beau glanced up at Nicole. "I've already told her," he said, breathing heavily. "A professor named Westover was lying in a puddle of sludge on the theater floor, his flesh eaten away. I mean all of it. Romano told me there was nothing left but bones inside his blood-soaked clothes. And it wasn't even blood, Romano said. More like black muck."

Ryan felt his body tighten. "Like the chimp in Krakauer's lab."

"Exactly."

"This is too much," Nicole said. "We're back to this melting thing, and I can tell you, nothing works that way biologically." She eyed them both. "Nothing."

"I'm just a cop," Le Beau said. "And I've heard lots of things—"

"People don't melt," Nicole insisted. "It's not possible. The *thermodynamics* don't even make sense."

Le Beau rubbed the stubble on his chin. "Can't say they do or not, but Romano told me he could see through the empty eye sockets into Westover's skull. It was hollow, like his brain had drained away." He looked up at Nicole. "So how'd that happen?"

Nicole opened her mouth to say something, but just shook her head, perplexed.

"There's something else," Ryan said. "The Mexican guys ... the cleaners in Krakauer's lab, I think they somehow got melted like the monkeys." He curled his lip in distaste before adding, "The outer skin doesn't melt, it kind of mashes up. Anyway, I thought I saw a tattoo from one of the cleaners through a biohazard bag."

"You didn't tell me this," Nicole said.

Ryan shrugged. "I'm not totally sure," he said. "But Krakauer has different cleaners now."

Le Beau hoisted his large body out of the chair. "Okay," he said, "I want you kids to back off this thing. Go to your classes, do whatever it is you do, but don't come to the police station reporting anything about Krakauer's lab. I'll give you a cell number, but call only if there's a genuine emergency. And don't leave anything on the voicemail—I'll see your number and call you back from a different number. Otherwise, I will check with you every few days for anything new. Agreed?"

"What's this all about?" Ryan asked.

"I wish I knew."

"But it's dangerous."

"Oh, it's dangerous, all right," Le Beau said. "Romano was yanked into the office the second he arrived to fill out reports. Our new captain, Barton, instructed him to say nothing about Westover, and less than six hours later Fred was found dead in an alley, a victim of a knifing. No suspects. Random, they said. I don't believe it. Romano was too smart to get knifed by some townie."

"But he talked to you?" Nicole asked.

"Yeah. Romano and I were close—joined the force about the same time. He met me in the bathroom and told me what he saw. He said Captain Barton was on the phone all afternoon, pacing around his office. And then he ordered Romano to work an extra half shift that night." Le Beau's eyes strayed to the door. "We don't work extra shifts after a full day and an incident like that, not unless somebody like a Supreme Court Justice comes to campus."

"You suspect the police captain?" Nicole asked.

"The report on Westover says he died from aspiration—choking— on his own vomit. It states that Officer Romano found him unconscious and called the medics. Nothing out of the ordinary." Le Beau shook his head. "It's a lie! Romano never filed that report." He shifted his eyes between Nicole and Ryan as if he was expecting them to say something.

Ryan didn't say anything, but inside his unease was growing.

"I'll tell you something else," Le Beau said, "I've checked out this Westover fellow, and he was into some heavy genetics stuff. My guess is he invented some kind of bug that—"

"Heavy genetics stuff? Invented a bug?" Nicole had a look of disdain on her face.

"Invented, created—whatever—I don't know what science types do in their labs, but I think this Professor Westover made something that turns people into soup, and Krakauer is continuing his work. How the captain fits in I have no idea, but I'll bet money changed hands."

"What about those guys in the lab?" Ryan asked.

"I saw them the morning of the break-in. They claimed to be military police and they might be—but no one has ever heard of them, and their license plate was bogus. They're probably some branch of government investigating Krakauer, maybe trying to get a fix on his research. I don't know. Best to avoid them."

Punctuated with protests from Nicole, Ryan told Le Beau about the mysterious death of Fraser Samuels. The officer stared at the floor, but said nothing.

"So what does all this mean?" Ryan asked.

"I don't know," Le Beau replied. "I just don't know. But I want you kids to be careful. This thing is rotten."

* * *

Lieutenant Karen Prator wended her way through the dining hall at Proskin Pharmaceutical and stopped in front of Donovan who was eating alone at a corner table. She fixed her eyes on him and folded her arms. "You didn't tell the general, did you?" she said.

He continued chewing, and without hurrying, placed his fork carefully beside the plate. He looked up and said, "I told him I had no desire to work with you."

"Did you explain why?"

"Nothing to explain."

She tilted down toward him. "That's the way you feel, Michael?"

"Exactly the way I feel," he said flatly.

"It meant nothing to you then?"

"Look, Prator, if we're going to work together, you need to understand a few things. First, we don't talk about personal—"

"Fine," she said, waving away his comments. "I don't want to hear it. But remember, it wasn't my idea to kill what we had. It was you, all you, and we both know why."

"We do?"

"You couldn't handle someone getting inside your guard."

"Are you finished?"

"I guess that's a good word for it."

"The general says you have some influence with Iverson."

She eyed him.

"First hand Intel. Quite valuable."

"I see," she said, nodding her head. "You know about Darryl and me."

"My only concern is that you get Iverson to open that gate."

"I'll do my best to sway him."

"I'm sure you will." He went back to eating.

Her lips parted to speak, then pressed closed. "Anything else?"

"The general has briefed you," Donovan said, "so you know the importance of what we're doing. This complex is secure. No outgoing comms so don't bother phoning or emailing anyone. Outside we travel in teams and everything is line of sight until Thermopylae. Understood?"She nodded.

"Understood?" he repeated more forcefully.

"Yes," she said in a strained voice. "Understood." She took a breath and frowned. "Everything is line of sight? Even a restroom?"

"Everything. The general has a severe restriction on information flow. He's determined there'll be no leaks, accidental or otherwise. So, yes, I will accompany you into the bathroom, and you will accompany me."

"If someone walks in?"

"A hypothetical, but if someone enters the bathroom we tell them we're federal agents, show our IDs and inform them they will have to wait." Donovan ran his eyes over her well-tailored suit. "You still carrying a Sig 229?" he asked.

"Yes."

"A great weapon. Get rid of it. Pick up a Five-seven downstairs threaded for a suppressor. And dump the suit. Jeans and a leather coat are better. You're not in the Secret Service anymore."

20

Midas, Nevada:

"Honey? Laura? Mail truck's come from Golconda."

"Okay, Mom."

"You awake, honey? Harvey's dropped the bags."

"Ah ... thanks. I'm up."

"You need more sleep."

"I'm fine."

"You're not fine, you're dead on your feet."

"Just need some coffee."

"Working at the diner all day, and slugging the mail."

"Mom, please."

"The mail's Ron's job, not yours."

"He needs a little help right now."

"He needs to stop drinking."

"He's trying."

"Ron's a bum. Never should have married him."

"We got Lisa ...."

"She is a sweetcake. Don't mind looking after her."

"I'll load the bags. Ron said he'd help me sort it at the Gold Circle."

"The Gold Circle? He's there in the morning?"

"He's trying, Mom."

"He's a bum."

* * *

Biggar, Saskatchewan, Canada:

"Mr. Mayor, as a councilor of this town, I have a right and a duty to speak my mind."

"You do, Bob. Let's hear it."

"It's about those signs."

"What about them?"

"You know what. They have to come down!"

"Not while I'm mayor. The signs promote our town."

"Promote our ... Mr. Mayor, I have been sending out flyers on this issue—"

"I know, Bob, and you're heading to the post office to view the results."

133

"That's right. The signs make us look like a bunch of hicks."

"We *are* hicks, Bob. Look at that plaid coat you're wearing."

"If you think that's funny—

"All I'm saying is there's nothing wrong with being who we are."

"Fine, but we are *not* hicks."

"Bob, we live in northern Saskatchewan in the heart of grain country, for heaven's sake. We've got Sandra Schmirler—who did a damn fine job getting us that gold medal in curling—and a barley processing plant. If this isn't hick country, what is?"

"That kind of attitude is killing us, Mr. Mayor."

"The signs stay."

"Those signs do more harm than you know."

"Those signs, Bob, were here before your grandfather was born."

"We have moved on from that time."

"There is such a thing as continuity with the past. The signs were erected in a quieter, less pretentious age—by good people—and I intend to preserve their legacy to us."

"Ten-foot signs that pump up New York and say we are worthless is an embarrassment!"

"You know what your problem is, besides the pole up your butt, I mean?"

"I object to that kind of language, Mr. Mayor."

"You take life too seriously."

"This is a very serious issue."

"Cancer is serious, Bob, drugs in our community are serious, but not the signs."

"You've been warned, Mr. Mayor, I am very determined."

"Yes, I see the powerful clinch of your jaw."

"Your ... sarcasm ... you will regret—"

"A joke, Bob, relax. Maybe you should go fishing."

"A referendum might change your mind."

"I doubt it."

"A growing number of people side with me."

"Well, Bob, you count them up."

"I will. I'm on my way to the post office right now."

"And I'm off to Jackfish Lake—catch a few tasty pickerel."

* * *

Carefree Dream Liner twenty-four miles west of Puerto Rico:

"Never fails, Zwag. Always rains on our day off."

"Yeah, and when the sun comes out we're stuck here in the maintenance room."

"This is crap."

"Total crap."

"I should have got that high-school diploma."

"I never had a chance, Zwag. My old man kicked me out the day I turned sixteen."

"Tough break."

"Yeah. I've never gotten a square deal my whole life."

"What's this?"

"What's what?"

"A package here for you, Kyle."

"A package?"

"Got your name on it."

"My name?"

"Maybe from your girlfriend."

"Don't have a girl."

"No return address, but somebody must love you."

"What's the postmark?"

"Philadelphia."

"Open it for me. My hands are greasy."

"Just a minute … look, Kyle, a cigar box. Hey! Twenty bucks! A couple of them. Somebody sent you some twenties in a plastic bag."

"So tear it open!"

"I am. Don't get your shirt in a knot."

"Hey! That's mine. Gimme it."

"You get all the breaks."

"Bloody time my luck changed."

21 [decorative border]

A huge roar shook the stadium as Syracuse stepped onto the field. Orange-shirted fanatics were everywhere, screaming and hollering, stamping their feet. Nearly three hundred miles from Syracuse, but still 'Cuse fans made the trip, as if they had no life beyond their lacrosse team.

From the opposite end of the field, Ryan watched them swagger onto the turf, walking, not running like other clubs. No, the 'Cuse never rushed; they walked two abreast in an unhurried manner, as if they wanted their opponents to get a good look at the best team in the nation. Halfway out they began to trot, but nothing so strenuous as to cause a sweat. Ryan grunted his admiration. Truth be told, he was relieved to be around people whose entire focus was lacrosse. Nobody cared about melting monkeys or lying police captains. They cared about lacrosse. Lacrosse and nothing else.

Ryan swept his eyes over the crowd and stopped at Nicole, who was waving her arms, trying to get his attention. He paused, noticing a hunched figure six rows above her. Ryan wondered why she and Basil weren't together, but he turned away, wanting to concentrate on the game. Waldhart had talked about centering one's mind before a contest, and Ryan intended to do that. He hated Syracuse.

He could hear the 'Cuse players talking as they paired off to throw the ball around.

"I told you this tourney would suck," one of them said.

"No doubt," replied a defenseman whose body resembled a tree trunk. He ran his eyes over Ryan and said, "This guy looks like he belongs in a library. I'll take him. I need a rest after last night's mixer."

Ryan ignored him and loosened up with a few stretches.

"Hey, braaain," the tree trunk said, drawing out the word with a sneer. "Don't get excited over there. You won't even touch the ball."

Ryan smirked. "Y'know, I find it amazing you're proud of not having a brain. What do you suppose that means?"

"It means we'll beat you by twenty goals, Einstein."

The other defenseman laughed. "Hey, Wexler, this guy doesn't have much respect for you. Tell him who he's dealing with, a first team All-American."

Wexler gave Ryan an intimidating look.

"Wow!" Ryan said in mock respect. "Your eyes are dull, but definitely forceful."

"We'll see," Wexler mouthed, keeping his eyes on Ryan.

Ten minutes into the game, Syracuse had already scored three times, and Ryan was feeling the power of the team. They were bigger, faster, and had a never-ending supply of players from their bench. Twice he had a reasonable opportunity to score, but couldn't finish. The square-bodied Wexler needled him constantly, challenging him to do something. Suddenly, Ryan cut hard toward the goal. He caught the pass at full speed and swept around the crease looking for an underhand shot. Wexler cut through the crease and stayed a half step in front of him all the way, despite his large body. It was obvious why he had made All-American: he was big and extremely fast. At the last second, Ryan rolled inside. Wexler instantly shifted toward him, pushing him away from the net. Too late. Ryan scored a clean shot in the top hand corner. He raised his hands in triumph and turned to smile at the beaten defenseman.

Something like a truck smashed into him.

Ryan's head snapped back and his body flipped through the air, slamming onto the turf. An explosion of red and yellow lights danced in front of his eyes as he lay on the ground, the field spinning around him. Wexler had crosschecked him in the helmet. Ryan struggled to his feet in time to watch the player head for the penalty box. Forty seconds later during the man-up Ryan scored a second goal, this time from the back side, and the pain at the base of his neck didn't feel as bad any more.

After Ryan's third goal, a hard rip to the stick side, the Syracuse coach began screaming at his defenseman. "Someone's gonna run tomorrow," Ryan said, jabbing his finger at the player.

"Are you taunting?" the referee yelled.

"No, sir. That's against the rules."

"You keep your finger out of his face, smartass!"

"Yes, sir."

In all, Ryan scored four goals against Syracuse and had two assists, but it wasn't enough. The Big Orange scored twice in the last minute to win by one, and Ryan had to endure a slap on the back from the defenseman. "Not bad, brain," he said. "You might even be 'Cuse material."

* * *

Ryan showered for a long time after the game, tilting his head back and letting the water beat on his face. He could hear players in the locker room talking about Syracuse and what they'd do if they had another crack at them. Ryan didn't feel especially good about losing either, but more than the game was bothering him.

Much more.

He remembered the look on Le Beau's face when he talked about his friend, Officer Romano. Le Beau had been nervous. Fearful, even. He believed somebody had killed a Yale cop, murdered him so there'd be no report about how the genetics professor had died. Now Ryan was thinking about Fraser Samuels and the cleaners, and whether Krakauer might be more than just a weird professor. The whole thing was getting out of control.

When Ryan finally opened his eyes the room was filled with steam, and he felt vaguely ill at ease not being able see the tiled walls across from him. A dozen people could be hunched over there and he would never see them. A silly thought, he knew, but still .... He grabbed his towel and beelined it for the locker room.

Once inside, he stopped. The room was dark; everyone had gone. He flipped on a single row of bulbs that burst to life over his locker, causing banks of shadows to spring up at the edges of the room. He eyed the shadows, as if they had malevolent intent, laughable in another setting but eerie in the deserted room. As a child he remembered being afraid to dangle his hand, worried that something under the bed might reach up and grab it. He glanced around, his imagination galloping. The darker shadows were grinning at him, like crouching gargoyles. It was definitely time to leave. Lately, he had begun to feel uncomfortable in lonely spaces and he wished he had left earlier with the rest of the team. He toweled off, threw on his clothes, and stuffed his equipment into his bulging locker.

A blast of cold air swept into the locker room. Ryan turned his head slowly. Someone was standing in the doorway, his face a rim of shadow. Ryan dropped to a crouch, reaching into his locker and wrapping his hand around his lacrosse stick.

"Ryan?"

"Who's that?"

"Carlson. Forgot my wallet." He flipped the switches by the door, filling the room with light. "What are you ... man, what's the matter with you?"

"Nothing," Ryan said, straightening, and trying to look natural despite clutching a metal lacrosse stick like a baseball bat. "Got spooked, that's all."

Carlson opened his locker, found his wallet and left, but not before saying, "You'd better take it easy."

Ryan waited until Carlson was gone before leaving. He felt stupid and didn't want to follow him up the stairs as if he were a big brother. But minutes later when he was ascending the stairs, and he heard the lonely crunching of his sneakers in the empty stairwell, he picked up the pace, relieved to push through the lounge doors. About thirty people were still in the reception area, including Coach Waldhart and several reporters. A fire burning cheerfully in the hearth banished his lingering fears, and gave him a sense of normalcy.

He plucked a Gatorade from an ice bucket that had been set up for the players, most of whom had gone. The cold liquid felt good in his mouth, and he ran his eyes leisurely across the room.

Then stopped.

Standing by the windows was Nicole, dressed in a brown leather jacket, jeans, and L.L. Bean duck boots for the wet fields. She had her back to him, gazing out the windows. Ryan traced the strong, athletic lines of her body, the figure of a dancer. He wondered whether she might be waiting for him, but dismissed the idea. Ol' Basil was probably lurking somewhere in the vicinity.

Ryan scanned the room. No Basil. He glanced back at Nicole, curious why she had come to the players' reception area, then on impulse he crossed the room, approaching her from behind.

"What a sexist place this is," she said as he was opening his mouth to speak.

He halted in surprise.

Still looking out the windows, she continued, "That coach of yours wouldn't let me in the locker room."

"Waldhart's like that," Ryan said, recovering. "For some reason he doesn't want nymphets running around while we're dressing."

She turned to face him and said coyly, "Is that how you think of me—a nymphet?"

He smiled. "I was talking about what Waldhart thinks. My thoughts are quite different."

"I see right through you, Ryan Taylor," she said, holding his eyes and making him feel—he had to admit—uncomfortable. The old Nicole was back.

"How'd you like the games?" he asked, changing the subject.

"I saw only the last one."

"We should have clobbered those guys," Ryan mumbled, then added, "We won the first two, against Notre Dame and Harvard."

"I heard."

Ryan still wondered whether Nicole had been waiting for him, but didn't want to ask. "I'm surprised to see you," he said, trying for casual indifference. "I thought we agreed last night to go about our regular business."

"We did. But my regular business takes me to the strangest places."

He gestured around the room and said, "Where's your pal, Basil?"

"I haven't seen him for a few days."

"You didn't see him at the 'Cuse game?"

"He was there?" She seemed shocked; it was the first time he'd seen her truly taken off guard.

"Six rows behind you."

"Really." She frowned and swept her green eyes over the faces in the hall before returning to the window.

Ryan took another swig of Gatorade and followed her gaze into the empty field, where an old man was walking a miniature Dalmatian. "So you and Basil having a lovers' spat?" he asked, wishing he could enjoy the moment more than he was.

"Maybe so." Nicole had recovered her usual composure, although a certain tension remained visible in the set of her shoulders.

Ryan nodded, thinking she might continue. When she didn't, he deposited the Gatorade bottle on the table by the wall and turned to go.

"I talked to Waldhart," she said.

He hesitated.

"Are you really the best attackman Yale's ever had?"

"What?"

"That's what Waldhart said—the best he can remember at Yale."

"You're kidding." Ryan turned back toward her. "Coach said that?"

"Yes, and he said you have loads of potential."

Ryan grunted in a combination of delight and disbelief. All he ever heard from Waldhart was criticism. He glanced over in the coach's direction.

"I think you have loads of potential, too."

For a second her words didn't register. He was still thinking about Waldhart.

"Ryan?"

Her hand was warm on his arm.

"I didn't just show up. I came to see *you.*"

Ryan looked at her warily. "Oh, yeah?" he said.

She squeezed his arm. "Relax. I just wanted to tell you, after hearing Le Beau last night ... that you should be careful. That's all."

Ryan said he would, but couldn't help wondering if there was more to her visit than what she said. Nicole always seemed to have deeper motives than appeared on the surface. "I'm glad you came," he said, trying to be nice.

"I wasn't sure I was welcome, after the horrifying scene I caused at your practice." She made a funny face as she said the word "horrifying."

"Of course you're welcome," Ryan said. "Your dad might have donated the stadium."

"You never know," she said, smiling. She glanced around and said, "Actually, this is the first lacrosse game I've ever seen."

"And?"

"It's exciting."

He grinned.

"And I must say, Ryan, I agree with your coach—you really are good. I had no idea."

"Yeah?"

"I could grow fond of lacrosse."

Ryan paused. He liked what she was saying, which immediately put him on his guard.

"What?" Her brow wrinkled.

"When you're nice to me ...."

"Yes?"

"I get this picture of jagged rocks and a siren singing her lungs out."

"Oh, Ryan," she laughed.

"I'm wrong?"

"Of course you're wrong."

"Now why on earth would I have such a wrong impression?"

"Because you really don't know me," she said, her fingers teasing through her dark hair.

"I know you well enough."

"Do you?"

"I think so."

"How can you know someone if you've never spent time with them? We just see each other in passing."

"That's true," he said, trying to sound fair.

"Yes, it is," Nicole nodded decisively. "Maybe if we got to know each other better you'd feel different."

If any other girl on campus had said the same thing, Ryan would have been escorting her into his room before she could finish her sentence, but this was Nicole. He continued to eye her cautiously.

A small smile curved her lips but she said nothing.

In case she was having fun at his expense, he moved closer to show he wasn't intimidated. "Let me tell you," he said, "I cannot imagine spending quality time with you."

"I know," she said softly, suddenly nestling into him, taking him off guard. "I make you uncomfortable."

"No, you don't," he insisted, his arms hanging awkwardly. He wasn't sure what to do with his hands.

"I'm probably making you uncomfortable right now," she said into his sweater.

Ryan glanced around to see if anyone was watching. He wasn't uncomfortable, just didn't like being manipulated.

"We could be friends," Nicole breathed.

"Yeah, right."

"We could, I think."

"Hmm."

"I know I've been kind of rude."

"Continue," he said.

"The truth is I don't mean to be that way."

"Look, Nicole, you can cut the act because it's not going to work."

"That's what you think, isn't it? That I'm always playing a game." She shrugged. "You're partly right. I do play games sometimes. I wish I could just say what's in my heart, but I'm afraid of ... of making myself vulnerable, I suppose."

Her voice had a poignant quality, her breath warm against his neck. He had no idea whether she was being genuine or not, a more than frustrating situation.

"There are things about me you don't know," she continued softly. "I mean, how could you? Nobody knows."

Ryan felt her body tense, and he instinctively put his arms around her.

"I had something happen to me when I was young that ... it affected me a great deal."

Ryan immediately thought about sexual abuse. He didn't know if he was ready for this.

"When I was eleven," she said, "my brother died—he was only eight. I was supposed to be looking after him and I, well, my phone rang. I got talking and forgot about him." She swallowed a deep breath. "Bobby took his bicycle onto the road ... I just forgot about him." She blinked her eyes and turned away.

Ryan glanced down at her, still wondering whether this could be another one of her manipulation schemes; after a few moments, he decided it was probably for real, and held her more tightly.

"Every day I see him huddled there on the pavement, and the people gathered round, and I remember the tires screeching. The worst is the tires screeching."

He softly rubbed her shoulder. This was a Nicole totally foreign to him.

"My father never talked to me for a year," she said, her voice trembling. "Not once in a whole year."

Ryan could feel the pain radiating from her body, and he imagined a little girl curled up in her room, sobbing.

"You have to understand," she said, pulling away slightly to look at him, "after Bobby died my father and I were alone. My mother had left the year before. I hardly remember her. Housekeepers came and went ... well, you can imagine. So, without Bobby, my father was devastated. He had big plans for his only son, but when this happened, well, I don't think he has ever forgiven me. And I have spent my entire life trying to make up for what I did."

"You were just a kid."

She shrugged limply. "After the accident I tried to replace my brother, you know, playing baseball and soccer, even kick-boxing for a time. I was actually quite good at sports, but it didn't matter. My father never came to watch. Always busy. It's only recently I took up dance. Back then I was a real tomboy." She smiled wanly. "I scared all the boys, I think."

"I can't imagine," Ryan said.

"I became a goal-oriented little soldier," she said, "determined never to fail my father again. Every night I dutifully marked out the next day's objectives and, come snow or freezing rain, I achieved them. Second place, as my father often says, is the dustbin of history." She shrugged. "That's why I act the way I do, sometimes."

"You didn't need to explain," Ryan said.

"I wanted to."

He nodded and kissed her lightly on the cheek, not a romantic kiss, but an intimate gesture of one who shares another's pain. "I am truly sorry," he said. He tasted the salt from her tears on his lips and pretended not to notice.

She laughed self-consciously. "Yes, Nicole Van Buren is crying. Isn't that a lark?" She rubbed away the tears forcefully with her fist. "So you see," she said, "now you know all about Ms. Van Buren and her pain-ridden little life."

He gathered her close to himself and for a tall girl, she seemed very small in his arms. The two stood quietly holding each other as if they were alone in the room.

She broke first, gently unhooking her arms from around his waist. "In short," she said, striving to sound matter-of-fact, "I sometimes stampede over people, but it's all a front. A defense mechanism, I suppose. So I really am sorry if I have made your life miserable."

"I've never noticed—"

"Hah!" she said. "You run when you see me."

"I don't run," he said. "I just walk quickly." He was trying to cheer her.

"You really don't hate me?"

"Of course not."

"I know I can be assertive."

"Is that what you call it?"

She laughed, and her eyes were dancing again. "Your problem," she said, "is that those Yorktown girls probably swooned at your every breath. "Oh, Ryan," she mimicked, putting her hand to her forehead. "You are so clever! Oh, Ryan, you are so brave on that lacrosse field!"

"I am amazed!" he said. "That's exactly what happened."

"And now you have to deal with me. How overwhelming!"

"It's difficult, but I am adapting."

She moved toward him again, and her lips grazed his ear as she whispered her next words: "I'm hard to take at times, I know. But in my heart I feel differently, I really do. I just wanted you to know that."

She wore the nicest perfume, he thought, and—

"Taylor!"

Ryan pulled away. It was Waldhart.

"Good stuff today," he said.

"Thanks, Coach."

Waldhart's eyes surveyed Nicole but he passed by without saying anything more.

"He likes to intimidate," Nicole said after the coach had left.

"He's not the only one," Ryan said lightly.

"You're not talking about little ol' me?" she drawled, playing the southern belle. "I never thought you would admit to being intimidated."

"I admit nothing."

Her face abruptly went back to its seriousness. "Thank you for listening," she said.

He nodded.

"Sometimes it's good, y'know, just to talk." She seemed to want to say more so Ryan waited. "Maybe," she said, "well, I was thinking maybe we should see each other a little more regularly."

The words floated around him, but he didn't know how to respond.

"Just a thought," she said. "We certainly don't need to rush anything."

"What about your pal, Basil?"

"A friend, I told you that."

"A friend?"

"Yes, a friend."

Ryan stared at her.

She stared back.

He felt strangely warmed as he gazed into her eyes, and he almost reached for her, wanting to feel her close again. But inside he knew that none of this was real. It couldn't be: not with Nicole. And even if it were, he was not ready to deal with it. He took a breath and folded his arms.

"Your body language tells me you have an announcement," she said.

"Nicole, look, I—"

"You're rejecting me."

"No ...."

"I throw myself at you and this is what I get?"

Ryan smiled. "Maybe you're out of my league," he said.

"Of course I'm out of your league," she said, poking him, "but that doesn't mean you have to reject me." She took his arm and started toward the door. "It's not so bad," she said. "At least we can be friends—you, me, and Basil."

22

Midas, Nevada:

"Ron, I've got the mail bags in the Chev."

"Yeah, so?"

"We need this job, Ron. You said you'd help sort."

"I just got to the Gold Circle, Laura. Can I at least finish my beer?"

"Ron, please."

"Okay, okay. All you do is bitch!"

"I'm not bitching. The bag's heavy. Could you help?"

"Unbelievable! I can't have a minute to myself …out of the way, I'll get your precious bag."

"Thank you."

"Hold the door open, I'll be back in a sec …. Okay, got it … I'll dump it on the table ... see, takes no time to sort. Now maybe you could get off my back."

"I just want Lisa to have a better life than us, maybe go to college—"

"You live in a dream world."

"If we could save a little every month—"

"Heard it all before. Pull the junk mail—we'll toss it."

"We can't do that."

"It's just junk."

"Not to the companies who paid for the ads, Ron!"

"Got a box here. Weird looking."

"What is it?"

"Dunno."

"It's addressed to the town hall."

"Town hall? What a joke. Must mean the Gold Circle."

"Ron, don't open—"

"Relax, it's just a cigar box—with no bloody cigars."

"What's that?"

"A plastic bag ... twenty bucks! Two of them, I think."

"You'd better leave it."

"Like hell, I will. Easy money. Hey! Another Bud here."

* * *

Biggar, Saskatchewan, Canada:
> "Hi, Bob. Come for your mail?"
> Well, I'm not here to admire you, Connie."
> "Nice."
> "Any response to my flyers?"
> "A big response. I put them over here ... yup, you have a hundred or so tear-offs."
> "I knew it! Give me them."
> "You won't like what they say."
> "Just never mind—"
> "Most of them want to keep the signs."
> "This is town business, Connie. You are not supposed to be reading ... oh, forget it, what else do you have?"
> "A box for the town council, from Philadelphia."
> "The States?"
> "No, Russia."
> "Why would someone from ... what is this, a cigar box?"
> "And not declared."
> "A plastic bag or something. Wait. A twenty dollar bill, US."
> "Hey! That's not yours."
> "I know what to do with unsolicited money, Connie; I don't need some postal clerk to instruct me. If anyone asks, I will be at Town Hall."

* * *

Carefree Dream Liner west of Puerto Rico:
> "Ah, man, Kyle, I feel sick."
> "Yeah, I'm seeing this bright halo."
> "I'm gonna throw up."
> "My eyes ache."
> "I must have eaten something—"
> "I can't swallow, Zwag, my mouth's so dry."
> "Gonna find the Doc."
> "Wait for me."
> "There's Jimmy."
> "Jimmy! Come here. Help me."
> "Ah, I'm throwing my guts up. Man ... sorry Jimmy."
> "Get the Doc, Jimmy. Hurry!"
> "It's blood ... oh, man, holy shit, look at this."
> "Call the Doc!"
> "Jimmy, clean your shirt later. Go!"
> "Legs won't hold."
> "My stomach ... can't take it ... the pain."

"Man, what's happening to me?"

"I crapped my pants, Kyle ... crapped my pants."

"I'm burning up."

"Oh, God ... help me."

"Head's pounding ... my tongue ...."

"Help me."

"Can't breathe."

"Please, God ...."

* * *

On the shuttle back to campus, Ryan listened to Nicole prattle on about Krakauer and his oddities. He wished she'd stop, because for a few hours that morning he had managed to forget about Krakauer's lab. The games had brought release, and even his unexpected encounter with Nicole had busied his mind with pleasant thoughts; he felt normal again. Now everything came rushing back like a recurring nightmare.

"He definitely has notes somewhere," Nicole said. "No one can conduct experiments without notes, not even Krakauer."

Ryan sighed. "What does it matter?"

"What does it ... are you serious? It matters a great deal. With notes, we can see what Krakauer is doing." Her face had an intensity that surprised him. "He must have them hidden in his computer."

Ryan laughed.

"What?"

"I seriously doubt it. Nobody hides secret notes in a computer—not if they want them to stay secret."

"Why not?"

"'Cause you can't hide them. Not from someone who knows how to look. Even if they're encrypted, if somebody has physical access to your computer he can break in. Maybe not like in the movies where he taps a few strokes and unlocks the files, but believe me, if those government types want what's on his computer, they'll get it." He snorted. "That's why Krakauer's notes aren't on his lab computer. He's too smart."

"Smart people often do foolish things."

"That's true," he said, shrugging. "I could check, I suppose, next time I go to the lab, but there's no way the notes will be there."

"If you could check, that'd be great."

Ryan said nothing, but he felt trapped and didn't like it. Then, almost under his breath, he repeated, "There's no secret notes in his computer."

Nicole lifted a hand to acknowledge his point. "You're probably right," she said, "but he has to have notes somewhere. He needs *written* notes, end of story."

"For sure?"

"Yes," she said, exasperated. "That's what I've been saying. No one can conduct series after series of experiments like his for years without keeping some type of lab notebook."

The bus lurched to a halt at Old Campus disgorging a half-dozen students, along with Ryan and Nicole, on the broad sidewalk. They headed toward Nicole's college, which was more or less in the direction of Sterling Library. Ryan had yet to complete his duties for the day and he needed to get back to the lab. A mist had begun drifting through the air and Nicole pulled up her hood, still muttering about Krakauer's notes.

Ryan's eyes roamed sightlessly across the castle-like walls of Old Campus; he too was thinking about Krakauer's notes. "I might know where they are," he said at last.

"Where?" She looked excited.

"I said I might."

"Where do you think?"

"He makes written notes during the day—I told you that before—and then he tucks them in his pocket so he probably takes them back to his apartment."

Nicole's excited demeanor changed. "I can tell you right now he doesn't keep them in his apartment."

"How would you know?" Ryan asked, irritated that his suggestion met with such contempt.

"Because," she said, "if Krakauer kept them in his apartment, those men wouldn't have been scrubbing around the lab looking for them."

"Maybe they tried the lab first."

"Breaking into a university lab before some old apartment?" She scrunched her face at the suggestion. "Anyway, he needs those notes *in the lab* while he's working. So if they're not in his computer, and he doesn't check a lab book during the day, then where are they? They've got to be somewhere." She squeezed his arm and said, "Think, Ryan, you must have seen something."

"I don't know," Ryan said, defeated. "I suppose he could be storing them on a remote server somewhere but—"

"But what?"

"I told you, he's a paranoid nutball. I cannot imagine him leaving his precious notes out there in the cloud where government types could find them."

"Okay, so where would they be? On a USB or something?"

"Maybe," Ryan said, "but all I've ever seen is his little scratch pad where he notes things during the day, and then the next day he starts over with a new scratch pad. But there are no bundles of notes, no flash drives, no nothing."

"Then what does he use his computer for?" she asked.

Ryan shrugged and said, "The regular stuff, I guess," but he felt like saying he didn't give a shit.

"Think," she repeated, the strain evident in her voice. "What have you seen him do?"

"On-line gambling," he quipped. "Krakauer's a big on-line gambler." He was tired of the questions.

"Come on, be serious!"

Ryan cut through a tour group crowding the sidewalk. He pushed one of them out of the way and felt good about it. "I'm sick of all this crap," he said, glaring back at the guy on the sidewalk. Then turning to Nicole, he said, "And don't tell me to be serious in that parental tone of yours. I'll be serious when I want to be serious. And right now I don't want to be serious, if that's okay with you." His voice dripped with sarcasm.

Nicole had a pensive look, as if she were assessing the situation.

"Do you get the picture?" Ryan asked with exaggerated patience in his voice. "I am sick of Krakauer, of the lab, and I am really sick of your questions. I'm just tired of everything."

Ryan saw Nicole's face change. Her eyes softened and a slight smile touched her lips when she said, "I can be pushy, can't I?"

Ryan didn't respond. He knew it was manipulation.

"Ohhhh, don't be mad at me again," she said, puckering her lips into a pout. Then, grabbing his hand, she said, "Okay, you've a right to be angry. I don't mean to be so, well, so overbearing. I just want to figure this out—don't you?"

"I'm not angry," Ryan said, withdrawing his hand.

Nicole lifted her eyebrows.

"Well, maybe just a little," he said, realizing how ridiculous it was to say he wasn't angry. He looked at her. "I want all this stuff to go away, to have a normal life again."

"I know," she said. "I feel the same."

"I came here for a good education and to play lacrosse, but now—"

"Now all these strange things are happening."

"Yeah." He watched absent-mindedly as a groundskeeper clipped vines overgrowing the walls of Old Campus. He wished he could do nothing but prune vines for a month.

"So Krakauer sits at the computer and listens to, what, classical music, you said?"

"Yeah, an old Mozart CD. Then he reviews his written notes."

"And then?"

"And that's it. He putters around for a while."

"He does nothing else?"

"With his notes?"

She nodded.

"No, nothing." Ryan rubbed his eyes.

She waited.

"Maybe he memorizes them, I don't know. Everyone says Krakauer's a genius." He added the last phrase trying to make his suggestion sound more reasonable.

"No," she said in a low tone, "if he could memorize everything like some sort of Savant, he wouldn't be taking notes in the first place." And then, as if thinking aloud, "He must be doing something with those notes. So-what-does-he-do?"

Ryan shook his head.

"Think," she said again. "What would you do if—"

"Wait!" He jerked around. "Krakauer listens to the same Mozart CD every night. The same one!"

"So?"

"And he reads over his notes as he listens," Ryan said, half smiling.

"What are you saying? That Krakauer transfers his notes to a hidden disc?"

"No, much better."

"Yes?"

"It's kind of sneaky. I can't say for certain."

"Go on."

"He plays this Mozart CD all the time, keeps it right out in the open with his other music CDs, as if it has no importance. I mean, who would know any different?"

"What are you talking about?"

Ryan turned to face her. "He has to have notes, right? That's what you said. Has to. And if his notes aren't in his computer ...." Ryan started to laugh. "Yeah, that's it." He continued walking.

"What?"

"Mozart might be more than a simple music CD. It could be a live DVD made to act like an audio CD. If you put the CD in the computer, it will play Mozart like any regular CD. But in the subchannel data, or some service area outside the file table ...." He began nodding. "All the hidden files are accessible even while the CD continues to play Mozart."

"Is that possible?"

"Sure. It would take some programming, but it's certainly possible. A CD with Mozart on the surface so to speak, and encrypted files underneath."

"How would he ...."

"He'd write his own driver so he could access a ... shadow volume."

"But without the password—"

Without the password it's hard to know what you'd find. Some tiny boot loader, maybe. Done correctly, it would probably just look like

Mozart and random bits."

"There's no way to see the hidden files without the password?"

"Look, I'm just sprouting an idea—it might be nothing. But if he actually took the time to do something like this, and if those government guys didn't notice anything, it's a good bet he was sophisticated about it. Outside the physical tracks of a CD, there are other zones you could write to." Ryan stopped walking. "The bottom line is that you don't need serious processing power to crack this thing. There's a much easier side door."

Her eyes lit with interest.

He looked at her and smiled. "I have physical access to his computer so I can just implant a keylogger to trap his keystrokes. It doesn't matter where he stores the data. If he stores them on his computer or on the Internet, I'll know. If he uses the Mozart disc and types a password, I'll have it."

She looked doubtful. "Are you sure it will work?"

"Of course. I might not know biology, but I've been programming since I was seven. This is code that's out there—some of it I've written myself—anyway, it's well tested and isn't picked up by any commercial anti-spy or virus software I've ever come across. I just need a few minutes to load the exploit." He glanced at her. She was impressed, no doubt about it, and he couldn't resist bragging a bit more. "There are a bunch of custom firmwares out there these days. It doesn't matter even if it's a live CD—I flash it at the hardware level and hook in. That's how I got into the Student Employment files," he said. "It loads before the OS. Even had Edwards's computer email me the password. Went right through Yale's firewall." He chuckled softly.

"Can't something like that be traced, if it's sent to your computer?"

Ryan shook his head. "Nothing comes directly to my computer. I have it tunneled to a throw-away that onion-routes the data through servers in Malaysia, India, and a half-dozen other places. It end-to-end encrypts it, then dumps it somewhere new every time. I know where it will land, and it never goes the same way twice. Then I go and pick it up. Once I touch the pick-up server, I never go back. So by the time it gets to me, there are no records to trace."

"Really?" She looked amazed.

"Really," he said, enjoying the moment.

Nicole's eyes began to glow. "Let's put your program in Krakauer's computer," she said.

Ryan blanched.

"This is great."

He nodded, but all he could think about was the actual danger he might be getting them into. If he was right that Krakauer was using the Mozart CD as a repository for his data, then almost certainly Nicole would want him to examine it, and who knew where that would lead? He wiped the mist off his face, feeling cornered.

She sensed his hesitation and asked bluntly, "What's the problem?"

"I need to think," he said, walking onward.

She followed. "Your wonderful program won't work," she said.

"It'll work fine," Ryan replied, giving her a withering look. She could really irritate him sometimes. "The password's not the problem."

"Then what is the problem?"

"I don't think you're taking this seriously."

"Sure I am."

"No, you're not. People have been killed, and you act as if this were an exciting new adventure. Now, you're asking me to commit a felony, okay?"

"It sounds like you've already done that a few times at Yale."

He looked at her closely. *Was that a threat?*

She blinked several times. "You're right," she said, her eyes growing earnest. "I probably should apologize. I have been entirely too cavalier. It's just hard to believe something sinister is going on. At the end of the day, I'm sure we'll laugh together at the weird coincidences that brought us to this point. But, you're right, and I'm sorry."

"I wasn't fishing for an apology."

"I know. But you deserve it. There is something unusual here. You said yourself how serious it is ...." She paused and gazed at him with imploring eyes. "Don't you think you should use your skills for good? All I'm asking, Ryan, is for us to get that password and see what Krakauer has been doing. If there are any concerns, we can let Le Beau deal with them. Okay?"

Ryan nodded, and scolded himself for getting into this mess.

23

Nicole had just bid Ryan goodbye when she saw a familiar figure scurry behind a Ryder truck across the street.

It was Basil.

A surge of anger swept through her. *He was following her.* She strode out into the road, keeping one eye on the traffic, and the other on the truck. *Spying on her!* She couldn't believe it. The old song by the Police floated through her mind, "Every move you make, every step you take, I'll be watching you." Well, this "watching" garbage was about to stop.

Once across the street she rounded the truck, eager to confront Basil. He wasn't there. She circled the vehicle. No Basil. She glanced up and down the road, scanned the clusters of students on the sidewalk, but he was gone.

Nicole scowled, running her eyes over the truck again. He hadn't climbed into the cargo area, because the door was latched from the outside. Not in the cab either because she had stood on her tiptoes to peer in. She even bent down to check under the truck, but still no Basil. She frowned. Then, on a whim, she pulled open the cab door. And there was Basil, stretched across the seat, his head under the steering wheel, hiding.

"What are you doing?" Her voice seethed with indignation.

Basil twisted his head toward her, his eyes uneasy as they roamed her face.

"You're spying on me!" she spat at him.

"Of course I'm not," Basil said, sitting up and straightening his leather jacket.

"Then why were you hiding inside the cab?"

"I ... I wasn't hiding," he said, stepping out onto the street. "I was just ...." He motioned toward the cars moving along the road and said, "This could be dangerous—"

"Basil, don't change the subject!" She was angry, and wanted him to know it. "Tell me why you were hiding inside this truck."

He smoothed his hair. "I wasn't hiding," he repeated. "I thought it would be better if you didn't see me when you were talking to Ryan. And you know what, Nicole? You could have been more forthright with me about this whole situation. If there's something between you and Ryan, at least you could have been honest about it." He was obviously trying to control the conversation.

Nicole took a breath. "This is unacceptable," she said. "You've been sneaking around—"

"I have not!" He moved toward the sidewalk, as if he were greatly concerned about being in the roadway. "You know, this is why I didn't want you to see me," he said in an accusing tone. "Right away you assume I was following you when I was not. I was heading for lunch, if you must know, when I saw you and Ryan talking. You started across the street, so I got into the truck to prevent you from thinking exactly what you are now accusing me of doing." He wagged his head to underscore his bewilderment that she could so wrongly accuse him.

"Were you at the lacrosse game this morning?" She wasn't going to let him squirm away.

Basil squinted his eyes tensely as if he were thinking of a reply.

"You were there, weren't you?"

"I was coming to see you," he said, finally.

"How did you know I was there, unless you followed me to the fields?"

"I just wanted to talk to you."

"I don't believe this," Nicole said, giving him a look of incredulity.

"There's nothing wrong with wanting to talk. You yourself said you wanted to talk."

"What were you doing, waiting outside my room? Watching, so you could follow me? You were, weren't you? Watching, like some stalker!"

"No, no, you have it all wrong."

"I want you to stop this nonsense," she said.

"Fine!" he said bitterly. "I won't ever bother you again. Does that make you happy?"

Nicole leveled her eyes and said, "I mean it, Basil. I don't like people spying on me."

He swallowed.

"Never again," she said.

"I ... I'm sorry," he said, not meeting her eyes. "I just wanted to see you. It was stupid. Okay? Let's put these last weeks behind us." He glanced up at her, his face radiating contrition. "Look, we used to have fun together. Maybe we could go to the Cayman Islands for the weekend or something. What do you say?"

"I don't think so, Basil."

"Just a day or two. Please. You loved the Caymans. We could snorkel—"

Nicole shook her head. "I think we should put things on hold for a while."

"I'm only asking for a weekend," he pleaded.

"We both know we need some time off."

"That's just a polite way of saying—"

"I know, Basil," she said quietly. "Let's not ruin the memories we have of each other."

"So this is it?"

"I'm sorry," she said flatly.

His lips grew thin. "I know what this is about. I know exactly what this is about."

"Basil—"

"It's this puerile idiot, isn't it?"

"Nothing to do with him."

"It seems funny that we were fine until he showed up. Now you're always busy."

"I don't want to pursue this conversation any longer," Nicole pronounced in a formal, distant voice.

Basil's face darkened. "Well, maybe I do."

"Then enjoy talking to yourself," she said as she turned to leave.

He grabbed her arm.

Nicole jerked back but he held firm, then squeezed tighter, hurting her.

"Stop it!" she yelled, but his fingers had clamped onto her arm like a vice. She swung around with her free arm and drove the heel of her palm into his face. His head popped back and she yanked her arm away. "Don't you ever do that again!" she shouted.

"He's low-class," Basil hissed, holding a hand to his cheek. "A Neanderthal, for heaven's sake." His eyes blazed as he stared at her, his body hunched predatorily.

Nicole started walking.

"He'll be pushing a broom at Yankee Stadium after he gets booted out of here. You know I'm right!"

As she cut through the cars she could hear Basil calling after her, "You're going to be sorry. You hear me? *Really sorry.*"

* * *

A sense of foreboding descended on Ryan as he punched the button on his computer and opened up his code library. Murphy's Law—anything that can go wrong usually does—wasn't born of idle minds; it came from hard experience. They were tinkering with a bomb, no matter what Nicole said.

The servers were up, the components compiled. He'd double-and triple-checked everything—loaded the flash key containing his keylogger program, a bunch of firmware, and included some general exploits just in case. But the feelings persisted.

It wasn't long before he was heading for Sterling Library and the basement lab, unease dogging his every step. He entered the lab cautiously, as if he expected Krakauer to be waiting for him, arms crossed, demanding to know what he was doing. But the professor was busy inside the main airlock chamber, and Ryan had no problem loading his software, and instructing the computer to send every keystroke Krakauer typed to a bot that would send it on where Ryan could pick it up. He then cleaned the memory, the logs, expunging every last bit of evidence. When the professor finally emerged, Ryan made a great show of washing and tidying the back labs. He left soon after, feeling better. Everything had gone smoothly. Apparently, Murphy wasn't always right.

Later that afternoon, Nicole showed up at his dorm bearing two coffees and four bagels. "So, this is where you live," she said, sweeping her eyes around his room. "Okay … not bad. I expected piles of rubbish."

"Of course you did," Ryan said. "You have a critical nature." He didn't mention the half-hour he had spent straightening up his room in anticipation of her visit.

She glanced at the computer. "Anything?" she asked.

"Nothing yet. Security over speed. It can take a while, sometimes."

They spent the next hour devouring the bagels and coffee, and debating whether Krakauer recorded his research at the end of every day.

Suddenly, a window opened on the screen.

Nicole moved closer for a better view. She was crouched over his shoulder now, her hips pushing into him, her fingers resting on the back of his neck. Ryan might have enjoyed the closeness, but he said nothing, just concentrated on the screen. He sensed she was in her manipulating mode.

"What's all this stuff—did it work?"

Ryan stared at the screen.

"What is that?" she asked. "The password?"

"Yes," Ryan said. "Brownstone9."

"Really? The password?"

"Yeah."

Nicole grabbed him and kissed him on the lips. "You are a genius," she said, her eyes gleaming.

"There might be another password," Ryan said, returning his eyes to the screen. Nicole's kiss seemed genuinely spontaneous and it took him by surprise. He never quite knew what she was thinking, but at least he was no longer just a jock stumbling around the biology lab. Today he had become a computer genius. The thought satisfied him.

He waited as several other passwords arrived. "Layers of passphrases," he mumbled.

"Krakauer is careful."

"He certainly is. This is a bit excessive." Ryan expelled a breath.

"Is something wrong?"

"Don't know." He stared at the computer. *Something was definitely wrong.* He watched with growing concern as dump files started filling the directory. Krakauer must have been browsing the Internet for something. Text was arriving from everywhere. "No, no," he said. "It shouldn't be doing this."

"What's happening?"

"Aw, jeez, it's looping through everything. It's only supposed to send text!" He had a sinking feeling in his stomach. If it did that ... he stared in horror. It couldn't have been worse. *User over quota.*

"What does that mean?"

Ryan couldn't take his eyes off the computer screen, frozen with panic.

Nicole had a studied calm in her voice when she asked, "Did we get the passwords?"

Ryan nodded. "But it seems like ...." He jumped up from his chair. "I gotta go," he said.

"What's the matter?"

For some reason his mouth wouldn't move. Only his mind worked, and it told him, *Anything that can go wrong, will go wrong.* He had made a crucial mistake and now he would pay for it.

"Ryan?"

He tore his eyes from the computer. "That first hop server account is full," he moaned, "and these files of Krakauer's, they shouldn't be coming through. They're coming in faster than they're going out to the next hop. And they're filling up that account as well."

"So?"

"So some sysadmin in Taipei, where this server is, is going to notice that. He's going to wonder where all this data is coming from, and realize I backdoored his system. Then he's likely to reach out to the host sysadmin at Yale and let them know they've been hacked, too." He mopped at his hair. "Oh, man, I should have guessed this might happen."

"Will they find you?"

Ryan groaned. "No. They can't find me, but the first thing the Yale ITS will do is email Krakauer and tell him that all this is coming from his IP and that his system has been compromised. I'm cooked! No doubt about it." He looked at Nicole. "Maybe dead for all I know, like your friend, Fraser."

"Talk to me," Nicole said, shoving her face toward his. "What happened?"

"It's like a flood in the basement, okay? I can delete the logs, but that's like bailing out what's there. Unless we turn off the water rushing in from Krakauer's computer, I can't clean this up—it will get found. And if Krakauer hears that somebody's been tampering with his data, it won't take him long to guess who that somebody is." He looked at his watch. "I've got to get over there and shut this off before it gets any worse."

Nicole sat down and said, "He records his information at the end of the day and then turns off his computer. Right? So you can't very well restart it while he's there."

Ryan felt sick. She was right.

"I don't see the problem," she said. "You have a key card. So we wait until he leaves, go into his computer, and stop it."

Ryan shook his head. "I can't get into the lab or the Central Power Plant at night. After eight my card doesn't work, and Krakauer always stays late." He glanced around his room in despair.

She rose with a determined look in her eyes. "Then we have no choice. We've got to chance it right now. You said he often does last-minute things in the airlock chambers—"

Ryan smacked his palm against his forehead. "The steam tunnels!" he said. "I could use the steam tunnels tonight."

"To get into the lab?"

Ryan's mind was racing. He had already unlatched the escape hatch that led to the lab. All he had to do was get into the tunnel system somehow. "You've seen the culverts around campus? They all lead to the steam tunnels," he said, as if his words explained everything. He felt his spirits lifting. This could work.

"I know about the steam tunnels," she said. "They run under the campus, like a giant maze."

"Exactly."

"If it's a maze of tunnels down there, how do you expect to find your way?"

"I've been down there before," he said.

"What about the padlocks on the grates? Do you have a key?"

"I'll need a hacksaw," he said, wondering where he could lay his hands on one. "Most of the guys who run the tunnels take several trips to saw through the chains, a bit at a time, you know, 'cause it's hard sawing. But I think I could do it in a half hour or so if I had a few blades. You'll have to watch out for me, though. Yale cops are everywhere at night."

"That's how you guys get into the tunnels? Hacksaw through the chains?"

Ryan half smiled. "I did it during my first year, kind of a thrill, you know."

"Kind of stupid."

Ryan flushed, recognizing her superior face instantly. He swallowed his pride and said, "I know Yale expels students who're caught in the tunnels. But as I said, it was my first year."

She snorted. "I'm talking about sawing off the chains. Whoever thought of that one, well, it's dumb, for sure."

"That's the only way in."

"It takes half an hour to saw through the chain?"

He didn't say anything.

"Do you have a hammer?"

"Sure, but you can't use a hammer to—"

"Follow me," she said as she started toward the door. "Bring your hammer and that thermos off the shelf. I have a surprise for you."

Ryan hiked behind Nicole until they arrived at the basement entrance to the library. She pulled the hammer from his hand and explained what she wanted him to do with the thermos. Ryan had serious doubts about her idea, but decided to try it anyway. He opened the door with his card and headed toward the lab.

Once inside Ryan was surprised to find Krakauer watching his television, the tiny set that the professor never turned on. Ryan tried to greet him, ready with a story about how he had forgotten class notes, but Krakauer hardly nodded, so intent was he with watching the news. Ryan made a quick detour into Krakauer's private lab, his eyes darting to the computer. But the professor had turned it off, fortunately, and Ryan resisted the temptation to restart the machine and unload the program. The gamble wasn't worth it. Krakauer could return at any moment, and then what would he say?

In the back rooms Ryan banged cupboards and thumped cages as he "searched" for his notes. Then he stopped beside a bottle of liquid nitrogen and removed the Styrofoam top. He took the ladle as Nicole had instructed, and slowly filled his thermos. With the thermos nearly full, he strolled past Krakauer—trying hard to look casual. As it turned out, it didn't matter. Krakauer never even looked up when Ryan said goodbye.

Outside the lab Ryan moved carefully through the basement halls passing the thermos between his hands as it got progressively colder. Nicole was waiting for him at the exit. She took the thermos and walked around the library, glancing both ways to make certain no one was watching. Satisfied, she sauntered over to the grate and sat down. "Now, watch this," she said as she poured the liquid nitrogen steadily over one entire link. Then, taking the hammer, she stood up and struck the link crisply. It crumbled as if it were porcelain. "Better than sawing?" she asked.

Ryan stared in disbelief.

"The nitrogen makes it brittle," she explained as she pushed the broken end of the chain into the grate.

"Amazing."

"The wonders of science," she said, widening her eyes in mock bewilderment. "Now instead of sawing, we can be eating dinner."

* * *

"Basil, how are you?"

"Fine, Dad."

"Anything wrong?"

"No ...."

"No? Sounds like you're hesitating."

"Well, I might have a slight problem, nothing urgent."

"What is it? You need money?"

"I couldn't spend all the money you give me, Dad."

"You're sure? I could add more to your account if you need it."

"Thanks, Dad, but I'm good."

"Well, if you need something special, just put it on the card."

"Okay, thanks."

"How're your studies? You're keeping your grades up, correct?"

"Grades are fine, Dad."

"Good, good. Remember you're the fourth generation Meryash to attend Yale."

"I remember."

"And Skull and Bones? You'll be tapped, correct?"

"I think that's going well."

"You think? You don't know?"

"It's ... it's going well, Dad."

"Make sure it is. We don't want any mistakes here. Skull and Bones will be central to your success. You understand that, I hope?"

"I do. It's going well. Don't worry."

"That's great, Son. Anything else? 'Cause I'm kind of buried here."

"No, I just wanted to say, 'Hello,' and, ah, you know, maybe ask your advice about something."

"My advice? Ask away."

"It's not that important, really."

"If it's important to you, it's important to me. Tell me the problem. But give me the short version. I'm in a bit of a squeeze for time."

"It's about a girl I've been dating."

"Pregnant?"

"No."

"Venereal disease? What?"

"No, nothing like that."

"Good. Got to watch that stuff now days. Always use protection. Things aren't like when I was your age. Serious consequences for the foolish. You understand that, don't you?"

"I do, Dad."

"Then what's the problem?"

"It's hard to explain."

"Just spit it out. Is she after money? I've warned you about that. Correct? Some of these women will do anything—trick you into getting them pregnant, blackmail, lawsuits, all kinds of things. You know that, correct?"

"I know, Dad, and I'm careful."

"So what's the problem with this girl?"

"Well, I'm just worried that, ah, you know ... I like this girl a lot and I think I'm losing her."

Laughter. "Doesn't sound like much of a problem. Any girl with half a brain would want someone like you."

"There's no doubt about that, but it hasn't been going well."

"I see. So you want to know what to do. Correct?"

"I'm not sure I've handled things in the best way."

"You've come to the right place, Son, because if there's anything your dad is good at, it's solving problems. Of course, I don't know the details, but I can tell you the bottom line, and it applies to every problem. *Every problem.* You understand?"

"I do."

"You want to hear the answer?"

"I'd like to."

"Before I tell you, remember, the simple answer is always the best answer."

"Okay."

"Apply this principle to any problem, and you'll solve it. So don't be put off by its simplicity."

"I'm listening."

"You do what it takes, Son. Whatever the problem. You do-what-it-takes to solve it. That's the secret."

24 ~~~~~~~~~~~~~~~~~~~~~~~~~~~~~~~~

The general watched them carefully, seventy soldiers spreading out across the grounds of the mock White House. Displayed prominently on the hoods of their pressure suits, on their backs, and on their upper arms, were brilliant red squares inset with black biohazard trefoils on white triangles. They moved with the practiced efficiency of professionals trained to deal with every eventuality. Behind them came four-man teams with FN P90s and M320 grenade launchers, the latter fitted to launch both non-lethal CS gas and deadly fragmentation grenades. Scattered among them were the liaison officers, whose instructions were to initiate contact with the easily spooked Secret Service and then determine how to avoid conflict. Friendly fire was the general's biggest fear, and he was determined to secure the White House without a shot.

"Everything's on track to achieve our mission," Donovan said, anticipating the general's apprehensions. He spoke quietly, never once taking his eyes off the coordinated movements of soldiers below the catwalk.

"I'm still concerned about transporting our people to the White House without raising suspicion."

"It is a concern. But both groups have standard vehicles common in the area. Group A will arrive first in special ambulance vans and EMS vehicles, no visible weapons."

"You mean the biohazard personnel."

"Yes sir, as well as the liaison officers."

"And the four-man teams in Group B?"

"More of a problem, but we have excellent staging areas."

The general knew that Donovan was a man who never bragged or exaggerated; he read missions with a cold eye. If it could be done, he'd do it—and with Donovan in charge, it usually could be done. The general scanned the crudely painted West Wing of the White House, the entrances to the building, the artificial trees and surrounding fence. "Scenarios?" he asked.

"Maxed at sixteen," Donovan said. "Four basic with twelve variations."

"Good. Keep it simple. The men have to respond quickly." He paused. "Composure," he said, looking at Donovan, "I can't stress it enough. We're all friends here."

Donovan nodded.

"And the Park Police?"

"Bit players."

"Still," the general said, raising an eyebrow, "they have jurisdiction over the sidewalks outside the White House."

"True, but with biohazard suits standing in front of them, they'll take their lead from the Secret Service."

The general scratched his face, thinking. "Okay, reasonable."

"As I see it," Donovan said, "everything hangs on you getting through to Mosley." He was talking about Glen Mosley, Director of the Secret Service.

The general nodded, well aware of his need to bring the Director on board. "Iverson might be more crucial to our operations," he said. "But be assured, the moment you approach the Southwest Gate, I will personally call Mosley at the White House. He knows me, but he goes by the book. He will definitely order us away, so the best we can hope for is that he'll hesitate before opening fire on defenseless EMS responders. Prator could be more important for us. She'll be calling Iverson, so I'm hoping with Mosley and Iverson in the mix, we'll gain you some precious seconds as you approach, and eventually get you in."

"Yes sir."

"Remember our role—a dedicated hazmat team trying to protect the President and others in harm's way." He paused. "And that includes the Secret Service. They have their job to do and we have ours. Even if they aren't expecting us, there's no reason we can't work together."

"Agreed."

"Your men need to understand that a hundred surveillance cameras point in every direction around the White House, and scores of sensors monitor sound and movement. The Service will be fully aware something major is happening."

"Both inside and out."

"Right," the general said. "Already the Service will fear that some kind of chemical or biological contaminant has been loosed inside the White House, and outside, of course, they will see us coming. Keep our liaison officers positive. Prator and I will be on the phone to Iverson and Mosley, but there'll come a moment of hesitation, and when it comes, the liaison boys will have to talk fast, and confidently. We're just firefighters from the DOT Hazmat Training Conference at Coral Hills, responding to a distress call from a special agent in the presidential protection division. The liaison officers need to avoid the question of how we responded so rapidly to an emergency call, and focus on the biological disaster inside the White House."

Donovan nodded.

"The officers have less than a minute to convince the Service of their inability to handle the situation. Less than a minute. Otherwise, we'll have squads of antiterrorism soldiers crawling all over us."

"Understood."

"The Service is well-trained to handle biological contingencies," the general said, eyes narrowing, "but they will recognize immediately that a threshold has been passed, that a potential disaster awaits them. They will have to rely on us—whether they want to or not."

Donovan grunted his agreement.

"Most important," and the general leaned forward to make his point, "everyone has to be dead calm in this business. Dead calm, you understand?"

"Yes sir."

"One mistake and all hell will break loose. We don't need that."

Donovan squared his shoulders. "If it comes to that, we have the firepower in Group B to contain—"

"Negative," the general said sharply. "The liaison officers must control the situation."

"Agreed," Donovan said, but his face registered a trace of anger.

The general eyed his chief officer, who had now transformed into something completely unreadable. Donovan didn't like correction, didn't like making mistakes, and especially didn't like others knowing what he thought. A good soldier, and indispensable at present, but his kind needed watching. The general decided to state the obvious. "Colonel, we don't want a firefight with the boys at the White House, or with the responders—it's just one more thing to explain. Your liaison officers are the key. How they handle things will determine the number of body bags at the end of the day. I want this clean and peaceful."

Donovan set his jaw before talking. "General," he said, "I meant to assure you that in the worst case Group B can handle the eventualities. But we'll rely on our liaisons—they've been over the possibilities a thousand times—and I expect the Secret Service to cooperate with our hazmat teams, especially when the bioagent will be wreaking havoc inside the White House."

The general nodded, satisfied. "Good." he said, "Remember, once on the grounds there's no point in tiptoeing around. The first group walks upright across that lawn—calmly—not rushing. Understood? It'll be hard to open fire on unarmed hazmat personnel without giving multiple warnings. But if something does go wrong, you break out weapons from the false seal under your tanks, and get to the entrance points of the West Wing. Group B in that case will provide support."

"Understood," Donovan said.

"Sir?" An aide had entered the rotating pressure doors behind them. "An urgent call from the CDC in Atlanta."

The general took the secure phone and listened to the terse comments of his informant at the CDC. "Thank you," he said, returning the phone to his aide, and waiting for the young man to leave. The general never violated his need-to-know policy; his aide had no need to know, so he was not in the loop. Nothing to do with trust, but information was a restricted weapon—those who controlled it exercised the power, and their numbers had to be minimized.

Donovan observed with inquiring eyes.

The general mulled over what he had just heard about Krakauer. He had misjudged the man, a fatal mistake. The professor, he had assumed, wanted recognition from the scientific community, an assumption that seemed to account for the risks he was taking. But releasing his trigger on the civilian population? He must be insane! The general took a deep breath. At least it was on a ship, which proved he was not out to destroy the world. Still, if his trigger ever hit a population center, would that be the end? He didn't know, but the thought made him shudder.

Donovan read his mind. "How bad?"

"Containable, so far. He released it on a ship. The CDC has a boatload of mush in the waters off Puerto Rico. They will hold the full story for fear of panic and because, frankly, they have no idea what they're dealing with. But they're scared, real scared. In the next hour or so, they'll issue a few lines about the catastrophe at sea. They have to say something, but I'm told they'll drag their feet for a few days."

"This changes our White House approach."

"It does. Can you get the men ready?"

"It's pushing it, but we'll handle it."

"Good. The Service now knows the kind of biological devastation they could be facing. CDC has almost certainly briefed the White House. It might work to our advantage."

"Orders?"

"We don't take chances with this thing. Wait until tonight. Then you and Gonzales get suited up and crawl over that lab a dozen different ways. Make certain it's clean. No traps the good professor can set off. If he's done this, he's capable of anything."

"And in the morning?"

"We'll have a talk with the man."

* * *

Before leaving that night, Krakauer snapped on the small television in the main lab, checking the news, as he had been doing all day. He settled into a chair, his eyes glued to the reporter who was broadcasting from the home port of Carefree Dream Liner.

"It's been hours now," the reporter was saying, "since communications with the liner have been severed." She gestured dramatically to an empty pier, to huge ropes sprawled uselessly across the dock. "This is where passengers kissed their loved ones goodbye. It was a once-in-a-lifetime vacation with the promise of luxurious accommodations, sumptuous dining, and perhaps even romance under the Caribbean stars, but now," her face turned grave and she paused histrionically, "now we can only wonder at the fate of those fourteen hundred souls." She turned. "I have here Elmore Simpkins, spokesperson for Carefree Dream Liner. Mr. Simpkins, what is going on out there?"

"Our passengers are like family to us," Elmore said, as if he had memorized a speech, "and you can be certain that Carefree personnel are pursuing, and will continue to pursue, every avenue possible to resolve the situation during this difficult time."

"Is it true there are hundreds of dead on that ship?"

"It's not helpful to speculate at this time, but let me say that the safety of our passengers is paramount to us and we are cooperating fully with the CDC, members of which are alongside the ship at this moment—"

"That would be the Centers for Disease Control and Prevention, in Atlanta, would it not?"

"Ah ... yes, exactly. Of course, we cannot be entirely certain about the specifics at this time—"

"Excuse me, Mr. Simpkins," the reporter said, cupping her ear. "We have pictures of the phalanx of government vessels surrounding the liner ... yes, there we have it, a long way off ... our helicopters are not allowed in the area, but viewers can see the many coast guard ships positioned as if they were blockading the area."

"I would like to assure everyone," Elmore's voice broke in, "that it appears the cruise ship is not in any danger, certainly sea-worthy. Relatives and friends of those on board should know that everything is being done that can be done. We have ... ah, we have a number to call—"

"It's on the screen now," the reporter said.

"Ah ... okay, it's on the screen now." He licked his lips and returned to his studied manner as the number scrolled by.

"Are you concerned that CDC Atlanta is involved?"

"No, we welcome them. As I said, the safety of our passengers is our first concern."

"Some are saying that the presence of the CDC indicates a serious outbreak of—"

"I don't think it's helpful to speculate at this point," the spokesman said, holding up his hand. "We'll just have to wait for the CDC and Coast Guard to report."

"Apparently, there was a Mayday distress call from the captain."

"I have no information on that, but we would expect the captain to call the Coast Guard, or even the CDC, if he was concerned about a communicable disease. A few years ago a British liner had an outbreak of measles, and if I remember correctly, the CDC was informed as a precaution before the ship put into port. There is no doubt that Carefree Dream Liner captains are among the best trained at sea and they are extremely vigilant—"

"And what about the communication problem?"

"The communication problem?"

"It's been several hours, as I understand it, since your last communication with the liner."

"Yes, well, ships are not required to send hourly communiqués."

"Reuters is reporting that the ship is not responding to *any* messages. Would you care to comment?"

Elmore licked his lips again. "As I say ... I have no information on that report."

"But you are worried about the fate of the ship and its passengers, are you not?"

"Of course. Any time there is an incident at sea, we worry. But again, every precaution is being taken. The safety of our passengers is our overriding concern."

"Thank you, Mr. Elmore Simpkins, spokesperson for Carefree Dream Liner." The camera returned to the reporter. "Well, there you have it," she said, setting her jaw. "What some are calling the *Ghost Ship* is positioned about twenty miles west of Puerto Rico ...."

Krakauer turned off the television and glanced around the lab, a profound calm flowing through him. Fire and pestilence had begun.

25

The 911 GT3 RS is the ultimate Porsche—0 to 60 in 3.1 seconds, top speed 204 mph. Basil Meryash chose it in basalt black metallic because he felt the color was impressive, and because the dealer gave him someone else's custom order on the spot, after a hefty surcharge. Basil didn't like to wait for things.

He pulled up to the Student Employment Office, parked at the side of the building, and pulled out his cell phone. "I'm here," he said, then clicked off. Within seconds, the door opened and an auburn-haired girl appeared.

"Hi! I'm Amy Tamerlane," she said, hurrying to the driver's side window while her eyes drank in his car. "Wow! Is this a Porsche?"

"911 GT3." Basil effected nonchalance.

"Must have cost a hundred grand!"

Basil smoothed his hair. "More than two," he said, "with the extras."

"No way!" She caressed the hood reverently with her fingers. "What I'd do for a ride in this baby."

"We can always work something out," Basil said, smiling. "Right now I have to deal with a little problem."

She fiddled with her sweater and said, "You talked on the phone about a hundred dollars."

"I did," he said. "But now that I see you, Amy, I think a couple of hundred would be more appropriate." He opened his wallet and handed her two bills.

"Thanks," she said, stuffing the money in her pocket. Hesitating, she then added, "You're telling me the truth, right? I don't want to get into trouble."

"I heard him say every word. You're just reporting it as if you heard it yourself. Nothing wrong with that. You saw Ryan Taylor, drunk, bragging about how he gets around Student Employment restrictions by working for Proskin Pharmaceutical. And then you tell Dr. Edwards there's a rumor that Taylor has a habit of picking up computers and stuff from offices, and that he intends to rob Student Employment to pay them back."

"Is he really going to rob—?"

"I don't know, Amy," he said, leaning forward and talking in a conspiratorial voice. "I've heard him say it, but he's such a braggart, you never know what he does. I wouldn't put it past him, though. You just tell Edwards the truth, that it's only a rumor, but you thought she should know."

"Yeah, I'll say I don't like spreading rumors, but I thought she should know."

"Exactly."

"Then Dr. Edwards can do what she wants with the information."

"That's it. Nothing wrong with that."

"Y'know, I never liked that guy from the beginning," she said, her lips twisting. "He was so pushy."

"He's a piece of work," Basil said with sudden bitterness, his gaze darkening for a moment. Quickly regaining his composure, he ran his eyes over Amy's compact form. "Tell you what," he resumed casually, with a half-smile, "After you finish up, why don't you drop by my place—it's not far—we can order in some pizza, and you can tell me how it went with Edwards. And if you're a good little girl," he said with a suggestive grin, "I'll take you for a spin in the Porsche."

"Cool! I'd love that." She smiled seductively as she took his address, then gazed again at the sleek-looking machine, before prancing back into the Employment Office.

* * *

Le Beau tapped his pencil nervously on the desk, his eyes on his watch, as he waited for his appointment with Captain Barton. "Be at my office 1:00 p.m.," is all the captain had said, but it was enough to give Le Beau a sick stomach. Minutes later, he took a large breath, and trundled off to see the chief.

"Take a seat," Captain Barton said, pointing to a wooden chair in front of his desk. Le Beau glanced at the four cushioned wingbacks on the other side of the room. No soft chairs today.

"Coffee?" the captain asked, his tone still neutral.

"I'm fine, sir," Le Beau said.

"Well, I'm going to have some," and he poured himself a cup. "Wife doing well?" he asked, stirring in cream and three sugar cubes.

"Yes, thank you."

"Good, that's good." He returned to his desk. "You been losing weight? You look ... well, good."

"I'm working at it, down about ten, I think, sir."

Captain Barton nodded, as if he found the information fascinating. "Elijah," he said, "I don't enjoy this part of my job. I sincerely don't. But that's why they pay me so much." He forced a smile.

"Is there a problem, Chief?"

"There could be, but I suppose it's up to you." He swallowed some coffee, sighed, and continued, "The whole world is run by corporations, huge companies in competition with other huge companies. They care about the money—the bottom line, you know—but I think it's more than that. I think it's about besting the competition, and pleasing stockholders. And when something disrupts their goals, they can be ruthless beyond belief. Know what I mean?"

Le Beau frowned. "Not really," he said.

"Your wife, Helena, has been participating in a trial of several drugs unavailable to the public. Right?"

"Yes."

"And it's going well?"

"I think so."

"The new drugs have suppressed her symptoms, I take it."

"So far," Le Beau said, and then he added, "Where are we going with this, Captain? What has my wife's condition got to do with my job?"

Captain Barton's left hand massaged his jaw. "I got a call from the administration late last night. Called me on my home phone. And then this guy from Proskin Pharma gets on the line. Seems like they're reconsidering whether your wife can continue with the trials. Reviewing her application, they say."

"I don't understand. They've already agreed she fits the profile," Le Beau said, taken aback. "They can't just, I mean, she was already enrolled—"

Barton shook his head, his face a mirror of disdain. "We're talking about major companies here, with fingers in all sorts of pies. And when you bite one of those fingers, well, it can tighten into a fist, and really come down on you. Understand?"

"You're saying I've bitten someone's finger?"

"Come on, Elijah," the captain said, raising his voice with some impatience. "Even I know you've been nosing around the Westover case. You've been in the vaults reading the reports, you've met with that research kid a couple of times, and you're just asking too many damn questions. And the so-called robbery outside Krakauer's lab. Pathetic!" Barton jerked out of his seat and started pacing. "You'd better listen to me. These companies don't want us stirring up old issues. They've got drugs in the pipeline worth billions. And they know what you're doing. Believe me, they've got people everywhere."

Le Beau rose.

"They even know about your plans for Arizona. That's where you and Helena want to retire, isn't it?"

Le Beau stared at the captain but said nothing.

"It's not going to happen, Elijah. This is real. If you keep it up, word will come down. You understand? No retirement package. No Arizona. No nothing. All because you didn't keep your nose out of things."

"I was just doing regular police work," Le Beau protested.

"Oh, don't be so naïve! These people could replace you and me tomorrow. One word and we're gone. And they'll do it, make no mistake.

Then, what happens to Arizona, and to your wife? What happens to me?

Le Beau felt sick, almost faint.

"Look," Barton continued, his voice softening, "I don't like delivering this message any more than you like hearing it. We're way over our pay grade, you and I, when it comes to dealing with people like this. Sometimes the only option is not the one we want to take, but the one we have to, for the sake of our families, our futures. I'm telling you this straight because I need to know you are hearing me loud and clear. No bullshit. You get what I'm saying?"

Le Beau nodded, but running through his mind was the sickening idea that this man with the sincere face and earnest eyes had sent Fred Romano to his death.

The captain moved closer, trying very hard to sound the elder statesman as he said, "Maybe these companies have made mistakes in the past, maybe they haven't. I don't know. What I do know is that they are serious about keeping a lid on things." He pushed his fingers through his white hair. "This doesn't concern us. They just want to keep moving ahead, and they can be very helpful to those who help them. You understand?"

Le Beau eyed the captain. "I don't take cream."

"For the love of Mike, I'm not talking about cream! If I thought you would take the bag, I'd fire you myself. Right now! Today!" He kneaded his face slowly, as if to banish the weariness of the day. Reaching automatically for his coffee, he brought it to his mouth then returned it to the desk, untouched. "I'm talking about preparing for retirement," he said in his quiet voice, "when we'll be a thousand miles from New Haven, and nobody will care whether we investigated this case or that. I'm talking about living in Arizona, in the deserts where the Apaches roamed, fishing in ... what is it, the White Mountains?" He approximated a smile. "Stop being so damn selfish. It's time to stop thinking about yourself for once, and think about Helena and her needs in the coming years. These corporate types are not bad people, Elijah, and they're eager to help. They'll meet you half way. If you want, I have a number to call—"

Le Beau raised his palms to say no.

The captain took a large breath and expelled it loudly. "Well," he said, as if he were talking to himself, "I tried my best to get through to you. They asked me to talk to you, and I have. But it's your call. So what do you want to do?"

"I'll think on it," Le Beau said, but he was wondering how far they might go.

"You do that," said the captain. "And remember, I'm your friend here. And you don't know how far I've already gone to bat for you. But if you don't stay away from this case, from the kids, and from anything else that involves them, I can't help you. I can't help your wife to participate in any drug trials, and the Arizona desert is just a dream you never had."

Le Beau gritted his teeth and nodded.

Captain Barton pulled open the door and said in a cheerful voice, adequately loud for the outer office to hear, "Thanks for stopping by, Elijah."

26

The night had come. Nicole stood guard at the crosswalk behind the library, like a spy in a B movie, ready to signal should anyone spot Ryan removing the grate.

Okay," Ryan mouthed, beckoning from the murky hole that led to the steam tunnels. She hurried across the pavement and down the metal ladder into the hole. After returning the grate to its original position, Ryan dropped to the floor without bothering to use the ladder. "Cool, eh?" he said, his face beaming.

"This is it?" Nicole asked, curling her lip. She ran her eyes along the huge steam pipes that crowded both sides of the walkway, wondering why the tunnels fascinated so many students. They were hot, dirty, and smelled like fried mouse droppings. At any moment she expected a brood of troglodytes to pour through a crevice in the wall.

"Don't bump the pressure gauges," Ryan said. "They're burning hot."

Nicole eyed the metal gauge protruding from a steam pipe not two feet from where they stood. She wasn't about to touch anything, not the scalding gauges, not the electrical cables that dangled from above, and certainly not the spider-infested rubbish stuffed along the walkways. The whole place reeked, on second consideration, of boiled sewer water.

Ryan set out for Krakauer's lab, seemingly confident of where he was going, Nicole following behind. As the tunnels twisted and turned, and branched in every direction, she wondered how he could possibly keep his bearings without the campus above as a referent. His scribbled notes marking the turns did little to inspire confidence, and soon his pauses grew longer, his face more pensive.

"Are we lost?"

"No."

She followed him to the next junction and waited as he studied his scribblings.

"We're not lost?" Nicole asked.

Ryan kept his eyes on his paper.

"I think we're lost," she said as she glanced up and down the half-lit tunnels.

"Well, we're not."

"Then why do you stop every time the tunnel branches?"

"Relax."

"I'm trying to, but I'm wondering—"

"What? What are you wondering?"

"Whether we should go through one of those escape hatches—"

"No way."

"Just to see where we are."

"I know exactly where we are."

"Really? What part of campus is directly above us?"

"I haven't got time for this."

"You don't know."

"We can't go through an escape hatch. They've got alarms."

"How do the workers navigate this place?" she asked, glancing around. "There must be something that indicates where they are."

"There's nothing."

"I don't believe it."

"Tribal knowledge, that's what they say."

"Well, it seems to me—"

"Nicole, please be quiet," Ryan interrupted as he started down the tunnel. "I can't think with you talking all the time."

"Yeah, we're lost," she mumbled under her breath.

"No more," he said, and something in his voice convinced her to keep silent.

Nicole surveyed the walls where the tunnels branched, looking for markings that might indicate where they were. *Nothing.* She feigned interest in one of her nails, hoping to ease the pressure. Already he was avoiding eye contact, which made her feel awful. Still, she remembered the fate of Milton's angels—wandering in endless mazes, lost.

Ryan pointed toward one of the walkways and said, "I think the library is that way. We'll be there in a minute or two."

She put on her most positive face. Lost or not, Ryan was trying very hard—especially with Ms. Judgmental at his elbow. The thought bothered her. She didn't mean to be judgmental but apparently she was, so she decided to applaud his efforts if and when they ever arrived at the lab. Twenty minutes and two backtracks later, they entered the escape door to Krakauer's lab. Ryan's face glowed in triumph as he helped her into the lab.

She waited patiently as he moved through the darkened room, searching for the switch.

"Ah," he murmured and light suddenly flooded the area.

Nicole blinked. The room was tiny, hardly a lab: a metal table with sinks, a few cupboards, and except for a shelf piled with large plastic tubes, blank walls.

"This is it," he said, gesturing. "We're here."

She smiled. This was her moment. "Well, I have to say, Ryan, you were right! The next time I explore the tunnels, I will insist on *you* being my guide."

He grinned in that unconsciously charming way he so often did, and she was glad she'd said something nice. Was that so hard to do? With a few positive words she had made him happy, and somehow, doing so had made her happy as well. She tucked that piece of information away. In the future she would be more generous with her praise and less on the offensive. Her aggression was just a mechanism to keep people at a distance, and she suddenly realized she no longer wanted to keep Ryan at a distance. Nicole didn't know exactly when her feelings had changed or what she wanted, but one thing was certain. She was tired of being the disciplined soldier, always suppressing her feelings, always achieving objectives. Why couldn't she just be another frivolous college student?

He was looking out the doorway of the lab now, and Nicole moved in behind him. She rested one hand on his shoulder to keep her balance and was surprised how solid he felt, quite different from Basil. She couldn't resist a slight squeeze on his upper arm to feel the hardness of his muscles.

He turned toward her, thinking she was trying to get his attention.

"This lab complex is huge," she said, craning her head both ways, trying to conceal her silliness.

"Yeah," he agreed, glancing down the murky corridor.

In spite of herself, she crowded against him until she could feel the line of his body against hers, and smell the after-shave on his shirt collar. It felt good to be close, and she might have brushed her lips across the back of his neck had not her brain prevailed. She tried to dump the juvenile thoughts from her head, but the feel of his body against hers proved too strong.

"You really did a good job finding your way through those tunnels," she cooed softly, not knowing what else to say. She hoped she didn't sound too ridiculous since she had already praised him for navigating the tunnels.

"It can get confusing," he said.

She rubbed his back affectionately, but he didn't seem to notice.

What was she doing? She had come to Krakauer's lab for a purpose but here she was pressed up against Ryan like some cheerleader at an after-game party. She needed to get down to business. "You control situations or they control you." That's what her father always said, and the thought of her father jolted her back to reality. She could just imagine his shock if he knew the secrets she had revealed about their family. "Tell people only what they need to know," that was her father's mantra. But she had been astoundingly careless these last few days. Abruptly, she took her hand off Ryan's arm and created space between them. "Where's Krakauer's computer?" she asked in a resolute voice.

"This way," Ryan replied, oblivious to her inner turmoil. He stepped out of the miniature lab and turned on a shock of hall lights.

She surveyed the gleaming white hall and the yawning dark beyond.

"Spooky at night," he said. "No one comes here after eight."

"And if someone did," she said with a smile, "you'd be my protector, right?"

"I don't weight-lift for nothing," he said, proffering her an arm.

She slid her fingers over his bicep, this time boldly, and laughed. He laughed too, but she could see concern in his face, and she knew he was thinking about the men in the lab, in this lab. A sudden outburst of chittering from the animal room made her jump.

"It's just the monkeys," he said, glancing around. "They'll settle down soon."

Nicole followed Ryan up the hall, eager to get into Krakauer's computer but not wanting to appear too eager, lest Ryan think that she wasn't taking the situation seriously. When they entered the private lab, Ryan went straight to the computer, but Nicole paused, running her eyes over the various pieces of lab equipment, and stopping at the freezers and sealed chambers. An airlock door? She had a sick feeling in her gut. Krakauer had been working on a dangerous pathogen, of that she was certain, probably trying to strip off its lethal properties. The confusing aspect of it all was Le Beau's comments. She didn't buy the melting bodies—that was ridiculous—but something odd was happening, something very odd.

"Okay, it's done," Ryan said.

"That's it? I was expecting it to beep or something."

He arched an eyebrow. "Everything is done," he repeated as he flipped through a pile of CDs. "I'll double check when I get back, but the logs should be clear, and this won't send any more data." He found something and popped it into the computer. "Now, let's see what's hidden in you," he muttered.

Nicole held her breath as he punched in the passwords, knowing that the disc could be just what it appeared—a Mozart music CD. A second passed. Then a few more. Ryan stared intently at the screen. Suddenly, he slapped his hand on the table, causing her to jump. "I knew it!" he said with a grin.

"You're in?"

"Yup, it's on the CD. There's a bunch of files ... here's map data, and in this other window some info about states, starting from the west. Let me see, cities and dates ... lots of them. Here is a spreadsheet with a list of shipments of something, and more numbers." He turned to Nicole. "Does any of this make sense to you?"

"Let me look," she said, bending closer and then switching places with him. She stared at the maps and skipped back and forth between the windows where Krakauer had recorded his notes. One document had a listing of neutralization assays where all of Krakauer's antidote tests came up negative or incomplete. She continued flipping through the windows.

Okay, she could see what he was doing. These were blood samples. And these were shipping invoices from cities all over the country. Here were some from Canada and Mexico. Lots of samples, that's for sure. She leaned back in the chair. Why was Krakauer collecting blood samples from people?

Nicole closed her eyes and let the pieces assemble. Ryan had always said Krakauer was working on gene therapy. She ran her tongue over her lips, thinking. A therapy? Is that what this research evaluated? Krakauer was definitely looking for something in the general population. Probably trying to make a name for himself, like every other Yale prof. But—she reread some of the notations—everything was wrong. It was immune research all right, but not the kind that would relate to gene therapy. Nicole opened and closed several windows, trying to understand the data. She expelled a long breath in frustration. Nothing made sense. What was wrong with her thinking?

Then something occurred to her. She pushed the ridiculous idea away but it persisted and she furrowed her brow, not liking where her thoughts were leading. Could she have missed the core of Krakauer's research? Could he be doing something quite different from what she had expected? Something ominous ... out of the lab?

Nicole snorted; she was becoming as bad as Ryan. *Can't jump to conclusions!* She would read everything again. She clicked on the folder called *Omega*. Aha! Jackpot. She began to read.

"No, no," she whispered, as she swept through the notes with growing alarm. *Got to read more carefully!* Her mouth was parched and she felt feverish.

She must have misunderstood. It couldn't be. Not possible. Nicole put her hands to her burning face and stared at the screen.

"What is it?" Ryan was leaning over her shoulder.

"I ... don't know."

"Does it say anything about—"

"Just wait!" she snapped. "I said I didn't know."

He moved away.

She looked up and waved her hand. "Ryan, I'm sorry. It's just that ... give me a minute. I want to reread these notes."

After a few more minutes, Ryan ventured a tentative, "Well?"

Nicole closed her eyes, incredulous. She had read Krakauer's notes three times to be sure. He had infected everybody. He had created a doomsday gene and put it into every man, woman, and child.

Ryan paced the room, glancing at her, concerned.

"Oh, God," she whispered, then turned away, as if that might change what was on the screen.

Ryan stared at her. "Nicole?"

"I don't believe what I'm reading," she said at last.

"What is it?"

"Epidemiological projections," she said, motioning to the screen.

Ryan returned to the computer. "Projections of what?" he asked.

"The spread of a pathogen."

"A disease?"

Nicole nodded. "Yeah. Sort of."

"Okay, that's not so bad. Krakauer told me he was studying gene therapy. That's what he's been studying, right?" His voice was hopeful. "He's been trying to find an antidote for a bunch of diseases."

"Ryan," Nicole said, "Krakauer has engineered something very contagious ... something that isn't stopped by the immune system. And from these invoices, it's outside the lab."

"A very contagious—what?"

Nicole took a deep breath. "It's a vector—a delivery system. And what he's delivering is some genes that—well, they don't seem to do anything by themselves. But if these data are real, the way it spreads suggests that everyone in the United States has it, except for maybe a few trappers in Montana." She pulled up the maps and showed Krakauer's tracking of his research. "Look," she said, "he's got blood samples from every state, gets them from the Red Cross for his studies—and this lower graph tracks the spread. From these projections I would guess he has infected the whole nation ... the world, I suppose."

"Us too?"

"I'm afraid so."

Ryan frowned. "I don't feel sick."

"It's not turned on yet," Nicole said, sounding calmer than she was. Unbelievable—a killer gene! What was the matter with Krakauer that he would create such a thing? She stared at the white tiled ceiling, as if that would help.

"Nicole?"

She tilted her head to include Ryan in her vision, but her mind was spinning in a hundred directions. "Nobody knows," she said. "He has driven his gene, or gene circuit, I guess—he calls it *Omega*—everywhere, and nobody knows." She half laughed and shook her head in amazement. "Everyone, including you and me, feels just fine. But our entire cell structure has been changed. It's been hijacked by this—"

"Wait. I don't understand. What does it do? Why aren't we sick?"

"The gene is latent. It's waiting."

"Waiting for what?"

"Waiting for a signal to trigger it. It's changed us, Ryan, every last piece of us."

Ryan's eyes showed his disbelief.

"Think of it as a delivery system," Nicole said. "Its payload is DNA. So Krakauer—that psychotic—has somehow created a vector that can evade the body's immune system. The body doesn't know it's there. That's why we aren't sick, because the body's immune system doesn't know there's anything to fight against. And so when we come into contact with *Omega*, it spreads through us like a silent wildfire, injecting every one of our cells with its payload of genes."

"And nobody knows."

"That's right. Nobody has a clue. There aren't any symptoms. And even if there were, they'd be so mild no one would notice." She glanced around wearily and continued talking in a mechanical fashion. "The genes are a set of instructions for how to build something. The body is the factory and it's been given a new product to manufacture."

"I'm not sure I understand. What exactly is *Omega* doing in my body right now? What's it manufacturing?"

"Right now, nothing."

"So it's just sitting there, doing nothing."

"Right. It lies dormant until something, probably a chemical, triggers it."

"And then?"

"It amplifies." Nicole motioned toward the screen. "It unlocks a bunch of molecular safeties and then tells the cell to begin releasing more trigger. Like a slave, the cell uses those instructions to destroy itself. After it makes enough trigger, the cell bursts, spreading the newly made trigger onto other cells. These cells in turn produce even more trigger, burst, and trigger other cells in a chain reaction. But Krakauer's notes show this thing moves at incredible speed. Not like a virus, which takes hours or days, but in minutes, seconds." Nicole bit her lip. "Oh, merciful God, I don't believe what I am saying!"

"So what I saw in the lab ...."

"A chain reaction, cells destroying themselves."

"We could melt like that chimp?"

Nicole said nothing. It was enough that Ryan was getting the idea. She returned her eyes to the computer. A quiet desperation was beginning to overwhelm her; the truth was becoming unbearable.

A water pump clunked to life in a back room.

"Can't we find this thing and kill it with some kind of antibiotic?" Nicole smiled wanly. "It doesn't work like that."

"This is bullshit," Ryan said. "There's got to be something that can kill it."

Nicole shook her head. "There's no 'it' to kill," she said.

"Sure there is," Ryan said, irritated. "The *Omega*! We stamp out the damn thing. Without it in us, we've got no problem. Right?"

"That's the horrible thing about what Krakauer has done," she said. "Once we contract the *Omega*, it becomes part of us." She took a breath. "Our genome is full of DNA that isn't really ours—most of it so ancient we don't even know what it does." She sighed. "Now, it seems, we have a new aspect to our bodies. Krakauer has managed to bypass our immune systems, and so now *Omega* is forever a part of our makeup. It's a genetic alteration, as much a part of us as the color of our eyes."

"So we can never rid ourselves of it?"

Nicole slowly shook her head. "We are it," she said.

27

"How fast now?" Amy asked as the Porsche streaked along I-95 south of New Haven.

"A hundred and five," Basil said coolly.

"Feels like thirty."

Basil cut around a tanker and tromped the gas. The Porsche bolted forward like a startled rabbit.

She grabbed his thigh and threw back her head, laughing. "Oh, Basil!" she shrieked. "This car is incredible!"

"Hundred and forty," Basil reported. "But I'd better slow down," he added, motioning with his head.

Amy glanced over her shoulder at the flashing lights receding in the rear window.

"If I kept this up," Basil said, giving her a smile, "we'd have to drop bread crumbs for them." He pulled to the shoulder, turned on his hazards, and switched off the ignition. "The gallant officers on our tail aren't stupid," he said, exhaling slowly. "They know what they're chasing. The 911 GT3 is an amazing machine, but quite rare, and in a day or two concerned peace officers would be sniffing around my door."

She looked at him with large, uneasy eyes and asked, "Are we in trouble?"

"I wouldn't worry about it," Basil replied, removing his registration from the glove compartment and placing it beside his license. He waited quietly for the police to arrive, unconcerned about the ticket he would receive. It had been a good day. Amy had proved astonishingly appreciative for a simple ride in his car and, more importantly, she had handled the situation at the Employment Office just right. Soon Ryan Taylor would find himself in an unhappy position with Ms. Edwards and the Yale police. He would have some tall explaining to do, and before long, he'd be packing his bags and heading for Loon Flats, or whatever backwater he came from. Basil's father was right. You do what it takes.

The police officer approached from the rear.

Basil lowered the window, placed both hands in plain sight on the steering wheel, and smiled pleasantly.

"Have you been drinking tonight, sir?" he asked.

"Sure have, officer. Starbucks Mocha Valencia, double shot of espresso. Rather tasty. Not all Starbucks make it well, but I suppose you know that." He gave the officer a thoughtful look and added, "You might try the one on Chapel Street. They have a talented barista."

The officer's face darkened. "I will ask again, sir. Have you consumed any alcoholic beverages tonight?"

"*Alcoholic* beverages? Dear me, I misunderstood. No, sir, I have consumed no alcoholic beverages this evening."

The police officer studied Basil for a moment, then flipped open his book. "Do you know how fast you were driving?"

"About a hundred and forty," Basil said matter-of-factly, handing over his license and registration. Yes, it had been a fine day.

* * *

Elijah Le Beau was worried. Even in the worst days of her illness, Helena had managed to keep a positive attitude. But tonight she had barely said a word since he arrived home.

He opened the hall closet, pulled out a shoebox labeled "Arizona," and carried it to the dining room table. "I think I'll check out the map again," he said, glancing over. The Arizona box always cheered her.

She turned her eyes toward her husband, but all she said was, "Careful with the candles on the table."

"All safe," Le Beau said as he moved each candle to the sideboard, and smoothed the map across the table. "Look at this, Helena," he said, beckoning his wife to come closer. "Arizona's White Mountain region, snow-capped mountains, streams bursting with fish. Is this not the most beautiful place on earth?"

She leaned over his shoulder. "It is, Elijah. It really is."

He nodded with satisfaction. "Can you believe it," he said, tapping his finger on the map, "we'll be right there!"

"We've had some good years here in New Haven," Helena said quietly, "but I wish we could pack our things right now."

"Four years," he said. "Four years until I retire."

She nodded.

Le Beau glanced up from his map and said, "You're worried, aren't you?"

"A bit. Four years is a long time."

"The medicines are working, right?"

"Yes, they're working wonderfully. I can move, I can see, but who knows what will happen a few years down the line?"

"I do," Le Beau said. "You'll be just fine. I really believe it. Dr. Mokosh says this Proskin company is incredibly innovative, and your clinical study is slated for five years, so almost certainly other medicines will come along. Right?"

She nodded.

He paused. "There's something else, isn't there?" he said. "You've been quiet all evening."

"Oh," she said, shaking her head, "it's probably nothing."

"Tell me."

Her eyes moistened. "I'm ... ah, a little concerned whether I'll be allowed to continue."

Le Beau looked at her. "What do you mean?" he asked.

"I'm Hispanic," she said. "Not African-American."

"So?"

"So, when they were filling out my forms, someone checked off African-American, and this might be a problem."

Le Beau took a breath, processing the information.

"Apparently, they need a certain balance in age, sex and race to evaluate the data properly, and mistakes like this create statistical problems."

"Who told you this?" Le Beau asked.

"A man called this afternoon, a Proskin representative. He said adjustments often occur in trials of this sort, and they would inform me in a few days whether I could continue."

"Did they—" Le Beau stopped. He could see that Helena was fighting back tears.

"I don't know what to do," she said miserably, the tears now trickling down her cheeks. "How can they stop the medicines if they're working?"

Le Beau pulled her close, wanting to shield her from the evil that was swirling around them. Captain Barton's words were galloping through his mind. Stay away from the Westover case, he had said, or Proskin would remove Helena from the drug trials, and turn the couple's Arizona plans into dust.

"Wait a minute," he said, forcing a smile. "When did Proskin call?"

"A couple of hours before you got home."

"Then there's no problem," he said in his most upbeat voice. "I thought they'd just called you." He mopped his face to show his relief. "Proskin left me a voice message less than an hour ago, and said they've cleared up the difficulty. You have a permanent spot in the trials, even when we move to Arizona."

28

Ryan finished with the computer and returned the Mozart disc in numbed silence. He understood every word Nicole had said, yet couldn't believe it. The idea that Krakauer had changed the cell structure of virtually everyone in the world was bizarre.

His mind just wouldn't accept it.

Like the theory that eighty percent of body heat is lost through the head, or you only use ten percent of your brain—these things always turned out to be wrong when he looked them up. None of this made sense. How could Krakauer have turned everyone into walking bio-bombs? It was absurd. Things like that didn't happen. He remembered when he was ten years old hearing about people bursting into flame. A woman sitting in her living room had suddenly caught fire, leaving only scorch marks on the fabric, and a man burned to a cinder in bed while his wife slept peacefully beside him. Ridiculous! At least, that's the way Ryan viewed it. And Krakauer's *Omega* was probably ridiculous as well. It couldn't be real. It was scientific bullshit.

"Ryan?

He turned his head but his mind was still processing a thousand conflicting thoughts. He could see Nicole's mouth moving, her eyes widening as she whispered, but he couldn't focus on what she was saying. There was no reason for panic, he told himself. Predictions of calamity always worked themselves out. Like the first atomic bomb. Scientists worried about a chain reaction that would destroy all matter.

Then there was the doomsday clock, set just minutes from midnight. Never hours, always minutes till destruction. Y2K, rogue comets, global warming, AI and a hundred other fears proclaimed the collapse of civilization. With every new supercollider came predictions of black holes and obliteration. Diseases like swine flu, bird flu and Ebola were always on the brink of engulfing the world.

The basic nightmare never changed, only the details: with Krakauer, hundreds of millions would die choking on their own blood. Alarmists were always prophesying The End Of The World As We Know It. But nothing ever happened. After every so-called calamity, you look around and more or less everybody's still here. Besides, even if Krakauer *had* infected the entire planet, surely some bright scientist studying the problem would come up with a solution. Isn't that what always happened?

"Ryan!" Nicole was shaking his arm.

"What?"

"I hear something!"

He looked around, his mind still churning.

Nicole dropped her voice. "I think somebody's in the lab."

Ryan stared at her vacantly.

"Outside that door!" she whispered urgently, pointing to the main entrance.

His mind suddenly engaged and his eyes darted toward the door. Krakauer? His heart pounded. No, not Krakauer. He turned slowly toward the door, breath growing shallow. The men! They had returned. He tried to think. The lights! He should darken the room, or block the door—do something! He grabbed Nicole by the shoulders. "We've got to get out of here," he said, and the words caught in his throat.

She glanced at the door.

"Now!" Ryan said, pushing her toward the back of the lab.

She looked confused, unsure what she was supposed to do.

"The tunnels!" he said. "Get to the tunnels."

"Who is it?" she asked, her body turning rigid. "The men?"

"Run!" Ryan said through clenched teeth, this time shoving her roughly. She turned and sprinted down the hall with surprising speed. He swept his eyes around the room, stopping at the main entrance. There was a muffled sound, then the creak of a hinge.

The door opened and two men in blue pressure suits pushed into the lab. Ryan tried but couldn't move, his body paralyzed by fear. All he could do was stare at the man with the dead eyes, like a doomed animal fascinated by a predator.

As they neared, the heavy sound of the door slamming jolted Ryan into action. He whirled around and started toward the hall. Too late. A heavy glove clamped onto his collar. Ryan jerked away, saw a blur of movement, and lights suddenly exploded around him. He tumbled to the ground, pawing at his aching head. For an instant he wondered whether he had been shot. He stared at his hands. "No blood," he heard himself say in a listless tone. He touched his head again. What was it about that awful phrase? He tried to focus his confused mind. That's what they'd said: *no blood*. They had wanted to kill him using the baseball bat! And now one of them had found that same bat and had crushed the side of his head with it.

Splotches of light danced crazily before his eyes. He had to get up. To stay on the floor meant death.

Above him the men swayed ponderously in their billowing suits, trying to grab hold of him. Even with hazy vision Ryan could see that neither had a bat. The shorter one had struck him with a fist; it just felt like a baseball bat. Ryan struggled to his feet, only to have the taller man wrestle him to the ground again. Then the other was on him like a rabid dog, pummeling him with his fists. Ryan thrust his head into the taller man's shoulder to avoid the blows, but the smooth skin of the air suit stuck to his face like plastic. He couldn't breathe.

Ryan panicked, fighting for air. Twisting, kicking and punching in a frenzy, his lungs screaming for oxygen, he wrenched free and skittered across the tile floor, smashing shoulder-first into the wall. Fire shot down his arm.

He scrambled to his feet. Something had popped in his shoulder, but that would have to wait—he had to get to the tunnels. Even in their cumbersome air suits, he had no doubts the two would soon crush the life out of him. Over the years Ryan had had his share of scuffles, and he'd always handled himself quite well, but these men were different. He knew he had no chance with them. They had been trained to fight. Probably to kill.

The shorter man rose to a crouch and banged his gloved fists together, his dead eyes staring at Ryan through the clear plastic of his protective hood. Then he abruptly stopped banging his hands and looked up, as if he had seen something. In spite of himself, Ryan felt his eyes turn upward. The man burst forward, driving his fist ahead like a piston. Ryan jumped back like a frightened cat, stumbled sideways and grabbed at the suit's breathing apparatus for stability. It ripped off, tangling in the man's feet.

Ryan darted to the opposite side of the room, gasping, trying to make it to the rear door. The taller man stepped into the open doorway. Ryan whipped his head around, looking for a way to escape. He saw the other man tearing off his twisted breathing apparatus, and Ryan knew he wouldn't be long at his task.

"Get out!" every fiber in his body screamed. "Get out now!"

Ryan fixed his eyes on the tall man in the doorway, dropped his throbbing shoulder, and charged across the room, as if he were a fullback. The man hesitated, started backwards, and tried to side-step out of the way. Ryan drove into him at full speed and lifted him into the air, slamming his body against the steel doorpost with a sickening thud. He slid soundlessly to the floor.

Ryan grasped at the fire radiating down his arm and wondered if he had separated his shoulder. He rubbed it deeply, trying to dull the ache. Something about the pressure made it feel better, as if rubbing diluted the pain.

A thick glove suddenly curled around his ankle. The taller man on the floor had recovered. Ryan tugged his foot upwards, pulling it free, but the man latched onto it again. Ryan spun around and kicked at him several times. Then lifting his free leg, he plunged it down, driving his heel into the man's chest. Even through the sealed air suit Ryan could hear the man's muffled scream as he clutched his middle. Several ribs must have broken when Ryan crashed into him.

Without another look, Ryan raced out the door and into the main hallway. He reached the tiny lab at full gallop, but was moving too fast, and crashed into the metal table with its four sinks. A bolt of pain shot down his leg, masking the ache in his shoulder. He touched the tender spot on his hip bone. And then he heard feet pounding in the corridor. The men were coming. He had to get out of the lab, and fast.

"Hurry!" Nicole called, beckoning with her hand. She was already on the other side of the steel door that led to the steam tunnels.

"Coming!" he shouted as he hobbled around the table toward the door. Pain throbbed in every part of his body, but he knew he had to get through the escape door and latch it closed. The yellow light of the tunnels was life.

The shorter man reached the tiny lab as Ryan stepped through the door into the tunnels. He had removed every piece of his ripped pressure suit, obviously no longer concerned with whatever was in the lab. He wanted Ryan. And he was coming straight for him. Ryan had often heard that the eyes were the windows to the soul, and if they were, the man bearing down on him had no soul, because those eyes were lifeless voids.

"Ryan!" Nicole shouted from the walkway, "Come, now!"

"Gotta bolt the door!" He reached in for the handle to pull it closed.

Dead-Eyes lunged, one hand grabbing the edge of the door, the other shooting out like a snake's tongue toward the plastic tubes on the shelf. Ryan swung the door shut, but it sprang back as if warped. He looked down. A pipe! The man had wedged a plastic pipe between the door and the metal frame.

"Leave it!" Nicole screamed.

Ryan knew he couldn't leave it. He kicked frantically at the pipe, his hand still firmly grasping the handle. The pipe barely moved. He hammered it again, this time with his full foot, and this time the pipe popped back into the lab. Relieved, Ryan pulled on the handle, but in that moment, gloved fingers squeezed through the opening at the top, and began tugging inward.

Ryan braced his foot on the wall and strained on the handle, but he knew it was hopeless. He swept his eyes across the floor. The hook! Where did he drop the ... yes, there it was on the cement divider beside the door. He scooped up the heavy piece of metal with his left hand and smashed it down onto the protruding gloves.

The man squealed. The thick gloves disappeared into the lab, but instantly another set of fingers, these ones without gloves, rammed through the opening. Ryan struck again with the hook, but missed. He swung again, wildly, but it caught the top of the frame and flipped from his hands, spinning out of reach.

"Ryan ...." Nicole's voice sounded frantic as she started back to help him. But the game was up, and Ryan knew it when the gloved fingers reappeared. He couldn't out-pull two men.

They began to jerk the door inward. Erratic jerks that threatened to wrench the handle from his grasp. He thought about letting go and trying to run. But they'd be on him before he reached the first bend in the tunnels.

The muscles in his forearms began to cramp, and he realized what he had to do. The only thing he could do. But he worried about the outcome. The door jerked inward again, the handle almost ripping from his grasp. He tried to shift his grip, but his fingers were numb and wouldn't respond. He had to risk it. The door jerked again. *Now!* He released the handle and drove his foot into the center of the door, which swung inward like a gate caught in a hurricane, crashing into the surprised men. Ryan seized the handle again and yanked the door closed, slamming the dead bolt home. He slumped against the door, exhausted, and breathed out in relief.

"Let's go," Nicole said.

"Yeah," Ryan said, rubbing his shoulder. He wanted to disappear into the tunnel system too. He knew Dead-Eyes wouldn't be satisfied until he caught and killed them.

They had barely started down the short walkway that led to the tunnels when something heavy hit the door.

Nicole clutched his arm.

Another thud. Then a loud *crack*.

"Whoa!" Ryan jumped back.

"What was that?" Nicole asked.

Ryan stared at the door.

"A gun?" Nicole had a stunned look on her face. "That was a gun!" she said. "This is insane!"

Two more shots came in rapid succession, one of them rattling the deadbolt. Ryan and Nicole flattened against the cement walls of the exit as a half-dozen more bullets splattered through the metal door near the deadbolt, rust and dirt spraying everywhere. The metal looked like tattered fabric, but the deadbolt held firm. Ryan's eyes drifted to Nicole. Neither spoke. Both realized the flying shrapnel could have easily torn through their own fragile bodies.

Then without a word they turned in the same instant and started toward the tunnels. Ryan needed time to think. Just running through the tunnels, hoping to escape, wouldn't do. Sooner or later these—whoever they were—would find them. He had to get the police involved, or maybe the FBI. And he had to do it fast.

Behind them came the sounds of something heavy crashing into a metal door, and Ryan knew they were using the steel table as a battering ram.

Nicole's eyes met his. "I'm scared," she said.

"Yeah," was all he could say. He scanned the narrow tunnel both ways, hoping to spot a worker. Where were the workers? The pounding was so loud that somebody on the night shift had to hear. Why weren't they checking out the noise? He took another look. Nobody. All he could see were the wrapped steam pipes running along both sides of the walkway, and the dim lights punctuating the gloom. Then reality forced away his hopes. Loud noises were common in the tunnels. Bill was always talking about this or that project underway, night and day. Even the gunshots would sound like staple or nail guns. No workers were coming.

Ryan took a last look back at the escape door before heading into the tunnel. What he saw made his blood freeze. The entire frame had been banged out from the cement walls, with the deadbolt still holding. Ryan swallowed hard. Another time or two and the whole structure would tumble like Jericho's walls.

He grabbed Nicole and fled down the twisting passageway. "Careful of those pressure gauges," he shouted as they neared an unwrapped section of steam pipe jutting into the walkway. They slowed as they passed the gauge and then continued at a trot until they came to an intersecting tunnel.

"This way," Ryan said, pointing to the left. He didn't care which way they went as long as they got two or three turns ahead. Even trained assassins couldn't guess right every time the tunnels forked and before long, Ryan reasoned, he and Nicole would be in the clear. They could contact Le Beau or the FBI and end this nightmare.

After four or five turns their clothes were soaked with sweat and they walked part way to catch their breath. Running in the tunnel heat proved tough and Ryan was amazed Nicole could even keep up. With every turn he felt better about their chances and decided to take the next escape hatch he saw. It didn't matter where it went or if it was alarmed. Yale's disciplinary committee was nothing. He just wanted to survive the night.

"There's one," Nicole said, pointing to a walkway that ended in a rusted door.

"I see it," Ryan said as he hurried down the pavement. He took hold of the deadbolt with both hands and yanked hard, but like the others, it was frozen from years of disuse. He glanced at the junk strewn along the walkway and picked up a ten-inch metal bar that had some heft to it. Aiming carefully, he hammered the end of the metal tongue and it jumped across.

"Good one," Nicole said.

"Okay, let's get out of here," Ryan said, butting the door open. The steel hatch swung inward eight inches and stopped. He gave it another push but it wouldn't move.

"What's the matter?"

"Something's blocking it," he said. He heaved with his full weight, but still it wouldn't open any farther than the eight-inch gap. He reached in with his hand and swirled it around, quickly finding the problem. Another wall of sorts. Behind the escape hatch somebody had placed a wall unit, maybe a cupboard, he didn't know, but it was heavy and bolted in place. "We have to find another hatch," he said, stating the obvious.

They glanced over their shoulders toward the tunnels, toward the yellow light and hissing steam that now seemed foreign and dangerous, no longer a refuge. Somewhere in those tunnels men were hunting them. Ryan tried one last desperate time to shove the wall unit out of the way, but it was solid. His shoulder was throbbing. He snatched up the metal bar, something to use on the next deadbolt if it was jammed. They returned to the tunnels, their heads jerking at every sound.

Five minutes later, at the intersection of three passageways, they spotted another escape door. Ryan gave Nicole a look of relief. He just wanted to get through the hatch and call the cops.

That's when they saw them, the tall man first, hobbling along the walkway with his left arm tucked awkwardly at his chest, holding his injured ribs. Ryan bit his lip. The tunnels must have crossed somewhere.

"Ryan!" Nicole was pointing.

"I know, I know." He swept his eyes desperately up and down the tunnel. If they went through the hatch now, the men would be right behind them. The pressure gauge! He had to chance it. "Go to the hatch," he said.

"What are you—"

"Just do it," he shouted. "I don't know where the steam will go." He turned and sprinted toward the gauge, stopping an arm's length away. The enormous heat radiating off the exposed metal deepened his concern about what would happen when he smashed the gauge, but what else could he do? The man was moving rapidly toward him, and fishing for something in his windbreaker.

Ryan tried to calm himself as he lifted the metal bar over his shoulder. He didn't want the steam to explode in his face, but he didn't want to miss either. He swung the bar down hard onto the exposed tip, and at the same time jumped backward to avoid the blast of steam.

A loud clang filled the tunnel, but nothing happened. He had struck it soundly, but it didn't even dent. The supposedly fragile metal of the steam gauge was tougher than he thought. He crashed down on it again, this time using his full weight, but still it remained intact.

The sound of feet.

Ryan jerked his head up.

The tall man was closing fast, and in his right hand he carried a large gun. Behind him, another figure appeared. Dead-Eyes.

Fear swept through Ryan's body, a surge of energy that sent him racing down the tunnel toward the walkway that led to the hatch. His heart was thumping so hard he could hear it pounding in his ears. He had to get through that emergency door, reach the safety of people—

Screams.

Ryan looked back. The tall man had dropped to the floor, his hands covering his face. Steam was spewing from the pressure gauge, a narrow spray, almost invisible, as it spewed super-heated water vapor into the air. The man seemed disoriented. He tried to stand but burned himself again, this time on the back. He fell to his knees, twisting like a lobster in boiling water, and shrieking his lungs out. Then, abruptly, he fell silent, as if realizing that the whole pressure gauge could blow. He started to crawl away, feeling with his hands like a blind man, but leaving his gun behind on the walkway.

Ryan stared at the gun. If only he could get his hands on it. He turned, part of him shocked at what he was doing, and dashed back toward the discarded weapon, toward the man with the dead eyes who was pounding toward him. Ten feet from the fractured gauge Ryan could feel the heat, even from so small a stream entering the air. He shifted his eyes to the running man. Only he was no longer running. He had stopped and braced his arm against a wrapped steam pipe.

Crack! Crack!

The second crack spun Ryan around and flung him flat onto the floor, as if someone had hooked him by the jacket. He felt a burning in his armpit and wondered if he had caught himself on a metal bracket or some other junk littering the tunnel. The whole thing was senseless, but he continued thinking about it. Then, slowly, it occurred to him he had been shot. His body seemed rooted to the floor, refusing to move. All he could do was stare up at the steel girders supporting the tunnel. There were two large girders and three small, he noticed, and the larger ones had a decorative edging. Someone, a long time ago, had thought the tunnels deserved adornment. Another useless thought. Was he in shock?

He focused his mind and tried to sit up, but couldn't. Heat radiated across his chest. Not pain. Just heat in his shoulder and chest. He took a full breath. His lungs seemed clear and relief swept over him. No bullet in the chest. He would be okay. Then he remembered the man running toward him, and the gun on the walkway.

The gun!

He needed that weapon.

He struggled to a sitting position, in time to see the man scoop up the gun and shove it into his belt. A petrifying fear engulfed Ryan. He had no weapon, no place to run, and no hope. He was about to die.

The man eyed Ryan coolly and then surveyed the tunnel, as if making certain there were no witnesses. He moved toward his prey in an unhurried way, pausing only to check on his partner. As he passed the spraying steam, he glanced at it briefly, but mostly he kept his eyes on Ryan.

Five feet out he stopped.

Ryan squinted at the pistol in his hand. Futile thoughts of grabbing for the weapon or of throwing dust in the man's eyes flitted through his mind, but in the end, all he did was sit on the walkway and wait to die. He knew he should say something, but his tongue was frozen as he stared into the face of his killer.

The man glanced up and down the tunnel again, then locked his lifeless eyes onto Ryan's.

Ryan tried to swallow.

The man put in a new magazine.

"Why?" Ryan managed.

"You're screwing the mission, kid."

"I don't know about any mission."

"I believe you." He raised his pistol.

Ryan turned his head and squeezed his eyes shut.

"*Stop!*"

The voice was earsplitting.

Ryan jerked his eyes open.

"What are you doing?" Nicole hollered. The sound of her voice echoed down the dimly lit tunnel.

"No, no!" Ryan wailed. He knew the man with the pistol had no compassion. He would put bullets in both their heads.

"Do you know who I am?" she yelled as she strode toward the man. "I'm Nicole Van Buren! And I called the police a half hour ago. They'll be here any minute." She was waving her phone dramatically over her head.

Ryan groaned. She had no idea ... the killer didn't care who she was. "Leave her," he said. "She's a silly—"

He never finished his sentence. The man was already moving briskly away. He pulled his fallen partner to his feet, grasping the man's windbreaker as they hobbled down one of the intersecting corridors.

Nicole ran up to him and thrust her face into his. "You okay?" she asked.

Ryan got to his feet awkwardly and said, "Are you out of your mind?"

She stared at him.

"What the hell did you think you were doing?"

"Saving you," she said.

"Saving me? Are you completely stupid? He could have killed you."

"Well, he didn't, did he?"

"You were lucky."

"Lucky? I told him I called the police."

"Did you call them?"

"No, of course not. There's no reception down here."

"See, this is what I'm saying. You think everything is a game—"

"Why are you so upset? I saved your life."

Ryan blinked his eyes. The realization of what had just happened was sinking into his brain. He twisted his upper body slightly. It felt odd, and he slipped his hand into his jacket. When he pulled it out it was soaked with blood.

"Ryan! What—?"

"I don't know. I feel all right, I think."

"Let me see," she said, opening his jacket and lifting his shirt.

"Well?" he asked.

"Oh my God, you're shot."

"I kind of figured that. It doesn't hurt too bad."

"It hit under your arm," she said as she studied it. "So much blood it's hard to tell, but it didn't go into your chest, I think." She blew out in relief. "I think it just went through the skin and fat. You're lucky. An inch or two over ...."

Ryan forced a smile. "What fat?"

She rolled her eyes and closed his jacket wordlessly.

Ryan struggled to his feet and they stared at one another for a moment. He reached for her and she stepped into his arms. "Thank you," he said. "I didn't mean to sound ungrateful."

"I know," she said, burrowing her face into his neck. "It made me furious to see that man pointing a gun at you."

He didn't say anything, just held her close and drank in the sensation of being alive. Over her shoulder he stared mindlessly at the narrow slip of hot vapor shooting into the air. The quiet hiss of the steam had grown louder and made him feel happy. It reminded him of his eighth birthday when his mother had hired a clown to fill balloons with helium.

The next second, panic seized him.

"We've got to move!" he said, grabbing Nicole violently by the arm.

Her eyes darted around as if she were searching for the men.

"The steam! The steam!" Ryan shouted. "It's gonna blow."

They spun around and charged down the tunnel toward the walkway that led to the escape hatch.

"The emergency door works," Nicole said between breaths. "I've already opened it."

When Ryan rounded the cement walls leading to the hatch, he felt better. At least they were no longer talking beside a broken steam valve. He watched Nicole climb through the door, and then looked back. The amount of vapor in the air seemed the same as before and he wondered if his imagination had been playing tricks. Maybe the fissure in the steam valve hadn't expanded at all.

Whoosh!

The sound shook the tunnel, and in seconds Ryan felt the first wave of heat, as if someone had opened the gate to a furnace. He bolted toward the escape door. Other waves were coming, he knew. Four hundred degree waves of steam, hot enough to cook your flesh. Already, the tunnel had darkened and smelled like sodden rags.

He jumped through the hatch and slammed it shut. His face was dripping with sweat—from tension, not the heat. He mopped his face and stared at Nicole, who had her head propped back against the wall.

"Too close," she said.

He nodded his agreement.

"Where are we?" she asked, glancing around the dimly lit room.

"No idea. But we're not in the tunnels, and that can only be good."

29

"Thank you for coming," the general said. "The hour is late."

Bruce Thomkins accepted a scotch and water, and snatched a handful of pretzels from a bowl on the coffee table. "Of course, sir. You know I would always come regardless of the time."

The general nodded. "There are few people I can count on," he replied with the ghost of a smile. "But you are definitely one of them."

"Thank you."

"Washington must be buzzing."

"Like nothing I've seen in my lifetime."

"We've got more than the ship, I hear. A couple of towns—in Nevada and up there in Canada."

The Secretary frowned. "Your sources are better than mine," he said. "I received word less than twenty minutes ago about Nevada, but there's been nothing on Canada. If another town's been hit with this thing, who knows where it's going to stop?"

"When will the Cabinet meet?"

"As we speak," he said, "but the full Cabinet meets the day after tomorrow."

"Where? In the Cabinet Room?"

"No, the Situation Room."

"I see. The President will include congressional leadership—the speaker and the president pro tem?"

"They'll all be there, yes, and several others. It'll be a little tight, but the President wants a full meeting. This is a national crisis. We'd meet tomorrow but we lack concrete information. Right now, nobody knows much of anything. It doesn't look like terrorism, but ...." He shrugged. "Catastrophic cellular failure—The Nevada Syndrome—that's what they're calling it, and it wipes people out in minutes. Turns them into black jelly."

"They're worried about panic?"

"Terrified would be the word. Even if rumor of this gets out, there'll be blood in the streets—the nation will implode with fear. No one at work, trade stops, infrastructure breaks down. Hoarding. Riots. Anarchy. Who knows the ramifications? The National Guard, of course, is being readied, but I've heard they're activating contingency plans for the other armed forces."

"On US soil? Interesting. Federal forces haven't been used as domestic police since the Civil War."

"The *Posse Comitatus* Act of 1878."

"Right."

"Well, at this point it's just discussion."

"Like after 9/11." The general chewed slowly on a pretzel, then said, "It's a wise precaution, especially since they have no idea of the extent of this thing, or the source."

The Secretary grunted his agreement, drained his glass and poured himself another. The general studied his old friend for a moment, then swallowed some Scotch. He hadn't yet decided on the right approach for his next subject, the real reason for meeting so late into the night. Bruce Thomkins might have been his adjutant once and accustomed to following his orders, but he was still a man of principle who would not blindly follow a course of action he deemed immoral. He needed to be convinced that the general's way was best for the country.

The general broke the silence. "Bruce, does your love for history go beyond American history? What do you know about Julius Caesar and the Rubicon?"

The Secretary pursed his lips, surprised by the question. "You're the historian, but as I remember, Caesar crossed the Rubicon River, the ancient boundary between Gallia and Italy, with a full legion."

"Yes, no Roman general was allowed to pass over it with a standing army. To do so was treason, punished by death."

"But Caesar crossed nonetheless," the Secretary said.

"He did. 'Let us go where the omens of the gods summon us,' Caesar is reported to have said."

"Brave words."

"But not foolhardy words." The general swirled his Scotch and continued, "Caesar had battle-tested veterans. No army in Italy could stand before his men, and Caesar knew it. It was his destiny to overthrow the corrupt Roman Republic."

"Destiny can be illusive," the Secretary suggested.

"Destiny," countered the general, "is what we make it."

The Secretary threw back his Scotch and filled the glass again, mostly with whiskey.

"We're facing our own Rubicon here," the general said, "and I need to know whether you're on board."

"You know you can count on me," the Secretary said, frowning for emphasis. "Whatever I can do, I will."

"Don't be so quick to answer," the general warned, "and go easy on the Scotch. I need your mind clear."

The Secretary pulled his hand away from his drink. "What exactly are we talking about?"

"We are talking about the Rubicon, Bruce, and how one man's decisions changed the world for five hundred years—a thousand, if you count the eastern half of the Roman world. That's what Caesar did at the

Rubicon. His decision to act made possible the magnificent Roman Empire, a light so brilliant it still shines today in all forms of government." He raised a finger, "But when the moment came, Caesar had to act."

"His decision created his destiny."

"Exactly so. And it also ended the Roman Republic."

The Secretary shifted in his chair. "You're saying that Caesar ended democracy."

"The rule of a corrupt mob, yes."

"A republic ended, an empire begun."

The general lifted his hand in agreement. "It was a huge break from the past. Before Caesar crossed the Rubicon nobody in Rome could imagine their country being run by an emperor—a dictator, if you will— but once the emperors began, no one could imagine anything else."

The Secretary took a long, slow breath. "Are you going where I think you're going?"

"I don't know what you're thinking, Bruce, but we definitely have our feet in the Rubicon."

"And our decision will change the face of American politics?"

"It will alter everything."

The Secretary traced his finger around the rim of his glass.

"Bruce, on reflection, I think some of that Scotch would do you good," the general said, his eyes glinting.

The Secretary smiled. "Are you confident my mind will remain clear?" he asked, taking a long sip.

"This subject has a way of focusing one's mind," the general replied quietly.

"It does indeed."

"We've been friends for many years," the general continued after a brief pause. "Slogged through some wicked swamps, you and I. But I want you to set that aside. Think only about the country. Nothing else. What's best for the people of this great land, that's your only concern."

"It's always foremost in my mind."

"I know that's true. But I also know," he paused to make his point, "that the decision we make here tonight will determine whether millions of Americans live or die."

The Secretary leaned back in his chair and waited.

"No society lasts forever," the general said, "but people always think they have more time than they do."

"Until the end is staring them in the face."

"Yes, and even then they can't believe what's happened. They cast their eyes around in denial, looking for miracles to save them, but none comes. And it happens over and over again. We look back in history and see citizens of once powerful nations lying dead in their streets, or on their knees begging mercy from people who will grant them nothing but a quick exit. History's patterns never change. The pictures are always the same, and our fate won't be any different."

The Secretary tilted his head in disagreement. "I would guess most Americans think the 'when' is a long way off, certainly beyond their lifetimes or their children's."

"True," the general replied. "Undoubtedly, they think we somehow deserve what we have—food, homes, freedom. But we both know that 'deserve' is a wretched stepchild. We have these things because we labored for them, and we can protect them. Otherwise, someone would take them away before the downing of the sun."

"Look at Hitler in the last century."

"A good example. His plan for the British was to cart the men off to the continent as slaves, and to use their women as breeders for the Aryan race."

"But American power protected the remnants of the British Empire," the Secretary said, nodding.

"Yes, otherwise the British would have suffered the same fate as many fallen nations before them." The general leaned forward intently. "Because Britain survived, the history of the world looks stable. But I ask you, who will protect America if its power is suddenly ripped away? Russia? China? Our European friends?"

"That's a non-question for most people because America will not lose its power," the Secretary said, cocking one eyebrow.

"Ah, yes, we cannot lose our power. That's what keeps us going to baseball games. Our position is secure."

"You can see why people think that way. Three generations have passed since we've fought a war for survival. Our citizens see all these police activities and forget what real war can be like."

"Yes. Peace on our own soil has lulled us to sleep."

"Are you suggesting that the unthinkable is possible?"

"Total destruction of our society? Not just possible, Bruce. I'm saying it's inevitable and likely soon. This nation is in grave peril." The general sat back again in his chair, but his face was taut.

"Our current situation is certainly precarious," the Secretary acknowledged, "but I don't expect many would believe our nation is on the verge of collapse."

"Think of it this way. Our society was constructed in a simpler age when the enemy was visible. Then we had to worry about approaching armies. Now we have terrorists living among us, hiding in the tall grass, and they're a determined bunch of bastards. They desperately want to kill every last one of us infidels, even if they die in the process. This would be of little concern, except for our own genius. We have given our enemies the tools to eliminate us. Nothing new, I grant you. Great societies are usually destroyed by the weapons they create. But ours has managed to miniaturize its weapons. Now one man can kill an enormous number of people by spreading a few chemicals, or by infecting himself with smallpox, or detonating a nuke. Add to that the incredibly complex and interdependent society we've built, and we are teetering at the edge of a chasm with no bottom. A few determined people can bring about the collapse of our entire society."

"9/11 redundancies should help."

"Not for what I'm talking about. Ten dirty bombs in ten major cities would probably destroy our economy, and us as a nation. Or one high altitude EMP. People will be starving in the streets. The truth is, we are living in a house of cards and Americans don't realize it."

"So you think sooner or later some crazy terrorist group will take down this country."

"Not later," the general said. "We're discovering new jihadist movements almost every month. And some of them have great aspirations. Intelligence thinks that this new group—*Ikhwaan al-Amin*, The Brotherhood of the Faithful—has finally gained possession of several fission weapons."

The Secretary's face registered shock. "I hadn't heard that," he said. "Do you think it's true?"

"Don't know. It's all very hush-hush. But the Russians believe it."

Well ..." the Secretary said, exhaling slowly.

The general leaned forward and said, "The Middle East has two things that frighten me. Boatloads of money—which we finance—and fanatics that want to kill us. Now that Iran's gone nuclear, we don't know where the game's going. And I've said it before, left alone, a determined enemy always acquires the weapons it needs to carry out its plans. There's only one way to survive such fierce determination: you destroy that enemy."

"We're trying to do that," the Secretary said. "We've used every tool we can, political, economic, diplomatic—even war. Other countries find it to their advantage to thwart our efforts. In all candor, General, I don't see how we can do more. We can't just nuke the whole Middle East."

"No, we can't. But we can destroy them nonetheless."

The Secretary frowned, not understanding.

"Every millennium or so," the general said in a measured tone, "a weapon comes along, so powerful that whoever commands it can determine the course of history for hundreds of years. In the last century it was the atomic bomb, but we chose to do nothing with it. We could have subjugated the world and denied the technology to everyone. But we sat on our hands and let our enemies take control of our weapon. Many think we made the right decision, and maybe we did. But the Cuban missile crisis and a half dozen other events could have been catastrophic, and a large segment of our population would have died, and those that did survive would have been shivering in a nuclear winter, chewing on rats' hides like our Stone Age ancestors, and asking why the hell we didn't act when we could. Bottom line: we were just plain lucky."

"Can't argue with that," the Secretary nodded.

"Think of it, Bruce, the Assyrians, the Greeks, the Romans—they all ruled the world in their turn, for good or ill, because they had the weapons to do it. We too have powerful weapons, but we can't use them."

"Because they might devastate the planet or create a major war."

"That's the fear," the general said. "But suppose we had another weapon, one so powerful that it could eliminate our enemies in a single day, and at the same time make it seem like an accident of nature. Should we use it?"

The Secretary looked intrigued. "Are we talking about what's devastating these towns?" he asked.

"We are old friends talking hypothetically."

"Well," the Secretary replied slowly, "if there's an enemy that intends to kill our citizens, and if that enemy has a high likelihood of doing so, then our moral duty would be to kill them first ... with our special weapon," he added with a wry smile. "But, as you say, this is all hypothetical because we don't have such a weapon, and even if we did, the decision to use it would not be ours. We don't have the power."

"Suppose we did have the power."

The Secretary reached for his drink and took another long, slow sip. "I've never known you to blather on in hypotheticals," he said. "What are you proposing?"

The general locked his eyes on the Secretary.

"Sir?"

"I'm proposing to make you the President of the United States," the general said flatly.

The Secretary cleared his throat. "Are you serious? The President's only a year into his first term."

"Quite serious. This is our Rubicon. Every few hundred years someone like you or me stands before the river, and decides which way history should flow."

The Secretary ran his tongue over his teeth. "You do know what's killing these people, don't you?"

"I do. It's the creation of a madman, but it won't stay in his hands for long. As it turns out, he's compromised everyone—you, me, your cousin's brother, even the President and the entire Cabinet. Release a drop of trigger material into the air, and everyone exposed experiences Catastrophic Cellular Failure. As you said, CCF turns them into black jelly. Then, after a half hour or so, the trigger substance degrades into harmless chemicals in the environment, untraceable."

The Secretary rubbed his face. "Is there an antidote?" he asked.

"Thus far, no."

"You're not proposing ...." He swallowed. "Judas Priest, General. You're not suggesting ...."

The general nodded.

The Secretary's eyes widened. "You want me to release this stuff at the Cabinet meeting?"

"You are the Secretary of Agriculture, Bruce, ninth in the presidential line of succession. The designated survivor for this meeting, I'm told, will be ...." He paused and looked at his friend.

"Diane K. Hanson," Bruce said, slowly, understanding. "She's Secretary of Education. Below me in line of succession."

The general gestured toward the Secretary's briefing notebook. "The lab boys will seal a drop inside the front cover, and a slow-acting acid inside the back. Fold over the inside pages and press the two covers together. Two minutes later the acid will expose the trigger. That's all there is to it."

"Then what?"

"Cabinet secretaries have portable biohazard suits, right?"

"Yes. In the last few days we've been carrying them in our briefcases."

"So you take your briefcase to the bathroom near the ground floor elevator, go into a stall, and put on your suit. Stay there until we come for you."

"But this thing ...."

The general eyed the Secretary. "Go on."

The Secretary took a breath to compose himself. "This thing spreads like wildfire."

"That's what makes it safe," the general said calmly. "It kills fast, and disappears fast, leaving no trace. Even the problem in Nevada burned itself out."

The Secretary nodded blankly.

"By the end of the day a small number of people in the White House will be dead, and you will be the President of the United States. The Chief Justice will administer to you the oath of office, and you will select me as your Vice President because I've had experience in these situations. Then, and only then, can we begin to get a handle on this thing."

"And the other components?"

"We will have to release the trigger in a few strategic US towns," the general said, "unfortunate, but necessary."

The Secretary sighed. "I presume you mean very small towns."

"Very small towns. We've targeted eight of them, but we've also selected five sporting events—containable venues, I assure you—in large cities, to create panic. We can stop whenever we reach the crisis state. When that happens, you will then have no choice but to declare a public emergency, and station regular army troops in US cities."

"I can see the protests now."

"Protests, yes, there'll be some—news outlets complaining, and legal briefs flying everywhere to declare your actions unconstitutional. There will be the inevitable debate on the *Posse Comitatus* Act, cries that the army cannot act as a police force within the borders of the United States. But we'll be ready for them."

"Desperate times require desperate measures."

"Something like that. But fear is an amazing thing, Bruce. People will, as you said, immediately start hoarding, mobs will prowl the major cities, looters will smash out store windows, and there'll be fires, rapes, murders on an unprecedented scale. The police will be overwhelmed, totally unequipped to handle the chaos."

"So the army will have to step in."

"And everyone will understand that. Welcome it, even. What the hell is the *Posse Comitatus* Act? they'll say. Bottom line? People want order, and they don't want to die. They would rather give up a few freedoms, than have chaos in their streets."

"True," the Secretary conceded grimly.

"It will happen fast. Within a few days, we'll be forced to declare martial law and take control of the streets, the distribution systems, and quietly the media. Once in control of the media, we'll flood the airwaves with rumors of new outbreaks, heartbreaking stories of the victims, and footage of the carnage left behind. This will keep the nation at a fever pitch, and allow us to act freely. After that we can enact temporary laws giving us sweeping powers during this state of emergency."

"Sweeping powers? Congress will never pass—"

"They will if the news has bags of black jelly—that used to be people—being thrown into dump trucks."

"Congress will still shout bloody murder!"

"Some, yes. But politicians possess no skill so finely tuned as saving their own necks. The few pontificators in the Senate and House will have no platform during this emergency because we will control the message."

"Politicians have a way of—"

"They do," the general interrupted. "But, I repeat, we will control the message." He leaned forward. "That's why it's important, though repugnant in the extreme, to sacrifice a small number of fellow Americans. It will create the fear we need to save our nation. We'll also have outbreaks pop up elsewhere in isolated parts of the world to keep people's attention on what the epidemic is doing, where it's headed, and not on a handful of self-serving politicians whining about the loss of freedoms. Everyone will be gripped by the drama unfolding nightly on the news. They will agree to almost anything because they will want to survive. All we need to do is keep the pot boiling and the nation fearful until we secure the controls of government."

The Secretary furrowed his brow. "But even then, with new laws enacted, I don't see Americans accepting a President with dictatorial powers."

"Not today, not in our present world. But the world is about to change. And so will the threshold for accepting a new order."

"It may but—"

"Don't misunderstand me, Bruce. I'm not proposing we overthrow our democratic form of government. No, not that. Never! I am sworn to protect and defend the Constitution of these United States. And I'll do that to my dying breath. But I don't see how we can defend ourselves under the current structures of government. We've grown too weak. Our enemies are determined to kill us, so much so that I believe in the not too distant future millions of Americans will suffer horrific deaths. Millions."

"So your ultimate goal is—"

"To take control of government. We suspend the Constitution three to five years, move against our enemies, and then, like George Washington, we return government to its rightful owners, the people."

The Secretary stared off into space. "Sainted Mary preserve us," he said quietly. He remained silent for long seconds as he fingered his glass. Then, making eye contact with the general, he said, "I now have greater respect for Julius Caesar."

"Indeed."

He nodded slowly. "I don't say you're wrong. And so then? We purge our enemies overseas by what, this accident of nature?"

"Exactly. This thing will appear to eliminate our enemies by fate. We will release the trigger judiciously, but it will seem to kill randomly across the world—even here in the States—like the Black Death during medieval times, hitting one area, and then another, and finally it will settle into extremist territories, eradicating everyone, including, of course, these extremists. Innocents will die, but that's the nature of war."

"Are you certain you can control this thing without an antidote?"

"I am. We won't risk sending trigger vials the way Krakauer did. Too unpredictable. Our people will be given the trigger once they arrive at their designated countries; it'll be hidden in, say, the plastic ends of shoelaces, or break away buttons. They transport the trigger to a designated area, crack the plastic and everyone dies, including the courier, who thinks he has immunity. So no witnesses."

"Isn't there a risk that some courier could crack open the shoelace en route to his destination, spreading Armageddon?"

"The couriers receive the trigger in the target country. They are simply moving to denser population centers."

"What if a courier gets cold feet and turns himself in to

authorities?"

"We always send a watcher to prevent that. The second doesn't know the mission of the first, just that he stays on plan."

The Secretary nodded. "And in the US, what happens here?"

"As I said, we have selected a number of target areas for the first few days."

"You'll also target other countries."

"Yes, containable areas in a dozen other countries, mostly western, to give the appearance of randomness, and then ...." He paused, narrowing his eyes. "Then we hit them. We loose hell on these radicalized regions in North Africa, the Middle East, Malaysia, Pakistan ... and North Korea as well for good measure."

"But it could spread beyond—"

"Believe me, once the dying starts, everything will slam shut. China, Russia, India, European and southern African countries will close their borders in an eye blink, as will we in the Americas. In a week, two at the most, the process will exhaust itself and the enemy will be neutralized. Large populations in neighboring regions will survive, of course, especially in southern Russia, India, and Turkey—they are not our enemies—but most of these extremists will no longer pose a threat to us."

"What then? Quarantine these zones? How long will that take?"

"Not long. A month should do it," the general said, "but practically I expect the quarantine will extend upwards of two years, which will cause some temporary economic disruption." He sipped his drink. "Unaffected countries will proceed with caution because they will have no way of determining what devastated the dead zone. We, of course, will know and will send in units to continue the flow of oil and other raw materials, and to secure weapons, like Pakistan's nukes."

"Whew!" the Secretary murmured as he played with the remaining Scotch in his glass. "A lot to take in."

"It is."

"Who's running the operation?"

"Donovan."

"I see." The Secretary dipped his head in concern. "Colonel Donovan's a bare-knuckled soldier and an incredible logistics officer, but I'm surprised he would sign on to the wholesale removal of an enemy."

"He knows only segments of the mission. When it becomes necessary, I'll bring him more into the loop."

"I'd be careful there, General."

"Duly noted. Now, we need to make a decision."

"More to the point, *I* need to make a decision."

"You do."

Bruce Thomkins drummed on the side of his chair, his body shifting first to one side, and then to the other, as he tried unsuccessfully to find a comfortable sitting position. He downed a fistful of pretzels and swallowed more whiskey. "Well," he said finally, expelling a long, slow breath, "we've got enemies beating at the gates. What choice do we have but to eliminate them?"

We could wait and hope for the best," the general said. "Maybe we'll last another thousand years."

"But that's not what history teaches us, is it?"

The general shook his head.

"They won't stop," the Secretary said, almost to himself. "They won't stop until they find a way to destroy us. And now that this new weapon is on the field, how long before someone else uses it?"

The general waited.

For a long time Secretary Bruce Thomkins stared at the black walnut floorboards. Then slowly, ever so slowly, he raised his head and said, "We're standing at the Rubicon, and we need—I need—to make a decision." He set his drink on the table. "What we learned in the military is still true. When you can't make peace with an enemy, you destroy him. We have a weapon that will protect our people, and I think we should use it."

"Are you certain?" The Secretary's old friend gazed at him, unblinking.

"I am."

The general rose. "Then, let us go where the omens of the gods summon us."

30

Le Beau brushed his teeth and readied himself for bed, his mind swirling with thoughts of retirement in Arizona, of Helena, and of Captain Barton's warnings. The man was an ass, sure, but he was probably right. Big corporations ran the world and as long as the product sold and the money flowed, no one cared what they did. Le Beau had been around long enough to know how the world worked. Why should he get involved in something he didn't even understand? The kids would be okay. They didn't need him trotting around like the Lone Ranger trying to save the day. Besides, the Van Buren girl had a rich daddy, probably with lots of bodyguards. No doubt he could handle things just fine without Elijah Le Beau's input.

Events had simply gotten out of hand. There was such a thing as over-policing a situation, and that's what he had done. He was angry about Romano's death and he had allowed that rage to turn him into a zealot. The truth was—and he might as well face it—he was obsessed with the Westover case. When in his sixteen years as a police officer had he ever met secretly with students? Or lied his way into the records office? Or pitted himself against his superiors? For that matter, when had he ever put his job ahead of Helena? Because that's what he was doing.

He stuck his head into the bedroom but Helena had already fallen asleep. The new medicines from Proskin had dramatically increased her energy, but she still felt exhausted at the end of the day. He walked over to the bed and gazed down at her, so small and vulnerable she looked. Did he really want to risk Helena's health in a battle he was ill prepared to fight? Elijah tucked the covers around her shoulders and she mumbled her thanks. His wife trusted him, and if ever she needed him to exercise wisdom, it was now. She could have married anyone—every guy on the campus had been after her—but she chose someone who ended up a cop. And never once did she complain about her outdated clothes, or their rusted Ford Taurus, or their less than modern house. All she wanted was a little retirement place in Arizona. Was that too much to ask of a husband?

He left the room determined to swallow his pride and heed the captain's advice. No more playing detective; he would keep his nose out of things. Descending the stairs to switch off the kitchen lights, he instead found himself opening cupboards and checking possibilities in the fridge. *It's not hunger, it's appetite*, he heard the cheery woman at Weight Watchers say. *Wait twenty minutes and the appetite will go.* He banged off the kitchen light with a resolute swipe of his hand and hustled himself into the den. A diversion was what he needed, something pointless to anesthetize his mind before sleep. Grabbing the remote, he flipped on the television.

A man named Elmore Simpkins was staring wide-eyed into the camera, trying to explain why his company had lost communication with one of its ships. Le Beau settled into his La-Z-Boy as the man continually evaded the reporter's questions, obviously trying to put the best face on a disastrous situation. The clips of Mr. Simpkins's interview were interspersed with commentary by experts who had no first-hand knowledge of the situation, but plenty of opinions. They speculated about terrorists, gas leaks, and pirates on the high seas, but with fourteen hundred passengers presumed dead, and the CDC crawling up and down the ship wearing biohazard suits, they all agreed, that the CDC was likely dealing with a pathogen.

Le Beau yawned, already growing tired. Then one of the scientists made a statement that piqued his interest. The layperson, he said, had no idea of the proliferation of unregulated genetics labs across the world. With proper training, a bio-terrorist could easily engineer something like smallpox, or avian flu that could spread very quickly. He admitted, however, that nothing biological could kill so many people, so quickly, and that a chemical weapon was a possibility.

The news broadcast switched abruptly to an unrelated story and Le Beau turned off the television, feeling mildly uncomfortable. Professor Krakauer, of course, had nothing to do with the cruise liner; but as he climbed the stairs, a cold draft followed him, prickling his skin.

31 〰〰〰〰〰〰〰〰〰〰〰〰〰〰〰

Ryan rested his head against the storage room wall, his eyes beginning to adjust to the darkness. Across from him on the dirty floor sat Nicole, legs sprawled in front of her, eyes glazed with exhaustion. Neither said a word.

At length, Nicole motioned to a sign lit by a small yellow light: *Silent Alarm Fire Door.* "Does that work?" she asked.

"Probably not," Ryan said, "but for sure the sensors on the steam valves work. Lots of people will be here soon, Power Plant workers, firefighters, police."

"Police?" Her eyes opened wide.

"I don't care," he said. "This thing's getting too dangerous."

"But even Le Beau said to stay away from the police."

"I know but—"

"They could take us away, shoot us for all we know."

Ryan glanced at her, his eyes acknowledging her point. "Maybe the FBI ...."

"Exactly," she said, scrambling to her feet. "We'll call my father. He's got lots of connections in the FBI."

"Let's call Le Beau too." He felt safer with the officer involved.

A door opened at the top of the stairs, the light creating shadows on the wall.

Nicole's eyes met Ryan's.

The door closed, the shadows suddenly disappearing. Then came footsteps, descending, and a beam of light dancing along the stairs.

Nicole raised a finger to her lips. "A night watchman," she whispered. "We can't let him slow us down."

Ryan nodded and moved to the opposite side of the door from Nicole. They waited as the footfalls grew closer, Ryan hoping the watchman would give a quick look in the darkened basement and return to his desk. He seemed nervous, his flashlight jerking everywhere, as if night duty spooked him.

He stopped at the bottom of the stairs, his feet shuffling first in one direction, and then the other, the light beam careening along the corridor walls to no purpose. It was clear the man couldn't decide which way to go. He poked his light into the storage room, and then returned to the hall. In those brief seconds, Ryan got a look at him—a pudgy man, moustache, mid-forties, wearing too much cologne and an undersized rent-a-cop hat, certainly not a threat, but somebody they would have to outwait. And already the delay was worrying. Nicole was right: there was no telling who might show up. The watchman was now plodding toward the end of the corridor, his big flat feet flapping along the tiled floors until eventually they slowed, then stopped. Ryan listened, hoping the man would disappear up the stairs, but no luck. He heard the boots shuffling again as he turned, then flapping the tiles once more as he moved with agonizing slowness to the central area.

Ryan closed his eyes in frustration as more precious minutes flitted by. Finally, after several movements one way, and then the other, the watchman started up the stairs, his light bobbing up and down.

Ryan sighed. He couldn't see Nicole's face in the shadows, but he could feel her relief.

Suddenly, the flashlight swung around and pointed back into the storage room, almost, it seemed, on a whim. As it hit the far end of the metal escape hatch, the reflected light looked like bursts of fragmented sun.

The watchman once again lumbered toward them, his light growing larger on the hatch.

Anger welled up in Ryan. This guy had no idea what he was doing, yet now he was back. And for what? To inspect the shiny door? He could hear the boots tramping closer, and knew that if the man entered the room, it was over.

The watchman stopped two feet from the entrance.

Ryan pressed against the wall.

The man shuffled forward and Ryan's body tensed.

With his flashlight filling the room, the watchman stepped inside, his head turning slowly, until abruptly he stiffened. He had spotted Ryan against the wall.

Ryan darted forward, grabbing the startled man by the collar, and yanking him off balance. The flashlight briefly lit the man's face like some campfire ghost story, two eyes glistening with fear, a mouth open as if about to scream. Then something crashed down onto his head, and he crumpled into Ryan's arms with a groan, his flashlight bouncing on the floor and rolling under a collection of chairs.

"I got him!" Nicole said.

"You sure did." Ryan squinted. The light had taken away his night vision.

She dropped a heavy metal object onto the floor.

He looked at her. "What did you hit him with?"

"A lamp."

"A lamp? One of those brass lamps in the corner?"

She didn't reply.

"Are you insane?" He shifted his eyes to the man heaped at his feet.

"Let's go," she said. "We've got to get out of here."

"No! Not until I look at him."

Ryan retrieved the flashlight and inspected the watchman's head. His hair was matted with blood. "We can't leave him like this," he said. "He could die."

She bent down and checked him over as Ryan held the light. "It's a minor cut," she said. "The scalp has a rich blood supply. Looks bad but it's not."

"We can't just leave him."

"The emergency people will find him. We've got to go!"

"Where's his radio?" Ryan asked, sweeping the light along the edges of the room. "We can call somebody when we're out of the building."

"Over there, I think."

He followed her finger toward the side of the room.

"*Arrghh!*" Suddenly, the man bolted upwards, fists swinging. Nicole threw her hands out, but they provided no protection. He punched her directly in the chest and face several times. She flopped backwards onto the floor, groaning.

Ryan took three quick steps back to the man, but it was too late. He had already jumped on top of Nicole and had his thick arms wrapped around her body in some kind of bear hug. Ryan tried to pull him off but he had hold of her like a wrestler. "Get your hands off her!" Ryan yelled, and bashed the flashlight across the already bloodied head. The bulb exploded with a pop and the cylinder split in his hand, scattering the batteries on the floor, but the man released Nicole. He rolled off and flattened onto the floor, howling and grasping his head with both hands. Ryan threw the broken flashlight away and dropped down on his good knee in front of Nicole.

"Are you all right?" he asked.

She nodded, but even in the dim light, she looked dazed.

Ryan glared at the man who was now sitting on the floor, his hands covering his head. He had seen the blood and was howling louder.

"Quiet!" Ryan said.

The howling continued.

"You punched a woman, you moron," Ryan said. "Shut up!"

The volume increased.

Ryan smacked the watchman's nose with the back of his knuckles, and the room grew silent.

"That's better," Ryan said darkly, then added, "the scalp bleeds a lot. You'll be fine."

Nicole pushed herself off the floor shakily. "We need to go," she managed. Ryan quickly bound the watchman with computer wires, stuffed his mouth with the soft part of his too small hat, and helped Nicole up the stairs.

* * *

After Basil dropped off Amy Tamerlane, he swung by Nicole's dorm to see how she was doing. He parked his car behind the Bursar's office, out of the way where Nicole wouldn't notice it. Then he ambled over to her college, followed some students through the gates, and waited in the shadows for her return. It was a familiar routine: Basil had been doing it for weeks.

He swept his eyes over the solitary light glowing in her apartment, a sure sign she wasn't home. She always left a light on when she was away, probably to discourage thieves. Two or more lights meant she was inside, and no lights meant she was in bed asleep. But the single light told him she was still out.

For the next several hours Basil hunched in the deeper shadows and waited. He thought about Nicole's characterization of him as a stalker. That of course was absurd. He was the furthest thing from a stalker. He checked on her from time to time, sure, but there was nothing wrong with that. Nicole was his girl, and had been for a while. Who wouldn't worry when a girlfriend became emotional or upset? She was simply having a few bad weeks, confused about what she wanted out of life. Not uncommon. He had seen it before.

But he wasn't a stalker.

He simply cared about Nicole and had a natural curiosity about what she was doing. Nothing wrong with that.

A voice made him turn his head, almost a whisper it was, as if the woman were trying to enter the college undetected. Basil squinted, knowing it was Nicole, and knowing she was ashamed to be bringing someone else back to her room. He watched them move slowly along the edges of the quad until they came to the oak door that led to the stairs. They paused, and then kissed. "Oh, Nicole, Nicole," Basil murmured, "how could you let someone kiss you?" He ground his teeth, knowing it was not just "someone" kissing his precious Nicole. It was Ryan! It was that ridiculous, smirking drunk who was now pushing into her, distracting her with one hand as the other slithered under her sweater. Basil stared, his blood like sludge pumping through his veins, his mind a swirl of rage as Ryan's hands greedily explored Nicole's body.

They started up the stairs.

Basil choked down some air. Except for his gnashing teeth and clenching fists, he hadn't moved since they entered the gate. He shifted positions to better view them when they reached Nicole's door. He could see them clearly now, Nicole fishing out her key, Ryan waiting, an oily smile on his face. Then, abruptly, Ryan turned and swept his eyes over the quad, as if he were a lord surveying his manor. Basil ducked back into the shadows, swallowing hard when seconds later Ryan ushered Nicole inside and closed the door.

A cruel wind swept across the quad, cold and wet, sending shivers through Basil's body. He turned up his collar and waited, although for what he didn't know. But to leave somehow suggested he was abandoning his lovely girl, and he would never do that. The minutes stretched into an hour, and still he waited. Another hour passed and Basil felt weary in body and soul. At least the rain had stopped.

Then a light went out in the apartment, and another, until it all went dark. Basil blinked his eyes. After a time he climbed the stairs and listened at her door. He could hear voices, very low, and he knew Ryan was still inside with his girl.

As Basil trudged back to his car, his mind smoldered like a burnt reed. It wasn't Nicole, he told himself. No, not Nicole. It was Ryan and his manipulative ways. People of his ilk were quite skilled at using others. No better than animals, sniffing out vulnerability in their prey. And then they struck. They twisted everything to their advantage, and little cared what destruction they left in their wake.

But for all his cunning ways, Ryan hadn't reckoned on Basil. Events were already in motion that would purge this pathetic parasite from Nicole's life. All Basil had to do was wait. Yet waiting was the one thing he could no longer do. Not now, not after seeing Ryan fondling his girl. Dark impulses coiled in his mind and he craved justice.

Ryan must suffer—and the thought excited Basil.

Do what it takes, his father had said.

He thought about his target pistol.

In an instant it all began to unfold before his eyes. He would take Ryan into an abandoned building—plenty of them around New Haven— and he would tell the miscreant exactly how he would die. At first, Ryan would dismiss the threat, maybe demand release. He might laugh nervously and tell Basil he couldn't be serious. But when Basil forced him onto his knees, and he felt the pistol behind his head, the arrogant Ryan Taylor would collapse into the slobbering coward he truly was. He would beg; he would promise anything in exchange for his miserable life.

And then Basil would dictate the terms on which Ryan would leave. One week, that's what Basil would give him. One week to get on a bus and head back to Bumpkinville. With Ryan gone, Nicole would return to her elegant self, and life would once again find its natural path.

32

By the time they reached Calhoun College, Nicole was in great pain. Ryan wondered whether the watchman's wild punches might have separated one of her ribs, and he was glad he had thumped the man's head with the flashlight.

"You need to see a doctor," he said, opening the gate.

"Says the man with a bullet in him."

"Not *in* me, through me," he said. "Basically, a cut and it'll heal fine. It's you I'm worried about. Promise me?"

"First thing tomorrow." She smiled weakly. "I guess I was a little quick with the lamp. I thought he was attacking you."

"He'll live to fight another day," Ryan said. "I'm just sorry I wasn't there for you."

"Weren't there for ... you pulled him off me!" she said, her face crinkling in disagreement. "He had my neck clamped in his teeth like an insane man."

Ryan peered at the bite marks and shook his head. "A tough night for you."

"For you too," she said. "I'm so glad you're alive."

He closed the gate. "I'm glad too," he said quietly. "But you should not have risked your life for me."

"I didn't risk my—"

"You did! And I don't want you doing that again." He took her hand and said in a deliberate tone, "I'm thankful for your help, and I know I'm still here because of you, but please, no more risks. Okay? If those men show up again, you run the other way."

"Ryan—"

"I'm serious. You run! If I die, I will die happy, knowing you're safe. But if something happened to you because of me—"

"Ryan," she interrupted, putting her hand on his chest. "You are so ... so ...."

He angled his head down and felt her breath on his lips. Then slowly he pulled away. "Too bad we're so beaten up," he said, feeling suddenly awkward.

"I suppose so," she sighed, then added, "I must look disgusting."

"No, no," he said. "That's not what I meant. You look fine."

They walked in silence along the edge of the quad, toward the stairwell. Under the light Nicole thrust her face out and said, "Tell me honestly, am I badly bruised?"

He moved closer and was surprised at the extent of the bruising.

"You look fine," he repeated.

"Really?"

"Minor blemishes on a beautiful face." He gave her a smile. "I'm more concerned about your ribs."

She lifted the bottom of her knit sweater. "Nothing's broken," she said. "It's just hard to breathe."

He touched the area gently. "You're in for some uncomfortable days. Rib injuries can hang on for months."

"I'm fine with that. I just don't want my face looking like a punching bag."

Ryan examined the worst areas of discoloration again. "Two weeks and you'll be like a new punching bag," he said, and gave her a tender kiss on the only spot he thought safe to kiss, the top of her head.

"You have such a way with words."

"Thank you," and he encircled her with his arms, knowing she needed comfort. "We'll ice it." His lips brushed against her hair as he tried to focus on being encouraging. "Ice is magic. It's amazing how it takes the swelling away—a day or two and everything will be fine."

"Seriously?"

"Maybe not the discoloration," he replied, injecting some honesty. "That takes a bit longer." He pulled away slightly and caressed her shoulder.

They climbed the stairs to her room. As Ryan took her key and opened the door, he happened to glance down toward the quad; for an instant the shadows seemed to flicker but he brushed away the impression and followed Nicole into the room.

* * *

Nicole snapped on the apartment lights then winced at the brightness. She needed some Advil. Her head ached, her neck throbbed, and her chest felt like an elephant had been rolling on it.

"Want some coffee?" she asked.

"Don't think so," Ryan said.

It was just as well. She didn't feel like making coffee. A hot shower then something to eat, that's what she wanted. In the bathroom she swallowed three Advil, glanced in the mirror, and let out a silent scream. She looked awful! No wonder Ryan had had second thoughts about kissing her. A swelling on the left cheek and a burst blood vessel in her right eye had turned her face into a Halloween mask. Gingerly, she pulled off her clothes to examine the bruising on her ribs and the bite marks on her neck. Just plain ugly, she thought, her face, her body—the whole package was nasty. Despite her best efforts, tears rimmed the bottoms of her eyes. She rubbed them away impatiently. Feeling sorry for yourself, her father always said, was admitting defeat, so she forced herself back to the mirror and took a good, hard look. Solve the problem, that's what she would do. She cracked the door and sounded almost cheerful when she called to Ryan, "Could you bring me a tray of ice from the freezer?"

Thirty minutes later she emerged freshly showered, her face twice iced, and makeup liberally applied. Except for her cheekbone, the ridiculously expensive Sisley-Paris makeup she had bought on a whim covered remarkably well. She had even slathered it on her ribs, though she supposed there was little point in applying it there. Wearing her toasty flannel nightgown and sheepskin slippers—comfort clothes—she strolled into the main area.

Ryan pushed himself off the couch. "You look a lot better," he said as he started toward the door.

"You're not leaving?"

"I gotta go," he said. "I was just waiting to tell you—"

"Don't be silly," she said. "You need to clean that wound. I have some fabric bandages, antibiotic cream—"

"I'll clean it when I get to my room." His eyes had that wary look—the old Ryan, the one who always suspected manipulation.

She looked directly at him and said, "*If* you get to your room. Remember, those men are still out there!"

"I think you scared them off," he replied, but his voice sounded less than certain.

Nicole blocked his way to the door. "Stop and think," she said, hardening her eyes. "Those men might be prowling the streets looking for you. Even if they're gone, don't you think after busting open a steam valve and clubbing a security guard that there'll be police everywhere? What are you going to say to explain the bullet wound in your side if they stop you?"

Ryan's eyes darted around the room. She had gotten him thinking.

"Here's what we're going to do," she said. "You shower and clean that wound, and I'll call my father."

"I think I should—"

"Then—" she held his gaze—"*then* I'll call Le Beau. Okay? That's what we planned to do anyway."

He hesitated.

"Don't say a word." She grabbed his hand. "You clean up. I'll make my calls and fix us tuna melts." Marching him into the bathroom, she made a point of handing him a new toothbrush. "Slippers and men's pajamas in the cupboard; bandages there as well. Just dump your clothes outside the door and I'll clean the blood off." With that she walked out and closed the door.

Nicole headed back to the living room, feeling better about having control again. She picked out a magnum of spicy Alsatian *Gewürztraminer*—a wine with a bite—and poured herself a generous glass.

The Advil seemed slow to kick in and she needed something further to dull her aching ribs. Then, sitting on a leather ottoman, wine in hand, she called her father on her cell. He picked up immediately but was too busy to talk, so he instructed her to bring Ryan to their Greenwich house the next day, where they could deal with everything systematically. She paused before calling Le Beau. Her father was a stickler when it came to dispensing information and would be upset at her involving the officer. But she had promised Ryan she would call and knew he would ask. The phone rang only once before clicking into voice mail. Relieved, she tapped off and left no message, as Le Beau had instructed. It didn't matter. She hadn't intended to say much anyway. Time to collect Ryan's clothes, and turn her attention to the tuna melts.

After the shower stopped, Nicole waited ten minutes before popping the sandwiches into the toaster oven. Ryan would need time to bandage his wound. Meanwhile, she sipped her wine, still finding it hard to believe what Krakauer had done. His genetic tinkerings had changed everything; she touched her fingertips together, knowing they were no longer her own. A new life form had burrowed its way into every living person, and had now become part of the human genome. If Krakauer triggered his deadly gene in a major population center, civilization could end. She wondered whether her father would even believe her when she told him.

She craned her head toward the bathroom. "The tuna melts are already in the oven." No reply.

Minutes later, with the cheese browned just right, she placed the sandwiches on a plate and set everything out on a table beside the couch. Tapping on the bathroom door, she called, "Food's ready!"

Still no reply.

She returned to the living room, paced across it twice and sipped more wine before returning to the door. "These are tuna melts," she said. "They get cold."

He mumbled something, but she couldn't make it out for all the banging and thumping going on, and the expletives.

"Ryan?"

"Just a sec!" he called back irritably.

"Toothpaste is in the cabinet."

"It's not the toothpaste," he muttered, opening the door. "Look at these things!"

She tried unsuccessfully to cover her smile. "A little floodwater in the legs, but they seem roomy enough."

He didn't return the smile. "What the hell are these?" he asked, looking down at himself.

"Pajamas."

"They're a joke. What else you got?" He wiped a trickle of water from his face, and Nicole wondered why she was finding him so sexy, despite the ridiculous pants.

"Only what Basil left."

"You must have something else."

"How many guys do you think I've had over here? That's all I've got." Then, smirking, she added, "I don't know what you're complaining about. Basil's nightgowns are charmeuse silk, the silk of emperors—quite comfortable."

"Pink and white?"

"Coral and ivory," she corrected sanctimoniously. "Some people find them fashionable."

"Where are my clothes?"

Nicole motioned with her head toward the sink. "I'm soaking the blood out."

"I can't believe this," he said, scanning the room. "Nothing else to wear?"

She shook her head.

He exhaled in frustration.

"Oh, Ryan," she said. "Please relax. You look great in pink." She couldn't help chuckling.

He grimaced.

His miserable face made her laugh harder, and then clutch her chest in pain.

"What?"

"Nothing. Hurts to laugh, that's all." She looked at him. "But you know what? It still feels good—to laugh, I mean. Don't you think? Especially after tonight."

"Yeah," he said, giving her a look of resignation. "You're right." He plucked distastefully at his silk pajamas and continued, "I guess pink it is."

Becoming suddenly serious, Nicole gestured to the bandages bulging under his arm. "How's the gunshot?"

He unbuttoned his pajama top and let it drop to the floor.

Caught off guard, she forced her eyes away from Ryan's torso. "Is it bad?" she asked, leaning forward to make it clear that she was interested only in the wound.

"I think it's okay." He pulled back a section of gauze.

"Ugh," she said. "The bullet really shredded the skin."

"I smeared Vaseline on it," he said.

"It's worse than I thought."

"Just ripped the skin a bit. Any closer and I wouldn't be here talking about it."

She continued to stare at the wound. "It must hurt."

"Actually, my shoulder bothers me more," he said, rotating his arm. "But I'm kind of used to being banged up, from lacrosse."

She ran her eyes over the curve of his shoulder as he rotated it slowly. His skin was smooth, supple, cloaking the swells and dips of his muscles like the charmeuse silk shirt he'd shed. Surprised by the observation, she again strove for objectivity: Nothing but bruising on the shoulder. Good.

"What about you?" he asked. "Your face looks better; a lot better."

"You think so?" She wanted the reassurance.

"Absolutely," he said, nodding, his eyes wandering over her face before they again met hers. "You look ... wonderful; you really do."

She tucked her lips up slightly at the corners, letting him know she appreciated his comment.

"I'm sorry you're so sore," he said.

"I've had a drop or two of wine," she said. "That helps, but I'm not used to being banged up. My whole chest aches when I breathe, and even when I don't." She paused, realizing she sounded like a complainer. "I guess I'm not as brave as I thought."

"Nobody's as brave as they think. But you," he shook his head in admiration, "you were incredible. The way you came at those men. I can't imagine anything braver."

Nicole felt her face flush. She knew the truth was far from how Ryan imagined it, and she was eager to redirect the discussion. "Nothing to do with bravery," she said, shaking her head. "I was scared out of my mind."

"Bravery is doing what's needed even when you are scared," he said as he retrieved his pajama top and pulled it on. He tried to say something more about her bravery, but she talked over him. His compliments were too uncomfortable—especially when she knew he would soon discover the full truth.

She turned away, the buttery aroma of toasted bread and melted cheddar reminding her. "The tuna sandwiches will be ice cold if we wait any longer," she said, striving to sound casual. "And you'll think I'm a bad cook."

They returned to the living room where Nicole sat on a hard-backed chair and Ryan sank into the couch across from her. She declined his offer to switch places, preferring an erect posture to bending her body, although the second glass of wine did much to ease the pain. For the next few moments they both sat quietly, eating their sandwiches and sipping wine.

"Good," he said, the verdict muffled by his full mouth. "Real good!"

She was glad she had opened two cans of tuna, again surprised by how much he could eat. Their conversation was pleasant, first about her modest cooking talents, then about the number of bottles filling her wine racks, and then, of course, about Basil's silk pajamas.

It was good to laugh, she thought, even if it hurt.

But the earlier events still swirled around her like dark water, threatening to suck her under if she yielded even for a minute. What would Ryan think of her in the coming days when he understood better how she had put him at risk? She had only been trying to help her father keep an eye on Krakauer and his supposed gene therapy research, but in the end she'd placed Ryan in a situation that was quite out of control. He would still be blissfully running around campus scrubbing for odd jobs if she hadn't sent him to Krakauer. But how could she have anticipated the insanity of the professor's research?

She watched Ryan polish off the last of the food. The image struck her as so ordinary: the two of them drinking wine and eating tuna melts, a harmless event at any college. A sigh escaped her lips. She wanted so much to be like everyone else—to go to parties, hang out, have fun. But her life had ended when Bobby died. She was not here to have fun. She was here to accomplish objectives. If her father wanted information on gene therapy, she found a way. A good soldier, that's what she was.

She poured herself a third glass, not a good idea, but at least a sensible amount.

"Nice wine," he said.

Nicole nodded absently.

"Hope it's not the thousand-dollar variety."

"Modestly priced."

"Ha. That probably means five hundred. Anyway, after tonight I feel no guilt," he said, grabbing the magnum and filling his glass to the rim. He sucked off the top inch, then grinned as he reached to pour some more.

"I need to tell you something," she said.

Ryan looked up, interested.

"From the beginning," she said, "you were right and I was wrong. You were right about Krakauer, about those men, and about this issue being too big for us."

He shrugged off her comment, but said nothing as he returned the bottle to the table.

"I talked to my father," she said, "and he's arranged for a car to pick us up tomorrow at noon."

His brows rose. "A car? To go where?"

"To our Greenwich house. My father will be there—"

Ryan shook his head. "I would rather just contact the FBI."

"The FBI will be at the house tomorrow," she said. "My father's arranged everything."

"What did you tell him?"

"Not much—he was in a meeting. But I did mention your gunshot wound and my bumps and bruises."

"And?" he asked over the rim of his glass. His eyes remained on hers as he took a sip. Not a gulp, she noted absently. Paying attention.

"He was upset, of course, but glad we're okay. He said he'd have a physician there—actually, several—to check us out."

He smiled crookedly at her. "The doctors come to your house as well?"

Nicole's smile felt limp. "I've told you my father is rich and important. Well, he's a little more than that. He has connections everywhere—in the White House, the military, in grass huts dotting the Patagonian hills. And unlike politicians or celebrities constrained by their visibility, my father does exactly what he wants. He operates behind the scenes like some shadowy stage manager. If it's a gaggle of doctors he requires, believe me, the best ones in the country will be flapping around us."

His eyes studied her face for a moment. "Every time you mention your father," he said quietly, "you have such pain in your eyes. He paused, and anger."

"Yeah, well ...." She blinked several times, surprised to be on the verge of tears, something she would never show to her father.

He shrugged, letting his eyes slide from hers, to give her privacy. "Didn't mean to intrude."

"No," she said quickly, and impulsively leaned forward. His eyes returned to her and she sat back, feeling awkward. "No, that's fine." She smiled, trying to mask her feelings, and knowing he could see right through it. She swirled the golden liquid in her glass a moment, then choked some down before gazing at him again. "There is an upside to my father. Want to hear it?"

"Sure."

"Those gunmen, they'll never bother you again."

Ryan stared at her.

"I'm serious," she said.

He grinned and snorted his disbelief at the same time.

"It's true. Never again."

"That's a pretty big upside," he said, settling back and resting his arm gingerly on the top of the couch.

"I suppose it is." She looked away, absently studying the scattering of crumbs on the plate, and wondering vaguely whether the alcohol was making her more confiding. She continued in spite of her thoughts, saying, "My father has a way of handling problems. No doubt about that."

Ryan frowned into space. "He works with scientists, right? Maybe he could find a way to handle Krakauer's *Omega*."

Her exhalation radiated pessimism.

"Why not?" Ryan persisted. "He's a problem solver; that's what you said. Maybe he could solve this problem—or get someone else to solve it." His face looked earnest, hopeful.

"Maybe," she said, but she knew there was no ready solution to the genetic alterations Krakauer had made. She dropped her eyes. A door slammed somewhere, and she heard a faint burst of distant laughter. Out there, in the rest of the world, things were proceeding normally. "The truth is, I don't want to think about it tonight. I want to crawl into my bed and wake up to the world I knew yesterday. That's what I want to do." She took a deep breath, felt it shudder over her lower lip. "But of course I can't, can I?" Her last words were barely audible and she couldn't conceal her melancholy.

He sensed her mood and fell silent.

For a while, neither spoke.

"Well," she said finally, "it's getting late. You'll need some blankets." She pushed herself to her feet, then gasped as a shredding pain flashed across her chest.

"Nicole?" Ryan was beside her.

"I'm fine," she said, hunching over. "I guess the wine didn't help as much as I thought."

His hands were on her arms, holding her securely, and his eyes searched her face.

"Really," she said, straightening cautiously. "I'm fine now." She squared her shoulders to bolster her words, but the change in position made her wince, betraying the truth.

"You should sit a minute," he said.

She looked around. "I need to clean up—"

"I'll do it." His hands on her arms moved her gently but firmly toward the couch.

She sank into the cushions; the warmth still lingering where he had been sitting.

"Do you have aspirin or something?" He glanced toward the bathroom.

"Vicodin. I have Vicodin in the medicine cabinet."

"One or two?"

"Two, please." She felt nauseous from the sudden pain.

Ryan returned promptly with the pills and a Dixie cup of water, both of which she gulped down.

Nicole then watched him clear away everything in one swooping trip—the wine glasses, the plates, the mostly empty bottle, even the folding table. Amazingly, he didn't break or spill anything, even with half-filled wine glasses tucked precariously under his wrist. He returned, paused to lean against the doorframe, and said with mock earnestness, "I also vacuum."

"There's a broom in the closet," she teased.

"A broom ... hmm." He shook his head. "Not trained on a broom. Sorry." He moved toward the hard-backed chair.

"Here," she said, patting the cushion beside her.

He glanced at the cushion, then back at her. She smiled benignly, feeling slightly foolish but striving to appear confident. Why she had invited him to sit on the couch, she didn't know. Loneliness, she supposed. Maybe a need for comfort, or to allay her anxiety about the future. Anxiety. That was it. No doubt she was still running from the sobering events of the day, still wanting to pretend to herself—at least for a few hours—that she was a normal college student sitting in her room with a normal guy. In pink silk pajamas. Her smile widened, threatening to spill laughter, but when he swung the chair out of the way she recovered. He did look better in them than Basil had. Filled them out in all the right places.

She watched him deposit the chair against the wall. Nicole liked him, she liked him a lot. The truth was, she enjoyed his company more than she wanted to admit even to herself, but this had nothing to do with romance. Not with Ryan. Certainly not with Ryan. Yes, she had made offhanded comments from time to time, little flirtations to ruffle him, throw him off balance. But they were just friends, no more; two people drawn together by a complicated set of circumstances. All they were doing—as friends—was enjoying each other's company and providing solace in the aftermath of a difficult day.

Nothing wrong with that.

When he returned to the couch, she glanced away to ease the pressure.

"I'm looking forward to meeting your father," he said. She felt the cushion sink as he sat down beside her. "Should be interesting."

"Be careful what you wish for," she murmured.

He bumped her playfully with his shoulder and said, "I might like him. Who knows? I like you."

She nodded, but the comment made her feel miserable inside. There was so much he didn't know. Why couldn't she talk to him more openly, unburden her soul! But, of course, that was impossible. She had already said too much about her personal life. They dwelt in vastly dissimilar worlds, she and Ryan, where different rules applied, and she could do nothing to change that reality. She groaned inwardly, thinking about tomorrow when he would meet her father. How could she ever explain to Ryan the way she had conducted herself? And how could she face him when he discovered that so much about her was a lie?

"You might not be understanding the dynamics of the situation," Ryan said with a twinkle in his eyes. "When someone says he likes you, you're supposed to say, 'Oh, that's nice. I like you too' ... or some variation of that."

"I'm sorry!" Nicole blushed. "My mind was ... I do like you, very much." She touched his arm to make her point, and immediately wished she hadn't. It signaled for him to continue, and despite all her flirting, she wasn't ready for this. Up till now she had played a game with Ryan, a shameless game of manipulation. In the beginning it had mattered little what she had to do—flatter him, tease him, bully him—as long as she got what she wanted. But somewhere along the line her feelings had changed, and she no longer felt she could play the game.

Nor could she hide from the blindsiding truth that she *wanted* Ryan to like her. And that changed everything.

He was looking at her now, and she knew that look. She needed to take possession of the situation.

"Thank you for cleaning up," she said lamely.

"Two seconds' work," he replied, shrugging away the comment. "Feeling any better?"

She nodded. "The Vicodin's kicking in. Should have taken some earlier."

"You're not much of a complainer, are you?"

"Ohhh, please," she groaned, covering her face.

"What?"

"I've been awful!"

He raised an eyebrow.

"I'm a complete whiner. I've been feeling sorry for myself all evening!"

"You've got reason," he said. "Some guys on our team whine about every little ache."

She chuckled. "I'd fit right in."

"Don't think so," he said, leaning closer to make the point. His eyes were locked onto hers.

"Well, I ...." She didn't finish her thought, and in fact she wasn't quite sure what her thought was because another had instantly replaced it. His shifting weight on the cushions had tilted them toward each other. They were sitting surprisingly close, and she could feel the warmth of his body through the silk pajamas—his arm and hip, the entire length of his leg—even though they were scarcely touching.

He remained where he was, his eyes still on hers. Hazel. She'd never noticed before that his eyes were hazel, warm, peaty brown rimmed in deep moss green. She jerked her eyes away, smoothed her flannel nightgown around her knees, paying undue attention to a wrinkle, stroking it repeatedly with her palm. She needed time to think, time to sort through her emotions.

His leg relaxed, settling fully against hers. She could feel the long, hard muscles of his thigh, the heat of his skin.

A little quiver of desire fluttered in her breast, and she knew she should move away. She needed perspective, resolution. Tomorrow was coming. And then what would Ryan think?

He shifted, leaned his arm on the back of the couch, and she tilted even closer to him. His breath was hot on her cheek. She rolled slowly onto one hip, trying to move away without revealing her effort to do so.

He moved again, and she slipped into the hollow of his shoulder.

And relaxed. The Vicodin was doing a fine job of deadening the pain, and apparently her good sense as well.

His hand slid from the back of the couch to trace up her arm, lightly, a fingertip caress. She shivered.

"I don't think this is a good time," she managed, but didn't pull away. The smell of shampoo drifted from his damp hair.

His hand eased across the back of her neck.

She shuddered again as her tense muscles softened under his touch. "We've had a big day, both of us," she whispered.

"Mm-hmm." His hand sifted her hair, exploring, tempting.

In spite of herself she pushed her head back into his palm; eyes closed, she turned her head slowly, deliciously, as he cradled her neck, gently kneading, replacing anxiety with pleasure, and a hunger for more.

She was floating on the edge of some invisible chasm; she could feel it. And any wafting of the wind, any wavering of her pathetic resolve, would carry her over.

His fingers soothed, enticed, moved lazily along the curve of her neck and around to the hollow at its base, then lower, trailing across the upper part of her breasts.

She caught her breath as a frisson of pleasure rippled outward from his fingertips. His touch electrified her nerves.

She had to get control! She blinked, twice, dizzied by her racing pulse, her ragged breathing. She thought to sit up, but her treacherous body abandoned her will, opened itself to desire. She *wanted* this.

His arms slid around her, drawing her gently toward him. He lowered his head to brush his lips across her cheek. "Ryan ..." she breathed in protest, but that was all.

He stroked her hair, nuzzled and licked her throat, followed her jawline with his tongue until he lowered his mouth to hers.

Her lips parted in welcome, moaning. Her hands moved up his arms and along his shoulders until they met, encircling his neck, and she pressed her body against his. She burned with the need to feel him, touch him, taste him. Her mouth moved eagerly against his, accepted his probing tongue, wet and hot, and she probed deeply with her own. Nicole ached with the animal need to couple, and she no longer cared about anything else.

When Ryan slipped his hand under her nightgown, she opened her legs for him; when he caressed her thighs, she arched her hips; and when he entered her and a tremor shook her body, she clung to him, and let everything fall away.

And not once did she think about tomorrow.

33 〰〰〰〰〰〰〰〰〰〰〰〰〰〰〰

Early the next morning Jozef Krakauer headed to his lab at Sterling Library. The night shadows had given place to shafts of light streaming through the trees, and the professor felt a deep joy welling up in his soul. A few had died, yes, but now untold millions had the hope of genetically pure lives.

Westover and other distorters of the human genome had lost. They had dangled promises of marvelous corrections to nature's supposed deficiencies, but Jozef Krakauer, one man, had cried from the watchtower, had alerted the masses to the awesome power of genetic engineering. Soon everyone would understand how close the world had come to a genetic holocaust. "The Nevada Syndrome," as they were calling it, was all over the news. People would finally know the terrifying potential of genetic engineering. And they would clamor for it to end.

Krakauer opened the basement door to Sterling Library, headed down the passageway, and entered his lab. He paused at the television, curious what reporters might be saying, but changed his mind, feeling uneasy. There was an unusual stillness in the lab.

He cocked his head.

Silence.

Not a single sound from the animal cages at the rear. Odd. He headed down the corridor and into his private lab. At the edge of his vision the darkness moved. Krakauer turned and let out a tiny gasp. A man was standing near one of the closets on the other side of the room, his face in shadow. Instinctively, Krakauer backed away, but then caught himself. This was his hour. He took a calming breath and moved toward the center of the room.

"Professor," the man said, "please remain where you are."

Krakauer felt his body stiffen. He recognized the voice. It was the general.

"We want to talk to you," the general said.

Krakauer swept his eyes over the other Proskin security people emerging from the support labs, six in all. They encircled him, their eyes gleaming like ravenous dogs, jubilant in their victory. He tried to speak but two men, one tall, his face wrapped in bandages, the other powerfully built with cold-looking eyes and clipped blond hair, grabbed hold of him before he could utter a word. They twisted his arms behind his back and cuffed his wrists, then wrenched his head back and yanked open his mouth to inspect his teeth with a flashlight. That done, a woman dragged a chair beside him and motioned for him to sit. When he hesitated, the men pushed him roughly into the chair, and the handcuffs bit viciously into his wrists.

"There is no need for this," Krakauer protested.

"You're a dangerous man," the general said.

"I don't understand."

"I think you do."

Krakauer met the general's teal eyes, but refused to wither under their scrutiny. The man was used to bending others to his will—breaking them, no doubt—but he would find no success today.

"You've been conducting research a bit differently than you've reported," the general said.

Krakauer lifted his chin and refused to speak.

"Field studies."

Krakauer said nothing.

"Not going to answer my questions?"

"Your questions will be answered in due time."

The general's face tightened. "You've been hiding your true intentions, haven't you?"

"I have hidden nothing."

"Afraid to speak the truth?"

"I fear nothing."

"Well, then," the general said, gesturing for him to speak. "If you fear nothing, this is your opportunity to help us understand your research."

Krakauer clamped his mouth shut. The juvenile manipulations grated on him.

The general folded his arms. "I'm waiting."

Krakauer smiled to himself. How pitifully inferior were these people with their presumed power! How utterly mediocre! Their only defense was their ignorance. He exhaled wearily and said in a steady voice, "You want to know about my immunological studies, yes? Read my reports. I included everything in my data."

"I don't think so. You've been working on a delivery vehicle, as Westover was, but you've had that figured out for some time, haven't you?" The general leaned forward. "You've been busy building something else. Hmm? Why don't you tell us about it?"

"The object of my research is beyond your understanding."

"You've disseminated it, haven't you?"

"You know nothing about what I've been doing."

"Really. These scientists here—" he motioned over his shoulder toward two men standing slightly out of the circle —"Drs. Wu and Hodsdon, understand your research quite well. They say the gene circuit you've engineered can be triggered to produce enormous amounts of that same trigger, which would then destroy the body in a chain reaction."

Krakauer gave him an empty stare.

The general motioned to a silver case on the table. "Recognize it? I think you do. That's the trigger."

Krakauer turned away.

"Ashamed to admit what you've done?"

"I have saved the earth," he said, turning back. And you bind me like an animal. The shame is yours."

"We've placed you in restraints," the general said, "to prevent you from triggering your unholy creation and killing everyone in this room."

"You think I would do that?"

"I think you're capable of murder. Yes, I do. What do you think?"

"I am a scientist."

"A mass-murdering scientist," the general shot back, stressing each word. "Does Biggar, Canada, or Midas, Nevada mean anything to you? Or maybe a cruise ship off Puerto Rico?"

Krakauer blinked.

"You've murdered hundreds of people in the last couple of days," the general said, his voice rising. "Hundreds? Maybe thousands! And the unbelievable part about this *thing* of yours, this putrefaction from hell ... is that it could have ended life on the earth!"

"My cause is greater than you know. It's the putrid sea of genetic engineering that endangers life on the earth. I didn't open that door. I shut the door. What was Alpha, is now Omega. An end to the age of man's arrogance. *You* are the danger. Not me. And there was no possibility of amplification. I sent vials to containable target areas."

"Containable! How do you know? A rat or a stray deer could have carried it out of town."

Krakauer gave him a superior look. "*Omega* affects primates only," he said with a patient voice. "I'm surprised with all your snooping you didn't know that."

"Wu and Hodsdon told me as much," the general said, "but your 'containable' *Omega* has amplified in Nevada."

Krakauer's face registered shock.

"That's right. Somebody carried it out, a truck driver they think, into the surrounding areas. Bio-defense teams from the army have secured the county, but nobody knows what'll happen now."

"It's a rural area. It'll self-limit."

"Let's hope so, you insane bastard!" The general moved closer. "Now," he said evenly, restoring his composure, "you are going to tell me *everything* about your research."

"I have nothing to say."

"Do you like pain?"

"Threats? You think threats will make me talk?" The dogs were surrounding him now, their lips taut across their teeth. "I've been faithful to my charge."

The general ignored him. "You've been working on an antidote to the trigger. I want that information."

Krakauer shifted in his chair, unsuccessfully trying to relieve the pressure on his wrists.

The general dropped his eyes to the handcuffs. "Are they bothering you?" he asked.

Krakauer looked away.

"Five seconds," the general said quietly. "That's what you have. I will—not—play—your—game." His words marked off the time.

Krakauer steeled his mind.

The big man with the bandaged face stepped forward and yanked Krakauer to his feet. Cold-eyes then unlocked the cuffs, took hold of Krakauer's hand, and twisted it savagely.

Snap!

Krakauer screamed. Fire exploded up his arm and seemed to jolt his heart. He stared in horror at his hand hanging limply, attached only by his rapidly purpling skin.

"I want to hear about the antidote," the general said.

"My time is over," Krakauer murmured.

"I agree with that. The antidote," the general repeated. "Tell me about the antidote."

Krakauer reached for his broken wrist but they twisted it again, grinding it back and forth. He shrieked but couldn't hear his voice, feeling only the fire racing over his body, and the air rushing out of his lungs. The dogs pressed closer, mocking, hurling insults, inflicting pain.

It was the end.

Soon they would count his bones.

* * *

The general grimaced. At times like this, he wished he had taken his father's advice and become a country doctor, helping people rather than hurting them. But whatever he had to do to protect the country—to safeguard hundreds of millions of people—he would do. He signaled for Donovan and Gonzales to take the professor into the main airlock chamber. The man was putting up more resistance than anticipated, and the general was worried that a janitor or some early bird worker in the library above might overhear his screams. The sealed chamber would solve that problem.

The general turned to Prator and said, "Inform the perimeter people we'll be an hour longer. The good professor needs more persuasion." Then he locked his hands behind his back and stood ramrod straight as the airlock chamber was stripped of its blue contact paper. He watched as Donovan and Gonzales sliced open Krakauer's shirt with a Delta knife, and bound him to a lab chair. Then they hooked a Bunsen burner to a gas nozzle and scorched a swath across the professor's chest.

The general muted the intercom, then spoke gently into the mic once Krakauer's screams had subsided, as if consoling a friend. "Tell me about the antidote," he purred, "and all this will end."

Krakauer's mouth moved in pain, but still he wouldn't cooperate.

The general blew out in resignation and said, "Professor Krakauer, you will talk eventually. Everyone does. Why go through this?"

Krakauer turned his face toward the glass and laughed, almost hysterically.

"Professor Krakauer, listen to me," the general said.

But the crazed laughter continued. Then his eyes rolled up in his head and he began to twitch.

The general turned to Wu and Hodsdon and asked, "What's going on?"

The two scientists moved closer to the glass. "I don't know," Wu said, his brow furrowed.

"Look at his lips," Hodsdon said. "They've turned blue."

"Oxygen deprivation," Wu murmured.

"What's happening?" the general demanded.

"His system is shutting down for some reason," Hodsdon said.

The general returned his eyes to the chamber. Krakauer had begun to arch his back and twist like an animal in extreme pain. The general flipped on the mic and said, "Talk to me, Donovan."

"I don't know, sir. He should be fine, just a broken wrist and a minor burn. But something's clearly wrong."

"What's he saying?"

Donovan leaned closer and listened to Krakauer's ramblings, then turned toward the general and shrugged. "Something about fire and pestilence, and the power of genetics."

"The power of genetics?" The general frowned.

Donovan spoke again. "*Omega* ... he's talking about the end of his mission."

Wu took the mic and asked, "Did Dr. Krakauer touch anything when he entered the lab?"

"Negative," Donovan said. "He flailed around a bit on the way in, but that's about it." He looked back at the professor who was flipping and twisting in his restraints like a salmon caught in a trap.

"Did he grind down on his teeth?" Wu asked.

"Don't think so ... I don't know, sir."

"Did he do anything out of the ordinary?" Hodsdon asked.

"Babbling, as if he were talking to someone. Chewed on his fingers."

"I see," Wu said. He turned his eyes to the general.

The general muted the mic.

"He might have released the trigger," Wu said.

The general looked from Wu to Hodsdon. "The trigger?" he said, mostly to himself.

"Not a concern for us out here," Wu said. "But in there, well ...."

The general returned his eyes to the vacuum lab.

"Dr. Krakauer understands the potential of his gene therapy," Wu continued. "He might have waited until he was inside a sealed lab before triggering it."

"How ... how could he have released the trigger?"

Wu pursed his lips, thinking. "Donovan said he chewed on his fingers."

"Go on."

"Most often people conceal poisons in teeth, but since we checked his teeth, and he was clean, it's possible he embedded the trigger elsewhere, maybe under a coating on his nails."

"Could he have taken poison or something?"

"Possibly," Wu said. "We found TTX this morning in his lab, and we know he's used another neurotoxin before, conotoxin. So it's possible."

"But you think it's more likely *Omega*."

"I'm afraid so," Wu said. "Even tetrodotoxin shouldn't compromise his system this rapidly."

The general flipped on the mic and said, "Listen, Donovan, we have a situation here. Wu thinks the professor might have consumed a toxin, but there's an outside chance he somehow released the trigger. If he did, we'll know inside ten minutes. That's how long it takes the substance to compromise the system."

"Understood," Donovan said. "We'll keep the doors sealed."

"Colonel?" It was Gonzales.

Donovan turned.

"He released the trigger?"

"They think he ingested a toxin."

"They're lying. It's the trigger!"

"We'll know soon enough."

Gonzales rubbed the unbandaged side of his face.

The general flipped on the mic. "Everyone take it easy," he said. "We'll get you out. Don't worry."

"There, you see?" Donovan said to Gonzales. "Just relax."

"Colonel, I don't think we should stay in here."

"We've no choice."

Gonzales nodded and took a deep breath before beginning to pace, his eyes darting around the room. Then he began to bite his lips and eye the chamber door.

"Take a seat," Donovan said.

"We might be okay if we got out now."

"Negative," Donovan said. "Sit down."

"You know how this thing kills." His pupils had dilated and he started to hyperventilate.

"I told you to sit," Donovan said. "Now!"

"I'm getting out."

Donovan stepped toward Gonzales but he bulled past and reached for the handle on the airlock door. Donovan grabbed Gonzales's arm, but the taller man pulled away and struggled toward the handle.

"Put him down!" the general ordered.

Donovan ripped out his knife and spun around in a semi-circle, plunging the blade into Gonzales's neck. The man reared up, his whole body stiffening, and then crumbled onto the floor, his fingers clawing at the blood spurting from his neck.

The general watched as Donovan bent over Gonzales and helped him to a sitting position against the wall. Gonzales was coughing out blood and speaking in strangled breaths, "Sorry, Colonel ... I'm sorry."

"It's okay," Donovan said, cradling his head. "It's okay."

Seconds later, Gonzales slumped over and fell silent.

Donovan rose and stared down at his partner for the longest time. Then he laid him out on the floor, straightened Gonzales's blood-soaked shirt, and took a lab coat from a shelf, tucking it under the corpse's head. Donovan's eyes remained unreadable, but his jawline was like stone and the veins in his neck throbbed.

He walked over to Krakauer, who was now shaking violently and dribbling bubbles of saliva off his chin, and booted the man in the stomach.

The general took a breath and turned on the mic. "I'm sorry," he said.

Donovan squinted through the glass and said, "I want the truth."

"Doesn't look good," the general said. "Wu thinks it's Krakauer's beast."

"How long?"

"Five to ten minutes Krakauer should start exhibiting signs of cellular collapse. Three to five after that for you."

Donovan nodded. He removed the watch the general had given him, flipped it over, and read the words: *With my shield or on it.* Then, setting his watch, he sat down.

Prator approached the general but addressed her question to the scientists standing beside him. "Is there nothing we can do?" she asked.

"We can wait," Hodsdon said.

"He has a pistol," the general said. It wasn't much comfort, but it was all he could offer.

Prator moved closer to the glass and peered at Donovan.

He raised his eyes.

She stared at him.

He stared back.

She flattened her palm against the glass and continued to stare.

He turned his head, checked his watch, and glanced at Krakauer. Then he turned back to her.

She was still staring, her palm against the glass.

He rose and came to the window.

She inclined her head toward him until her forehead rested on the glass. He stood there, his eyes on her, but not moving. Then, finally, he reached toward her hand and mirrored her palm, and silently gazed into her eyes.

The general looked away. He had seen enough.

* * *

Krakauer was dead. He had died fifteen minutes after entering the airlock chamber, not from his engineered creation, but from a fast-acting toxin concealed in a false fingernail. His body showed no signs of cellular lysis, and if there was an antidote to the trigger, the professor had taken it with him to the grave.

The wordless meeting between Donovan and Prator had proven interesting to the general. Donovan's usual icy demeanor evaporated in the presence of Karen Prator, and he'd had difficulty tearing himself away from the glass. When he finally did return to his chair, it took a full minute before he was able to don his calm exterior. But then—like the soldier he was—he managed to sit quietly, checking his watch from time to time. Not once did he glance up at Prator.

The general was pleased. Donovan had a weakness.

* * *

But now loose ends were bothering him again. Captain Barton of the Yale Police reported that a student named Meryash had been in the university's Employment Office, stirring up questions about Proskin Pharmaceutical, to such an extent that a Yale administrator had talked to several police officers about the situation.

The general dispatched Donovan and Prator to deal with the problem.

34

Ryan scrambled down the stairs at Payne Whitney Gym, eager to exit the building. He had just stuffed a note into Coach Waldhart's box to apologize for missing so many lacrosse activities, and he had no interest in bumping into the man in the hallway. Ryan's note explained everything. He had pneumonia and would be in bed for a few more days. His periodic cough, which he seemed to have picked up at the lab, would give him, he hoped, a reasonable chance of being believed.

Outside Payne Whitney, Ryan swept his eyes across the parking lot, checking every open space, every darkened corner for danger. When the sun suddenly peaked out from behind a cloud, his mind flooded with optimism. He was eager to meet Nicole's father, somebody at least he could trust to clear up this mess. Nicole herself had turned out to be far more loving and sweet-natured than he had expected, and the thought of being with her excited him, muting the events of the past few days.

He paused, noticing a black Porsche moving slowly along the edge of the lot. The vehicle suddenly bolted forward, rounded a row of cars, and stopped. Ryan eyed the silky machine. He'd never expected to be impressed by a car, especially one that had Basil Meryash seated behind the wheel.

The window slid open.

Basil smiled, all teeth. "I thought that was you," he said with exaggerated excitement, as if he had discovered a childhood friend. Short of being an actor, it's hard to fake a smile. But Ryan thought Basil's cheery face could have won an award. "How you doing?" Basil chirped.

"Okay," Ryan replied, eyeing Basil casually. Something about his face—the set of his jaw, the hooded eyes. Ryan wasn't sure, but something told him Basil had been in the quad the night before.

"You like my Porsche? Just got it." Basil's voice still oozed cheer.

"Nice."

"Hop in. I'll take you for a spin."

"No, thanks. Got things to do."

"I'd like to talk," Basil said, an edge creeping into his voice. "About Nicole."

"There's nothing to talk about."

"Just fifteen minutes, over coffee."

"I don't think so."

"Well, I've decided to move on and ah ... I, ah, wanted to say a few things, that's all. Will you give me that?"

Ryan exhaled in frustration and glanced around the parking lot. He checked his watch; plenty of time before his meeting with Nicole and her father, but a chat with Basil wasn't high on his list.

"Fifteen minutes is all I ask," Basil said.

Ryan shrugged. "You've got five." He pulled open the door, settled into the bucket seat, and ran his eyes over the dials. "Impressive," he said coldly.

"It moves, too," Basil said, tromping the gas. The Porsche squealed out of the parking lot and onto the road, plunging Ryan deep into his seat. He pulled the safety belt across his chest and snapped it into place.

Two minutes later they were shooting down Whalley Avenue, darting in and out of traffic as if they were on a NASCAR speedway. "You don't worry much about tickets, I take it," Ryan said.

"Never seen a radar trap on Whalley. But you're right. We should get off the main road." Basil jammed his foot on the brake, wrenched the wheel around, then punched the accelerator. The engine roared as they streaked across the intersection in front of the oncoming cars.

"Are you nuts?" Ryan hollered over the sound of blaring horns.

"Watch how she handles," Basil shouted back. The Porsche flew down the side streets, swaying and rolling as it weaved through the vehicles.

"Slow down!"

"What's the matter? Afraid to die?"

"I don't want to be in a wheelchair, jerkoff! Stop the car!"

Basil cornered the next intersection almost on two wheels and rocketed through three stop signs into an industrial area.

"Hey! Did you hear me?"

"Nobody much out here," Basil replied, accelerating. "There's no danger of—"

"Stop the fucking car! Now!"

Basil jammed on the brakes so hard it felt as if the Porsche were standing on its front wheels. "You ask, I do," he said in a singsong voice, and allowed the car to roll slowly to the curb.

Ryan stared straight ahead, his entire body rigid with fury. He wanted to bounce Basil's head off the steering column, and it was all he could do to control the urge. The Porsche stopped in front of a derelict sewing factory, a crumbling brick structure burned at one end, with a huge painted façade, barely visible, of a smiling fifties-style woman seated at her sewing machine. Above the woman in faded block letters, he could see the words: Tompkins Sewing & Embroidery Co.

Basil eased himself out of the car. "Happy now?" he asked, banging the door shut before Ryan could answer.

"Yeah, I'm real happy," Ryan said acidly. He ripped open his door and got out.

Basil pressed the remote lock as he strode off toward the empty building.

Ryan started after him. It was time to deal with this ass.

Basil rounded a brick wall, and disappeared.

A humorless smile crossed Ryan's face. The rich kid wants to fight, he mused. Probably took Kung Fu or some other crap at summer camp. Not a problem; even with his shoulder and the wound under his arm, he'd drop this guy like a duffle bag. He pressed his bandaged armpit for a couple of seconds, then shook his arms loose and turned the corner.

Ryan froze.

He was looking directly into the barrel of a .22 caliber pistol with a target sight on top.

"You are dead!" Basil shrieked in a psychotic voice.

Ryan stared at him, at the gun, at both.

"You think you can do what you want? Huh?" He was standing with his knees slightly bent, two hands on the gun, and pointing it at Ryan's face. "Answer me!" he shouted, his hands shaking with rage.

"Take it easy—"

"You slept with Nicole last night, didn't you?"

Ryan glanced around at the vacant building and grimy courtyard, and knew he was in trouble. He raised a hand calmly and said, "Look, we can—"

"On—your—knees!"

"Okay," Ryan said. "Okay. Just relax." He started to bend.

"You thought you'd get away with this, didn't you? You're so stupid—"

Basil never finished. In desperation, Ryan bolted out of his half crouch and came up under his outstretched arms, crashing into him so hard Basil's feet flew off the ground. Ryan leapt on top and banged the gun out of his hand. It skidded across the paving stones into a jumble of papers and bottles against the wall. Ryan scrambled away and darted for the weapon, to make sure Basil didn't get it and do something utterly stupid. He clawed through the bottles, snatched up the gun, and whirled around, half-expecting Basil to be charging toward him. But Meryash was still on the ground, gasping for air. He had lost his wind in the fall.

Ryan turned the pistol over in his hand. He didn't know much about guns, but it felt odd to him, as if it were out of balance. He examined the grip. No magazine. He pulled back the slide. Empty. Basil had brought an unloaded gun. It was all a bluff.

A car door slammed.

Ryan shuffled toward the wall, peering out through a broken section of the divider, and saw a brown Chevrolet with a red light flashing on its dash. He craned his neck for a better view, then immediately ducked down, his heart rate increasing. A woman was standing by the Chevy, and she was talking to the man with the dead eyes. Ryan shot a glance at Basil, who was only now getting to his feet. "Give me your cell," he said in a hoarse whisper. "And don't make any noise."

"What?"

"Shish! Your cell phone! Give it to me."

"I'm not giving you my phone," Basil said, his eyebrows knitting into a tight slash, but his voice muted.

Ryan took some quick steps toward Basil and snapped the phone off his belt.

"Hey! You can't just take—"

"Quiet!"

Basil objected again, this time pawing at Ryan's arm, trying to get the phone.

"I don't have time for this," Ryan muttered, driving his fist into Basil's chest, and knocking him backward.

"Don't call the police," Basil said, his gasping voice suddenly morphing into a solicitous tone. "The pistol wasn't even loaded. I just wanted to—"

"Shh!" Ryan hissed. "This has nothing to do with you." He looked over the wall again, this time through a crumbled V where he wouldn't be easily seen. The man and woman were talking quietly as they walked toward Basil's Porsche, the man stopping in the middle of the road, scanning the neighborhood, the woman checking the license plate as she rounded the car, stopping at the driver's side door. She bent down, gazing in the window with shielded eyes. When the man arrived, he flipped open his jacket and pulled out a large black pistol.

Ryan jerked his face back from the wall and fumbled with his wallet. He was looking for Officer Le Beau's phone number.

* * *

Elijah Le Beau had just written his fourteenth parking ticket. Not bad for ten in the morning. He liked to fill his quota early. Not that the Yale police had quotas. No police force did. They had "suggested numbers" for each month. Failure to meet the said number meant you could forget about taking time off on special occasions, choosing vacation dates, or getting promotions. Le Beau had never liked passing out tickets, especially traffic and speeding tickets, but he kept his number at an acceptable level. The standard parking ticket, on the other hand, was different. He actually enjoyed slapping them on windshields. He felt like an extra parent, telling the students that, yes, the rules do apply to you. He especially liked catching them when they double-parked. He could never quite figure out why, after leaving their vehicles in the middle of the road, they should be so shocked at receiving a ticket. "I was only gone a minute." That's what they always said. He slipped the ticket under the wiper blade and patted it fondly. Yes, it was turning out to be a good morning.

His cell phone rang.

The number wasn't familiar, but he knew the voice: Ryan Taylor. He exhaled in frustration. Try as he might, he couldn't stay away from these two. Last night he had managed to ignore Nicole Van Buren's call because of caller ID, but with Taylor it was different. The kid didn't have a phone, which meant that caller ID didn't help. Now he would have to talk to him.

The phone crackled. Poor reception. "Can't hear you," Le Beau said, relieved to have an excuse for not responding. He felt bad about avoiding the kids, but what choice did he have? He needed to keep his nose out of things. They could easily handle their problems by other means.

"... Centennial Avenue," Taylor was saying, "abandoned tenements ... sewing factory." He continued speaking in garbled tones, but most of his words were lost.

"Hello! Speak up!" Le Beau said several times. Then he stopped. Something bothered him. "Repeat," he said. He plugged an ear to block the street noise.

"... a man ... gun ... at a vacant sewing factory ..." Taylor said.

Le Beau stared at the cracks in the cement road, thinking. Centennial was only minutes away, and although he never patrolled that area, he remembered the old sewing factory and the derelict tenement complexes. Taylor seemed to be talking about the men who had entered Krakauer's lab, the ones carrying guns, but he couldn't be sure.

Le Beau sighed. He had to sidestep this one. He couldn't even call friends on the force because, as Captain Barton said, Proskin would know. If he cared about Helena, about his pension, or their retirement plans for Arizona, he had to be focused. He had to start putting his family first. Besides, the two men were probably law enforcement. He had been around long enough to know that most of these things worked themselves out. It was probably a false alarm, and he shouldn't risk everything for a goose chase. Truth be told, none of this was his business. None whatsoever. He snapped off the phone.

* * *

Crash!

Basil's head whipped around.

More noise. Somebody was smashing out a car window.

"Let's get out of here," Ryan said, dumping the phone and gun on the ground.

Basil refused to move. "What's going on?" he demanded.

Ryan ignored him and managed to pull him a few steps.

"No!" Basil said as he strained toward the wall. "My Porsche! Somebody's breaking into my Porsche."

"Forget your Porsche!" Ryan said, clutching at him.

Basil wrenched his arms free and sprinted to the wall, popping his head over the first broken spot to look. His mouth twisted in anger. "It's the police," he said. "They're breaking my windows!"

"It's *not* the police."

"It is. I can see them." He started toward the opening in the wall.

Ryan dragged him back. "Basil," he said, clutching his face. "Listen to me!"

But Basil wasn't in the mood to listen. His face darkened and his lips stretched across his teeth like an enraged animal. "They can't do that!" he shouted, flailing his arms toward the street where he had parked his car. Then, abruptly, he squirmed away from Ryan and charged along the wall, screaming, "Get away from my car!"

Ryan chased after him, then stopped. There was no point. Basil was already beyond the wall and halfway to the road. Ryan groaned, and cast his eyes around the courtyard frantically, as if somehow that might help.

"That's a Porsche GT3, you imbeciles," Basil was yelling. "It cost more than your yearly salaries combined!" He had one of those shrill voices that pierced the air, and Ryan could hear every word as he threatened civil suits against them, the police department, and anyone else connected with them.

Smack!

A man was speaking in a low voice to a suddenly very quiet Basil. Ryan swallowed, his throat dry. He tried to think as he jerked his eyes around, searching for exits. He knew he had only seconds.

The archway! He could escape that way. It connected one building to another, and with luck, he could move along the corridor and out the other side of the complex.

He started toward the arch.

Something moved and he froze.

The woman from the street had circled around and was standing to the right of the arch, arms folded and holding a pistol with a long, black cylinder attached to the muzzle.

"Get on the ground," she said.

Ryan turned his eyes slightly, looking for a place to run.

"On the ground now," she said calmly, "or I will shoot you." She rotated the weapon toward him.

He took a knee, as he would for a coach.

"On your stomach, legs crossed, arms by your side."

Ryan obeyed, but he could feel his heart hammering against the paving stones. He tried to calm himself. The woman had a serious look about her, but she was also attractive, like the newswomen on television, and somehow that helped, as if it diluted the situation. Whatever the reason, he was glad she was here. The man with the dead eyes terrified him.

Ryan could hear Basil again on the other side of the wall. He was complaining in a breathy voice, as though in pain.

"Okay, okay," he was saying, as the man half-dragged him around the wall, one hand twisting Basil's arm behind his back, the other grasping his monogrammed collar. Basil's face had a red welt where the man had evidently hit him, and he was stretching up on his tiptoes, trying to ease the angle of his arm. They wobbled to a halt and the man threw Basil to the ground. "Get on your stomach," he growled.

Basil did so, but immediately began screaming about how he intended to report them to the highest authorities. "Your careers are over," he shrieked. "You understand? Over!"

"Your name is Basil Meryash?" the man asked.

"I already told you that."

"What's your address?"

"This is stupid," Basil said, lifting his head. "You know my address. You smashed my windows to get my registration."

"I need to confirm that you own the car," the man said.

"I own the car, okay? I own the car!"

"Then tell me your address."

"I also know a lot of lawyers."

"*Your address.*"

"2439 Flurry Boulevard, Short Hills, New Jersey, 07078," Basil rattled off insolently. "Are we clear on that now?"

"Confirmed," the man said, looking up from the registration. The woman nodded and walked over to Basil Meryash, then placed the pistol with the long cylinder two inches behind Basil's ear, and squeezed the trigger.

35

Le Beau pulled alongside a car in a tow-away zone. A two-foot-square sign shouted in bold letters: PARKING BY PERMIT ONLY. Vehicles Without Valid Permit Will Be Towed At Owner's Expense. Le Beau shook his head. Tow-away zone, and this guy is parked right under the sign. He climbed out of the car and opened his book.

"Hey! Wait!" A student with pierced ears and nose scurried toward him, flailing both arms.

Le Beau kept writing.

"Hey, man, don't give me a ticket," he pleaded. "I was just making a quick phone call."

"Sorry," Le Beau said, tearing off the ticket, "but you've got a no-parking sign bigger than Yankee Stadium above your car."

"Ah, man," he whined, "I was just calling my mother." He gestured weakly toward a pay phone.

Le Beau glanced at the lonely payphone, probably the only one left on campus.

The student gave him a pathetic look meant to engender sympathy and said, "I'm really broke … couldn't even pay my cell phone bill. Can't you give me a break?"

"How do I know you've learned your lesson?"

A glimmer of hope sprang into his eyes. "Oh, I have," he said earnestly. "Till the day I die, I will never park illegally again. I've learned my lesson. Really learned it well."

Le Beau smiled. "You were calling your mother? Is that what you said?"

"Yeah, she wants me to call, like every day."

Le Beau furrowed his brow.

"It's the truth."

"Cross your heart and hope your mother turns into a spider, or something like that?"

He crossed his heart vigorously.

"You'd better get your car out of that tow-away zone," Le Beau said as he crumpled the ticket in his hand. "Trucks prowl this area all the time, and once they hook on, you're in for a three–hundred-dollar impound fee. And they don't care about mothers like I do."

"Ah, man, you're the best," the young man shouted as he hustled across the street. He got into his car, mouthing," I love you," and left.

Le Beau shook his head and started toward his cruiser. He paused, glancing back at the phone, debating with himself. Seconds later he was picking up the plastic handle and dialing 911. "There's a fire on Centennial Avenue," he said, "in an old sewing factory." He hung up before she could ask any questions.

Then he piled back into his car, feeling better, and continued on patrol. The fire trucks would arrive in fifteen to twenty minutes, and if Taylor were in trouble, he would be okay. Le Beau turned onto Elm Street and groaned. Just what he didn't need. Four black SUVs had parked straddling the sidewalk, two on one side of the road, two on the other. Each vehicle had at least one man standing nearby, eyes constantly moving, watching the street, and several other guards were seated inside. Le Beau had seen it before. Somebody powerful—probably an actor or senator—was waiting for his kid. These people had plenty of money for bodyguards, and plenty of influence to cause him trouble. He sighed and pulled up behind a large armored SUV parked directly in front of Calhoun's gates.

Le Beau eyed the man standing beside the car. He had a body like chiseled stone, and a no-nonsense demeanor to match. A thick, ugly scar covered a two-inch square under his ear where his jaw had been reconstructed. Shrapnel or a bullet wound, Le Beau would bet his paycheck. He switched off the ignition and slowly got out.

The man came around the SUV to meet him. "Can I help you officer?"

"You can." Le Beau walked calmly toward the man. "I have to ask you to move these vehicles."

"Of course," stone-man said, his eyes examining every inch of Le Beau as if he might be a threat. "We'll be gone in a few minutes."

Le Beau nodded, and glanced around at the other SUVs parked on the street.

"They will be gone too," stone-man said evenly. "Now if you don't mind, sir, I would like you to move your cruiser away from this area."

Le Beau turned slightly toward his car, stunned by the request, which sounded more like an order.

"It's the age of terrorism, sir," the man said, softening his approach. "You understand."

Le Beau frowned, perusing once more the cars accompanying the armored SUV. Guard escort. No doubt about it. He wondered who was in the SUV but knew that at this point it didn't matter.

"I need you to move your vehicle now, sir. Loop around the block and we'll likely be out of your hair." The man's face remained pleasant, but Le Beau had no doubt there was another side to his personality.

* * *

Her father's voice was unusually warm, which made Nicole wary. "It's nice to talk to you, too," she responded. "Is anything wrong?"

"Everything's fine," he said. "But we do have a bit of a time constraint."

"I see. When will you be here?"

"I'm here now."

"Now? It's only ten-thirty."

"I apologize," he said. "The plan's been altered. I'm in a car outside the gates."

"Ahh ... okay." She cast her eyes around the apartment, thinking what she had to do. "I can be there in three minutes," she said. "What about Ryan?"

"He's not with you?"

She paused. Her father knew that Ryan had stayed the night. She wondered how closely he monitored her life. "Ryan had to see his lacrosse coach," she said. "He'll be back by noon."

"Fine. What's his cell? I'll have someone pick him up."

"He doesn't have a phone."

"No problem. We know what he looks like. Someone will find him."

Nicole didn't reply. Her father knew what Ryan looked like. Did he have pictures? She didn't know, and elected not to ask.

"As soon as you can," he added affably. "At least this way we can talk in the car, as I promised."

Exactly three minutes later Nicole exited Calhoun's gates. She immediately spotted Clarence, a former Navy pilot, standing by the armored SUV with his arms folded. He looked very unhappy, and then she saw why. Officer Le Beau was striding toward him, ticket book in hand and writing furiously.

"I moved my car," Le Beau was saying, "but I want a record of your visit. This is not a ticket but a warning notification." He ripped it off his book and handed it to Clarence.

"Officer Le Beau?" Nicole said.

He turned. "Ms. Van Buren."

She smiled in disbelief. "You're giving my father, what, a warning ticket?"

"Your father?" He shifted his eyes to the car, and back to her again. "It's just an infraction notification," he said. "Nothing major."

Clarence was already by the rear doors of the vehicle. He paused. "Thank you, officer," he said formally. "We'll be leaving now."

Le Beau nodded and headed back to his cruiser, but not without eying Clarence and the surrounding SUVs.

Clarence waited until the policeman was a good distance away before opening the door.

Nicole gazed at the retreating officer, who had now reached his car and was looking back. She waggled her fingers at him, which prompted a half smile. Then, returning her eyes to the gaping door, she swallowed a breath and entered.

Her father was seated in a rounded leather chair, especially constructed for the SUV, his head turned away and talking on his phone. "Good morning, sir," she whispered to his profile. He flicked his hand toward her as an acknowledgement, but continued talking. Nicole was glad he hadn't noticed her greeting, overly formal as it was. But she didn't know what else to say. She hadn't seen her father in almost a year, only talked to him by phone.

"General?" Clarence intoned from the front passenger seat.

Her father pointed his finger down the road. Clarence nodded to the driver and the SUV lurched forward. The privacy window to the front seats slid closed and her father snapped off his cell. He turned toward his daughter, inspecting her as one would a soldier. "You'll be fine," he said. "But just in case, I have medics waiting at the house. Are you in pain?"

"I'm loaded with Vicodin," she said. "Don't feel a thing."

He nodded, still examining her with his eyes. "Aside from the rough spots, you seem quite well."

"I am."

"Excellent grades, I've heard."

"Highest in the class."

"I expected no less."

The words hung awkwardly. Nicole knew he meant them as a compliment, but once again she had merely met expectations. Number one in her class, but it was only satisfactory.

"So, school agrees with you, I take it."

"I like Yale," she said.

"Good," he said. "That's very good." He reached out and touched her arm in a half caressing sort of way.

Nicole felt her body tighten. Her father's hand on her arm seemed so foreign. She remembered, before Bobby died, how her father would often wrap his strong arms around her, and kiss her, and tell her he loved her more than his own life. But that was before Bobby died. He hadn't kissed or touched her since. He hated her and he would till the day he died. At least that's what she thought. Now, with his hand still lingering clumsily on her arm, she wondered: was he trying to reestablish the father-daughter relationship lost so long ago? She was confused. He was reaching out to her, and somewhere deep inside she was struggling to reach back, but the best she could do was give him a superficial smile, and shift slightly to unhook her arm.

"I need to debrief," she said in a detached tone, a mannerism learned from her father.

He squared his shoulders and said, "Proceed."

"Last night I tried to tell you about Krakauer's—"

"We'll get to that," he said. "Any other developments?"

"It's urgent—"

"Other developments first," he said.

She took a breath, irritated he wasn't allowing her to speak. "I found Krakauer's notes."

His face changed. "That is interesting. Our teams came up blank. Where were they?"

"On a Mozart CD in the lab," she said. "He hid his files under the music. Ryan figured it out. He really understands computers." She couldn't help letting her admiration show. "We've become good friends, Ryan and I. You'll like him, I think."

"Do you have the disc?"

"No."

"Where is it now?"

"On Krakauer's computer desk; we left it undisturbed."

"It has a Mozart label?"

She nodded.

He snapped on the intercom and instructed Clarence to have someone secure the CD.

Nicole glanced out the window at the concrete divider on I-95. He hadn't even responded to her comment about Ryan. Nothing ever changed. For a moment she had foolishly dared to believe he might be interested in her life, maybe even still loved her. But far greater priorities occupied his mind, as they always had.

"You've read through Krakauer's files, I take it," her father resumed.

"Yes, but I—"

"Did you see any data relating to the antidote?"

Nicole waved away the question. "I want to talk about what Krakauer's done," she said. "He's not conducting the gene therapy experiments you and Proskin are so concerned about. He's engineered—"

"First, the antidote," he said.

"No! Listen to me!" she said through clenched teeth. "Last night you said we'd have time to talk. Do we or don't we?" She no longer cared how blunt she sounded. The issue was too important.

"We do," he said after an appraising pause, leaning back and stretching out his long legs.

"Fine." She took a breath to calm herself. "You seem to think that Krakauer is trying to find an efficient gene therapy vehicle. Well, he did. Or Westover did, a long time ago. What he's done since then is engineer an extremely deadly gene circuit, put it in that vehicle, and released it out into the open!"

"I understand," he said.

"You *don't* understand," she shot back, her voice rising. "This thing—*Omega* he labeled it—has affected everyone in the entire world, probably. He has altered our cellular structure! You, me, everybody! And now, because of Krakauer, the human race is on the road to extinction. Did you hear what I said? Extinction! Once triggered, this new gene set will continue ordering our cells to produce more trigger until all the cells in our bodies burst."

"I know about Krakauer and what he's done," he said quietly.

She stared at him, stunned.

"We've been monitoring his research—"

"You know?" she said in hushed voice. She tried to say something more but the words stuck in her throat.

"As I say, we've been monitoring—"

"Stop," she said, blocking his explanation with her hands. She leveled her eyes at him. "You *knew* about his research and yet—" She broke off, upset. "Why didn't you do something? Why did you let me send Ryan in there?"

"We didn't know the full picture until a few months ago," he said, "and by then it was too late."

She screwed up her face in disbelief. A few *months* ago! And he'd done nothing in all that time? Knowing her father, it hardly seemed possible. And now, sitting here in the car, he sounded unconcerned about the whole situation, as if Krakauer's research was just another event in the lab. Didn't he realize what this could do? She leaned forward, demanding his full attention. "Okay," she said, "I understand the part about it being too late to prevent *Omega* from affecting everyone, but surely you must have been worried that Krakauer might release the trigger."

"We were worried," he said.

"Then why didn't you stop him?"

"He was doing research on the antidote," her father replied, "and we wanted him to continue."

"On which antidote? For the trigger? You told me he was doing research on epitope mapping, and might keep some pathogens in the lab. *Very dangerous*, as I recall you saying." Her voice dripped with sarcasm.

"I know what I told you, but most of Krakauer's research these last few months had to do with finding an antidote for the trigger."

"Why didn't you tell me the truth?"

"It was a need-to-know situation," he said, "and you didn't need to know."

"I recruited Ryan and nearly got him killed," she snapped.

"That's unfortunate, but I don't dispense unnecessary information. You know that. It's nothing personal. Just a rule."

"So you kept me out of the loop."

"I did."

"Nice," she said, glowering at him.

He looked uncomfortable but said nothing, probably debating what avenue to take, Nicole guessed. She could scarcely control her anger, but couldn't maintain eye contact either. Exhaling in frustration, Nicole shook her head and turned away, disgusted.

The general cleared his throat. "Let me explain," he said. "I never filled you in on Krakauer because I didn't think recruiting you as a spy was the best way to handle the situation. I told you that Proskin's board was concerned about Krakauer's research, and that way I could keep an eye on him and still maintain mission integrity."

"Bottom line," she said, "you didn't trust me."

"It's about predictability, not trust. I can never predict your response to something. You have a mind of your own, and this issue is too important to be left to chance. You yourself have already said that Krakauer's research could lead to our extinction. I wasn't sure you could handle the reality of it."

"I'm handling it now," she flared. "You should have told me."

"It was a need-to-know situation," he repeated.

"I *did* need to know. You asked me to find someone for Krakauer's lab and I did: first Fraser Samuels and then Ryan. You asked me to keep a close watch on Krakauer's research, and I did that too. You said Proskin's board was concerned about Krakauer's procedures, so I scrubbed for every tidbit of information I could get from Fraser and Ryan. But you lied to me from the beginning. Krakauer's research had nothing to do with gene *therapy*—"

"Nicole, listen to me—"

"No—*you lied to me.* I'm your daughter. Fathers aren't supposed to lie to their daughters."

"This is not a personal issue."

"I think it is."

"You're wrong."

"I think you excluded me because you have never forgiven—"

"Nicole, please."

"You push me away, always."

"I do nothing of the sort. I handle all matters in the same way. It was a confidential issue, pure and simple."

"Really? Would you have left Bobby in the dark if he had been in my place? Or is it just Nicole the murderer you keep at a distance?"

He stared at her.

She turned her face toward the concrete divider, her eyes now a blur from the tears. She was determined not to cry in front of him.

After miles of silence, he looked at her and said, "I don't expect you to believe this, but I never wanted to keep you at a distance. We both know I did—there's no denying it—and maybe there's no forgiveness, but I didn't want it to happen."

Nicole kept her eyes on the divider, as if some comfort could be found in the endless wall of concrete.

"Bobby's death was an accident," he said, "one of those tragic things in life. I was angry, I admit, and for a long time most of my anger got channeled toward you. That was wrong. Terribly wrong. Bobby's death was not your fault. I should have told you that long ago. I don't know why I ...." His voice trailed off.

She blinked the wetness away from her eyes.

He cleared his throat again. "Catastrophic events do have benefits," he said. "They focus our minds on what's important."

Nicole didn't respond.

He sighed. "Well, what's done is done. You might never forgive me but at least you know my feelings." He paused. "I'm proud to be your father, Nicole, and I value your company. I sincerely do."

She glanced at him, wishing she could say something, but the words wouldn't come.

He opened his hands. "Accept it; don't accept it. It's up to you. But you know I don't puff flowery words at people. I say what I mean. And I'm telling you that Bobby's death was not your fault. The only one at fault here is me, for treating you shabbily all these years. There's no other word for it."

She turned toward him.

"You deserved better," he said.

Nicole found herself looking everywhere in the cavernous SUV but her father's face.

"You are my daughter," he continued, "my precious daughter. There's no one more important to me than you." He exhaled a long breath but the tension in his voice remained. "I might not have said it for a long time, but it's still true. I love you more than my own life. I just haven't showed it very well."

Without looking up, without a word, she unhooked her seat belt and moved across, leaning into him; the feel of his arms around her made the years fall away, and together they sat for an unmeasured amount of time, listening abstractedly to the hum of the tires on the road.

Five minutes later, maybe ten—she didn't know—her father said, "Krakauer's notes, did they contain anything on the antidote?"

She sat up and said, "Nothing helpful. One document had a record of his neutralization assays, but the tests were either negative or incomplete for an antidote."

He nodded, as if expecting the answer. Then he patted her shoulder and said, "I'm glad we talked."

"I am too," she said.

"We have a ways to go to mend fences, but at least now I have you with me." He looked at her. "I do, don't I?"

"Yes, you do," she said, pressing closer and feeling an inner peace she couldn't quite identify. The world was tottering on the edge of oblivion, yet a secret joy surrounded her like a bulwark, holding back the fear. She wondered how long it would last. Not long, she soon discovered. Minutes later, after they had talked more, and after he had kissed her on the forehead—actually kissed her—he said, "We have to make decisions, you know that, don't you?"

"I suppose so."

A grim smile creased his face. "Hard decisions," he said. "Decisions that will cost people their lives."

"What do you mean?" She returned to her seat, eyes riveted on her father.

"I'll tell you straight," he said. "It's the only way I know."

"I want it straight."

"A true daughter of mine. You make me proud."

She gave a half-nod to his compliment and motioned for him to continue.

"Krakauer's experiments have changed the direction of history, and we need to recognize that fact. The question is, where are we headed? The Black Plague killed two-thirds of Europe's population, yet they recovered. But my scientists tell me there'll be no recovery for the human race if this genetically altered *creature* residing in our cells gets triggered in our population centers. We have to find a way to control it, or it will destroy us."

Nicole sighed. "I don't see how we *can* control it, short of finding an antidote to the trigger. This genetically altered creature, as you call it, is now part of our genetic makeup. It not only resides inside us, it has become part of us. It's no longer external; it's who we are. We are now a species that can be destroyed in a violent chain reaction if somebody sprinkles a few chemicals in the air. How do you control something like that?"

"You control the information about the trigger."

"But somebody might stumble on—"

"Stumble on the trigger? You mean some high school kid in a chem lab? Anything's possible. But the lab boys think it's unlikely. They had supercomputers chewing on it for months, but it wasn't until we found it in Krakauer's lab that we figured out how to assemble it. Krakauer used a complicated process to construct the trigger. If you search hard enough you might find it, but you're not going to stumble over it. The point is, if no one knows the composition of the trigger, we avoid catastrophe. It will simply lie dormant in our cells."

"But Krakauer could release the trigger today!"

"He's already released it," her father said. "It's all over the news."

Nicole opened her mouth but nothing came out.

"Fortunately, he released it in containable areas, on a ship and in two small towns."

"What happened to the people?"

His face answered her ridiculous question.

"They're all dead," she said, looking away.

"I'm afraid so."

"What about Krakauer? Couldn't he release more—"

"He took his life this morning."

"He's dead!" She stared in shock.

"A neurotoxin to avoid answering questions about *Omega*."

"Won't the police—"

"A concern, for sure. Our agents have already sluiced the lab. They've emptied his fridges and replenished them with materials appropriate for his field of research. As a precaution, we sent an email early this morning from Krakauer's computer to Proskin, indicating that he was depressed over certain setbacks in his research. That will give Proskin officials reason for visiting him in his lab and finding him dead. I'm hopeful we can bury his actual research, but with the chaos in the country over these bizarre deaths, and a genetics professor committing suicide in a distinguished university's lab, well, I just don't know. We'll be monitoring it closely."

"You're worried that somebody—maybe the police or a news organization—will discover the true nature of his research."

"Ordinarily, no. But every law enforcement agency in the country is on this thing. It's the number one priority."

Nicole shifted uncomfortably in her seat. "Then what you're doing is serious. It's obstruction of justice."

"Yes, a serious crime. I am concealing information about Krakauer's death, the *Omega*, and the trigger he used to activate it."

"But why? They'll slap you in prison ...." She knitted her brows. "Just to save your pharmaceutical empire? Why not hand everything over and work with them?"

His lips twisted in scorn. "Forget the pharmaceutical empire. I risk everything because if I don't there will be nothing left anyway." He paused and lifted a finger. "I've learned from a lifetime of experience that information gets out. It *always* gets out. Especially with the government."

"You think someone in the government would leak—"

"Washington?" He snorted. "The place runs on leaks. If any arm of the government learns the actual composition of Krakauer's trigger ...." He shook his head. "Might as well paint the recipe on a bridge over the interstate. They'll all have their noses in it—researchers, department heads, elected officials—the whole bunch of them. And believe me, it won't be long before the information leaks or gets stolen. Then some maniac or terrorist group will manufacture the trigger and release it in our cities. It'll slice through us like a modern Death Angel, until every last one of us melts into the ground. Just like that, the people of the United States will be only a pleasant memory," he concluded in an ironic tone.

Nicole closed her eyes. She understood exactly what her father was saying, and though she knew *Omega* wouldn't kill everyone—pockets always survive—he was right that America as a nation would be no more.

"There is a way out," he said.

She looked at him.

"It's not an easy road. It requires hard decisions."

"What do you mean?"

"The first step is to recognize the seriousness of the problem."

"I think I understand how serious this is," she said somewhat acidly.

"Do you? Because most people, even when faced with the certainty of death, have an amazing capacity to deny reality."

"Hope springs eternal."

"It does. Like the passengers on the Titanic. Few recognized the seriousness of the problem. I imagine many of them refused the lifeboats because they couldn't believe that everything around them—the beautiful ballrooms, the sumptuous dining rooms, the endless decks—would be at the bottom of the ocean in two hours. Right now, you are finding it hard to believe that the world we knew is gone. I know you feel like that, because I do too. We are like the people on the doomed ship, afraid to leave our familiar surroundings, even with lifeboats bobbing in front of us."

"But getting in the lifeboat means breaking with the past, doesn't it?"

"It does."

"And that'll require hard decisions."

"I think so," he said.

"And these decisions need to be made quickly, while you control Krakauer's lab materials. Is that what you're saying?"

"Speed is essential, yes."

Nicole took a measured breath before her next words. She knew her father was leading her to a conclusion of momentous import, and though earlier she had loudly protested against being kept out of the loop, now she wasn't altogether sure she wanted to know the tough decisions he had in mind. "Your plan," she said, "means people will die. Right? A lot of people."

"Not a huge number. But important people. People we feel we know because we've seen them on television," he said in a compassionate voice. "But if we do nothing, we put America at risk—maybe even human civilization."

"People we know! Who do we ...." But she shook away the question. "Just tell me what you intend to do."

"Not just me," he said. "I want you by my side, every step of the way, if you can reconcile yourself to it."

"Go ahead." But Nicole was struggling to maintain her matter-of-fact exterior.

"I need to take control," he said. "It's the only way. If I could trust some branch of government to bury this thing, I would. But we both know what will happen if we leave it to chance. We need to lock this down, and that can only be done from the top."

She frowned. "What does that mean?"

"It means we have to take drastic measures."

"Okay, what?"

He studied her face briefly.

"Tell me!"

"I intend to replace the current President of the United States—"

"*The President?*" She mouthed the words, as if she were thinking his name.

"Replace him," he continued, "with the Secretary of Agriculture, Bruce Thomkins. He will then select me as his Vice President and I personally will take charge of all investigations relating to this whole thing."

"When you say *take over* do you mean—?"

"Yes."

"Doesn't the White House have Secret Service and military people to prevent that?"

"Secret Service, marine units, snipers, scores of anti-terrorism personnel on standby, the whole ball of wax. But except for the Service, most of these assets are four to seven minutes away. We intend to move faster than they do."

Nicole sat in stunned silence as her father explained his plan for taking over the government. He spoke calmly, as if outlining a business venture, but she knew he was serious. She also knew his plan would proceed whether she supported him or not.

"The bottom line," he said, "is that hundreds of millions of Americans likely will die if we do nothing but hope for the best."

She nodded, but her mind was numb.

He moved his hands slightly, indicating he would like her to respond.

She still said nothing.

"Nicole?"

"I don't know what to say," she said, half smiling her astonishment. "There must be another way besides killing the President and his Cabinet." She felt a desperation growing within.

"I've studied this problem for months," he said. "There is no other way. If we had an antidote, maybe, but my scientists say it will be years before any progress can realistically be made on that front. We simply can't take the risk. Too much is at stake. It's foolish to act as if Krakauer hasn't reformed the planet with his doomsday gene. He has, and before summer, the Internet will run riot with speculation on the composition of the trigger. Every lab in the world will be working on discovering it, and eventually someone will. I'll say it again: the world we knew is gone. We cannot pretend otherwise. We have to act, and we have to act now."

"When will this happen—at the White House, I mean—when will you release the trigger?"

"Tomorrow."

She opened her eyes wide.

"Speed is essential."

Nicole looked at him, her mind swirling. "I agree we need to do something," she said. "But I'm not comfortable with such extreme measures."

"Of course you're not," he said. "How could you be? I've been pondering this for months and I still despise what fate has laid at my door. The President is a friend. A good man. I've worked with him a dozen times over the years. He has three lovely teenage daughters who will lose their father, but I know this President well, and he will take a political approach to *Omega*, and put millions on the path to destruction. It's not pleasant to be at the eye of the storm where you have only minutes to make decisions before everything erupts around you, but we're here, and God help us if we do nothing."

"I can see your course is set," Nicole murmured. "What I don't understand is why you're telling me."

"I break my need-to-know rule because I want you at my side, the way I would have wanted Bobby to be there."

"I see."

"These next days will be the defining moment of my life. I need my only child with me."

"Need?"

"Yes, I need you with me, Nicole. I'm not ashamed to say that."

"A familial urge, I guess."

"What is life without the people you love?" He took a breath before answering his own question. "Duty. That's all it is. But that's not a bad word. With or without you, I will discharge my duty to the American people, to protect and defend them, but how much more meaningful to have my daughter standing with me."

Nicole winced. "You're asking too much of me," she said. "I don't know how to respond."

"You understand the issues at stake," he said, brow furrowing.

"I do, but ...." She rolled her head back, wishing the world would go away.

"Am I doing the right thing?" he asked, perplexed by her reaction.

She stared into eyes she had never seen before, intense eyes, seeking—for what seemed the first time—her opinion. "I don't know," she said finally. "I just don't know."

He patted her leg and said, "Whatever conclusion you reach will be acceptable to me. And I don't say that lightly."

She covered her face with her hands and moaned, as if the gesture would help her reach the right decision. Then she massaged in wide circles her brow, her eyes, her cheeks, until slowly she drew her fingers down to her chin. "Has it come to this?" she asked. "Killing the President?"

"Sometimes there are no good choices," he replied. "In my mind, survival of the nation comes before any individual or group of individuals. If we do nothing, we summon the Apocalypse."

"I agree, of course," but her mind was a whirl of thoughts.

"Well," he said at length, "we can talk again in a few days when we have more time to—"

"I'm with you," she said quietly.

His eyes searched hers.

"I am," she said in a steady voice, "to the bitter end."

He closed his eyes in what could only be relief.

"But I need to be honest," she said. "I don't think I'm ready for this."

"No one is ever ready when these moments come," he said, "but believe me, you have my strength and more. Of that, I'm certain."

"What can I possibly do?"

"You can start by helping us interrogate Ryan Taylor."

36 ᵕᵕᵕᵕᵕᵕᵕᵕᵕᵕᵕᵕᵕᵕᵕᵕᵕᵕᵕᵕᵕᵕᵕᵕᵕ

As the dark SUVs disappeared down Elm Street, Officer Le Beau marveled at his own stupidity. What was the matter with him? Was he completely self-destructive? Everybody knows you leave people like that alone—just tip your hat and keep going. You don't give them warning slips, for heaven's sake!

Eventually, he climbed back into his car, intending to resume patrols, but for some reason found himself heading across town, to Centennial Avenue and the sewing factory. He tried several times to connect with the phone Ryan had called him on, but had no success.

You'll end up with nothing—the captain had said, but Le Beau pushed the man's face out of his thoughts and kept driving.

More thoughts came.

He could see Helena standing in the living room with a bewildered look on her face. *They fired you? What about Arizona?* Le Beau jammed the accelerator to the floor. It was as though his integrity as a human being were at stake. If he turned his back now, he could never look in the mirror again. Job or no job, he had to do what was right. He couldn't let somebody die.

The neighborhood was worse than he remembered: mostly industrial, a few bars, a pawn shop, some three-story row houses with tiny yards, and plenty of vacant lots, plus now and then the ghostly frames of homes whose occupants had long since gone. He pulled up behind a burned out van with no tires, popped his trunk, and got out. He hadn't worn a Kevlar vest for years, but this seemed like an appropriate time. It looked smaller than he remembered, but he fiddled with the Velcro fasteners until he was able to shove his arms through the holes and secure most of the ties.

Elijah Le Beau took a breath, checked his 9 mm for a full complement of rounds, then jumped back into his car and headed for the sewing factory.

* * *

Ryan had never seen a dead body, even at a funeral, much less watched someone die. For long minutes he had lain on the ground, his face turned away from Basil's lifeless form. He couldn't erase the horror of seeing his body bounce in response to the woman's shot, jerking up, and then flattening onto the paving stones like warm clay. The blood had leaked out from Basil's hair and glistened a brilliant red in the morning sun, pooling around his head and shoulders, snaking slowly down to the lower lying stones.

That's when Ryan saw the woman turn toward him, her leather boots slowly approaching, the pistol with the silencer hanging loosely in her right hand, pointed toward the ground. She stopped a few feet behind him where he couldn't see, the way she had with Basil. Ryan stared at a tiny pebble inches from his nose and thought a prayer; any second he expected to feel the *thwack* of a bullet behind his ear.

It never came. Instead, the woman leaned over and said, "If you stay on the ground, you live. Get up, you die."

The pair moved about their tasks quickly, never speaking. The woman bound Ryan's hands with his belt, stuffed his mouth with newspaper, and secured it with torn strips of cloth. She went through Basil's pockets, retrieved his car keys, and several minutes later returned, driving the Porsche up the walkway and around the brick fencing into the central courtyard. Scooping up the empty gun and pieces of smashed phone, she threw them into the back seat of the car. Then the man drove the Chevrolet into the courtyard and dumped Basil's body into the trunk. The two of them scraped dirt and mortar from the base of the crumbling wall and spread it over the blood.

From time to time, Ryan could hear vehicles approach, pass by, and continue down the road. Then one stopped and cut its motor. The woman paused, and walked over to the crevice in the wall where Ryan had looked out earlier. "Police," she said expressionlessly.

The man dusted off his hands. "Yale or New Haven?"

"Yale," she said. "One officer. I think it's him."

"Okay, get some height."

She nodded, and moved rapidly toward a set of slate stairs that led to the building's main entrance. The man hauled Ryan up by his bound hands, and towed him toward the open trunk. "Get in," he said.

Ryan hesitated. Basil was lying on his back in the trunk, facing upwards, except that half of his face was missing and in its place was a tangle of bones, brains and dark-red congealing blood.

The man pulled out a pistol with a thick silencer and said, "One way or the other."

Ryan climbed into the trunk and lowered himself gingerly onto Basil's body, trying to keep his face from touching anything wet. It was no use.

In the darkness, after the latch had clunked and his face had slid across Basil's to a comfortable but sticky resting place, Ryan counted his breaths and imagined they were waves breaking on a warm sandy beach.

* * *

The old sewing factory stood starkly against the morning sky, the grounds littered with cigarette butts, broken glass and twisted rubbish. Weeds grew in clumps where once there had been grassy borders, and bits of green sprouted from spider cracks in the cement.

Le Beau swept his eyes over the broken facade with its smashed-out windows and charred walls, and his concern grew. Not the smartest place to be strolling around without backup, he thought grimly.

He had never put himself in this kind of situation before and he knew he should at least call in his location. But he couldn't risk it. Any report would surely find its way to Proskin, and that could jeopardize Helena's drug trials. He had to gamble. But on a last-minute impulse, he unhooked his radio from his belt, ready to make a call if need be.

Jaw set, he rounded the brick wall that screened off the facility.

In the center of the courtyard sat a fancy Porsche and a brown Chevrolet.

Le Beau scanned the courtyard before returning to the Chevrolet, his eyes narrowing. He had seen this car before, across from Sterling Library ... the military pair that knew Captain Barton. He pressed his lips together, thinking, then moved closer to get a better look. A pigeon suddenly beat its wings off a window ledge, and Le Beau jumped. His eyes darted to the ledge, to the nearby doors and windows, but he saw nothing. Easy does it, he said to himself, taking a long breath and slowly inspecting the whole building, then the courtyard.

Still nothing.

He glanced at the cars again, and then the paving stones to the rear of the Chevrolet. Something about the scattered sand and bits of mortar troubled him. The area looked discolored, as if someone had tried to soak up oil. Then he noticed a piece of cloth, maybe part of a jacket caught in the trunk latch.

Popping sounds—and movement at the far end of the courtyard. A man with a gun! Then a woman suddenly appeared above him on the stairs, and he saw her raise a weapon.

Le Beau swung his arm around, reaching for his 9 mm, but his body jerked sideways, as if he had been hit by a linebacker. He took a step to maintain his balance, his chest burning. Then something struck him in the stomach. His ear and cheek turned to fire, and his mouth filled with warm blood.

Officer Le Beau stumbled to the ground, realizing he had been shot. He felt no pain, not really, just a rush of adrenaline pumping through his body, and the fear he would die. The popping sounds continued. A bullet smashed his left thigh. He rolled over on the stones, grasping his leg. A voice inside his head screamed, "Move or die!" He twisted around and clawed at the 9 mm on his belt, but he had trouble pulling it out. Suddenly, it was in his hand and he fired several shots blindly, exactly what he had been trained not to do. Then, with every ounce of determination in his soul, he hauled himself off the stones and lurched toward the nearest doorway.

Two more bullets smacked into his back, again penetrating the Kevlar vest.

Le Beau stumbled through the entrance and collapsed. His body felt as if a hundred bees had stung it. He lay on the tile floor, face down, confused by the large drops of blood splashing onto the tiles, inches from his face. He touched his hand to his chin, and it turned red with blood. Several teeth were missing. And part of his ear. He tried to gather his fragmented thoughts. A bullet must have passed through his mouth and out his cheek, and another clipped the top of his ear.

He coughed, and his chest heaved like a bag filled with water. He tried to sip the air, but felt as if he were drowning. Four or five bullets had somehow pierced his vest. His hand went for his radio, but he remembered unhooking it, and then dropping it in the courtyard. Le Beau glanced around the tiny room and couldn't help wondering if this would be the place he would die. A dirty, foul-smelling space where once a proud doorman might have stood, but now reeking of decomposed excrement. More significantly, the room had no exit. Helena's face fluttered through his mind and he worried about how she would take the news.

A wave of dizziness swept over him and he knew he was losing blood. He made a supreme effort to focus his mind. None of the bullets had severed an artery, he guessed. More likely, he had just suffered too many wounds. Either way, he was in trouble and had only minutes of consciousness, if that. He needed to convince the pair outside that he was not worth the effort, that any attempt to storm the room would prove costly. It wouldn't be easy. These were military types on a mission, and apparently, part of their mission was to eliminate witnesses.

He crawled behind a plastered column, braced his pistol, and waited.

Seconds later, he heard footsteps outside.

"Are you ready yet?" Le Beau called as robustly as he could, but his voice sounded weak. "I'm waiting!"

No reply.

"Think it's easy to kill a cop?" He broke off in a fit of coughing, patches of darkness threatening to overwhelm him, but he pulled himself back. "Not so easy killing a cop," he muttered, as blood dribbled from his lips. He coughed again to clear his throat, but it didn't help. He forced some air into his lungs and continued in the loudest voice he could muster, "Whatever you're trying to do, better do it fast. Backup's on the way."

Silence.

He repositioned his gun hand in an effort to keep alert. His eyes had begun to feel heavy, as if he had taken a sleeping pill, and his body was strangely cold. He squinted at the open door, wanting something to happen, but with every passing moment, he could feel the warm waves of sleep beckoning him from the darkened shores of his mind. *Concentrate,* he whispered to himself. *Focus your thoughts.* His eyes drifted closed and he dragged them open again. *Focus!* But he was slipping into the darkness.

A shadow flitted past the open door.

Le Beau stiffened, readying himself. *When the going gets tough,* he said to himself, but he was too tired even to think the rest. He stared down the barrel of his pistol, waiting. Long seconds passed.

Was that movement on either side of the entryway? He blinked his eyes a dozen times. Tentacles of fog wafted across the door. "Let's get on with it!" he hollered, squinting through the gathering haze. He pulled the trigger and the *boom* of his weapon shook his mind awake. It took several breaths to ready himself for his next words, but he managed to shout, "First one through the door dies!"

Le Beau rested his head against the column, gasping for air. The shouting had utterly exhausted him, and the room was spinning in a giant circle around him. Another jolt to his mind, he mumbled thickly—that's what he needed. He fired his pistol again, but this time the *boom* seemed muted, as if from a distant hill, and his mind swirled more violently. He squeezed his eyes shut, trying to control the spinning, but when he did, he seemed to spiral into a deep well, and an overwhelming tiredness descended on him. His limbs felt heavy, like dead trees—and then suddenly they were incredibly light.

He was drifting on a river, with soft water washing over him and the sun warming his skin.

Le Beau could see Helena now.

She smiled at him and he smiled back.

A quiet breeze brushed across his face, and Officer Le Beau floated away.

37

"Interrogate Ryan?" Nicole asked, straining against the seat belt.

The general held up his hand to forestall her concern. Now that she was on board with his plans—which pleased him enormously—he was not about to lose her over something this trivial. He needed to bring her along slowly. "Not quite the word," he said. We want to interview him. We need to know about the antidote, if it exists."

"Well, whatever you call it, I don't want Ryan subjected to—"

"I know," he said as gently as possible, "I know. But he'll not be hurt in any way. We're simply covering our bases. You can be there the whole time to help him remember."

"He doesn't know anything about Krakauer's neutralization assays," she said, settling back in her seat. "I've talked to him several times."

"You're probably right," the general nodded, "but on the chance he knows something he's not aware of, it's worth the effort to debrief him to get to that answer quickly. You understand the stakes."

"Okay," she said, still wary.

"We did learn something from Krakauer's release of the trigger."

"Something good, I hope."

"Something very good. Krakauer might have been a reckless fanatic, but he was right about *Omega* containing itself before it could spread beyond targeted areas. It amplified in Nevada—hit a number of areas north of Midas where it was released—but exhausted itself rather quickly."

She looked at him. "That's why you think it's safe to use at the White House?"

"None of this is safe, but it's a necessary risk." He paused, giving her time to think. She still had lingering doubts, that much was clear, and needed to express her reservations or she would never fully be with him. And he wanted his daughter with him. He gestured for her to speak and when she did, her strength of character made him proud.

Nicole looked him squarely in the eyes and said, "You call Krakauer, reckless? At least he released the trigger in so-called containable areas. You're planning to use it in the middle of Washington, DC!"

"Not in the middle of Washington," he said. "In the Situation Room, behind closed doors."

"It could still amplify—seep out to the guards, then staffers, and so on."

"Actually, it's worse than that," he said. "The first symptoms are sweating, nausea, and headaches, so although this thing works fast, they'll have time to call the Secret Service."

"So you agree. It'll amplify."

"Yes, but not beyond the White House. If it breaches the Situation Room—a reasonable expectation—it'll self-limit. The West Wing will take a hit, but the White House response to any threat will be immediate lock down. At the end of the day, our soldiers will be there to secure the entire area and limit the spread."

"It's still a risk," she said.

"A risk, yes, but doing nothing presents an even greater risk, given the circumstances."

Her eyes showed that she understood. "The circumstances being that some politician or bureaucrat might leak information about the trigger."

"Exactly. No one knows quite what to make of this Catastrophic Cellular Failure, Nevada, as they call it, but they will soon enough. And when extremist groups get hold of that information—and they will, believe me—death and hell will follow in their wake. Does anyone think that these fanatics won't release the trigger in American cities?"

"They probably will," she said grimly.

"Damn right they will. And then it'll be too late to control the situation." He glanced out the window at the buildings and parks lining I-95 and added, "At this very moment our cities are still intact, the people productive. We can still protect America."

She followed his eyes. "It all looks so normal." The traffic had begun to slow, and outside, two elderly women were watching children chase each other around a playground.

"It does look normal," he acknowledged. "Normalcy bias. The familiar lulls us into believing that what we see is permanent. But it's not, Nicole, and soon—very soon—the familiar will disappear, and just like the Titanic, all of this could be at the bottom of the ocean. We need to act."

She said nothing, just stared out the window.

"You know we have to do this," he said, keeping his voice matter-of-fact, not wanting to appear as if he were pushing her.

"I know. It's just ... hard."

"We've been meticulous in our planning. If we move now we can limit the damage to a fenced off area—the White House—and reduce the cost in American lives."

"And Secretary Thomkins, he'll be President." Her eyes still lingered outside.

"Yes, and that's critical, because with Bruce Thomkins at the top, we can control information about *Omega* and its trigger."

"Makes sense," she said quietly. "Hard to believe, but it does make sense."

He was about to respond when his cell phone buzzed. He raised his hand in apology and snapped on the phone. It was Donovan.

"We've eliminated Meryash," Donovan said. "Got rid of his car. But we have some situations."

"Go on."

"The Taylor kid, we picked him up, but he got loose. I have vehicles scouring the area. I don't think it'll be long."

"Understood."

"Also, the black cop, Le Beau, showed up and we took him down."

"Witnessed by anyone there?"

"If you mean Taylor, negative. He did see Meryash cash in."

"Go on."

"The problem is we had to leave the cop's body. Sirens were closing."

"I see." The general spoke deliberately. "Either of you observed by civvies?"

"Don't think so, sir."

"Tomorrow we launch Thermopylae. After that it won't matter." He clicked off his phone.

The general felt his daughter's eyes on him, enquiring.

"Bumps in the road," he said brusquely. "Nothing major." He opened the console on his chair and asked, "Would you like to see the news?"

"Yes, I would," she said, her demeanor sharpening.

"I thought you might." He tapped the console and a television rotated into place behind the driver's seat.

"This is Fernando Sanchez for CNN in Biggar, Canada," the reporter said, "where disaster has befallen a rural farming community."

"I watched this a half hour ago," the general said quietly.

"Biggar is a small town," continued the reporter, "of roughly 2000 people, nestled in the province of Saskatchewan." He pointed down an empty highway. "The Montana border is 225 miles in that direction—not far, but I can tell you, that's a lot of empty farmland. To get here you pass by such metropolises as—" he checked his notes—"Swift Current, Moose Jaw, Eyebrow, and Saskatoon." His smile morphed into a grimace to indicate he understood the gravity of the situation.

Glancing around, he continued, "In the distance you can see where two highways intersect, the 4 and the 51, just outside Biggar's town limits; we're set up about a mile away. That's as close as the Canadian authorities will let us come. The Canadian version of the CDC has sealed off the whole town—but you can still see the famous sign in the distance." He turned and said, "Terry, cut to the sign." The camera zoomed in on an eight-foot sign that declared:

NEW YORK IS BIG
BUT THIS IS BIGGAR

"For over a hundred years those words brought smiles to people's faces," the reporter told the camera, "but now, as the magnitude of the situation becomes apparent, no one is smiling."

"Fernando," the anchor broke in, "what do we actually know about the situation in Biggar?"

"An excellent question, Bert. At this point, we have very little information. We've seen a number of self-contained fully ventilated vehicles arrive all morning—the kind associated with outbreaks of disease—and some have reported sightings of personnel in positive pressure suits going from building to building. The airspace has been closed and no one is being allowed to get anywhere near the town. Beyond that, as I say, we simply don't know. Canadian officials have been promising an update since early morning, but so far they've given us nothing."

"It's hard to deny the similarity to the cruise ship off Puerto Rico, and the growing situation in Midas, Nevada."

"It certainly does appear similar, Bert. Officials at this point refuse to confirm any connection and seem to be keeping a very tight lid on all information coming out of the affected areas."

"I've never seen anything like it. We can't even get a news crew into northern Nevada." Bert shook his head in disbelief before asking, "Have there been any communications with residents of Biggar? Any phone calls or text messages?"

"Not that we know about. It's as if they were sealed off from the rest of the earth."

"A tragedy, especially for loved ones desperate for information."

"Indeed."

"As you know, Fernando, CNN doesn't like to speculate, but are you hearing any rumors as to what's happened?"

"The whispers are ominous, Bert, and the feeling here on the ground is that something horrible has happened in Biggar. One Canadian source who asked not to be identified said that as far as he knew, there are no first-hand accounts of what occurred, and that there might never be."

"Unbelievable. Our hopes and prayers certainly go out to the families."

"For certain. Fear and anxiety is written on everyone's face here, Bert."

"And the fear is growing, Fernando?"

"It is. People are questioning where this thing will strike next."

"I'm told you got a statement from the mayor of Biggar."

"A declaration of shock is a better way to put it. Mayor Roger

Conley had just returned from his cottage in the Battleford area north of here when he got the news. He is reported to have said, 'God help us,' before Canadian officials whisked him away."

"You also have something on the mayor's family, I understand."

"I do, a tragedy like so many other stories today. The mayor's wife and two boys, who were scheduled to join him, never got out of Biggar."

"Defies imagination, Fernando."

The reporter nodded slowly and said, "The only other bit of information we have comes from a spokesperson for Saskatchewan's Health Ministry. She describes the situation as exceedingly grave."

"What reaction have you received from—"

The general turned off the television. "I need to brief you on a couple of items," he said, "in case your friend Ryan calls."

* * *

Ryan sprinted down the roadway, looking for help. He had seen only two cars, and both sped away when the driver noticed Ryan's shirt was soaked with blood, no matter that his hands were bound. His escape had been sheer luck, the trunk latch catching on the bottom of his jacket and popping open. He fully expected a bullet in his back as he dashed across the courtyard, but he made the wall, and then the street, and he never stopped running, nor did he look back.

He could hear the engine of another motor vehicle in the distance, a black SUV. Ryan waved his bound hands and the vehicle slowed, then stopped. Two men--one black, one white--with military-style haircuts and a serious bearing stepped out.

"Your name Ryan Taylor?" one of the men asked.

Ryan tried to say that he was, but his words were muffled by the gag.

They removed the belt from his hands and cut the cloth stripes covering his mouth. Ryan spit out the newspaper, retching slightly, then said, "We've got to call the police. Do you have a phone? There's been a shooting—"

"Easy, take it easy," the black guy said, a solid man with piercing eyes. He poured some bottled water on a napkin and wiped Ryan's face clear of blood. That done, he opened the back door to the SUV and said, "Get in. We can talk on the way."

Ryan hesitated. "On the way where?" he asked. "Who are you guys? How'd you know my name?"

"We work for Nicole Van Buren's father," came the reply; the other man remained silent. "We were told to find you and bring you to the Greenwich compound."

Ryan glanced around at the burned out houses and vacant lots, and felt uncomfortable. "How did you know I was here?" he asked, debating whether to blitz through the houses away from these guys.

"We didn't," the man shrugged. "We've got a half dozen cars looking for you, most of them on campus." He handed Ryan a phone and said, "Press number four."

He saw no reason to object, and pressed the four.

"Ryan?"

"Nicole! Where are you?"

"I'm at home in Greenwich with my father."

"Listen, those men showed up this morning—one of the men anyway—and a woman and they—"

"I can't understand you. You're talking too fast."

"They killed Basil," Ryan said loudly. "Shot him in the head."

"Wha ... they killed ... oh, Ryan, that's awful!"

"It was. It really was. This is getting ... I don't know .... We've got to call somebody, the FBI ... maybe Le Beau. He might have been here ... somebody was shooting—"

"You're not making sense, Ryan, but listen to me," she hesitated. "The police are here at the house."

"The police?"

"Yes, and the FBI. A bunch of doctors, too, just as I said there'd be."

"Ah, okay. Be there soon." He handed the phone to the man and climbed into the back of the SUV. As the door closed, and he sank into the cushioned leather seats, the locks clacked shut.

* * *

Nicole clicked off her phone and locked eyes with her father.

"Better this way," he said. "You don't want him forced into a car. It's upsetting. This way you can explain everything when he arrives at the house. I'm sure he'll understand."

"They killed Basil!" she gasped.

"I know."

"You know? Why didn't you ...?" She turned away, preferring the traffic crawling along I-95 to her father's detached expression.

"Get it all out," he said.

She faced him squarely. "I can't believe this! Why would they shoot ... did you order this? I want to know. Did you authorize them to kill Basil?"

"I did not. But you have to understand, the boy was—"

"Basil. His name was Basil. Basil Meryash."

"Okay," he said. "Basil was creating problems—"

"For that he gets shot in the head?"

276

"He had a gun, Nicole. He had taken Ryan to some abandoned factory. The team did what they thought they had to. Not my wishes, but in the course of operations, these things happen fast."

She heaved a huge, unfathomable sigh, unable to control the tears welling up in her eyes.

"I know this is hard," he said, "because it's personal."

Nicole let out a small moan.

"Do you still want to be kept in the loop?"

Her body tensed. "I said I did."

"Then I need to tell you that the police officer you've been meeting with ...."

"Le Beau?"

"Yes."

She held her breath.

"I'm afraid he's been killed, too."

"Le Beau?" She swallowed, not comprehending. "Officer Le Beau? No," she said, shaking her head. "No, I don't believe it."

"I'm afraid so. While they were protecting Ryan, he opened fire on our people. Nothing else they could do."

"Nooo," she groaned, clasping her hands in front of her, as though in prayer. "Not Officer Le Beau!" She began shaking her head, trying to push away the truth, and feeling sick in her stomach. "It can't be. It ... can't." She stared at her father. "I don't believe this! I saw him this morning. How could ... I mean, where did ...?" She groaned again, louder this time, and covered her mouth. Officer Le Beau, dead! She could still see him coming around his desk, a twinkle in his eyes as he offered his hand, enjoying her discomfort. How could he be gone?

"I know you liked the man—"

"I can't believe this. Basil and Le Beau dead!" She shot an accusing look at her father, unable to control her anger. "Why don't you keep a tighter rein on your people?" she demanded.

"Agents in the field need freedom to act," he said in an unruffled voice. "The downside is that sometimes they make decisions differently than you'd want. But what's done is done. We have to move on."

"Yeah, I guess we'll just move on," Nicole said sourly, wishing she could escape this nightmare, turn the clock back a couple of weeks.

He paused and said, "Ryan is alive. Safe. Heading to meet us at the house right now. Focus on that. And don't forget about everything that is happening. These were collateral deaths—yes, unfortunate, but collateral events in a much larger drama. If we don't get control of *Omega*, hundreds of millions of other people will die in America. Do you understand? They're all going to die. Your friends at Yale, your dancing instructors, mothers and children everywhere across this land are going to die unless we put our feelings aside and complete this mission. Do you follow what I am saying?"

She lifted her hand to acknowledge his point.

"That's not good enough, Nicole. I need more. Much more." His voice was gentle, but he clearly wanted a commitment.

She raised her head and his eyes searched hers.

"I understand," she said, her voice lifeless. "I do."

He waited.

"It's just difficult to deal with the practical consequences. I knew these people, okay?"

"I'm amazed you're doing as well as you are," he said quietly. "It's not easy keeping the larger picture in view when the immediate constantly obscures it. But that's what we have to do in the coming weeks, and especially today with Ryan."

"What do you mean?"

"When we interview him, you need to keep in mind the larger picture."

38

Late that morning Ryan rolled through the gates at Nicole's Greenwich home, a broad expanse of green with sculpted trees, dazzling flower gardens, and Greek statuary lining the walkways. The massive residence was built of limestone blocks, a seventeenth-century style castle, complete with blue and red turrets, arrow slits, and a moat fronting the towering walls. The SUV snaked through the grounds and over a bridge until it stopped at an enormous arched doorway. Nicole was standing in the entrance.

She stepped into the sunlight.

The man with the piercing eyes opened Ryan's door and then retreated to the rear of the car.

"Welcome," Nicole said neutrally.

Ryan climbed out but stopped when he saw a sudden shock on Nicole's face. She had noticed the blood splatters on his shirt.

"From Basil?" she asked, her composure returning.

"It was bad," Ryan said, shaking his head.

She nodded.

He stared at her, waiting for her to speak.

"Hard to believe," she said finally. "Poor Basil."

"Yeah," Ryan said, not sure what else to say, and puzzled by her muted reaction.

"Glad you made it here safely," she said, moving down the stairs and kissing him robotically on the cheek. "How do you like the castle?" she asked. "Built in the 1890s by a Romanian land baron trying to emulate the past."

"Impressive," Ryan said, frowning.

"My father hates the place. Pompous ostentation, he calls it."

Ryan glanced at the men talking behind the SUV, their eyes on each other, but clearly aware of every movement around them.

"My mother desperately wanted to live here," Nicole continued. "A year and a day after we moved in, she left. But we stayed because my brother, Bobby, liked living in a castle."

"It's certainly big, no doubt about that," Ryan said, trying to say something that would fit with their bizarre conversation. It was as if they were strangers.

She stepped through the arch, saying over her shoulder, "I'll introduce you to my father."

He followed Nicole into an entrance hall with huge chandeliers and sweeping staircases that ascended to the upper levels. A servant took his jacket and ran off to fetch a clean shirt, returning almost instantly with an assortment of five, apologizing that he hadn't a better selection. Ryan chose a blue hiking top, took a few minutes to wash up before he and Nicole headed for the library to meet with her father. On the opposite side of the entrance hall, they turned into a broad corridor, cut through a sitting room, then down another corridor until they stopped at a door elaborately carved with reliefs of animals and foliage, bordered by leaded glass on either side. Nicole tapped the knocker before entering.

A tall man with gray hair rose from his chair by the fire. Though he was thin, his shoulders were powerfully built and every part of him seemed like it was cut out of wood. His steel gray eyes smiled warmly as he extended his hand.

"Good to meet you, Ryan," he said before Nicole could even make introductions. They shook hands and Ryan took a seat across from Nicole.

"This is a beautiful library," Ryan offered, running his eyes over the walls of books, the enormous paintings, and glistening plank floors.

Her father nodded and said, "I hear you two have had quite an adventure."

"I wouldn't be here if it hadn't been for your daughter," Ryan said earnestly. He took a breath, ready to extol Nicole's bravery, but her father moved the conversation to another footing.

"Well, we're all glad you're here," he said. "You're probably hungry—Nicole has already eaten. What can I get you? Steak? Fish? A hamburger?"

Ryan shrugged. "Anything's fine," he said.

"I think I'll have a burger," her father said, cheerfully. "Is that okay for you?"

"It's great. Thank you."

"French fries? Coke? Beer?"

"Fries and coke are fine, thanks."

"Got that, Pamela?"

"Yes, sir," said a woman standing behind him by the rear door. She had slipped in without Ryan noticing.

"Maybe a lager for me," her father said. "Negra Modelo with lime."

The woman dipped her head and left.

Two doctors came through the carved door unannounced and examined Ryan's shoulder, listened to his lungs, dressed the wound on his side, and pronounced him lucky, but fit. Lunch arrived next, as if part of a closely controlled schedule. Pamela placed an impressive platter on a swing-table next to Ryan; she had heaped it with steak fries, onion rings, assorted fruits, and a handful of finger chocolates. In the center, on a raised circle of glass, sat two large hamburgers.

Ryan made polite remonstrations about the amount on his tray, and then promptly tore into the burgers; he was starved. Through all of this, Nicole remained silent, reclined almost motionlessly in a large wingback chair. Nicole's father nibbled a piece off his hamburger and said, "Pamela is a fine cook, wouldn't you say?"

"Amazing," Ryan admitted as he crunched a mouthful of onion rings.

"Ryan," the general began, "Nicole has told me all about these last few days, and I want to thank you for everything you've done."

Ryan nodded.

"I trust you understand how serious this is."

"I do, sir. Professor Krakauer is a madman who's altered the DNA of everyone on the planet with some sort of a doomsday gene."

"Yes," the general said, studying him. "Hard to accept, isn't it?"

Ryan swallowed the last bite of his burger. "Yes."

"And you understand the implications. A lot of people are going to die—your friends at school, your teammates, professors, even your parents, I hate to say—if this *Omega* thing gets triggered."

"I know," Ryan said, downing a fistful of French fries. "It's unbelievable."

"Fortunately, the professor was exploring an antidote to the trigger, which could eliminate most of the problem."

"There's an antidote?"

"That's what he was working on while you were in his lab," her father said.

"Really?"

The general pushed his food aside and fastened his eyes on Ryan. "I don't like games."

Ryan frowned, perplexed.

"Especially when lives are on the line."

"I don't understand."

"I think you do."

Ryan glanced at Nicole, but her eyes were on the floor.

"You told my daughter you knew nothing about Krakauer's research on the antidote, but that's not the whole truth, is it?"

"Yes, it is. The complete truth," Ryan said, his eyes widening.

"I'm waiting."

"For what?"

"The truth. You know more than you're saying. Don't you?"

"No ... no, I—"

"You were there with Krakauer for months. You were his only research assistant. Somehow you knew exactly where he kept his research notes." The general leaned forward and raised his eyebrows. "I can understand your reluctance to talk about it. Perhaps you're concerned that others will question whether you were involved? I can assure you, Ryan, that we're all focused on solving the problem, not assigning blame. We're on the same team here. Tell me about the antidote. Whatever has come before isn't important."

Ryan gestured toward Nicole with open hands, bewildered. "What is this?" he asked, screwing up his nose.

She lifted her eyes but said nothing.

"Look," Ryan said, turning back. "I don't know anything about *Omega* or the antidote or ... whatever."

"So you're telling me that the whole time you worked at Krakauer's lab, he never once spoke about his research?"

"Well, sure, at times ...I guess ... he said things. But nothing about an antidote, or trigger. I mean, I didn't even know this thing existed until we got into his computer."

"I find that hard to believe, Ryan, especially since you helped Krakauer dispose of those dead maintenance workers."

"I didn't ... well, I saw a tattoo but—"

"You put bodies in an incinerator."

Ryan's tongue felt thick.

"That system to hide files inside the reserved areas of a disc. Pretty clever. Did Krakauer design that?" His eyes narrowed. "I didn't know his expertise ran in that direction."

"You can find most of the code for that online," Ryan said softly.

The general nodded. "And am I right that you designed a custom firmware to pluck it out, in what, an afternoon? The experts I have here say that's a hell of job in a few hours. Hell of a job."

Ryan's eyes glanced around the library. "I had most of it built before."

"I see. How are things back home? Any financial troubles?"

Ryan said nothing.

"You can understand why I have concerns, Ryan. And frankly, so do the FBI agents waiting downstairs. They think you're a terrorist." He paused. "Now, I don't believe you willingly did anything wrong, Ryan, and I'd like to help you. But you need to help me, too."

"I'm not sure what you want me to say."

"Surely Krakauer must have told you something."

"Well, he didn't!" Ryan said without trying to conceal his anger. He felt pressure building in his abdomen.

"Think carefully about your answers," the general said heavily.

"I am, but there's nothing to think about. The man never talked to me even once about anything." He stopped, took a breath to calm himself, and said, "Okay, listen, you're Nicole's father, and I don't want to be disrespectful, but I'm getting a little frustrated with these questions. I don't know what you want me to say. I just cleaned the labs. That's it. That's all I did. She's the one who sent me in there. Why are you asking me this stuff, anyway? If you want to know something, ask Dr. Krakauer. He knows everything."

"We did, this morning."

"Okay ...."

"Unfortunately, the professor died during our questioning period."

Ryan gaped at him, incredulous. Krakauer was dead? Died during the questioning period? What the hell did that mean? Ryan tried to focus. He had heard the words but somehow couldn't comprehend them. How could the professor have ...?

"He refused to answer our questions. We had hoped you'd be more cooperative."

Was that a threat? Ryan turned to Nicole and said, "What the hell's going on?"

"You'd better tell him what he wants to know," she said in a low voice. "It's important."

He half smiled his disbelief. "What are you talking about?"

She sat stone-faced, her eyes lifeless.

"Jeez, Nicole, what's wrong with you? Can't you even—"

"You don't have much time, Ryan," she said, glancing toward the library door.

Ryan followed her eyes, but saw nothing. He pushed his table aside and stood up. "You said there were police and FBI here. I'll take my chances with them. Where are they?"

Nicole didn't respond.

"Okay, that's it," he said. "I'm gone."

The door opened.

Ryan whipped his head around.

A man built like a freight train pushed through the door, his jaw clotted with purple scars, his black eyes menacing as they locked onto Ryan.

Ryan retreated several steps.

The man stabbed a thick finger at him and shouted, "Don't move."

Ryan instinctively held his breath, his eyes darting in Nicole's direction, thinking they had to get out. Then, suddenly, he realized she was part of whatever this was.

"There's still more to talk about," she said blandly.

Ryan looked at her, stunned. He opened his mouth to say something, but instead pivoted and headed for the rear door. He stopped. A second man! Striding toward him. "Oh, no ... no ...," he gasped. Blood surged through his veins, hammering in his ears. It couldn't be! Not here. Not with Nicole. Not the man with the dead eyes. Ryan lurched back and collided with his table of empty dishes, scattering it across the plank flooring. Hands reached for him. He stepped sideways, wrenching away his arm. Something flashed, like a gun. Only it wasn't a gun. A curved, black device with sparkling electrodes at the end. A blue light flared, and a surge of electricity hit him.

He screamed.

More electricity.

His muscles bunched up in a violent contraction and he collapsed to the floor. They shoved the electrodes into his stomach, his mouth, and the back of the neck. He couldn't think. They yanked him to his feet and shocked him again. His legs buckled under him but they had him propped up between them. The shocks never stopped. His mind reeled and he didn't know where he was. All he felt was pain, and the sensation of being dragged out a door and down a set of stairs.

* * *

"You shocked him!" Nicole shouted, her eyes blazing. "You never said anything about doing that."

"I know," her father said gently, "but believe me, it just looks scary. It's the safest way to subdue someone. Standard practice used by every police force in the country. He'll be fine." He paused before adding, "Of course, we need to keep talking with him. You saw how combative he was."

"Combative?" She raised her hands in agony. "I saw him get frustrated with your questions."

"He knows more than he's saying."

She opened her eyes, speechless. "Father," she said, pleading, "he knows nothing."

Her father raised his index finger and said, "Yet to be determined."

"No, you're wrong. Please ...."

"Are you willing to gamble hundreds of millions of lives on it? Your life? Mine? His? The stakes are serious, Nicole." The general opened his hands in an appeal. "Let's give him a chance to cool off downstairs. We can't let him walk out of here in any case. It's not safe for him, and we can't take the risk that he might talk to someone about this. Not until it's under control. You know that."

Nicole exhaled in frustration. "I know this is serious," she said, "but I don't want him hurt."

"Of course. That's not our intention."

"And I want to talk to him."

"Ooh," he said, puckering his lips. "I don't think that's a good idea. Give him some time to calm down. And you get some rest. I will let you know the minute anything changes."

"Well ..." she said, hesitating."

"Trust me, Nicole. It's for the best."

39

Nicole Van Buren had the worst night of her life. She flipped from side to side, searching for a comfortable sleeping position, but succeeded only in tangling the covers around her legs. Several times she drifted off, then jerked awake, her forehead cold and damp. Nightmares of Bobby's death—which had always plagued her—had merged in some horrible way with images of Ryan lying dead on a highway, like a neglected animal. She told herself Ryan was fine—just downstairs resting as her father had promised, but the tossing continued.

At four o'clock in the morning she wandered out to the medicine cabinet, downed two Ambien pills, and fell into a fitful sleep, still laced with horror.

* * *

Donovan slept well. He had arrived in Washington late that evening, met briefly with his senior officers, and bedded down on the concrete floor of a loading dock, his sleeping bag zipped around his neck.

Before turning in, he thought about talking to Prator, who had taken a spot at the end of the dock. Several times she had looked at him, inviting him to speak, but each time he decided against it. He would talk later. For now, it was best to focus on the mission.

* * *

The general rose at dawn. He drank his coffee, ate scrambled eggs and apple slices, and boarded a helicopter for his ride to Westchester Airport. But the general never just went along for the ride: he took the controls from Clarence on both the Black Hawk and the Gulfstream jet that arrived at Reagan, 0800 hours. Another short helo ride and he was at the DOT Hazmat Training Conference at Coral Hills, Maryland. A sizable group from Proskin was undergoing hazmat training, though not the team that would very soon approach the White House. They were already in position, only minutes away.

The general wandered through the tables, pausing to take questions from the press about the need for pharmaceutical companies to be vigilant in an environment of radical extremism. He stopped to congratulate DOT officials on their execution of the conference, and nodded his understanding when they apologized for the Secretary of Transportation's absence; apparently he had a Cabinet meeting at the White House. During the conversation, a message came through on the general's cell that Secretary Bruce Thomkins had called his wife to say he was about to enter the Situation Room and would be unable to meet her for lunch. The general noted the time and forwarded the message to Donovan.

Exactly thirty-five minutes later, the general called Glen Mosley, Director of the Secret Service. "This is Garrett Van Buren," he said. "I have urgent information."

"Garrett? How'd you break into my—"

"Listen carefully, Glen."

"Can't talk now." The line went flat.

The general redialed.

Mosley came back on instantly. "Make it fast," he said tersely.

"I know what's going on at the White House."

Silence.

"I have information you need."

"Go ahead," Mosley said. "You have fifteen seconds."

"Iverson's on the line from the West Wing, isn't he? People getting sick, headaches."

"In ten seconds I'm blocking you."

"You've got a serious problem."

"I'm at the White House right now," Mosley replied, "and everything's fine."

"You're breathing hard, Glen. You're leaving your meeting with the First Lady in the East Wing, and heading for the Situation Room. Right? Listen carefully. You need to seal off the West Wing immediately. It's the Nevada pathogen, Glen. Somebody's triggered the thing in the West Wing."

"Bloody hell!"

"I've dispatched a hazmat team to the White House from our training program in Coral Hills—"

"What?" Mosley roared.

"They're wearing Level A suits—"

"Hold on."

The general waited.

Within seconds, Mosley was on the phone again. "I've instructed Iverson to seal the plant," he said, his voice ragged. He was clearly running now and the general could hear Secret Service agents shouting orders in the background.

"Glen, listen—"

"You'd better turn your team around—this second—and tell me what's going on."

"You've been compromised. Someone in the Service has released the trigger in the Situation Room."

"How do you know?"

"A special agent in the presidential protection division—"

"Give me a name."

"Don't have a name, Glen, but listen, those hazmats of mine are unarmed—"

"Turn them around!"

"Tell Iverson to hold back his sniper units—"

The phone went dead.

The general immediately signaled Donovan that he had talked to Mosley, hooked the phone in his belt and strolled over to the central tent. He wanted a hot coffee before Secret Service tracked him down.

* * *

Donovan eyed the clock taped to the arm of his positive air suit. He had a go-ahead from the general and was nearing the drop-off point, but his team was thirty seconds behind schedule. He glanced over at Prator, who had opened the vapor-tight visor on her hood. Like the liaison officers and Donovan himself, she would keep her visor open until permission came to enter White House grounds. But Donovan was growing concerned. Special Agent Darryl Iverson, in charge of White House Operations, had not yet answered Prator's call.

Donovan glanced at his watch again. Thirty-five seconds behind. Time was against him. He weighed his options. Go in now with only the general's call to Mosley, or delay a minute or two longer, gambling that Prator would get through to Iverson. They needed to establish some kind of communication with the Director of White House Operations, but they couldn't wait much longer. Even with their intricate driving patterns, they had too many vehicles near the White House not to be noticed. Donovan pointed a finger at Prator, ordering her to break off.

Prator lifted her hand.

Donovan waited.

She raised her thumb. Iverson was on the line.

"Darryl," she said. "Thank God! Listen to me ... yes, it's Karen. I'll be brief. You've got a condition red. I repeat. A condition red. It's Nevada. Suit everyone up immediately! I understand, but ... yes, I'll hold." She held the phone inside her hood, her back rigid.

"It doesn't matter what Mosley said." Iverson was back. "Well, I am telling you it is the Nevada event .... No, that's not the problem. You're losing communication because they're down from Nevada. Put your suit on now, Darryl, please! What? That's right, General Van Buren ... he sent us ... because I was down the road with Proskin's hazmat unit, that's why. The general's already talked to Mosley ... no, wait! Mosley's making a mistake. You have to let us in." She looked at Donovan and waffled her hand. Iverson was proving difficult.

Donovan flipped the switch on his wrist to activate his hood mike. "Group A, we're going in," he said. "Group B on standby."

Prator kept talking as EMS vans, ambulances, and fire vehicles descended on the walkway that led to the Southwest Gate. Scores of men in positive air suits disembarked. Donovan and the liaison officers led the way.

"No rushing," Donovan said into his mike. "Be calm. We're trying to get permission from the Service right now." He turned to Prator, who was directly behind him, and gestured with his hands for information.

"Don't know," she mouthed.

He snapped off his mike. "We need that clearance now," he said.

She became more insistent. "Darryl, just a few more seconds. You have to instruct the agents at the gate to—yes, that's what I'm saying. I'm with the hazmat team right now. We're approaching the Southwest Gate. What? We're already on the walkway. ETA immediate. No, we're not turning around."

Already Donovan could see a cadre of Park Police running in their direction. He sent two liaison officers to intercept them, hoping to delay them with arguments that all was well, that Mosley and Iverson had been expecting their hazmat team.

"Darryl!" Prator screamed into her phone. "You'd better do something quick or they'll take us down .... Damn it! I know what Mosley said. There's no time for procedures .... If you've lost communication with him, then you have to act. Your sworn duty is to protect the President .... I understand, but we're already here, ready to go. No! Your response unit will take fifteen minutes to suit up and .... Negative! By then it'll be too late. Pass us in!"

Donovan swept his eyes the length of the fence. Secret Service guards were drawing their weapons and taking defensive positions.

"Stay where you are!" one of them roared.

Donovan signaled everyone to stop. Beyond the gate, he could see the rapid response team from the Service's Uniformed Division suddenly appear on the lawn. There was movement in the trees and along the roof of the West Wing. Iverson's sniper teams were positioning themselves.

"Darryl, don't hang up," Prator said. "You need to ...." She stopped abruptly, her eyes widening. "Oh, God, no! Darryl, please, listen to me," she said, her voice growing more urgent. "You're already coughing, I can hear it. You know what that means. No! You're not fine. It's affected you! You've got very few minutes. Oh, God," she said softly, "I am so sorry, Darryl. So very sorry. Yes, Biggar ... I know ... I know ... I do too. But you have to help us. You need to pass us through the gate, and you have to do it now. Instruct the agents at the gate to— Can you hear me? I'm sorry, what did you ...? Darryl, you're not making sense .... Hello? Darryl?" She groaned. He was gone.

"Let's hear it," Donovan said curtly. He didn't like the affectionate tone in her voice when she was talking to Iverson. She had wasted too much time on personal things instead of concentrating on the mission. He pushed away the possibility that he himself might be reacting emotionally to their conversation.

"Well," he said as Prator took a breath to compose herself.

"Mosley's down, maybe Iverson," she said, her voice now thoroughly professional. "Everyone's sick. They're evacuating the President."

"Take him," Donovan said, pointing to a liaison officer, "and get us inside."

Prator and the liaison officer stepped out from the group and started up the walkway.

"Hold your position!" an agent shouted.

They continued toward the gatehouse with raised hands.

"Stop now or we'll shoot!"

The liaison officer called out, "We need to talk to you—"

"Drop to your knees!"

They continued walking, more slowly.

"Stop, now!"

The liaison officer made a friendly gesture with his hands and said, "Hear us out. We're the hazmat response team from—"

A short burst of a submachine gun ripped the air and the liaison officer doubled over on the ground. Prator dropped to her knees and spread her arms. She glanced at the officer. He was clearly dead. "Kristofferson!" she shouted. "Are you there? It's Karen Prator."

One of the agents peered around the edge of the guardhouse.

"It's Prator," she repeated. "You know me."

"Can't let you approach," Kristofferson called back, still in his defensive position.

"I just talked to Mosley and Iverson," she said. They've given us clearance to enter."

"My communications are down," he said. "You will have to wait until—"

"We can't wait! People are dying inside the White House!"

"If anyone moves, we will shoot," Kristofferson said.

Donovan spoke quietly into his mike. "Group B take positions."

Your communications are down," Prator said in a deliberate voice, "because Mosley, Iverson and the rest of them can no longer respond. They are sick from the same thing that happened in Nevada. The same as Canada, and the cruise ship. That's why we're here. *They* sent for us!" She rose gingerly to her feet. "Think about what's going on," she said, taking a few tentative steps toward the gate, her arms still spread wide.

"Back on your knees!" an agent bellowed.

"I'm former Secret Service," Prator said. "You owe me at least a second to explain. I am not armed. Someone in the White House has triggered the Nevada contagion that's already killed hundreds of people in those towns and on that ship. Mosley thinks it might have been a dark agent in the Secret Service. He's worried that the Service has been compromised, and that there might be other—"

"Ma'am," came the same voice, "stop your forward progress or we will shoot."

Prator stopped. "Mosley's worried he's been compromised," she said in a louder voice, "and so he sent a distress call to our hazmat unit— the logs will bear this out. And, Kristofferson, you intend to shoot us?"

"You know I can't violate procedures," Kristofferson said, glancing at the agent who had been issuing the warnings.

"Don't look at him! You're in charge here," Prator shouted, "not these other agents. You need to pass us through. Now!"

"I–can't–violate–procedures," Kristofferson repeated, his voice strained.

"Then tomorrow every news outlet in the country will broadcast your picture. The Secret Service agent who refused entry to a hazmat team while the death bug, Nevada, killed the President."

Kristofferson mopped his face. "Who did Director Mosley call?" he shouted.

"General Garrett Van Buren," she said. "An impeccable reputation."

He wagged his head. "I don't know," he said.

"People are dying in there!" she screamed.

Kristofferson sucked on his lip.

"You've got to do something," she said. "Mosley called General Van Buren for help. The logs will be clear."

"I don't have the logs," he said plaintively.

"Agent Kristofferson, sometimes you have to make a decision without all the confirmations. *You* are in charge. What's your call?"

Kristofferson surveyed the hazmat team and then with agony on his face, he turned to the other agents and said, "Pass them through."

Donovan flipped on his mike. "Group B stand down," he said. "*I repeat.* Group B stand down."

40

Donovan's hazmat teams moved across the White House lawn calmly, not rushing, doing exactly as they had rehearsed. Donovan could feel the tension in the air; one twitchy agent and the whole peaceful veneer would explode in a storm of bullets. Everyone knew something very bad had happened inside the West Wing, and liaison officers were everywhere soothing anxieties. They were also making it clear that no one should enter the White House complex without a positive pressure suit. Still, with the breakdown in communications, and the loss of leadership—no Mosley or Iverson—events could rapidly spiral downward.

At the White House entry points, Donovan signaled the hazmat teams to use their codes to open the doors, and they stepped inside. Immediately, they broke out their Five-sevens from under their tanks and set off to secure their pre-assigned areas. They had been briefed to expect bodies—scores of bodies, the depleted remains of bodies—but they found nothing. Not one victim. Nothing in the second floor offices, and nothing on the main floor, the nerve center of the Executive Branch.

Donovan and Prator's teams were having the same curious problem on the basement level, locating only the Secretary of Agriculture, Bruce Thomkins, who had taken refuge in a bathroom by the elevators. They escorted him—safe in his yellow hazmat suit, but frazzled in spirit—to a nearby office where they could keep him out of harm's way. It was obvious that fear had emptied the complex; it was not clear where everyone had gone.

Seconds later Donovan found the first victims.

Pushing open the door to the Secret Service Office, he paused in the entrance, astonished by the effects of *Omega*. About five or six agents—it was hard to determine how many—lay heaped under the rows of computers, their sagging clothes sodden with black goo. Donovan closed the door and continued his sweep through the adjacent offices and Mess Hall. All empty. He started toward the Situation Room, but paused to hear a report from the main floor of the West Wing, a report he had been expecting, but one that stunned him nonetheless. They had solved the mystery of the missing White House staffers. The Secret Service had herded personnel from the first and second floors into the Press Room and locked them inside with members of the White House press corps. The room was ankle-deep in liquefied flesh.

Donovan briefed Prator on the report and looked directly into her eyes when he said, "Conditions in the Situation Room will probably be the same. Keep your team focused." And then he added, "Best not to think of the victims as people."

Prator nodded.

He pointed a gloved finger toward the complex of offices that made up the Situation Room, and then moved rapidly along the hall, opening and checking the smaller video conference rooms. As expected, he found nothing until he arrived at the polished wooden door of the main conference room. "They're in here," he said.

Prator and her team took up positions outside the door, weapons ready.

Donovan turned the brass handle. Locked. He examined the panel beside the door and tapped in the code.

The lock clunked open.

Donovan turned the handle again and pushed, but still it refused to move. He shuffled closer, giving the door a solid shove. It moved slightly, but not enough to see into the room. He glanced around, thinking.

"It's not locked," Prator said, stating the obvious.

"Put your team on it," Donovan said.

Prator directed three men forward. They laid aside their pistols and pushed hard, taking care not to tear their pressure suits on the door's decorative edgings. It held firm, as if something had been piled against it. Donovan waved them away. He'd have to find another entrance. He motioned for Prator to follow and they backtracked to a briefing chamber on the other side of the Situation Room. Donovan signaled Prator and turned the handle. The door swung open and Prator's team surged into the Situation Room.

Donovan followed. He eyed the cream-colored fabric walls, the glistening boardroom table, the cherry cabinetry ... before taking in the mounds of black sludge soaking the carpet. His eyes stopped at the shiny wooden door where they had tried to enter. He had seen a lot of sickening things in his military career, but nothing like this. Banked against the door were dozens of yellow hazmat suits smeared with black slime, some filled like sausages, others split with bones and goo hanging out. The Cabinet members had managed to don their hazmat suits, but too late, and from the looks of things, they were climbing over each other in a desperate attempt to escape.

Prator was out of sight now, in one of the side rooms, but he could hear her breathing hard in his earpiece. "We've got a live one," she said. "Don't know if we can contain him."

Donovan started toward the inner rooms when a man dressed in a yellow hazmat suit burst through the door. Behind him came Prator's men, pistols in hand, but their arms outstretched in a non-threatening way as they tried to herd him along the wall toward the corner. "Easy, easy," they were saying, their voices muffled by their plastic hoods. "Nobody's gonna hurt you."

The man's eyes darted around in a frenzy. "I want out of here!" he shrieked.

"That's fine," Prator said. "Just calm down." She had switched on her outer mike as she moved toward him, to project her voice clearly.

The man turned toward her, spotted the open briefing room door, and bolted toward it. Prator raised her Five-seven and pointed it directly at his face. "We have orders to shoot hostiles," she said. "Stop or I will consider you a hostile."

The man stopped.

"Where's the President?" Prator asked, her pistol still eye level.

The man stared at the pistol and licked his lips.

"Where-is-the-President?" Prator repeated.

He glanced at the crowd of hazmat suits gathering around him, and said in barely a whisper, "I'm Wilson Johns, Secretary of the Interior."

"The President," Donovan said through his mike. "Where is he?"

The Secretary shook his head. "I don't know. They took him."

"Secret Service?" Donovan asked.

"Yes, Secret Service."

"Speak up," Donovan said. "Can't hear you through your suit."

"The Secret Service took him," he said louder. "They pulled the President out of his chair, and left."

"They take anybody else? The Vice President?"

"No. Just the President. They said we'd be safe in our pressure suits. They locked the doors and promised to come back. But they didn't come back. And then everyone started dying."

Donovan pointed to Prator and said, "Follow this officer. She'll lead you out."

When the Secretary turned toward Prator, Donovan smashed his pistol across the back of the man's head. Then, bending down, he unzipped the Secretary's hood, popped the top off a glass vial taped to his arm, and held it above the open hood. "Secretary of the Interior," he said. "Can't leave him—he's above Agriculture in succession."

* * *

Donovan sent Prator's team to inspect the sub-basements below the Situation Room, not because he thought the Secret Service might have taken the President there, but because he wanted to clear the entire West Wing before a White House Biohazmat response unit arrived.

Meantime, he and Prator headed up the tunnel that led to the bunker under the East Wing. It was the logical place for the Service to have taken the President. At the first sign of sickness, they would have tried to isolate him from the others, and the best place to do that was in the Presidential Emergency Operations Center, the tube-like bunker under the

East Wing.

They hadn't traveled more than fifty feet along the tunnel before the bodies began to appear, first one or two at the guard stations, and then collections of three or four, all in business suits, all Secret Service agents, and all reduced to black muck on the cement floor.

"No pressure suits," Prator observed as they passed another station.

"They stayed at their posts," Donovan replied, nodding his approval.

Almost immediately they found the first agents wearing full gear, but their formless bodies inside their pressure suits looked no different from the others who had fallen to *Omega*. Complete cellular failure.

Donovan touched Prator's arm. "Ground zero," he said. They were approaching a dozen bodies sprawled on the floor, some with pressure suits, some not, and they seemed to be clustered around the remains of someone important in a yellow pressure suit.

"The President?" she asked.

"Secretary Thomkins wouldn't have released the trigger unless the President was there," Donovan replied.

"I'll check it out," she said, starting up the corridor.

"Wait!" Donovan said, trying to restrain her. But she was already a step away. Donovan saw the boots first, orange with black smudges from his decomposing comrades, and then the weapon, a pistol dangling from his hand. The agent was standing in a niche across from the fallen President, as if he were still performing his guard functions. But in his delirium, he had removed his hood, and his face glistened with sweat as he stared robotically at the clustered bodies.

Prator saw him too, and dropped to a crouch as she brought her weapon around and squeezed off a shot. But it was a hard angle, and she missed. In that second the agent's training kicked in. He jerked his pistol toward Prator, helpless in the center of the tunnel, and fired a dozen rounds in her direction. Donovan was beside her, throwing her out of the way, and firing his P90 at the small target hidden in the niche. But something burned into his body, like a finger of fire that knocked him to the ground. Prator was already on her feet, darting toward the niche and firing as she moved. Donovan could hear the *crack! crack!* of her weapon, and then silence. He rolled sideways and picked up his firearm.

"Nothing living up there," Prator said as she returned to Donovan, who was sitting on the floor. "The President didn't make it to the bunker, and it wouldn't have mattered if he did. I found three collapsed bodies inside." She paused. "What's the matter? You hit?"

Donovan grimaced. "In the shoulder. Not too bad, I think."

She dropped to her knees. "You took a bullet meant for me."

"Yeah, well ...."

"Michael!" Her face was filled with concern.

"Relax, Prator, I'm okay."

"No, you don't understand ... oh, Michael, I'm sorry. Your suit has a hole in it. *Omega*—it's fresh down here."

Donovan glanced at the bullet hole. "Only one hole?" he asked. "No rips?"

She inspected his suit. "Just the entry hole," she said.

"Tape it," he said, motioning to the tape on his glove. "Trigger won't get in as long as the suit's blowing out. I'll be fine."

41

Nicole pressed her ear against her father's office door, feeling guilty about listening secretly from the residence side of the house, but also feeling troubled that she had left Ryan locked up downstairs for several days now. Her father had been busy but had assured her that once things were done in Washington, he would release Ryan.

Men had been returning to the house all day, including Donovan. Despite this, her father still refused to let her see Ryan, and a sense of foreboding had now gripped her. She knew her fears were preposterous—her father would never kill Ryan—maybe some out of control field operative, but not her father. Even so, with Basil and Le Beau dead, that little flicker of doubt just wouldn't go away. The office had been buzzing all day with people discussing one issue or another, but now she could hear Donovan speaking in low tones, and he was clearly not happy. "These couriers are headed for population centers," Donovan was saying. "Not the rural areas I plotted."

"The plans have been modified," her father replied. "We have no antidote. Or am I wrong?"

"The Taylor boy gave us nothing," Donovan admitted.

"And I assume you're confident he's been sufficiently motivated."

"The kid's tough—no doubt. But we used the whole inventory. If he knew something, we would have gotten it by now."

"Then we have no choice. This is now a contest of speed. And the trigger works best in densely populated areas."

"We knew that, sir. We chose areas that were self-limiting to minimize the spread, areas where our enemies maintain their networks, camps—"

"Terrorists cannot exist without support from the cities. Eliminate the cities, you eliminate the threat."

Silence.

Nicole stopped breathing, trying to hear.

"With respect, sir," Donovan said, "I'm a soldier, not a butcher. A soldier doesn't exterminate a hundred million people."

"A soldier kills when he has to," her father replied. "The numbers are irrelevant. This is a different fight than we've ever faced. One side will die. I guarantee it. We better be damn certain it's not us."

"Yes, sir."

Pause. "Is there a problem?"

"No, sir."

Nicole heard the door open and close. She took a deep breath and tried to sort out what she had just heard. Another door opened, one of her father's inner offices, she guessed.

"You heard?" her father asked.

"Yes, sir, through the intercom, every word." It was Prator.

"Impressions?"

"He's resolute," she said.

"He'll try to stop us?"

"Without doubt, sir."

Another silence. "See the monitor? Toward the billets. He's headed for his room."

"He's considering his options, sir. But it won't take him long to make up his mind. Removing you is the simplest solution." *Pause.* "Let me go. I can talk him down."

"It's too late for that. We have to take him out."

Hesitation. "Yes, sir."

"Is something wrong?"

"No, sir. I'll call Clarence."

"Negative. Better if it's someone he trusts."

"Yes, of course ...."

"You should go now. He's injured, but he'll move quickly."

"Yes, sir."

"Can you handle this?"

"I can, sir."

"Good. My aide has a master key. And, Prator, don't hesitate, because he won't."

"Yes, sir."

Nicole heard the action of a pistol slide back and snap into place. The door opened and closed.

"Clarence?" Her father was on the phone. "Donovan has gone rogue on his mission. Yes ... yes, that's what I'm saying. Prator's on her way ... officer's quarters ... right, but I'm concerned about her ability to handle Donovan. What? Of course, let her proceed, but if something goes wrong ... right, no problem in taking them both ... that is correct. My concern is her usefulness after this. Certainly, yes, exactly. How could she be? Her effectiveness has been compromised. Okay, good. No loose ends. Understood? Fine. Get it done."

Nicole clasped her arms around her body, tightly, and felt her world crumble.

42

Ryan had been locked in his room for three days. His only communication—if you could call it that—was with the bull-necked guard who brought him his meals. The man said the same two words every time he entered the room: "Chow time." That's all he ever said. He brought the food, said his words, and left. As it turned out, that was the best part of his day.

The rest of it was a blur of shouting, threats, and slaps to the face. And blur was definitely the right word, because whatever it was that they kept injecting him with, it made everything seem distorted, as if he were in a horrific nightmare.

So when Nicole walked into the room that morning, he wasn't sure for the first minute or two whether it was really her, or some hallucination where she would turn into a giant red spider and try to eat him. He was so exhausted, he no longer cared what happened to him.

"Are you okay?" she began.

He lifted his head, his swollen face contorted in pain. "Go away," he said dully.

She winced. "I'm so sorry, Ryan."

His eyes blinked slowly, but he didn't have the energy to respond.

"Please believe me," she said, her voice flooding with anguish. "I didn't mean for any of this to happen."

"You're so full of shit, you know that?"

Nicole stopped short. "I would feel the same if I were—"

"Yeah, yeah. Just go!"

"We need to talk," she said, her voice shaky.

"Is this a different phase of the interrogation? You gonna shove bamboo shoots up my nails, or blowtorch my back? Cause I don't know anything about an antidote to the trigger. I wish I did," he mumbled, "because I'd tell you everything."

"I'm not sure what to say except I'm sorry. I had no idea. I honestly didn't."

He glared at her through bloodshot eyes. The lack of sleep was playing tricks on him. *Was this more bullshit?* He shook his head. This was the same girl who had sent him into Krakauer's lab, who had talked him into coming here. Her father, and his thugs had been working him over for days. And she expected him to believe her? He snorted. Not a second time.

"Things have happened," she said, "serious things."

He remained silent.

"Everyone at the White House is dead," she continued. "*Omega* has hit several cities."

"What am I supposed to say to that?"

"Nothing." She leaned closer. "But I need you to understand—"

"Enough. I've had enough. I don't want to hear anymore from you or your crazy family." Ryan straightened up in his chair. "I thought Krakauer was nuts, mumbling to himself, walking around the lab with his mask soaked in solvent, crazy eyes all the time." Ryan curled his lip. "But he's nothing compared to your father. Nothing compared to you—"

"I am not my father," Nicole said, an edge in her voice.

"I think I have a pretty good idea of who you are."

"You have zero understanding—" She stopped, and withdrew her finger from his face. "Soaked in solvent," she said, frowning. "Yours was too, right?"

"What?"

"The mask. Krakauer applied solvent to your mask as well, didn't he?"

"Yeah, so?"

"Never mind." She stood, talking to herself. Then abruptly, she said, "I am going to get you out of here."

He laughed darkly. "Cut the bullshit, Nicole. These guys are going to kill me—I know that. So spare me the lies. There's no FBI here. There's just guys that work for your father. *Colonel* Donovan. That's his name, isn't it? Donovan. The one you saved me from in the tunnels." He laughed again humorlessly.

"I didn't want any of this," Nicole said softly.

"Yeah, well," he said, rolling his head back so he could see her through the eye that wasn't swollen shut, "neither did I."

"My father is *not* going to kill you," she said firmly.

"Are you sure about that?"

"I am."

His voice was only a whisper. "Then I know your father better than you do."

* * *

Prator hurried through the passageways toward the officers' wing, slowing only when she caught sight of Donovan's billet, one of twenty identical sleeping rooms along an L shaped corridor. She beeped the general on her phone.

"I'm watching the main halls," he said. "He's still in the billet area."

"Understood," she said. She slipped past several doors until she came to one marked, Donovan. She paused, listening for movement. Hearing nothing she treaded soundlessly to the point in the L and peered

300

around the other side. Empty. She returned to Donovan's door, listened again, and gently rotated the knob. Locked. She pulled her Five seven from inside her jacket, took out the master key, and inserted it into the lock. Then, glancing up and down the corridor, she turned the key. *Click.* She paused, her ear to the door. Still nothing. Five seconds passed, ten, and no sound from inside. She opened the door and crept into Donovan's room.

A dull light bled through the window shades, casting faint lines on the floor. Prator swept her eyes across the room, the empty table, the single lamp, the gray blanket stretched like a drum across the bed. She glanced into the bathroom and then the closet. Puzzled, she inspected the window, but with dried putty cracking along the seal, she knew it hadn't been opened in years. She rechecked the bathroom and closet, holstered her pistol, and exited the room.

She called the general again and received the same word. Donovan had not left the billet area.

"One of these rooms," she said to herself as her eyes raked every inch of the corridor. She stood silently, thinking. There was no reason for Donovan to be in any of the rooms except his own, yet he was somewhere in the billets. Her eyes moved from nameplate to nameplate until she came to her own. She wondered. There seemed to be no purpose. She moved closer and gazed at her door. She reached for the knob and slowly turned.

Open!

Someone had opened her door with a knife, a credit card, she didn't know. But she had to move, and fast. If Donovan was inside, he would have heard even the softest touch on the doorknob. She swung her hand down to her jacket pocket, and in one motion extracted the key and jammed it into the lock, jerking it loudly one way and then the other, hoping to convince an intruder she had no idea her door had been breached. She was simply returning to her room.

She paused for the briefest of moments, thought she heard shuffling inside, and decided to gamble. With a calmness she didn't possess, she pushed open the door, coughing to announce her entry, and tramped in. She entered as she would have normally, turning to close the door behind her, only this time she deliberately exposed her back to whoever might be lurking inside. She knew she had no way to recover if the intruder chose to attack, and it took the greatest effort to keep her breathing regular as she flipped on the lights, and deposited her keys on the hook beside the door.

She felt a presence beside her, turned her head, slowly, and stopped. A gun was inches from her temple. Her instincts told her to remain still. She couldn't see the man's face, but she knew who it was. "Michael?" she asked.

"Yeah," he said, lowering a .22 magnum pistol and shoving it into his sling. "I popped the lock." He hobbled over to the table and picked up a note. He took a breath, seemed nervous. "Look, Prator, I was leaving you a message. Hard to write with my left hand. I thought that maybe we could...."

She turned slightly, allowing her jacket to fall open.

"I need to deal with some business now ... with the general, but if you'd like I could contact you in a few days."

She slipped her hand into her jacket.

"That's what I was trying to tell you ... in this note."

Her fingers slid over the ridges of the grip. *Don't hesitate, because he won't.*

He glanced away, as if he were thinking of what to say next, then returned his eyes to hers.

She scolded herself for missing the opportunity. *Don't hesitate.*

"I didn't write much," he said, shrugging. "Wasn't sure how to put it." He let the paper fall to the table, following it with his eyes.

It was her moment. She yanked out her pistol, dropped to a crouch, and fired twice. Donovan jerked backward, careened off the table, and hit the wall. She fired again, but in the same instant felt something smash into her chest. He had pulled his pistol from the sling and managed to get off a shot before the weapon fell from his hand. Still doing her best to stand, she stared at his body slumped against the wall, a red stain blossoming through his clothes, and then her legs weakened, and buckled beneath her.

"Prator," he gasped, "what the hell you doing?"

"My job," she choked out. Her chest felt heavy and wet.

"Protecting the general?" His laughter ended in a gut-wrenching cough. "Have you any idea what he's planning?"

"No. But I know what he's done for me. I wouldn't be here without him."

He sighed, taking a long time to respond. "Sorry I shot you. Instinct. You okay?"

"I think so ... if they get here soon."

"Good," he said, coughing again.

"And you? How bad?"

"You have talent," he said.

"I'm sorry."

"Don't be. You're the best thing ... ever, in my life."

"Now you tell me," she said, pushing herself up against the opposite wall to see him.

He struggled to lift his arm toward her as he spoke. "It was always you, Karen ... only you ... should have told you that long ago."

"You're telling me now."

"Yeah."

"And you used my name. I like that."

He smiled, then closed his eyes.

"Michael? Are you ...?"

"Fine," he said, "just praying."

"Praying? *You* praying?"

"Find that surprising?" He smiled sadly. "Yeah, I know, but I often pray ... mostly for forgiveness ... for choosing this kind of life."

"Oh, Michael," she said, and clenched her teeth, half crawling, half dragging herself across the floor until she reached where he lay. Then, slipping her hand into his, she rested her head on his shoulder.

"I wish we could go back," he said.

"We'd do things differently."

"We would," he said. "I'd ... I'd try to ...."

"What? Tell me."

"... to treat you ...."

"Michael? Can you hear me?"

The door opened. Prator glanced up. Clarence crossed the room, pistol in hand. He stopped in front of them, pushed her out of the way, and fired two shots into Donovan's head.

"Why did you—?" She groaned.

"General's orders," Clarence said. He turned toward her.

She stared into the pistol as it rose up to find her face.

"Sorry, Prator."

She sighed, and nodded. "Give me time to pray?" she asked.

"Sure," he said.

She squeezed closer to Donovan's warm body, closed her eyes, and whispered her first prayer in many years. She asked for mercy on her wayward soul, knowing that she deserved nothing at all. Then she heard Clarence's feet shuffle impatiently, and suddenly her mind exploded in a brilliant light.

43 ᛩᛩᛩᛩᛩᛩᛩᛩᛩᛩᛩᛩᛩᛩᛩᛩᛩᛩᛩᛩᛩᛩᛩ

Nicole stood by the fire in the library, warming her hands. Night had come and with it the inevitable chill of drafty rooms in an old castle. She remembered as a child—in rainy autumn days—how they'd build a roaring fire and toast themselves in front of the cozy flames. She loved the smell of burning wood, the crackling logs, the heat that warmed you to the bone, but tonight all she felt was sorrow, and an icy cold at the center of her being.

She had ruined everything with Ryan. They were on opposite sides of a chasm, forever separated by her lies, and never again would she see a smile on his face or affection in his eyes. It was as if she had crossed some phantom bridge and now had no way to get back. She bit her lip, holding back a flood of tears. Tomorrow, in all its misery, had finally come.

The rear door opened. Her father entered, and she knew he wanted to talk about Ryan. Pamela followed with a tray of coffee and assorted cookies and fruit. She poured her father a cup, and left as he sat down by the fire. "Busy day," he said, and gestured for Nicole to sit. "I suppose you've heard about Donovan and Prator."

She nodded and sat in the same chair Ryan had days earlier.

"One of those things," he said, "not much anyone could do." He sipped his coffee. "Turns out Donovan had been collecting files on Thermopylae—all our deliberations on the White House. Not sure what he planned to do with them, probably wanted them as a CYA chip he could bargain in the event something went wrong, I don't know. I sent Prator to talk some sense into him so we wouldn't have to lower the hammer." He shook his head. "They ended up shooting each other. Damn shame, the whole mess. I blame myself."

"I didn't know Karen well," Nicole said quietly, "but I always liked her."

"She was a special person," her father said. "No doubt about that. Committed to the American ideal. The best way to honor her is to turn the page and keep going, get control of things so millions of other Karen Prators don't die needless deaths."

Nicole studied her father's face—the smile creases around his mouth, the thin eyebrows and nose, the graying hair and intelligent eyes— and she found no traces of cruelty. None. No one would describe his face as cruel. Yet this was the face of a mass murderer. He intended to kill a hundred million people.

"I know you went to see Ryan," he said. He picked up two walnuts and crushed them between his fingers.

"I did," she said, gazing at her father and feeling a deep sadness. He loved her—probably, as he said, more than his own life. She didn't doubt it. But he had the soul of a demon. He had killed Donovan and Prator with no remorse, allies and friends, and although he had denied it, was probably responsible for murdering Basil and Le Beau as well. She couldn't even imagine the horror that had taken place at the White House, and she knew that by her failure to act, she was just as responsible. The guilt was unbearable. But none of this seemed to bother him. Worse, the killings at the White House were only the beginning; he was planning millions more.

Nicole's mind felt numb. She had no emotion at the core of her being, and she didn't know why. But she knew what she had to do.

"You shouldn't have visited him," he continued. "Not without talking to me first."

"I know, Father. I am sorry."

He nodded. "I understand. I was going to let you see him soon. I just didn't want you to see him—like that."

"It's what had to be done," she said coolly. "There is so much at stake."

"I am glad you can appreciate that," he returned, studying her. "It takes a brave person to see someone you care about in pain."

"Bravery is doing what is needed even when you are scared."

The general leaned forward. "I've never thought about it like that, but I guess it's true." He reached for another handful of walnuts. "I've been a soldier all my life," he said, "and the hardest part is sending good men to their deaths." He gestured, listlessly. "Do you know what stiffened my resolve on the White House mission?"

She waited, listening.

He wrapped the broken shells in his napkin and placed them on the serving dish. "Knowing that millions of other Americans would die if I failed," he said. "That's how I followed through."

"We had a speaker at school," she said, her eyes glued to the serving dish, "who said that you might not know what's right, but you'll always know what's better."

"A wise man."

She looked up. "I don't think he was talking about killing people."

"Probably not, but his point is nonetheless true."

"So if you had to decide who lives, a single person or a large number of people, you would choose the large number."

"Always."

"And if that single person was someone you love?"

"I would hope I had the strength to do the right thing."

"I'm struggling," she said.

"These last few days have been difficult," he said, "but I'm proud to have you at my side." He gave her a smile of encouragement and reached for his coffee. "Tomorrow I go to Washington and you can stay here. Give you time to sort things out."

"Sort things out about Ryan, you mean."

Her father locked his eyes onto hers.

"I understand," she said. "This whole thing has been about controlling *Omega*. Controlling the trigger. Keeping its existence a secret."

"It's the only hope we have."

"But Ryan is a problem. Because we can't control him, right? That's what you think? Because sooner or later, he'd talk," she said bluntly.

"It is a problem. But, as I promised you in the beginning, I won't harm him, maybe send him away for a while."

"We both know what has to be done," she said, her voice lifeless.

He stared at her.

"I'm struggling," she repeated, "but I've made my decision. No point in delaying the inevitable a few weeks or months. The world has changed, and I have to change with it. So tomorrow I will turn the page, and leave Ryan behind." She fixed her eyes on him and said, "I intend to be on that plane with you in the morning."

"If it's any comfort," he said, "you have shown incredible courage. I'll send Clarence—"

"No," she said. "This is something I have to do myself. I'll never be free from the past unless I participate in its destruction."

"No," he said, setting his coffee on the table. "That's not a good idea."

"I need to do this," she said. "And if you want me with you, that's the price."

He shook his head. "It's not easy to shoot someone," he said. "Not up close like that."

"I am not going to shoot him. We have vials of trigger," she said. "I'll use one of the sealed labs downstairs."

He hesitated. "Not a pleasant way to die. Are you sure? I really think—"

"He hurt me, Father, in ways you don't even know." She placed her hands on her knees, her eyes hardening. "We discovered *Omega* together in Krakauer's lab ... it's how I want it. It's how it has to be."

44

The bull-necked guard arrived the next morning while it was still dark. He clomped into the room, and tossed Ryan's clothes onto the bed. "Let's go," he growled.

Ryan blinked, trying to gather his mind. "Go where?" he asked.

"Move it!" the guard said, booting the bedpost.

Ryan followed the guard across the basement complex to the opposite wing, pulling on his clothes as they moved. The guard stopped in front of a stainless steel chamber with rubber seals, opened the door, and said, "Get in."

"Why are you putting me here?" Ryan asked.

The rubber seals blunted the sound of the door as it slammed shut.

Ryan took a deep breath of the fusty air, and ran his eyes over the gleaming walls and curved ceiling. The lab was empty except for a single steel chair. He scuffed the floor with his foot, a kind of molded material with a center drain, then checked the door, knowing it would be locked. He surveyed the walls and ceiling again, for what reason, he didn't know. The single chair reminded him of the interrogation room where the big guy with purple scars had stuck him with needles.

Five minutes later he was finding it hard to breathe. "Hey out there!" he shouted, pounding on the door. There was no response. The lack of air was making him feel antsy, and he began to rub his shoulders and neck, and to clutch his arms across his restless body. He tried to gulp the thin air, but it didn't help. Seconds later, the lever on the door clunked down.

Nicole entered. "I don't have much time," she said, glancing toward her father who was outside talking to the guard. "He wants us at the helipad in a few minutes."

"It's hard to breathe in here," Ryan said.

"I know. The room has a self-contained ventilation system which hasn't been switched on yet. I'll do that when I leave."

"Why did they bring me here?"

She shrugged and said, "In about an hour someone will come by and take you back to school."

Ryan couldn't hide his surprise. "I'm being released?"

She nodded. "Here, let me clean you up." She wiped his face, cleaning the sweat and traces of blood away from his stubble.

"What is that?"

"Rubbing alcohol. Someone will bring you a change of clothes. I'm sorry I don't have more time."

"You know," Ryan said, unable to control his anger, "this whole thing—keeping me here …."

"Some things are beyond my control," she said, "and I'm very sorry—" Her eyes shifted to the door and her voice dropped when she said, "I don't expect you to forgive me, but I'm hoping ... maybe ... in time, you'll understand."

"Fine. Better hurry. Your father's waiting." He lowered his volume as a concession, but he intended his words to cut. They did. He could see the hurt in her eyes.

"Nicole?" It was her father

"Coming," she said. She turned back to Ryan, her face desperate in its concentration. "My time's gone," she sighed. "I know I've made horrible mistakes ... I want so badly to make up for what I've done. Please ... try to understand." Her lips quivered slightly.

He said nothing, confused by the sadness he could feel flowing out of her.

"Don't forget me," she said, grasping his hand, and releasing it quickly. "This is the end ... for us, and I …." She broke off, unable to speak, her face filled with agony.

"Nicole," he said, tilting his head, "what's going on?"

Her eyes burned into his, and she opened her mouth, but nothing came out. Then, abruptly, she said, "Goodbye, Ryan," and joined her father without looking back.

After the door had closed, and after the ventilation had kicked on, a rectangular drawer in the wall slid forward. A glass vial rotated, popped open, and exposed the contents inside.

45

The Gulfstream streaked through the skies toward Reagan National in Virginia, the general and his daughter sitting across from each other in big leather seats. They were alone, except for Clarence in the cockpit. The general eyed his daughter, concerned. She had barely said a word since leaving Greenwich, where she had released the vial of trigger to kill her friend.

"You want to talk about it?" he asked.

She looked up from her magazine.

"You've been staring at the same page since we climbed aboard," he said.

She swiveled her chair to face him. "I'm not sure what to say," she said, "but I know I can't delay any longer."

"Is this about Ryan?"

"About us, mostly."

"I see," he said, guessing she was blaming him for Ryan's death. And she'd be right. He was responsible. Letting her eliminate a school friend was a bad decision. Especially like that. "Ryan was my problem," he said, patting his chest. "I should have handled it."

"I'm glad you didn't," she said. "I needed to protect Ryan."

He frowned.

"Ryan's not dead," she said.

"Not ... you released the trigger."

"I did, but he's immune, at least for a short while."

"Immune! You mean an antidote?" He was in total shock.

"Krakauer's personal version—not perfect, gives you headaches and nausea—but for a few hours it stops the trigger from activating *Omega*. He administered it to Ryan and himself, but apparently not to his lab cleaners."

"Why didn't you tell me?"

"I didn't know myself until yesterday. That's when I put it all together. I remembered that Krakauer got sick about the same time his first undocumented workers disappeared. I'm guessing they were all exposed to the trigger, except Krakauer didn't die. Ryan always complained about the mask Krakauer made him wear, a mask soaked in what he thought was disinfectant. But it was the antidote, carried in a solvent to penetrate the skin."

"Interesting." He gave his daughter an approving look and said with a light scolding in his voice, "You shouldn't have hidden this from me, but you've done well. Where is it?"

"In the storage room under the house."

"With the materials from Krakauer's lab?"

She nodded. "It's in a rubber tub marked, 'cleaning supplies.'"

"We had it all the time," he said, his mind racing. Any kind of antidote to the trigger, imperfect or not, would change everything. It was the break he had been looking for.

"I have something else to say," she said, "quite serious, I'm afraid."

"Okay."

"About Colonel Donovan."

"Go on."

"I heard you talking to him in your office."

"Yesterday?"

"Yes. At the residence door."

"I see."

"You were talking about releasing the trigger."

"Hmm."

"To kill millions of people."

He stared at her.

"I can't believe you'd do that."

"Nicole," he said, shaking his head, wanting her to understand.

"Millions," she repeated, her brow furrowed with incredulity.

"I don't expect that high a number," he said quietly, "but it is true I intend to eliminate extremists who are plotting our deaths."

"Not just extremists. You'll exterminate whole cities, everyday people who have done nothing to deserve such a brutal end."

"You don't realize—"

"Even Donovan wouldn't go along with you. He called it butchery."

The general suppressed his growing anger.

She leaned forward in her chair and said, "You told me if you had to choose between someone you loved and a large number of people, you would choose the large number."

"I did. But the choice here is between two peoples, two ways of life. Eventually, one group will destroy the other. I'm making certain that we are the victors, not the victims. I take no pleasure in killing non-combatants, but unless we act—and soon—millions of Americans will die in our streets."

"You don't know that."

"I do," he snapped. "History bears me out."

"No! It's nothing but conjecture. Speculation about the future. That's all it is. Even if you're right that extremists will one day kill us all, that day could be centuries away. I will not stand by and let you massacre whole nations on a hunch."

"I'm sorry you feel that way," the general said. "I expected more from you."

"And I believed you'd stop after the White House. I guess we were both wrong."

The general set his jaw. "I would never harm you," he said, "but you must know I will protect the mission—restrain you for weeks, months, even years if need be."

"I know," she said. "That's why my heart is aching. May God have mercy on us ... I'm ending this madness here, and now."

"Nicole—"

"I have no options," she said. "Nothing I can say or do will change your mind." She slipped a hand into her jacket pocket, and her mouth opened in anguish, and a desolate sound escaped her lips, like the sound of a dying animal. "What choice did you give me?" she asked, her eyes filled with sorrow. "I had to stop you."

"Why are you talking like this?"

"So many," she said. "I couldn't let them die."

"What are you saying?"

She removed her hand from her jacket, and opened it.

A jolt hit his body. His eyes darted to the tiny glass cylinder in her palm. "The trigger! You released it? When?"

"Just now," she said.

"Nicole ... what have you done?"

"A hundred million people," she said. "A hundred million."

"Nooo," he said, seizing the vial and examining the open top.

"I took two cylinders this morning," she said. "One for Ryan, and one for us."

He ran his eyes feverously over the vial again, looking for something—anything—that would prove himself mistaken. Anger seized him. "What were you thinking?" he roared. "Do you know what you've done? You've killed us! You've killed countless Americans by this reckless act. Consigned them to the grave."

"I've stopped a mass murderer," she said.

"Don't be absurd! You've just made it possible for mass murderers to destroy this nation." He raked his fingers through his hair, and tried to stave off tendrils of hopelessness slithering over him. He had told her things she didn't need to know a catastrophic error in judgment—and now he, his daughter, and an enormous number of unsuspecting Americans would suffer the consequences.

"I don't share your view of the world," she said. "I don't believe terrorists will destroy us. Hurt us, maybe. But not destroy us. We can't simply go out and kill people because they might do us harm."

He laughed bitterly. "Have you learned nothing from me? If your enemy has the will and the money, they'll get the weapons to do the job."

"Wholesale murder is evil. Pure evil."

He stared at his daughter and shook his head, his face showing extreme displeasure.

She returned his look, her eyes clear and unwavering. "I would do it again," she said in a resolute voice. "I would trade my life, and yours, for a hundred million people."

"A hundred million," he sneered. "The number is preposterous."

"Okay, one hundred thousand," she said in the same resolute tone. "I would trade our lives—gladly—for one hundred thousand people."

"That's all you've done, Nicole. You've traded peaceful American lives for militant, extremist lives." He turned away, knowing his anger was a useless emotion, especially now when time was so short. He remembered the bitterness he felt the day his son had died, and how poorly he had treated Nicole. She had followed him around the house, begging for forgiveness, her little face streaked with tears, and her body convulsed in sorrow. But he turned his back. And when he couldn't take the anguish and tears any more, he locked her in her room. That's what he did, pushed her in the room and locked the door, and never again did he see her cry. He glanced over at her now, and she was wiping a tear ... and the anger drained out of him.

"I'm sorry it has to end this way," she said.

He nodded and said without resentment, "But you're not sorry for releasing the trigger, are you?"

"No," she said.

The general opened his mouth to register his disapproval one last time, but caught himself and gestured futilely with his hand.

She said nothing, just sat quietly, staring off into space.

"Well," he said after a silence, "You and I are very much alike. Uncompromising in our beliefs. I was determined to eliminate a deadly threat to our country, and you were just as determined to rescue innocent lives from my oversized net. I was the avenging angel, you the guardian." He sighed. "Who will God find more pleasing, do you think?"

"I suppose we'll soon find out," she said.

"Yes, we will. But I think we both know the answer."

She smiled wanly.

He opened his arms, and she came to him, pushing into him so hard it hurt. He stroked her hair, knowing he could do nothing to change their predicament. Life was over. He had tried and failed. Now he must accept the situation and salvage what he could. He was a general, and he would act like it. He sucked in some air, and forced his mind in another direction. A sudden thought occurred to him.

"The antidote," he said. "When you gave it to Ryan in the basement, were you exposed as well?"

"Yes."

"Then you're still immune," he said, thinking.

"It doesn't matter. I can't fly this plane and it won't be long before you and the pilot ...." She broke off. The reality of their situation had finally hit home. "I can't fly this plane," she repeated quietly.

"No, but I can," he said, rising, "and I can get you off."

"How?"

"A parachute."

"This is a jet!"

"I just need to reduce air speed, that's all." The general opened his briefcase and removed a chrome-plated Beretta.

Her eyes widened.

"First," he said, turning the weapon over in his hand, "I have an unpleasant duty. You'll know when you should turn away." He stuffed the Beretta in the back of his trousers and tapped on the cabin. "Clarence," he called, "drop to 12,000, knots 250, and engage the autopilot. I need to show you something."

Seconds later Clarence emerged from the cabin. "Sir?" he said.

The general motioned to the chair in front of him. "Sit down," he said. "I want you to see something."

Clarence sat, his hard face filled with questions.

"Page fourteen," the general said, handing him a magazine.

He reached for the magazine, but the general let it slip from his hand.

"I got it," Clarence said, bending forward.

The general pulled out his Beretta and fired one shot into the back of Clarence's head.

Nicole screamed.

"It's over," he said. "Wait here." He entered the cockpit, pushed a button on the overhead panel to depressurize the cabin, and set the flaps at ten degrees to slow the aircraft. He returned to his daughter, who had her back to the dead pilot. "Come with me," he said. The general led her through the bathroom to the rear baggage compartment, selected a parachute, and strapped it on her. "That's the rip-cord," he said, pointing to a handle on her left side. "Count ten and pull. That's all you do. Once it opens, you can steer with the toggles." He grabbed the lever in the center of the aft-door and yanked up. The door folded down and a rush of air screamed in their ears.

"I love you," she shouted. "I'll never forgive myself."

He kissed her forcefully on the cheek. "There's no need for forgiveness," he said, "and nothing wrong with doing what you think is right. I'm proud you're my daughter, and I love you too." He tried to turn her outward for the jump, but she shuffled to the door, and with her eyes locked on his, fell backwards into the shrieking wind.

The general closed the aft-door and returned to the cockpit. He

315

reset the flaps and disengaged the autopilot, and then made a hard left turn out to sea. After watching Nicole's parachute open, he called his aide and instructed him to release Ryan Taylor, then sent an email to Bruce Thomkins about the temporary antidote to the trigger. He also mentioned that he was no longer a nominee for Vice President.

Leaning back in his seat, the general pushed away the symptoms he was feeling, and one last time he enjoyed the smooth draw of an OpusX cigar. One last time he pictured himself as the new Caesar, who might have provided safety for a vulnerable people. And one last time, one last haunting moment, he recalled the look in his daughter's eyes, and prayed she would find peace. Then, with his hand on the yoke, the general thrust forward, and entered a steep dive toward the ocean.

Three Months Later

46

Ryan hurried past a handful of students still wandering the sidewalks outside Watson Hall, a four-story brick Romanesque building trimmed with terra cotta and sandstone. Many thought the building's exterior boasted of strength and beauty, but to Ryan it looked like a prison.

The new semester was turning into a disaster. No matter how hard he tried, he couldn't seem to concentrate on his work. Even a course on Robotics & Artificial Intelligence, something he thought might fire his imagination, had barely kept his attention, and things weren't going much better on the lacrosse field.

All he could think about was the past, about decisions he had made, about Basil and the poor souls at the White House, about whether he could have done something to save them.

Basil bothered him in particular because if Ryan had been alert, he could have hauled the kid out of there. As unlikable as he was, he didn't deserve to die. Neither did the people at the White House, but at least Ryan didn't see it happen. The thought of how they perished—their grisly end—was bad enough. The West Wing of the White House still remained closed "for maintenance," as the Press Secretary put it, maintenance that required the building to be completely sealed in what looked like plastic wrap, because inside, as everyone acknowledged, they were still boiling bodies off the floor.

The whole thing was mind numbing, and Ryan knew he needed to dwell more on the good things that had happened, rather than the bad—like Le Beau's remarkable recovery. The doctors had told his wife to prepare for the worst, but somehow the officer managed to survive. After weeks in a coma, he sat up in bed and declared he was going fishing. One month later and forty pounds lighter, the hospital released him, and he and his wife left for Arizona, and retirement.

There was other good news, especially about *Omega*. President Thomkins had announced that the mysterious events in Nevada threatening America had run their course, and were no longer a concern. Life, he said, could return to normal. Ryan knew it wasn't true, that the *Omega* gene could be triggered at any time, could slice through entire cities, countries, reducing the population to mounds of sludge. But no one really understood the danger. So as the months passed with no alarming events, people gradually returned to their lives.

Ryan too wanted to get on with his life. But often he found himself walking the campus, staring at the other students, and wondering why they seemed so alien. He climbed the broad steps of Watson Hall determined to get back on track. It was simply a matter of centering one's mind, as Coach Waldhart always said—concentrate on robotics for the next hour, robotics, and nothing else. It was the best way to get beyond what had happened. Focus on the moment. Be fully engaged in everything he did. He pushed open the doors and wended his way through the students still choking the hallways.

He passed a group of students from Europe who were visiting the Computer Science facilities, started down the corridor toward his class, and then froze. Nicole was standing across from the lecture hall, her eyes examining every passing cluster of students. Ryan turned, hoping to avoid her, but before he could move, she'd spotted him, her eyes instantly locking onto his. She lifted her hand in a tiny wave. Ryan expelled a breath, and despite himself acknowledged her with a nod of his head. *Damn it!*

The students continued milling through the hallways as classes let out, and Ryan perused some of their faces, trying to think. He hadn't seen Nicole since the day she'd left for Washington with her father. Ryan had read a dozen articles about the general's death, mostly bullshit stories about an explosion on board that killed the pilot and crippled the plane. Rather than trying to land an unstable aircraft, and risking lives on the ground, the heroic General Van Buren had insisted his daughter jump while he ditched the plane at sea. All they found were oily scraps on the water.

And now here she was. Walking towards him. Nicole was probably the last person in the world Ryan wanted to see. He desperately wanted to run, to bolt down the corridor and out the door, but his feet failed him. Like a statue he just stood there, watching her get closer. Finally, she reached him.

"I know you've been avoiding me," she said softly, "and that's okay. I'm not here to strike up a friendship, just to say again—now that it's over—that I really am sorry."

"Fine," he said.

They stood like that for a silent interval.

"Do you believe me?" she asked quietly.

"What should I believe, Nicole?"

Her eyes welled up suddenly, and she turned to leave. "Whatever you want, Ryan ...."

Incredulous, he stormed after her. "What did you expect?" he asked. "A big, happy reunion?"

Her eyes hardened. "I don't expect anything from you."

"Unbelievable! You locked me in a fucking dungeon, Nicole, and had me tortured for half a week."

"I had nothing to do with that," she said, glancing around at the few remaining students. "I didn't even know it was happening."

"No? You didn't see your father's henchmen Taser me? Missed that moment, did you?"

"Ryan, you were about to walk out the door—talk to the FBI. What did you think would happen? The whole world was ready to explode." She furrowed her brow. "You should think about somebody besides yourself for once."

"Holy shit," Ryan blinked in amazement. "You actually think you didn't do anything wrong."

"I did what I could."

"Which was *what*, exactly?"

Nicole started to respond, but instead calmly smoothed the dark blouse she was wearing, eyed Ryan briefly, then, without a word, turned and walked away.

Ryan watched her leave, her shoes clacking down the now empty hallway, her hair bouncing back and forth with each step, clearly angry. *She* was angry with *him*! The whole thing was insane, and it was more than he could bear.

"What did you do, Nicole?" he called loudly.

She kept walking.

"You must have done something," his voice boomed down the corridor. "Just can't imagine what it was."

She turned suddenly and said, "You're alive aren't you?"

"Alive?" He laughed harshly. "Are you talking about your little mock-execution with the empty vial?" He took a few steps towards her. "I'm supposed to be grateful for that? You and your father head off to the plane, and leave me in there to watch an empty vial pop open—so I think I'm about to die!" His face twisted in scorn. "Was that for your father's benefit?"

She was walking back to him now, head lowered, eyes on fire. "It wasn't empty," she spat. "And yes, it was a big show for my father. I was trying to protect you."

Ryan paused, and shook his head in confusion. "What are you saying?"

She slowed as she grew closer. "The antidote," she said in a whisper. "Krakauer had found something that worked for a short time. That's why I came there, to rub it all over your stupid face." Her eyes bore into his. "Krakauer's *antidote*. I thought you'd understand what I was doing."

Ryan's body straightened. *Was it possible?* He searched for something to say, but all he did was stare.

Her eyes suddenly grew moist, and she turned away.

He caught her arm at the elbow and pulled her closer.

She resisted.

"Nicole," he said, knitting his brows, "your father was intending to kill me?"

She looked away and groaned. "Oh, Ryan," she said, "you have no idea. He was planning to kill a hundred million people! And so, yes, I'm sure in a very short time he would have seen you as a problem."

"Jeez," he said slowly.

"That's why I had to get on that plane, so I could put an end to it." She exhaled, lifting her eyes upwards to clear them.

Ryan licked his lips. "What did you—?"

"I killed him," she said, limply.

"What?"

"I killed my father ... on the plane."

He stared at her, incredulous. "And the news accounts I've heard—"

"Made up," she said. "By the administration. They wanted to take charge of the situation ... minimize questions, I guess."

"Oh, man," he murmured, and glanced around to make sure no one was listening. "What happened?"

She closed her eyes before speaking. "I was also immune that morning."

"*The trigger?*"

"It was the only way," she said, pressing her lips together. "I loved him, I really did. But what he wanted to do ... he wasn't finished, Ryan …."

He looked at her, stunned.

"Well, I really did it," she said, shaking her head in disbelief, "killed my own father. But what else could I do?"

Ryan blew out slowly.

"I expected to die in the crash," she said quietly, "but he saved me … got me a parachute." Her lips were trembling.

"Nicole—"

"He forgave me," she said, swallowing a sob. "That's the worst part."

"Yeah," he said, his voice barely audible.

"I needed you to know," she said.

Ryan nodded.

"And I can't talk to anyone," she said, lowering her voice, "about anything. The President made that very clear."

Ryan could see the pain in her eyes. He gestured lifelessly and said, "I don't know what to say. I'm sorry."

"It's okay," she said. "I did the right thing. I know I did. The world is better off without him. He was obsessed with terrorists, as if they were the end of history. But his solution—kill ten thousand innocents to eliminate one enemy—was sick. He was sick, I think. I know that now." She sighed. "Well, that's all I wanted to say. I'd better go."

He restrained her with his hand. "We should talk."

"I know," she said, "but I'm not sure we're ready—"

"We're ready," he said, squeezing her arm gently. "Just a cup of coffee?"

She hesitated.

"Nicole, I can't talk to anyone either."

"It is hard," she acknowledged.

"We'll go out somewhere ... I'll pay."

Nicole arched an eyebrow.

"Someplace cheap," he said, smiling.

She smiled back, and nodded.

That afternoon as Ryan was studying in his room, the newsfeed on his computer blinked on, and a newscaster appeared from the Emergency Broadcast Network. Someone had detonated three nuclear devices on U.S. soil. Phoenix, Chicago, and New York were gone.

ABOUT THE AUTHOR

William V. Crockett is a writer, scholar, and professor in New York. A graduate of University of Winnipeg, Princeton Theological Seminary, and University of Glasgow (Ph.D.), he has lectured and written extensively on theological issues. With his expertise in classical antiquity, Crockett has written two other novels, *Worlds Apart* and *A Celt in Rome,* set in the second century Roman Empire. He lives with his wife, Karen, in rustic Sussex County, New Jersey, where they often kayak and ride their motorcycles.

www.ingramcontent.com/pod-product-compliance
Lightning Source LLC
Chambersburg PA
CBHW060514180626
46817CB00002B/363